The Age of Larkspur

by

Aleighsha Parke

Cover Art by *Kristian Norris*

The Wild Rose Press, Inc.
PO Box 708
Adams Basin, NY 14410-0708
Visit us at www.thewildrosepress.com

Publishing History
First Edition, 2024
Trade Paperback ISBN 978-1-5092-5690-7
Digital ISBN 978-1-5092-5691-4

Published in the United States of America

Dedication

To my Auntie Arlene, thank you for always
encouraging me to keep writing.

Acknowledgements

A huge thank you to entire team at The Wild Rose Press. Especially my editor Dianne, and my cover artist Kristian Norris. Thank you so much for loving Larkspur and choosing to publish it.

Thank you to my mom who has been so supportive and encouraging! Thank you to my twin sister, Karrah, for getting so interested in our Icelandic heritage and inspiring me to learn more about Iceland and its rich and expansive history of folklore that helped inspire this book. Thank you to Jón Árnason, Eiríkur Magnússon, George E.J. Powell for preserving and sharing Iceland's captivating legends back in the 1800s. Thank you to my three amazing aunts—Arlene, Betty, and Elaine—for reading my first drafts, enjoying it, and pushing me to fulfill my dreams of publishing it. A special thank you to my Auntie Arlene for always encouraging me to never give up on my writing.

Thank you to my beta readers and friends—Avery, Jude, and Megan—for giving me feedback and helpful comments. I appreciate you all!

And the most important thank you, is to you, the reader. Thank you for picking up this book and giving it a chance. Thank you for helping me fulfill my dreams. I really hope you like it!

Prologue

The world can change from the actions of one person. It can send ripples and waves throughout history with effects that will not truly be felt until decades later.

One such woman changed the course of Woodvale. Her kind actions, with only the intention to help those around her, would create the beginning of a powerful issue our country had yet to face in such a blinding, uncontrollable, and unignorable force: greed.

Some say this woman is a goddess, our savior. Others see her as a demon in disguise, dispatched to destroy the Kingdom of Woodvale.

No one is ever truly right or wrong—you must decide for yourself who is the hero and who is the villain, if there is a clear-cut concept of such an enigma at all.

-*The Age of Larkspur* by Cassius Muscari, IV

Chapter One

A sage leaf flourished from the stem sprouting out of her ankle. She sighed, glaring daggers as the leaf bloomed into a perfect, purple-stained bulb.

Flora let out a huff, her birch-shaded bangs jumping from the release of air as she sank onto the damp, mossy log. Her fingers curled into the squishy texture, calming her for a second. Meanwhile, the flower bloomed and flourished, straining to catch the rays of sunlight streaming through the thick tree branches.

"Stop that, you," she said, flicking it with her finger. It shrank in response before ignoring her and growing bigger. Soon enough, a spike full of purple buttercup-shaped flowers bloomed and swayed to the side at the weight.

With another sigh, this one far sharper than the first, she snapped the stem from the base and dusted off the remaining stalk. It crumbled down into the forest floor, mixing with the twigs and dirt. Her ankle was now bare, save for the deep indigo birthmark of a larkspur. The stem thrummed in her fingertips, pulsing to a beat of the words: *look at me.* She refused to look at the enticing purple and instead focused on her ankle. Her marred, beastly ankle.

Flora's jaw clenched in the waning sunlight. Her birthmark served as an ugly reminder—a warning. *Stay good and stay hidden.* The words she lived by for the last seventeen years of her life. The constant reminder grated on her nerves, but she knew they were necessary. Besides, Flora did enjoy rules—they kept the chaos in order, and let life be fair. It was just, in some moments, some snapshots in time, she wished she could be free. Although, her personality wouldn't necessarily lend to that desire either way. But, at the core of it all, she longed for *more*.

A snap of a twig carried by the wind hit her ears, and her spine stiffened into a board as her heart beat a breath faster. The birds' lilting chirps silenced, casting the forest in an unnatural, eerie quiet. She yanked her skirt down, shielding the birthmark from the lurking forest eyes. She let the larkspur slip from her fingers, the humming in her veins immediately ceasing. Flora yanked on her supple leather boot she had discarded when she felt the niggling stem poke through her skin and bone. With the heel, she crushed the larkspur into the dirt, then scattered leaves and twigs and moss overtop, burying the vibrant evidence. Her gaze lingered on the space, chewing on her lip as she worried it looked too obvious. Except, she had done the best she could, and it was highly unlikely someone was in the forest with her. Even if her rapidly beating heart and other half of her brain did not get that memo of logic.

Flora's gaze darted around the forest, greens and browns creating a kaleidoscope of color, making it impossible to find the source of the noise. She laced her boot, drawing the strings tight enough to cut into her circulation before she rose, low-hanging branches grazing her head tenderly. A cold finger ran down her spine as she scanned the trees. Uneasiness blossomed in her middle, lingering even when she couldn't observe anything out of the ordinary.

The woods were largely unused as everyone was terrified of them. The very sight of a tree, growing high and mighty into the sky, struck deep, bottomless fear into the hearts of those who lived in Woodvale. Because they knew—everyone knew—the trees were where the witches lived.

Step one foot, even a toe, into the treeline and you would be devoured whole or cursed into oblivion. Except those who didn't blindly follow fallacy, like Flora, knew that you had to cross the *right* treeline. But the superstition about the woods lived on, despite the misconceptions littering history, fables, folktales, anecdotes, and gossip.

No one went into the woods. Not on a sunny day, and certainly not when the moon was high and the shadows thrived as the monsters awoke in the breathing blackness.

It amused Flora how much the woods evoked such unease in others. They weren't *all* scary. Many copses of trees grew in Woodvale—those were all safe. It was the woods surrounding Woodvale where you had to be careful. Woodvale was a rectangular country encased by a writhing sea, ginormous mountains, a green forest, and a black forest. There was no escape. Even when the land died and dried out, the only option was to stay and starve or risk the certain death of travel. It was an impossible choice, with a solution most folk in Woodvale feared too greatly to even entertain the idea of seeking help in that realm of life.

Magic.

Magic was a solution to many problems, but it was

too unknown with an undertone of insidiousness that made everyone cower away from it, instead of using it to solve their ailments.

As much as she knew she shouldn't, Flora liked Woodvale. Even with its faults, she was happy with where she lived. Even if all she wanted to do was run across her town's border and into the Sage Woods. Her heart was drawn there, but she was forbidden from ever stepping foot out of her town in her province of Sanarbre. It was even a struggle for her to be allowed in this copse, but her mother knew how much her body needed to be surrounded by the aromatic green.

Flora liked being inside the woods for the comfort it provided, the homey feeling it sparked in her. But she mostly liked it because it was the one place no one would bother her. She hated talking to people. She was always worried about saying the wrong thing or even saying anything at all. The words climbed into her throat, and she practiced for hours on end to make sure they sounded acceptable—but somehow, they ended up sounding *wrong*. She would spiral for weeks and relive the conversations that didn't go as she planned. Sometimes, she felt it was easier on herself and everyone around her if she just disappeared for a while. The forest never talked to her or made her feel like she didn't belong or cause waves of anxiety to plague her. Flora liked the plants, and the plants liked Flora.

If she had things her way, she would live in the trees and live off the land. But until things changed, that wasn't an option.

Another twig snapped, the crack sounding louder in the quiet, striking Flora's heart. A steady burst of fear hummed in her veins as she rose and began her retreat. Flora deftly moved through the forest, bypassing fallen branches and protruding roots with ease.

No hidden shadows or creatures jumped out at her, and as the full force of the unobstructed sun hit her face, she relaxed, muscles softening in the warmth. She glanced back into the trees only once, but there was nothing but greenery stretching their limbs to follow the girl that lived and breathed plants.

****

It was a short walk back to her village. The road was covered in wagon wheel dents and hoofprints, dust lingering in the air that Flora skirted around lest she dirty the hem of her skirt even more. The sides of the road were barren, the few copses only grew in small acres, not along most roads. Flora longed for the roads to be how they looked in old paintings, trees creating a canopy over weary travelers. But if her world were how it looked in old paintings, no one would dare step foot onto the roads in fear of the trees coming alive. Or worse, a witch leaving her domain to snack on sapped travelers.

Years ago, optimistic people would cross their fingers for a witch to appear so a boon could be granted. Except, this witch had only ever granted one boon known to history, and while it allowed Woodvale to blossom beautifully into a picturesque land with a full-bellied population, it ultimately sent their country into ruin.

Soon enough, stone and copper cottages cropped up. A lot of the homes used to be made of wood—but that was before the calamity. Flora's heart ached in her chest as too-thin children ran in the dirt, their clothes stained, without a care in the world. Giggles and happy shrieks carried on the wind to Flora's waiting ears.

Her heavy skirt swished through the dust, completely covering the beacon on her ankle. All her skirts were filthy and never lasted long as they were continuously subjected to the rough elements. But Flora would rather go through a million skirts than let anyone lay eyes on her cursed ankle because it would ruin her life as she knew it.

A scream filled with skin bursting and blood spilling reverberated through the air, sending Flora's heart to become acquainted with her stomach. The children stopped dead in their tracks as doors opened and her neighbors spilled into the street like water rushing in a stream. Flora's feet carried her forward with the masses until they reached the town square. It was a quaint, tragic focal point for the town with a water well framed by the gallows.

The crowd swallowed her whole as she moved closer to the gallows. Whispers of whose wrists were strapped inside—Timothy Row—and why Lieutenant Arbour was cleaning a glistening scarlet whip with his fingers: a stolen loaf of bread.

It started with blood—as everything does.

A single crimson drop hitting the dusty cobblestones caused bile to rise in Flora's throat. Her heart sank as she watched the man's face contort in pain and agony as the harsh squelch of the whip hitting his back rang through the ears of the crowd. The man had stolen a loaf of bread for his hungry family—a criminal offense with the drought and the curse sucking the life from their land that worsened everyday. But a whipping was a cruel punishment. Everyone was hungry, and desperation clawed at people's throats in such a tight grip it was hard to breathe, hard to even entertain the idea of living another week, another year. Flora couldn't understand why this was the action taken against those who just wanted their children to live another day.

Even still, most of the town came to watch. There was little entertainment, and they all knew that watching someone experience such soul-crushing agony would remind themselves not to make his mistakes. It was easy to want to steal, even amongst people whose throats filled with bile at the thought. Because they were *hungry* and *tired.* The King stole from the people until they had nothing left, except blood and skin and bone. And if he could use the blood and skin and bone from his people to force his world back into good health and wealth, he would do so in a heartbeat.

Flora had never personally met the King. Most of the people living in the provinces never had, but she had heard enough foul rumors and whispers to know the consensus about him. He would take everything from someone who made a mistake if it could fix what was broken.

Flora's roiling stomach forced her to step away, leaving the spectacle behind for fear she would lose her lunch—there wasn't enough food to spare for her to let that happen. As she left the square, the hairs on the back of her neck stood on alert, but she couldn't find the cause even after scanning and peering into streets and alleys nearby. The tingle in her spine begged her to stay longer, to figure out who was watching her, but Flora had to get home, lest she cause her mother's face to grow more wrinkled with worry.

****

A warm hug of baking bread, inviting and delicious, enveloped Flora as she stepped inside her home. The space was filled with knickknacks and knitted blankets in soft pastels in a variety of colors. A soft sigh escaped her lips as the tense emotions dripped from her tight body. Her mother always needed to keep her hands busy—hence why Flora was constantly treated with baked goods and warm blankets. Flora, her mother, and her best friend were some of the few people in their town who weren't skeletal skin and bones. Somehow, amidst the struggles of everyone else, her mother always found a way to ensure Flora had enough.

Flora knew it was because she felt guilty. She felt guilt for not being Flora's true mother—her biological one. But to Flora, Rosie Hendricks was more her mother than the one who cast her away at birth. It was for Flora's own safety, but it still cut Flora like a knife. A wound that could never fully heal, but she tried her best since she loved Rosie and her life, even with its disappointments and downfalls.

Rosie was her biological mother's handmaiden and was tasked with keeping Flora safe and out of reach from those who wanted her power. Rosie loved Flora like her own, but she was eaten up with guilt that Flora was cursed to spend her life in a small cottage in a tiny village at the edge of the country, just scraping by. To Rosie, Flora should have been drenched in riches and living in a grand palace, like her mother did. But Rosie did her best—she showered Flora with love and attention, protecting her from everything with all her might. A mother's love was the most powerful protection of all, and Rosie would lay her life at the Pitch King's feet before letting a lick of harm fall on Flora. It was a conversation the two had countless times, until Flora knew without a shadow of a doubt just how much love Rosie held for her.

"Oh, darling, you're home! Just in time," Rosie called from the kitchen. She had a flour-covered apron strapped over her wide hips and a grin that lit up her softly lined face.

"Are those honey buns?" Flora exclaimed, mouth salivating at the sweet aroma calling her name. Sticky syrup glistened in the dying light and Flora couldn't think of a better way to end her day.

"They're mostly for tomorrow—big day," she said, her smile dimming slightly. "Is Anise still coming over?"

Flora nodded, heart beating faster and growing warmer at the thought. Anise was her best friend in the entire world—the only one besides Rosie who saw Flora and didn't think her a slow, shy girl not worth any time or effort. Anise saw past Flora's thorny vines and saw her for what she was—a kind friend who longed for adventure and fun, just like Anise. Both girls were tied to the village in different ways but longed for *more*. They wanted different sky over their heads and new ground bursting beneath their feet.

"Just…be careful, darling. You know what happened last year," Rosie said, lines creasing her soft, worn face.

"Mom. It'll be fine," she said. "I haven't experienced anything weird since—just the normal weird, and no one has found me. It's been eighteen years and basically nothing has come for us. You have to stop worrying so much."

"It's my job to worry."

"I know, but please try to just take the day off tomorrow—that can be my birthday present—you, *relaxing*," she said, placing her hands on Rosie's shoulders.

In the last year, Flora had sprouted like a stem, growing taller than her mother and most of the women in her village. Flora liked being closer to the sky and being able to see more, but it was also another way she was different. It attracted more attention when she wanted none. She wanted to be like a tree in her forest: tall, beautiful, and eye-catching to the right people for a few seconds only, then fade into the background.

"Oh, Flora. What am I going to do with you?" she said, smiling sadly. Flora hugged her mother tightly, filling them both up with love, before they broke to their normal routine.

As Flora tidied the house, sweeping out the dust and stale air, her necklace thumped against her chest. Her locket, a gold circle engraved with a leafy floral design, housed her greatest protector. Rosie had been given it shortly after Flora was born, when everything was falling apart at the seams. Every once in a while, her locket pulsed against her chest, beating in time with her heart. It was because of the protection spell embedded inside—a cloaking device. When it beat, it meant someone was trying to find her. It was the perfect warning and the perfect barrier to getting any rest from anxiety as it pulsed against her chest fairly frequently. And even then, she could never get used to it, even after experiencing the sensation her entire life.

Because it meant someone was looking for her, and that was the last thing she wanted.

The spell warding the locket—or what Flora's mother was told anyway—kept her hidden from those who sought her so long as she kept the necklace wrapped around her neck. But Flora worried the necklace wasn't just a cloaking device because sometimes it shocked her instead of pulsing, and almost seemed to tease the stems growing out of her leg. The locket was sealed shut, its secrets locked away forever, unless she risked breaking it open. But she would lose her protection, and Rosie told her time and time again—*never take it off, and never let it break, for it could shatter you.*

Her fingers tightened around the locket, the warm metal digging into her soft flesh. Flora was worried about tonight; she just didn't want her mother to know. She didn't want to place another burden on her sagging shoulders. Almost exactly one year ago, just before the witching hour closed, Flora woke to find herself standing on the edge of the Sage Woods. The Forest called to her, whispering on the wind. But she couldn't even step a toe into the thicket before her mother found her. She yanked her away, scolding her, like Flora had any control in the matter.

Flora lived in the province of Sanarbre, tucked away against the mountains and shouldered by the Sage Woods, where the Sage Witch lived. She cursed trespassers and rewarded heroes with a boon. The boons were rare—there was only one known to history, and even though it was a gift, it was also a curse. It was also a prime example of the most important warning to the people of Woodvale: *Do not enter the woods, and do not tangle with the Sage Witch. Nothing good can come from dangling your tempting self for the wicked Witch to find.*

Her heart thrummed and her blood danced at the thought of going into the Sage Woods. As much as it called to the very marrow of her bones, it also filled her with terror. Her lungs seized and her limbs stiffened. She may have been called to it, but she knew in her bones just how wary she should be regardless. Especially for her—the Sage Woods was no place for a Larkspur Lady.

Chapter Two

The King was enamored by the beautiful, elegant woman who promised him a prosperous kingdom. So, who is really at fault here?

Is it King Desmond, who only wanted the best for his people? Who only wanted his crops to be plentiful and his people to have full bellies and healthy hearts? King Desmond is a saint—he spends his life ensuring his people will be happy, but he trusted the wrong people. Now, he rules a desolate wasteland, dying a breath more each day.

Or does the blame fall on a witch of a woman? She may have been granted a bountiful boon, but it was her power that ruined the country. It was she alone who caused the crops to fail and our land to be flattened to a crisp. Because she didn't know how to use her power to its fullest—didn't understand the rules she was bound by.

But is a slave at fault for her actions? Shouldn't we direct the blame to the man conducting her power?

-The Age of Larkspur by Cassius Muscari, IV

The dream started like any other. Flora was in her copse of trees, soaking up the nature before she was forced to return to the dying world yonder. Before she could do so, the dream shifted in a blink. A pitch-black forest appeared before her eyes and a figure darted past her, sending Flora to the ground in a swirl.

The man ran as fast as he could, running for his life in the nightmarish landscape. Flora gaped at the sight of black trees with branches that loomed over her like knives dipped in blood. Caws sounded in the distance before a crack of lightning broke through the sky and Flora flung herself from the ground and followed the man. Branches whipped against their skin, blood pooling and dropping to the hungry floor below. Phantom lights winked in the distance before the forest continued on in an endless stream of green so dark it was almost black. Flora followed the fleeing man, her curiosity piqued and a sense of urgency thrumming in her veins.

The man's foot connected with the unhinged root, and he went toppling to the ground with a soft thud. His lips loosened and a cry of pain and terror tore out of his mouth as a figure in a cloak of night, shadows covering his entire body, appeared before the fallen man. Flora watched with wide eyes, rooted to the ground.

"Please don't kill me—I have information," the man begged, hands pressed to his bleeding limbs. Scratches of varying depths and severity littered his skin. A nasty, scarlet slash of crimson blood welled and dripped down his forearm steadily.

"Do you think I care?" the shadowed figure asked in a husky voice, sparking fear in Flora's heart as her brain screamed that he was the Pitch King.

The Pitch King was shrouded in shadows save for a sliver of silver moonlight streaking across his face. He was smirking at the fallen man in a cruel imitation of a smile—all teeth and snarl.

"It's about the girl!"

The Pitch King remained silent, but the fallen man

was undeterred, as he quickly said, "I know who she is and where she is. I can help you. Please don't kill me."

"Tell me," the Pitch King said.

"Her name is Flora. She lives in Sanarbre." Flora gasped, her mouth dropping open as all of her greatest fears were presented to her. She hated her mind sometimes and the nightmares it produced, each one plucked from her terror, highlighting just how much she needed to worry about the possible situations she could find herself in.

The Pitch King hummed, fingers steepled against his chin. "Why, thank you. That is most helpful."

"So…you won't kill me?"

"Oh no—I won't kill you—but as a human with such loose lips, you aren't useful enough to me," he said, stroking his chin before his arms flew out like he was on a cross. The shadows surrounding him caressed him like a lover. The Pitch King muttered foreign words under his breath as the fallen man's body began to shift. His bones cracked and skin burst as sinewy feathers grew from the bruised, battered, and bleeding tissue. Ebony exploded violently from his skin, growing faster and furiously before everything human fell away. Gone was the brown hair and alabaster skin. His bones had crumbled to ash and where was once his hulking figure was a beautiful, terrified, and confused bird.

A grin of pleasure and malice overcame the victor, teeth bared and snapping at the animal, his eyes gleaming in satisfaction. The Pitch King could never tolerate loose cannons. Everyone long suspected his darkly shadowed self had secrets to shelter and plans to protect. And magic, murder, and mayhem were all ministrations in his arsenal, pillars of his domain ready to be invoked. He clucked at the bird, raising his shadowed eyebrows before sweeping his coat into the air and forcing the newly made bird into flight.

Flora watched, body quivering, as the Pitch King swept away, deeper into his forest domain, back to his palace of bones and shadow, with a crow following in his wake as he prepared to go hunting for *her*.

And then the nightmare was over, shifting to something new in the span of a breath, her fears of the malevolent man that terrified everyone in Woodvale dispersed to the recess of her mind.

Her world was gone. In its place was lush vegetation so blindingly green and healthy it stabbed Flora with an ache of despair deep in her core, blinding and white-hot. Her world didn't even remotely look like that. Gone were the fields of dried-up crops and cracked soil. Gone were the dirt roads and crumbling buildings of her village. Gone were the malnourished people and animals little more than skin and bone. Instead, she found silky vines and thick trees with colorful flowers littering the forest floor. A spark of recognition rang like a bell, but she couldn't place it—all she had grown up with was hard earth and desolate landscapes.

Her chest ached from the desperation rising in her for this to be real. For her to experience this in real life. A marrow-deep longing gnawed at her, all-consuming as she looked at the beauty surrounding her, hugging her close and welcoming her home. She wanted lush, extensive forests to be tangible, not just the copse she was used to. Birds sang in her ears as little critters scurried in the underbrush and trees. A gentle breeze flew into the forest, her hair twirling in the wind like swathes of starlight.

Sweet Flora…you're running out of time.

"What do you mean?" she asked, the wind caressing her arm. Her heart thumped in her chest.

Your body can only sustain the binding for so long.

"What binding?"

Hush, child. When your birthmark has reached its potency, and the color has been fully leeched from your body, your time will be up. You will join the other Larkspur Ladies, like pretty dolls on a shelf.

"I don't understand," Flora whimpered, a crease forming between her eyebrows. "Who are you?"

Someone who cares—someone who has waited long enough and saved enough strength up over the years to finally be able to speak with you. Even in this paltry version.

"But—"

Listen to me, Flora. There is one way to save yourself, and Woodvale. Find the Króna—the witch who made your necklace. Find her and she'll help you.

A frown tugged at Flora's chewed raw lips. "But where is this *Króna*?"

She is hidden in a cave at the base of the Norn Mountains where it hugs the Sage Woods. Find her, child. Save yourself and Woodvale.

With that, the whispering wind whisked away, back into the void it came from. Flora gasped a staggering breath as the hold it held on her lungs released. Suddenly, a dark shadow was closing in on her as stars blotted from behind her eyes.

The dream of darkness slipped away from Flora, transforming into a fantasy of a sunny afternoon with Anise. But the fear closing around her heart loomed, burning so bright it burst alive when her eyes opened the next morning.

A jolt of surprise hit Flora's bloodstream when her rose-colored room appeared before her eyes. She had the vague memory of a nightmare she hoped was just a figment of her imagination, but she couldn't catch the slipping strands before they were gone entirely. The only lingering remnant of the nightmare was a coil of fear deep in her belly, a warning that sang in her veins that danger lurked closer than she realized, but as she couldn't recall any specifics, she brushed aside her terror because she could remember her second dream.

With the dream of the whispering wind lingering at the forefront of her mind, she had convinced herself she must have sleepwalked again. That was the only explanation she could think of for the odd dream. Flora knew why it looked familiar—it looked like the Sage Woods, or at least what she could glean from the treeline last year.

Flora groaned, her head dropping into her hands— what a way to start her eighteenth year. But the dream offered some comfort if it was real, though she couldn't decide the veracity of it yet. Regardless, her ankle, the stipulations to her health, and her preceding legacy were a cause for concern. If she was being honest with herself, she was deteriorating more and more each day.

Once, Flora's locks were the color of honey, supple and sweet. But now, her hair was a shade away from being bone-white. Her skin was discoloring, her entire body seeming to shed any color that wasn't associated with stark white and the cool, paleness of death. Her hair mirrored the dead birch tree in her backyard, and her skin appeared almost ghostly in the right lighting. She was being leeched of color, year after year. And yet, her birthmark living on her ankle grew more vibrant and potent each year. All her color was draining into the cursed purple tattoo marring her body.

Flora just couldn't figure out exactly what it all meant or why it was happening. Her mother, Rosie— because to Flora, Rosie was her mother—told her the basics about her birthmark, but only enough for Flora's incessant questions to cease and for her to understand the risk her ankle posed should anyone see it.

The story went that many years ago, her ancestor saved the Sage Witch's forest, and thus, she was granted a boon. After her encounter, she received a jeweled necklace and a tattoo of a white larkspur appeared on her anklebone: a talisman of the magic granted. This allowed her to grow plants and nourish the land, keeping everyone safe and healthy. It was a useful gift, one that kept the Kingdom of Woodvale prosperous for many years, the power being passed down to the first-born girl of each generation.

Until Flora's mother. Anneliese Larkspur. High Lady Larkspur, consultant and rumoured mistress to King Desmond Vale.

No one truly knew what happened between Anneliese Larkspur and Desmond Vale. There was great speculation, mostly about who the instigator of the calamity truly was. Most believed it was Anneliese, and her wicked, witchy powers going to her head. They claimed her powers failed when she proved herself to be unworthy of the Larkspur boon as she was overcome with greed and selfish desires. A small group believed it was King Desmond, that the power at his right-hand's fingertips was too tempting not to play with, to test its limits and see how bountiful Woodvale could become.

They said his avarice split the world in two.

Rosie always told Flora it was complicated, that like everything, there were two sides to the story. Not each side necessarily had a good and bad side, just two fickle people whose swaying emotions got the better of them. Rosie insisted Flora try her best to be good, to not follow in her mother's footsteps, regardless of who was to blame for the calamity. She didn't want to taint Flora's opinions of her mother, or of the King, because he was still alive and well, and upturning every stone in his search for Flora. So no, Rosie wasn't sure who was to blame for the disaster all those years ago. She had theories, but she kept them close to her chest so Flora could be unbiased.

Flora had a cursed, tarnished legacy to fix, but Rosie was too protective for Flora to fulfill her role. And Flora didn't mind. She liked that Rosie kept her sheltered and wrapped in her mom's embrace. Rosie's heart would shatter if the babe she saved was twisted and rotted by the cruel world or killed and sapped dry for no reason other than being born to Anneliese Larkspur. Flora couldn't endure her mom's heart breaking.

Flora apparently had the potential to help the land flourish again, but her power never bloomed. Besides her birthmark sprouting purple larkspurs and draining her color, she had never performed *magic*. She had never thought much of it, when the years passed and nothing ever happened, because Rosie always stressed how important it was to stay hidden. If they were found out, Rosie would be executed, and Flora would become a consort, if she was lucky, or a slave if she wasn't— and Flora didn't want either of those things to occur.

All Rosie knew was the birthmark meant Flora had magic, but Flora assumed the magic must have dried up in the calamity. She wanted to help, but fear and anxiety kept her tongue clamped, her lips sealed, and her legs locked to Sanarbre. She always hoped one day her power would just burst out of her, and she could save Woodvale from complete destruction.

But she never even imagined there might have been a time limit. That was, if the whispering wind told the truth.

"Happy birthday, darling," Rosie said, bursting into the room with a pink ceramic plate holding a rich chocolate cake. Eighteen candles jutted out at the top, flames flickering from the draft.

"Thank you, Mom," Flora said as she lifted herself from her cozy sheets. She leaned in and extinguished the flame, causing smoke to waft into her nose.

Flora and her mother moved to the kitchen, spending the dusty orange hours talking and devouring the cake—a yearly tradition both cherished. Flora longed to tell her mother of her dream, but the words wouldn't go past thoughts inside her skull, sealed up tight behind her lips. She didn't want to worry her mother, and she also didn't want to be discouraged. But as they talked and relaxed, Flora was theorizing how to get to the Norn Mountains.

Flora may have hated talking to strangers, and even acquaintances, sometimes even friends, but she longed for adventure. She was scared—she had never left Sanarbre for a reason. But she was eighteen now, and with the prospect of her birthmark draining her of life, she had never felt more valorous. The part of her that feared people and change was dying with each breath as the sun began its rise into the sky. She would have to be braver than she had ever been, and she wasn't sure it would even work, but she had to try. She had known for years that eventually she would have to do *something*. And now, here it was—an answer, a quest, a *reason* to leave her village behind and throw on her lionheart.

Her heart beat faster, excitement and nerves humming in her veins. *But what if it all went wrong?* Flora thought, scenarios racing through her mind.

She could get captured on her way to the Norn Mountains. The King or the Witch could find her. Maybe that magnetic attraction she had to the Sage Woods would finally call her home. Or maybe she would get trampled by a stray horse, never to be seen or heard from again. She would break her mother's heart and soul.

No. Calm down.

Flora closed her eyes for a brief second, trying to calm her sprinting thoughts. If she kept her head and her wits about her, she would be fine. Probably. But probably was better than nothing. She had to do this; she finally had a reason. And if the whispering wind spoke the truth, she may not have long for this world.

She didn't want to die in her miniscule village, among decaying trees. She wanted to see her country, wanted to feel healthy grass and roots under her fingers. To do that, she had to leave her bubble. It felt like a weight was pressing on her lungs at the thought, but Anise had been saying for years that eventually she would have to work at healing the cracks in her mind. Figure out a way to live with her anxiety, instead of letting it rule her mind and body.

It was, of course, easier said than done. But she

was finally willing to try.

"Mom, Anise and I are going to explore today—not too far, but we want to spend some time with just each other for a few hours."

Rosie sighed, eyeing Flora as she stuttered through her sentence. She knew Flora well enough to know she was up to something. Rosie was just wrong about what exactly. Rosie clasped Flora's hand in hers, and said, "As long as you're back before nightfall."

"Thank you!" Flora said, a smile lighting her face in the warm morning glow streaming in from the window.

"Just be careful," Rosie said. "Don't let your heart get ahead of your mind."

"I know. I'll be careful," she said, giving her mother a reassuring smile.

Flora went to her room to dress for the day. Her wardrobe consisted of long trousers and long skirts. Today, she decided, was a trouser day. The masculine cut to the pant attracted her that day, and it would be much easier to travel to the mountains without a skirt snagging on loose rocks or thistles.

Trousers were uncommon for women in Woodvale, but in her small village, people didn't care as much as they did in Vale Centre, where women dressed in gold and jewels and men in cravats and rare minerals. Even with their world falling apart, the men and women rich enough to live in the capitol city somehow managed to find spare riches to flaunt. But in her small village in Sanarbre, the townsfolk were used to the unusual Flora. The girl who wore long frocks in the dead of summer, who liked trousers some days, and dresses and skirts the next.

She may have turned heads when she was little, but they were used to Flora by now. She was allowed her idiosyncrasies without question, even when they should have questioned why she wore long stockings and dragging skirts in boiling weather. She was allowed to be herself in the small corner of the country, where they had bigger things to worry about than a girl who liked dressing as she pleased. Or so she thought.

Flora longed for more girls to follow her lead—she hated being the odd one out as it cast more eyes her way. But as much as she hated the attention, she hated being restricted more. Some days her legs needed to be free, and no amount of eyes on her could snuff that desire out in Flora.

Although, there were two people who could make Flora bend and curve to their desires and overpower her own. Rosie was one, and the other was Anise.

"Flora!" Anise's lilting voice called down the path. Her huckleberry hair streamed in ringlets behind her as she raced up the path to Flora.

A broad grin bloomed on Flora's face at the sight. Her heart warmed in her chest as her cheeks flushed in cherry circles. Flora flung her arms around the other girl as they connected, her smile softening against Anise's shoulder.

"Hi," Flora murmured, a perpetual grin resting on her lips.

"Happy birthday!" Anise exclaimed, hugging Flora tight. She lifted Flora's feet from the ground and swung her around—a feat Flora was unsure how she managed to accomplish each year as Anise stayed the same and Flora sprouted taller.

"Thank   you,"   Flora   said   as   their   limbs disconnected.

"So, what are we doing today? Birthday girl's choice." Anise winked, grinning from ear to ear. Every year on each other's birthdays, they would spend the day together. Usually, they would explore the surrounding desolation or the copse and pretend they were adventurers on a quest.

Anise was the only girl in their village who took a chance on Flora. When Rosie and Flora first arrived, a weary handmaiden and a sleeping baby, they found the empty cottage, just waiting for an owner. The darkness of the dead of night enveloped them in protection as their journey was long, but successful. Although the cottage was ownerless, a woman waited for them. According to Rosie, she gave Flora her locket, and then she vanished. And in the morning, the village accepted the new residents without question, like they had always lived there.

Flora was a shy child, always hiding behind her mother's thick skirts. So, the other children paid her no mind. Except Anise. She saw Flora for what she was, underneath the brick walls surrounding her—a curious girl who longed for an adventure and a friend. Anise was loud and outspoken, and immediately swooped Flora up, creating a bubble of safety for the two to share. Flora eventually became comfortable around Anise, and the two had been inseparable ever since.

Things had been shifting between them for the past couple of years as their differences finally caught up to them. It was easy being friends with anyone when you were young, but the more you grew up, the easier it was for differences to break relationships in two.

But Flora didn't want to let Anise go. She would

hold onto her as long as she could. Until her grip turned to stone in the sun, like the trolls from her beloved folklore. She would remain by Anise's side—she needed her like she needed air in her lungs.

"Fancy taking a bit of a longer journey today?" Flora asked, wringing her hands before she stopped dead in her tracks as she realized what she was doing. She dropped her hands into fists by her side and tried to look more confident than she felt.

"Sure. Where to?"

"The Norn Mountains," Flora said. Anise blinked at her.

"But…that's like a two-and-a-half-hour walk and that's only one way. What could you possibly want there?"

Flora took a deep breath, steadying herself before she released it and her reckless desire into the world. "I want to meet the *Króna*."

Chapter Three

The Norn Mountains are a treacherous place—not for the faint of heart. They keep Woodvale locked in tight. There is no historical record detailing the perilous peaks. Whatever is on the other side of the mountain—if anything—no one alive knows.

The peaks rise high in the sky, so tall they blot out the sun. No one has ever reached the tallest peak and returned. Many brave souls have tried, and the Norn Mountains are sure to be filled with bones of the poor souls.

A warning for those foolish enough to try: it is said there is an old woman, a spirit, who may be powerful enough to help you. But like any witch, nothing she does is for free. She may ask for your very life in return for what you seek.

One last note: be careful around the stones.

-An Adventurer's Guide to Woodvale: Warnings and Suggestions by Gísli

"What? You want to meet the *Króna*? Who is that?" Anise said, her dainty eyebrows furrowing as Flora dragged Anise off the main path. She guided them east, in the general direction of the Norn Mountains, dust kicking up from their heels.

"She's an old woman who lives at the Norn Mountains."

"Okay, but *why* do you want to meet her? And on

your birthday? Really? That's how you want to spend it? The *one* of two days per year we're both free to do whatever we want?" Anise asked, crossing her arms over her chest, and Flora's stomach tightened as the guilt tried to burrow in.

A cat had captured Flora's tongue. She had never told Anise about her ankle, or who her mother was. Anise only knew Rosie was Flora's adopted mother. Rosie and Flora always alluded that her biological parents were dead, and Rosie was a generous family friend who loved children.

Flora wanted to entrust her secret to someone, and as much as she trusted Anise, she wasn't sure how much Anise could handle about her past. Or about how tumultuous her future appeared.

But she had to give Anise a reason, and a good one lest Anise not understand the importance of visiting the *Króna*. Flora herself was still unsure of this frenzied adventure, but the whispering wind's words were too ominous to ignore. The insidious seed of doubt had been planted and now there was no turning back. Flora had to act, sooner rather than later. She needed to dispel her anxieties and power forward. She needed to figure out the truth and somehow save herself and Woodvale, because doing nothing was not an option any longer. Self-preservation was an aggressive beast spurring her onward.

While it was true they had two days a year where both were free to do whatever they liked, they usually did something Anise enjoyed most. Because what Flora wanted was to spend the day lying on the forest floor, soaking up the earthy aromas. Unless they chose to go on an adventure, then, both girls had fun. But only if it was the two of them. Sometimes Anise roped in some relative stranger, and Flora's day and mood sank like a stone in water.

"The *Króna* knows something about my birthparents. Rosie told me." The words escaped Flora's lips before she could dwell on them. It wasn't the perfect lie. It caused a box to erupt around Flora that concerned her, shutting Anise out. But it also wasn't a complete lie. The *Króna* knew something about her magic, which was technically about her birthparents by association. Her gut wormed in guilt regardless—but it comforted Flora to remind herself that it was not a complete, total lie.

"Oh, Flora," Anise said, a sympathetic frown forming on her bow lips. "Of course, we can go then."

"Thank you."

"This'll be fun! A real adventure. We have a purpose this time," she said, her face glowing in the morning light, as her eyes gleamed. "Maybe she'll tell you something exciting about your parents. Maybe they were rich and lived in Vale Centre. Could you imagine?"

"That would be exciting, I guess," Flora said, a grimacing smile attempting to grow on her face.

"Oh, Flora." Anise laughed. "Stop that face. It'll be fine."

The two set off for the Norn Mountains. Flora had packed provisions for the journey: honey buns, dried apples, and as much water as possible that would fit in her knit sack. Flora's stomach was in knots as they walked. She was worried they wouldn't even be able to *find* the *Króna*, let alone convince her to tell Flora everything she needed to know. And out of Anise's earshot as well. Or, she would just have to take the leap of faith and tell her. Expose a part of Flora's soul only one other person knew about.

Flora knew Anise wouldn't give her in to the guard or anyone else for that matter. But it would change their relationship. Gone would be the lazy days in the sun, and in its place would be magic-filled days of worry and paranoia. It already weighed on Flora too much to let another person in on that suffocating secret.

Eventually, the cool morning sun burned to its midday peak, causing sweat to bead in glistening droplets on the two girls. Their legs were stiff from the constant walking, but instead of silence filling the air, laughter did. They had grabbed dried twigs they found on the dusty, cracked path, and were waving them around as swords. So far, Flora had won each "battle," knocking Anise's stick out of her hand with ease. Although, she suspected Anise may be letting her win on account of it being her birthday.

Flora and Anise had been playing with pretend swords for as long as they could remember. Because being a good adventurer meant knowing how to slay threatening monsters. Flora wasn't sure she could actually slay a monster, even if it was trying to kill her. But she was safe in her bubble, so what could possibly go wrong?

"What are you going to say to her?" Anise broke the silence they had been harboring since their stick swords snapped in two.

"I'm not sure yet. Something about how I know she knows something, and I want her to tell me."

"Good. I'll be here if you need help." Anise's words caused a flutter of warmth to erupt in Flora's belly.

"Thanks," she replied, a soft smile resting on her pink lips.

Flora often got too tongue-tied to speak with strangers, and Anise was always there to swoop in and save her. Flora did want to grow out of that, but it was so *hard* and letting Anise do it for her was so easy. Nevertheless, Flora vowed to try delving down the road of personal growth. Even if she didn't actually accomplish anything, it was a healthy feat in and of itself.

The two girls ventured down the overgrown and jagged path in limited conversation for the remainder of their journey, both caught up in the tangles of their own minds. Before they knew it, like a dream come to life, the Norn Mountains rose towering into the sky, cresting far above the horizon. The granite, rocky peaks loomed menacingly over their heads. The mountains were visible from their village, and they looked tall there, but standing a foot from the base was a whole other story. Flora's chest squeezed at the view. One earthquake and she would be crushed alive in an instant. And if she didn't die on impact, then it would be a brutally slow death of suffocation and agony.

Stop that.

Flora pushed aside the thoughts, her fear cresting over her. She needed to focus on the matter at hand, not worry once again about how she might die.

At the base of the mountain, carved stone structures cropped up from the earth, jutting out of place in the barren, smooth rocky surface. The stones looked naturally carved by weather and erosion, but there was something about them that kept catching

Flora's eye. She felt a presence from the stone, like something was lurking beneath the crusty surface. Behind the structures were pockmarks cut into the rough stone of the mountain and yawning pits of black. There were several cave entrances, but most were small and stout, save for one. The peak of the cave was a few feet taller than Flora, and a faint glow emitted from the depths of black.

"I guess it's that one?"

"Guess so," Flora murmured. Her stomach clenched at the sight of the dark maw of the cave, fear spiking her heart, racing through her bloodstream swiftly as a cool sweat broke out on her skin.

"We should have brought a real sword," Anise said, with a harsh laugh that was all false levity.

"We have a lot to learn as adventurers," Flora said.

"We'll be great. Besides, every adventurer has to start somewhere—this can be our somewhere. In a super creepy, dark cave with some old lady called the *Króna.*"

With Anise's attempt at making light of the situation, Flora started walking forward. Her legs felt like lead, like she was dragging them behind her as she struggled to move forward. Fear ate away at her very marrow, forcing her to be slow, and to wonder if she would ever get to the mouth at all and step past the sharp teeth and into the shadows.

"Together," Anise said, extending her palm toward Flora.

Flora nodded, steeling herself, and slipped her hand into Anise's. The warm contact of her friend grounded her—kept her calm enough to push away the encompassing fear and put one foot in front of the other toward the yawning mouth.

The two girls strode toward the cave, the smaller, bold one a beat ahead of her tall, quivering counterpart. The second their feet passed the first stone structure, the scenery changed, eliciting sharp gasps from the girls.

Gone were the sharp, craggy stone structures and in their place were chiseled statues. They had carved faces with sharp fangs and snarling features, and bulging stone muscles ending in honed swords that looked razor-sharp, even in stone.

Trolls.

The word rang through Flora's mind like a bell. Frantically, she tried racking her brain for the stories she had grown up with. Her mother had given her a book when she was six and starting to show an interest in adventure. It was a book of folklore from Woodvale, stories and warnings to the brave souls who wandered where humans didn't belong. Rosie thought it would help keep Flora in check, keep her from exposing herself to magic even as it hummed dormant in her veins. In reality, it did so much more. It opened her up to a whole new world of magic and mischief, of beauty and wonder, of the power of stories.

"Those are trolls," Anise whispered, eyes wide with terror.

"It's okay. They stay stone in the daylight—the sun binds them," Flora said, hastily as she squeezed Anise's hand. "If that's even true. They could be statues. Right?"

"I'm sure they're just statues," Anise said in a soft, soothing voice. "This *Króna* probably had it done to scare off trespassers."

"Right."

"But if they are real, how do you know they're stone in daylight?"

"Remember that book Mom gave me of the folklore? There was a section on trolls," Flora said, her stomach a knotted jangle of nerves. "I'm pretty sure I'm remembering correctly, and they are still stone so it lends credence to the tale. I know it's probably not true, though."

"Wow, I forgot about that book," Anise said, gawking at the statues. She gave Flora a cutting grin. "I mostly remember the stories about the heroes and adventures—not trolls."

"Good thing we're together then. I remember more about the…creatures."

"Ah yes, my little scaredy-cat," Anise teased, and Flora stuck her tongue out at the mocking girl in jest.

"We should hurry though," Flora said, taking note of the sun high in the sky. She had no idea how long it would take, and if she was right, and those were actually *trolls*, not just carved statues, they would have a limited to time to talk with the *Króna*.

"Let's go."

The two crept toward the mouth of the cave, a flickering flame casting the walls of stone in moving shadows. They shared a nervous glance as the sun winked out behind them, and the cave welcomed them in a dark embrace.

"Who goes there?" a croaking voice boomed, sending echoes bouncing to their quivering ears.

Flora's heart jumped and she clung onto Anise's arm, dragging the other girl close to her body. Flora wasn't sure if she was shielding Anise or forcing Anise to shield her. Flora hoped it was the former, but fear was clutching her heart so tight she didn't care. Terror had a death grip on her, cutting off her rational and altruistic self and replacing it with a selfish desire to cut her losses and run for her life.

It was the second time such a deliciously despicable desire had crossed her mind. And just like last time, disgust filled her so full she almost vomited from the sour, rotting taste creeping into her mouth.

When she was ten, Rosie had let her and Anise go to the village market alone. They were to buy some ingredients for her stew and return home immediately. It took a lot of begging and convincing to let them go, as the King's Guard presence was higher than normal due to reasons Flora wasn't sure about. Her only guess was that King Desmond was getting more desperate to find her as the years passed and Woodvale deteriorated more by the day. But the trip went fine, they found what they were looking for, and even treated themselves to sweets and iced tea, the mugs covered in beads of condensation that allowed them to draw pictures in the dirt. The two girls were smiling and giddy from the indulged sugar and were just about to leave when it happened—when their trip almost took a disastrous, dangerous, detrimental turn.

The guards were corralling people into a checkpoint. They wanted to inspect each child in case one was the long-lost Larkspur Lady. Flora and Anise were hiding in an alley, and it was only Anise's stubbornness that kept her from questioning why Flora was hiding. Anise didn't want some stranger inspecting her without her parents as a buffer. She didn't trust the palace guards—they came from the city and were usually quite cruel. They had almost killed her older brother once in a misunderstanding.

But then, a guard walked by their hiding spot. And it was then that Flora had the strongest urge to shove Anise out to the wolves so she could run to safety. However, Flora kept her hands to herself, and the guard passed by without spotting the cowering little girls. Since both were shaken and wary, Flora and Anise waited for hours until the guards had dismantled their checkpoint.

Everything had been fine in the end, but it had forced Flora to look deeper at herself. Forced her to start thinking about who she was, and who she wanted to be. What her values were, and how far she was willing to go for herself, and for those she loved. She hadn't figured out every answer that night, and she was still figuring the answers out, but it forced her to see a shade of black in her soul that left a bigger mark in her mind than she cared to admit.

"We come in peace," Anise called, grabbing Flora's hand in an attempt to calm her.

"Who are you?' the voice boomed again as shadows danced on the walls.

"My name is Anise, and this is my friend Flora," Anise said, tugging on Flora's hand—trying to coax her to open her mouth.

A shuffling of footsteps echoed toward their waiting ears, and a shadow of a hunched old woman erupted on the wall to their left before coming into view. Her deep umber skin was sallow from lack of natural light and wrinkled galore.

"Finally," she said. "You two are slower than I am."

"What?" Anise asked, a note of fear creeping into

her voice as her hand tightened around Flora's.

The woman came closer, until they could see her clearer in the firelight burning brighter. Her silver hair was matted, and her clothes were filthy and threadbare. Flora cringed away, the dirt and grime so thick she was concerned for her own health and that of the old woman's. The only part of her that wasn't filthy or ragged was a thin gold chain looped around her neck, a shining gold medallion swinging on the end. In one hand, she held a flame in a glass jar, and in the other, she held a moss-green powder spilling out of her wrinkled fingers.

"I don't want you, though," she muttered, looking at Anise. Then she blew the powder into Anise's face. She dropped like a sack of potatoes and Flora gasped, falling to her knees to catch Anise before she cracked bones against the stone floor.

"What was that for?" Flora shrieked, eyebrows flying high at her tone. She hadn't intended for it to come out so sharply. But her friend collapsing had driven a wedge of ice in her heart for the *Króna*.

"Oh, so you want her to hear all the details, child?" She sent Flora a sardonic smirk as a flush crept onto Flora's cheeks.

"You could have warned me. Or her. She could have waited outside," Flora protested, the words spilling from her lips. Something about the old woman hurting Anise loosened Flora's usually sealed lips.

"Something tells me that girl wouldn't go willingly," she muttered, causing Flora to frown.

"What?"

"Never mind that, child. There are more important things to discuss. Namely that leech on your ankle."

Flora gulped at the words. "Leech?" she squeaked and the *Króna* let out a cackle.

"In a way, yes. It is a leech unless you use it."

"Use it? But I can't. I've never done magic."

"I know. There is a reason for that—an insurance policy courtesy of the Sage Witch."

"But why?"

"Because your mother broke her rules and was hung before she could feel the Sage Witch's wrath. You were Lady Larkspur's only offspring, so you get her punishment."

"But the magic was a gift, right? To help Woodvale? Why would the Sage Witch take that away?"

"To teach people a lesson that she is not to be underestimated, obviously." The *Króna* shuffled around the cavern as Flora held tight onto Anise.

"So, how do I get my magic back? Something told me you could help me," Flora said.

"Are you sure you want the burden? It is a heavy responsibility to bear."

"You said it yourself—my ankle is a leech. I'll die if I don't, won't I?" Flora asked, a note of hope sparking in her chest. Maybe she could get out of all of this easier than she thought, without dying because of the actions of her ancestors.

"Yes, you will," the *Króna* said, squashing Flora's hopes, "but sometimes death is a blessing, not a curse."

"I don't want to die," Flora whispered.

"If you want your powers unlocked, you must find where she scattered your family legacy. The Sage Witch cast your family's amulet, where the power stems from and molds with Larkspur blood, into four shards. Find all four and you'll regain your full magical potential."

"Where are they?"

The *Króna* flicked her fingers up and said, "Vale Centre, the Svart Sea, the Pitch Woods, and the Sage Woods."

"But those places are huge!"

"Flora, you have Larkspur blood running in your veins and that boon tattooed to your skin and bone. The shards are drawn to you, and you to them. You'll hear their call when you're close," the *Króna* said, raising a disdaining eyebrow in Flora's direction as Flora's mind caught up with the string of places the old woman listed.

"Wait, you said the Pitch Woods? Are you insane? I can't go there! No one who's ever entered has returned," Flora cried, terror seizing her lungs as her eyes bugged.

The Pitch Woods were notorious for stealing people away and never letting them go. They were dark and treacherous, not an ounce of sunlight breaking through the blackened trees. It was said a sorcerer lived there, the Pitch King, who loved setting his monsters on trespassers. If the Sage Witch was feared because of the Larkspur curse or boon, the Pitch King was feared for simply existing. The entire Wood was a stain on the land and the map of Woodvale, cutting off life to the southwest in darkness and shadows. The one blessing was that his monsters and Wood never extended past his border, and there were no written or verbal sightings of him.

The only reason the people of Woodvale knew about him was because of one man. The only one in the hundreds of years of the Pitch Woods existence that went into the savagely vicious Woods and survived. He was a hollowed-out man, scars littering his body, and was more blood than skin when he escaped. He spoke of monstrous horrors and said the Pitch King let him go so he could tell Woodvale one thing: never enter his domain unless you'd like to die a painful death.

Flora couldn't even begin to imagine setting foot in his forest. One person had lived, and only long enough to dispel his warning. Flora scoffed at the fools who entered the Pitch Woods willingly, those desperate idiots who thought the Sage Witch was worse than the Pitch King purely because she was known to grant a gift only to revert it. The Pitch King was worse; he only bled death and destruction.

"You'll be fine—just don't go there first. Once you get one shard, your magic should start responding to it. Just keep your wits, child, and you'll survive the Pitch King."

"How do you know all this? And why are you helping me?" Flora asked, pushing through her thickening tongue. The longer she spent in this cave, the tighter her chest ached.

"The Sage Witch isn't the only one who knows the secrets of magic," she said. "As for why I'm helping you? Your mother asked me to—it was her dying wish and I don't like my debts to go unpaid, especially not with her."

"My mother asked you? She knew this would happen?" Flora's voice was small and careful, her fragile heart wavering at the unexpected information and kindness from the one woman she had the most complicated feelings about.

"Of course. She grew up with a woman who lived with the Larkspur curse, unlike you," she said. "That is all the information I have for you. Find the shards and your magic will be yours to wield. You can fix the burden your mother left you and save Woodvale from ultimate decay. Fail, and you'll turn into a colorless husk, before blowing away with the wind."

Flora swallowed thickly, fear and anxiety clogging her throat. She wanted to ask a million more questions, but the *Króna* had turned her back on her dismissively. Flora knew a lost cause when she saw one, and the *Króna* had given her information, more than she had when she arrived. So, she rose, holding Anise's limp body in her shaking, quivering arms. Flora gritted her teeth, a faint flush of sweat breaking out on her forehead as her neck clenched. She was about to drop her friend, the weight almost too much to carry for her frame, but she could not, would not, let Anise down. She owed it to her friend to get her out of the cave in one whole piece.

Something stopped her from stepping toward the exit. She was at war with herself, half of her telling her to hush and run away and the other half pushing her to ask her question—call the old woman out. She gently lowered Anise to the ground.

Flora closed her eyes tightly, letting an eternal black comfort her senses before asking, "Why are you telling me this now? I've been a short walk from you for almost eighteen years. Why now?"

The *Króna* sighed, and Flora's eyes snapped open to find the old woman pursing her lips, the skin whitened as she cast a shrewd gaze on Flora. "Your locket is breaking—the one I gave your adopted mother. It shields you and prevents those searching for you from finding you—witches, Kings, and commonfolk alike. But just like Woodvale, just like you, it's deteriorating—dying. Now is the only time I could seek you out, and it's not a moment too soon. The strength and stipulations of the enchantment on the locket evidently got away from me. Woodvale, and yourself, won't see another year if you don't fix your mother's selfish actions."

Flora swallowed thickly, working through the lump in her throat before nodding softly. "Thank you," she said quickly, her voice sounding hoarse and tired after her battle with her mind.

The *Króna* waved her off and shuffled backward, deeper into the shadows. She was dismissing Flora once and for all.

"I wish you luck, child. You're going to need it—the Sage Witch plays games to torture her opponents," she said, eyes piercing Flora as she looked back one last time. "That necklace won't save you anymore, child. You're going on a path in which it cannot shield you. It's done its duty, served its purpose. You don't need it anymore. Your path is laid out in full now; only the end is truly unwritten. You get to play the game at long last."

Flora's hand had unconsciously snaked up to clutch at the locket, and as she looked down at it, she could almost feel its dying breath at the *Króna's* words. It had been a shield for her growing up, but the time for hiding was over. Flora had to be brave and bold now. She dropped the locket, letting it bounce against her waiting chest, and met the *Króna's* burning gaze.

"A word of advice and warning." The *Króna*

sagged, shaking her head as she stared at Flora. She sent her one pitying smile before turning away.

"Women like the Sage Witch always win."

Chapter Four

Be kind to the Witch
And she'll grant you a boon
Be cruel to the Witch
And she'll tear you in two
-Nursery rhyme

Flora's arms burned and her lower back ached from carrying Anise's heavy, limp body out of the cave and away from the troll statues. She had forgotten to inquire more about them—she was curious, but she doubted the *Króna* would have revealed all of her secrets.

Flora sat in the baking sun, her exposed forearms turning from white to pink to a dusty shade of red as she waited for Anise to wake. Her mind raced with possibilities about everything the *Króna* had revealed, what it all meant and what would entail as a result.

Her heart pounded and her chest clenched from fear, but she was also partially excited. It was a real adventure at her fingertips—something she and Anise had talked about for years. And not just an adventure—a quest. She had a goal and a purpose, something to win or lose.

At that thought, her excitement dwindled. If she failed, she would die. And it sounded like a painful death. There was so much that could go wrong, and so much she didn't know. She needed to get home and talk

45

to her mother, figure out a plan from there. If anyone could help her, it was Rosie.

Maybe she should just give up now. It was a daunting task, traveling all over the country for shards of her family legacy. Maybe the Larkspur boon, gift, or curse, should just perish with her.

"Flora?" Anise murmured, slowly blinking her eyes open.

"Anise! Are you okay?" Flora flung her arms around the smaller girl and hugged her tight. Relief flooded her veins that she was alive and speaking.

"What happened?" she groaned, head lolling on her neck as she struggled to rise from the ground.

"The *Króna* doused you with something."

"That hag! My head feels like a horse trampled it," she complained, pressing her palm to her forehead as Flora's face fell in sympathy.

Flora felt awful that Anise was hurting, but she was thankful to the *Króna*. She could tell Anise on her own terms, or not at all if that was what she pleased.

"I'm sorry."

"Don't apologize—it's her fault," she said, with a wince. "What did she say to you anyways? Anything helpful?"

"Sort of. Can I explain later? We need to get back before my mom starts worrying," Flora said, and as Anise was struggling with her head pounding, she complied.

The two set off for home, sweat pooling in crevices and silence following their wake as neither was in a chatty mood. Flora spent the grueling walk in the beating sun thinking more about what the *Króna* said. And in the end, she still had no idea what she wanted to do.

****

All it took was one afternoon for Flora's entire world to come crumbling down into a decimated pile of rubble. It was such a short amount of time for such an all-encompassing annihilation.

The cottage was dark when they rounded the corner, sparking a flame of worry inside of Flora. The horizon was just starting to turn from a charcoaled ember to a mottled bruise. Rosie should have a candle lit in the kitchen window as she cooked dinner. But it was dark, a stark contrast to the homes beside hers, candles flickering behind discolored windowpanes.

Flora's heart was in her throat as she grabbed onto Anise's arm, steadying her as they approached her home. The closer they got, the more details Flora could make out. The very last trickle of the dying sun reflected off the ground—shards of glass. Flora made a choked noise as she released Anise's grasp and jumped to the door. Glass crunched under her boots as she pushed on the half-open door. The stained-glass window in the wood was shattered beyond repair, a glinting rainbow haloing the stoop.

Flora's heart stopped when she saw the inside of her home. Everything was in tatters and splinters. The furniture was destroyed, and seemingly every ceramic in the house was crunching under her boots as she moved in a daze deeper into the house. The blankets and knitting were cut up and dangled in the breeze wafting through the broken windows.

Her whole life, where she had grown up and made so many precious memories, was gone in one afternoon. The one saving grace was that not every single thing was ruined. Some clothes, books, and food were still intact. But everything else was a mess of a million pieces.

"Oh, Flora. I'm so sorry," Anise said, her voice thick with emotion. She too had spent a lot of her childhood roaming the small rooms, free and safe in the warmth from the oven always baking sweets and breads. They always had full bellies with Rosie around even when others didn't. It was a blessing Flora had never questioned, never allowed herself to wonder how she and Rosie were somehow able to thrive in their desolate province with little coin.

"Mom," Flora whispered, horror coating her throat as her stomach dropped.

Rosie was nowhere to be seen, but if the house was any indication, a struggle had occurred. She must have fought back when whatever happened started. She was normally docile and kind, but in the face of harm coming to her family, she fought like a mother bear protecting her cub.

Flora sank to her knees in front of her bed, the sheets ruined, but the blanket was untouched. And sitting on the blanket was a folded piece of paper with *Flora* written in flowing, sage-green script.

"Is that a note? Open it!" Anise encouraged, and with her heart in her throat, Flora unfolded the crisp paper, her fingers smudging the stark white.

Flora Larkspur,

I have something you love, and you have something I love. A fair exchange, no?

In a moon's time, I will trade you Rosie for your family's restored amulet. I will be waiting with your mother at the well near the base of the Línu Mountain

Pass at sundown—sharp.

Fail to show up, and your mother's life is forfeit. Fail to bring me the amulet, and I will destroy everyone you've ever loved.

Bring anyone, and their life, as well as yours, is forfeit.

The letter held no signature, except for a waft of a musty, earthy aroma when Flora's eyes reached the bottom of the page. Partnered with the color of the ink, Flora had a guess who the letter was from.

The Sage Witch.

Except it didn't make sense. From what Flora knew, it was the Witch who gave her family magic. And now, here she was, kidnapping her mother so Flora could retrieve something that once belonged to the Sage Witch herself.

It was then that Flora was filled with a deep sense of longing for her birthmother, so deep she could drown in the feeling. She had so many questions for her that Rosie didn't know the answers to even though she had been her handmaiden for years. Flora was usually content with the fact that she would never know pertinent information about her birthmother, but now? Now, she regretted her actions, wished she had fought harder to find information. But her mother was dead, and the only other person who could truly answer the intimate details was the King. And Flora was told he had ominous, perilous intentions. So, she was out of luck. If she wanted answers, she would have to search unturned stones for them, dig deep into the past—what she thought might be the only way for her to complete the quest shoved at her feet.

And Rosie, her poor, innocent mother, caught up in

a tangle of thorns since she took Flora on as a baby. Guilt ate away at the pit growing in Flora's stomach, a sheen of sweat dotting her brow and she struggled to swallow with the lump in her throat. Her mother was gone, kidnapped and held as ransom with the threat of death. She had a moon's cycle, a month, to find four shards in a vast country of ruin. Vines of despair and worry wrapped around Flora as tears burned her eyes.

"I don't understand," Flora said, glancing at Anise who also read the letter over Flora's shoulder.

"Do you think it's really from her? *The Sage Witch?*" Anise said, whispering the Witch's name. Even she feared the power and wrath of the Witch. Ever since the boon turned into a curse for the land, everyone feared the Witch. Folk were careful not to say her name, lest it conjure her out of thin air.

"It must be—who else would write this note and steal my mother? Unless it's a red herring?" Flora said, mind working a mile a minute to conjure up other possibilities.

"I don't know, she's a Witch—she's cruel, it has to be from her. But what is she talking about? What is the amulet and why would she go to such lengths to force you to get it?" Flora's heart sank like an anchor at Anise's words. Even trying her hardest, somehow, the choice to tell Anise on her own terms was snatched away from her.

"You have to *promise* me you won't freak out, that you'll stay here and let me explain," Flora said, clasping the other girl's hand as they mirrored wide eyes. There was a war raging inside of her head, part of her screaming at her to just tell Anise, get it over with and never have to hide such a massive secret from her friend again. But the other part of her begged her not to say anything, to let it all lay wrapped in shadows. Except, Flora knew she couldn't go on much longer without Anise knowing the truth. There was no other explanation for her behavior or her theories, for the true reasonings behind her desire to inquire and lunge after situations frothed with danger and far out of her comfort zone.

"What is it? You're scaring me." Anise gasped. "Tell me you're not the lost Larkspur Lady?" Anise snorted, as Flora's eyes widened comically large. Anise's smirk dropped, like it was on fire, as she stared at her best friend. The girl she had known since the cradle, the girl she had grown up into a young woman beside.

"Oh my Gods, Flora. You can't be serious?" Anise's jaw dropped open as the words escaped Flora. Something had caught her tongue, forbidding her from attempting to rid the horrified look on her best friend's face.

"*Flora!*"

She gasped, her tongue finally loosened even as her chest still clenched and squeezed her lungs. "I'm *so sorry*, Anise," she sobbed, tears stinging her eyes as they ran in rivulets down her burning cheeks. The words came out blubbering and spit-filled as Flora's very being squeezed her tighter, fear Anise would hate her rearing its ugly head.

"Flora, calm down. Breathe with me," Anise said, clasping Flora's quivering upper arms in hers. "In and out. That's it now."

Flora's gasping, stuttering breaths finally came out cleaner, air fully reaching her lungs and releasing with ease. Her eyes and nose burned from the pressure in her sinuses as Anise looked at her with large eyes filled to the brim with pity and worry.

"I'm okay," Flora said, softly as she swallowed the lump in her throat.

"Flora, what is going on?" Anise asked, squeezing her hand.

"I'm the lost daughter of Lady Larkspur," Flora admitted, squeezing her eyes tight. Anise clasped Flora's cheeks in her warm hands until Flora's eyes fluttered open to reveal her pale green eyes.

"Flora. You can tell me, but you can't hide when you do that," Anise said, stern, but soft.

Flora gave her a shaky nod before continuing her story. "All I know is my mother was Anneliese Larkspur, the one who caused Woodvale to turn to dust and ruin. Her handmaiden, Rosie, saved me before the King or anyone could take me for themselves."

"Everything makes so much more sense now," Anise whispered, awe in her eyes.

"Not that it matters though, I can't use my magic. There's some block on me."

"Oh! So the amulet thing is what will help you? Is that what the *Króna* said?" Anise had always been almost too clever for her own good because she rarely kept her revelations to herself.

"Yes. If I want my magic back, I need to restore my family's amulet. Then I can try fixing Woodvale, all because of my mother's actions," Flora said, shoulders sagging as the weight of the task before her sank in.

"Incredible! We can go on a *real* quest! We can set out in the morning, and oh! We'll need supplies, and I'll have to give my parents an excuse, but oh it will be *so fun!*" Anise said, talking a mile a minute as her eyes glowed and her hands shook. A blinding grin formed on her cherry lips before falling at Flora's blank face.

"Anise, you can't come—it could be dangerous."

"Flora, seriously? You can't go alone. You need me, and we're a team. End of story," Anise said, hands falling to her wide hips.

"Anise, I have no idea what this all will entail, and I'm the only one who *has* to go if I don't want everyone I love to die. So, you don't need to come," Flora insisted.

She couldn't live with herself if something happened to Anise. Even though she knew it would probably be easier and more fun with her best friend tagging along.

"*Flora*. I. Am. Coming." Flora glared at her best friend, trying her best to put her foot down, but her stern eyebrow quivered and her lip wobbled. Gods, she was weak.

"*Fine*. But if anything happens to you—I am sending you home."

Anise shrieked and jumped up and down, throwing her arms around Flora. "This is going to be so *amazing!*"

A quiver of unease took root in Flora's core, her eyebrows furrowing at Anise's reaction. She half-heartedly joined Anise in her excitement as she could see where her friend was coming from, though she didn't appreciate the sentiment when Flora's life had just been turned inside out and was slipping through her fingers like sand. It was impossible to join in with her friend's misplaced joy when her stomach had a pit growing and eating away at her organs. She was so worried something bad would happen on this quest. Ever since she and Rosie had arrived that blustery night, she had never left this small corner of Woodvale in her eighteen years of life.

Who did she think she was? Going on a quest like this—of course something terrible would happen. Anise would probably die because of Flora's stupidity and then Flora herself would die by tripping over a stone on a cliff, falling to the sharp rocks guarding the sea below, her blood splattering and her body trapped in a precarious location where she would decay and rot for eternity. And Rosie would be murdered all because of her.

Stop. That won't happen.

Flora took a deep breath, hugging Anise tighter, trying to banish the heart-thumping thoughts from taking over more than they already had. It was so difficult to quiet the voices in her mind—they were just so loud and had good points. She wasn't a warrior or hero or adventurer. She was a scared little girl with a heavy heart, and a desire to help people. But that wasn't necessarily enough to make things right.

She wasn't her mother—powerful and regal. She was just Flora. She liked dirt under her fingernails and helping her elderly neighbor walk to the market, even if it took all day. She liked playing pretend with Anise, even at eighteen, and she liked lazing around her house while Rosie made delectable honey buns and sugared sweets.

But adventure? Flora didn't know what that truly was. She was sheltered and may have had a big imagination and lofty dreams, but would that be enough? She didn't think so. But maybe, she could prove herself wrong. With Anise by her side, and the right provisions, she had everything she thought she would need in her arsenal. Or at least she hoped. But she couldn't think about that—she had to focus on being positive until her inevitable negative thoughts resurfaced and tore her asunder.

And really, if she failed, that meant her mother died. A painful, slow death by the Sage Witch, who seemed to have gotten crueler and colder as time went on. Flora had to succeed—if not for herself, then for Rosie. Because the alternative was unacceptable and far too heartbreaking for her to consider any further.

Chapter Five

The final gift Lady Larkspur left to Woodvale was a screaming babe with a birthmark identical to hers. But, as with every action she did, it was a gift as much as a curse. Before the King could get his hands on the baby, she was whisked away into the unknown, never to be seen since.

Guards, bounty hunters, and common folk alike vowed to find the girl. But it was as if a veil had fallen over her screaming head. No one found her. She stayed undetected for many years. By now, she would be a grown woman if she survived, and the questions on everyone's lips remain: Where is she? Who is she?

-*The Age of Larkspur* by Cassius Muscari, IV

Anise left shortly after their conversation so they could get a good night's sleep before beginning their journey the next morning. Flora wasn't sure how Anise could convince her parents to let her go, but that wasn't her problem to worry about.

Flora dreamed in nightmares that night, shadows crossing her mind as she fantasized horrific tragedies that could befall Rosie should she fail her quest. A moon's passing didn't seem like enough time with everything at stake. Then her dreams shifted with the oncoming breeze streaming through her broken window.

She began in her copse before she left, expecting to

see the dusty, desolate land of her village. Except her world was gone. The little light left was leeched from the expanse, shadows encasing the steps beyond her thicket. The pitch-black sky expanded as far as her eyes could see—forever, an eternity of night. The low-hanging moon cast silver beams into the shadows as it kissed the horizon so much it looked like it could be plucked by a tall enough hand.

A gasp escaped her lips, echoing in the hushed space as a stem broke free from her ankle. A stalk of deep purple larkspur grew faster than she had ever seen. It danced up her leg, cutting a slit in her long skirt as it twined up her calf, then thigh.

Her breath came out in short gasps as the darkness surrounding her closed in before a figure appeared. Its frame was tall and thick, wearing a coat of writhing shadows, effectively hiding their appearance.

Before she could blink, a hook sunk into her navel and dragged her toward the figure. She threw her arms up to protect herself before they collided. Except, they turned to shadow and ash the second they connected. The motion forced her to wake, gasping for breath as her room opened before her eyes. It was exactly how she left it—broken, but hers.

Her dream, or perhaps nightmare was a better word, concerned her, but she figured it was just her overactive imagination running wild with the terror and worry boiling inside of her. It was a crushing force she wished she could banish once and for all.

The sky was still starry and dark like the navy Svart Sea she had only seen in paintings. A flicker of excitement burst to life at the thought, overshadowing her worry in that moment. Soon she would view the sea with her own eyes. If they lived that long.

Flora rose from her bed as she wouldn't be able to fall back to her dreamland now that her mind was awake and racing. She would pack, she decided. It would be a good use of her time so they could leave bright and early.

A niggling at her ankle stirred her attention and another stem broke free from her skin. The green stalk rose and twisted in the night breeze before sprouting deep indigo buds, transforming into a perfect larkspur.

Flora sighed but let it grow longer as soon enough her ankle would be encased in a stocking and unable to breathe fresh air for a while. She gently brushed a flower petal, her fingertip smudging a dark purple as she realized what she needed to pack.

Over the years, Rosie put Flora's larkspur to good use instead of letting it be a complete burden. When it bloomed at home, Flora would yank it out of her skin, dry it, and grind it into a fine powder. Because larkspur wasn't just a pretty flower and could be an excellent weapon in the right circumstances. Larkspur was poisonous. Not to her, but to everyone else it was. It could cause death in the right dosage, or paralysis or blindness, but it mostly caused abdominal pain or rashes in smaller doses.

Larkspur was a dangerous plant, a juxtaposition with her magic that was supposed to be able to cause the land to grow bountiful with plants. According to history books, the Sage Witch based the magical birthmark off her ancestor's name—Alouette Larkspur—and it would pass down to her female descendants. Instead of giving her a poisonous power, she gave her the opposite—the ability to heal and flourish the land and grow plants.

Flora wasn't sure why her ankle sprouted actual larkspur. She had a history book, *The Age of Larkspur*, but it didn't go into in-depth details. Flora always assumed her larkspur was a curse because of her mother's actions that caused the land to begin the long process of dying.

Under their kitchen sink were vials of purple larkspur. Some were ground into a fine dust, and some were a liquid concoction with water and alcohol. Flora packed them all into her rucksack with a couple of changes of clothes, and her history, folklore, and botanical books. Then she snapped the larkspur off her ankle, twirled it in the soft glow of the sun just starting to crest over the horizon, before placing it on her mother's bed—a goodbye for now to Rosie.

****

"I'm sorry I never told you. I just didn't want it to change our friendship," Flora said, bumping her rucksack higher on her already aching shoulder. The books may have been a bit of a mistake—they hadn't even left the cottage yet.

"It's okay. I understand why you didn't. I mean, everyone is after you, and I know he's our King, but I wouldn't want to be under his thumb either. I just can't believe Anneliese Larkspur is your biological mother. You're so different from the stories about her, I can't believe you're related," Anise said, putting the last of the food in her own rucksack. Flora nodded along, tugging at her skirt so it fell closer to the floor.

"Wait—you're not wearing your trousers?" Anise asked, glancing over Flora.

"I have some packed. Why?"

"We can't be two young women traveling all over the country. At least not at first glance," Anise said, shaking her head. "It's the only way I convinced my parents to let me come—if we dressed the part of a young couple traveling."

"You know, *you* could wear trousers too," Flora muttered, even though trousers were sounding more appealing by the second. Free legs would be easier to run in if they needed a quick getaway.

"If I played the man, I would die of agony. *I* can't bind my breasts! Look at me—it would be *painful*. But for you, it would barely be a discomfort," Anise said, gesturing to herself, as Flora flushed crimson. Her tone was barb-free, but it still cut into Flora all the same.

It was true. Flora would have an easier time binding her breasts and playing the man. It wasn't even a big ask for her—she liked dressing both ways, in whatever was most comfortable for that day. Anise's comment didn't necessarily hurt her; it just dug into one of Flora's sore spots.

To Flora, Anise was a beautiful, voluptuous girl who caught everyone's eye with her shine. It killed Flora that so much attention was on her—that everyone wanted her. Because Flora knew no one would ever look at her like that, as she was too plain and shy. She was beautiful in her own way, but Flora kept to herself and hid too much for anyone to take notice. Not that she was even convinced she wanted romance, but jealousy was a green beast that didn't always follow logic or reason. It snuck up on unsuspecting folks and dug its thorns in deeply.

"Fine. Let me change and then we can go."

Flora changed into her hickory-colored trousers,

handsewn by Rosie, in record time and the two set off. The sun was just creeping over the horizon, washing the world in a honey glaze of morning light. The dusty dirt road was empty as the two began their trek to the town beside theirs. They needed to stop there first so they could purchase two horses. Their village was too small for a horse peddler, which was even more frustrating as it required them to walk farther and exert more energy. Although, it was not the first time the girls had made the trip. On their birthdays some years, their parents were kind enough to pay for them to have lessons and ride around the deserted countryside for an afternoon.

They were just outside the outskirts of town when Flora broke their comfortable, tired silence full of yawns and crusty eyes. "Do you really think it was the Sage Witch who took my mom?"

Anise pursed her lips, furrowing her eyebrows, before nodding. "It must be her."

"But if it is her, why can't she get my family's amulet? She was the one who created it."

"Maybe she can't leave the Sage Woods long enough to acquire each shard. Think of the Pitch King—he never leaves his realm, so maybe there's a reason for it."

"That's true. Maybe their domains trap them more than we realize," Flora said, before sighing. It was all theory and hopeful assumptions, but no concrete information. She wished she could just ask someone instead of having to search for hidden and unturned stones.

"So, where are we going first? And there's four, right? Where are they?" Anise asked, perking up.

"The *Króna* said the shards were in Vale Centre,

the Svart Sea, the Pitch Woods, and the Sage Woods," Flora said, casting her gaze away from Anise as she mumbled the last two locations.

"*What*! The Pitch Woods *and* the Sage Woods? Like inside or just, like along the border?" Anise asked, eyes wide as she forced Flora to look at her.

"I don't know. She said I would know when I get closer," Flora said, wringing her hands. "You don't have to come. I would understand if you wanted to go back."

"Don't be stupid—I'm coming. It's just a little daunting, that's all."

"Are you sure?"

"Of course, I'm sure. You're my best friend, and I would follow you on any adventure you go on. You need me," Anise said, as Flora swallowed thickly, eyes watering.

And so, the two continued on toward the town. They arrived as the glowing horizon gave way to blue skies and puffy clouds blotting out the sun. They were able to purchase two horses from the coin Flora found in Rosie's safe, money saved from the remnants of her former life.

Flora's horse was a chestnut mare that complemented Anise's tawny stallion. The two flew out of town, Anise's long hair flowing in the breeze while Flora's was tucked under a cap. Their ride was full of smiles and laughter and aching backsides and thighs.

They made excellent time, barely stopping that first day, trying to get as close to Vale Centre as they could while still being careful. Flora's ankle tingled all day, growing warmer the closer they got to the city. She hoped the first shard would be easy to find and easier to retrieve.

But she was happy as long as Anise rode beside her, keeping her calm and grinning. The two were finally embarking on the adventure they wanted to go on for years. Anise kept telling tales of how their story would go down in history, their names written beside the great adventurers of Woodvale, their legacy written in permanent ink.

Even though their legacy would be remembered on paper and in minds, Flora knew legacies were rarely written as planned. Flora had a gut-wrenching ache that their quest would not be easy, and it would not follow the script laid out by the *Króna*. All she hoped was that she could save her mother and keep Anise safe.

Chapter Six

Vale Centre is a maze.

Set in the middle of Woodvale, it houses the King's castle and rows of mansions and estates of the wealthy in circling droves. The citizens who live in Vale Centre never go hungry, unlike the provincial townsfolk. Their houses are full of riches and jewels, and luxury more severe than the average imagination.

It is said those who enter Vale Centre find it difficult to leave. Whether it be the cafes with seemingly never-ending food, or the vast luxury and jewels. Or it was the fact the city streets were endlessly confusing, trapping and tricking unsuspecting travelers into never leaving. To spend all their coin in the city, until their pockets were empty and their tankards were dry, and the city guards would appear to banish them until they refilled their pockets with golden and silver coins.

-An Adventurer's Guide to Woodvale: Vale Centre by Gísli

Rays and speckles of gleaming sunlight broke through the horizon, blotted out by the city looming before them. Vale Centre was full of buildings with towering spikes shooting into the sky, mingled with sprawling mansions encased in a stone brick wall protecting the city from unwanted visitors. It was raised several feet above the land with bricks and iron covered in brown, shriveled, and flaking vines. The closer they got, the more Flora thought her eyes were playing tricks on her as she spotted peculiar patterns. She squinted and inspected the stones because it almost looked like carved into the bricks were depictions of giants. She could see the scraggly faces encased forever in time and gasped as she faintly recalled a story about such creatures.

With a braced core and mighty effort, she dove her hand into her satchel and deftly pulled out her book, keeping an eye on their journey toward the city as she read. Long ago, Woodvale was protected by a horde of giants when it was threatened by earthquakes and tsunamis. That was why the city was elevated. It was said the giants raised it above the earth to protect those in Woodvale. The people lived and expanded their land into four provinces and a city center for the rulers, while the giants turned to stone under the city, creating a platform of protection until they started eroding.

That was how the story went anyway. There were hundreds of stories in Flora's book, and many more in the libraries scattered throughout Woodvale, but even then, so much was lost to time. Language, stories, myths, truths, fables, folklore, all lost to the one thing no one could escape. It broke Flora's heart that so much disintegrated from nothing more than not writing it down and moving onward without remembering the history that brought everyone to the present. It was why she adored and cherished the stories and history she did know.

The dirt road had turned to stone a few paces back, and Flora and Anise were enjoying the change of soundtrack from the hooves hitting the stone. The road took them traveling up a slight incline before a gold gate bursting open met their eyes. Other folks were on the road ahead, just walking into the city. There were several King's Guards loitering around the gate, gleaming swords strapped to their backs and glittering guns hung on their hips, but they didn't stop a soul from entering. From the guidebook, Flora assumed they were mostly there to keep people *inside* rather than out. Because if the King and his precious subjects wanted to keep living in their lap of luxury, they needed provincial folk to spend their hard-earned money in his city.

A heavy stone settled in Flora's stomach as they approached the golden gate. This was where her mother had lived and died. She had walked through these streets and socialized with the people who lived here. She would have even spent a lot of time in the King's castle, before everything fell to ruin at her hands. And probably his, too.

With a shaky breath, Flora and Anise slowed their tired horses to a trot. Flora was stiff in her saddle, trying not to glance at her ankle. It was warm and humming, and she could feel a stem trying to break through her skin and sinew.

But she had nothing to worry about.

They passed into the city without any guards calling for them to halt and lift their skirt and trousers, to inspect their ankles for a larkspur. Flora's forehead was wet with sweat and her throat was closing from the anxiety piercing her navel. She couldn't believe or trust they could enter the city so easily. It was where the King lived. But clearly, they knew something she didn't.

"Where to first?" Anise asked as they approached a

stable to store their exhausted horses while they explored Vale Centre.

"Well, the *Króna* said my birthmark would guide me, and it's warm, Anise," Flora said, her chest constricting like someone was sitting on it.

The city was too loud and big for Flora. She was used to wide open spaces and air that wasn't perfumed and metallic. She liked living in the outskirts of the country, even when it wasn't the lush land it was supposed to be. Meanwhile, Anise looked at home. She was striding through the cobblestone city streets with her head held high, gawking at every golden light fixture and shop boasting expensive wares.

Anise turned, almost causing Flora to trip, before extending her hand to Flora. With a smile of thanks, Flora slid her hand in Anise's, and the two glided through the city streets. Anise's handsewn dress and Flora's dirt-covered trousers and hair twisted into a brown cap looked completely out of place in the sea of vibrant colors and gemstones.

Flora and Anise walked through the rose-gold city streets with wide and gleaming eyes. Anise tugged Flora down thin veins and into wide squares with fountains and peddlers advertising their wares. She dragged her through markets and past taverns and cafes and dress shops. All the while, Flora had one hand tucked inside her bag, fingers clenched around a vial of powdered larkspur. She had read the guidebooks—thieves and pickpocketers were prominent in the markets, and the city was crawling with guards.

Flora felt like she had a bullseye dangling around her neck. Every pair of eyes that glanced at her felt like an eternity under their stare. She couldn't stop thinking a King's Guard was following them and would grab them and demand for her to lift her trousers and cut into her stockings, exposing the burning birthmark splashed on her ankle. They would peel her away from Anise and drag her through the streets and people would heckle her—she was the daughter of the woman who cursed them all—and then she would be before the King. At his mercy. He could do anything to her, and she couldn't do anything to stop it.

And *breathe*.

Flora let loose a stuttering breath as she attempted to collect herself. She hated when her thoughts got away from her, when she went down the dark veins in her mind to places she had no business being, imagining things that hadn't happened and probably wouldn't if she were *careful*. And she was always careful.

In what felt like a blink of an eye, the sun had completely passed over their heads and was sinking beneath the city, the sky stretching from a bright blue to a burnt orange, cascading the city in shadow and a warm glow from streetlamps. Although the invention was clever and useful, it was something her village didn't have. They used candles to light their way— streetlamps were for the wealthy as it was a tedious and extravagant design that required far more resources than they had on hand. The streetlamps could have been for everyone, had the calamity not occurred, sending Woodvale back and stagnant in time instead of forward.

Flora felt no closer to the shard. Her ankle buzzed with a tingling warmth, but it didn't grow hotter or colder during their trek throughout the city. The warm breeze turned biting, cutting like a knife into their exposed forearms and cheeks.

"We should find a place to stay tonight," Anise said, cheeks flushed and eyes glazed as she watched the intoxicating city pass her by. Flora cast a concerned gaze at her friend, a niggling in her mind that something was odd here.

Time slipped through their fingers like sand. It was already dusk, and their legs barely hurt even though they spent the day wandering the streets. Vale Centre was strange, and Flora's belly was beginning to wiggle and worm with the notion that not everything was right here. But their purses were still heavy with their coin, so Flora wasn't too worried yet.

At the end of the gilded street was a tavern called The Blóm Inn, with a sign boasting rooms at an affordable rate, so the two girls headed there. A murder of crows sang their caws overhead, welcoming the dusky and starless night in full force.

The tavern was empty save for a person in a black cloak with a hood and a woman playing a lute. A grisly man hunched over the bar, scrubbing at a plethora of stains and scratches.

It was perfect. This was the kind of place they wouldn't stick out like a sore thumb and shouldn't cost an arm and a leg to rent a room.

"Good evening," Anise said, approaching the bar as Flora lagged behind.

She was admiring the large tapestries coating the four walls of the main room. They were of the four provinces in their glory, in such vivid and vibrant detail Flora could imagine herself standing in the scenes.

One depicted Whaelmere, the sea province, with rice fields and sandy beaches stretched toward the churning obsidian sea. Another painted Myrkurden, sister to Whaelmere except it shared a border with the Pitch Woods, with thick pine forests and stone cottages. Next was Skógur, the province lucky enough to share a border with the Pitch Woods *and* the Sage Woods. It had rolling hills of wheat fields and pastures stuffed with fat animals and a contrasting dark and light forest in the backdrop.

Lastly, Flora found Sanarbre, where she had grown up. It was beautiful, with dense, bright forests and stony paths to vast and plentiful diverse fields of crops. There were the cottages she knew, with the addition of enchanting wisteria, and kind folk who wanted to live an honest life under the sun and come home with dirt under their fingers at the end of a long day. In the distance, she could see the Norn Mountains and the Sage Woods, painted in such crisp detail it was like it had been stolen from her own imagined memory.

Her heart burned in her chest for the painting to be a reality. She longed for luscious forests and healthy crops, full bellies and happy smiles on everyone's faces. It was up to her. She could do it. Apparently. As much as she wanted to—desperately wanted to—fix Woodvale's problems, they seemed too daunting to fix for one girl with no practice. She had never actually *done* magic.

She needed to find the shards, and fast—it was the only way to calm her racing heart.

"Flo!" Anise called, snapping Flora out of her reverie. They had agreed to call Flora, Flo, on their travels in an attempt to follow their ruse. Flora gave them a week tops at using the nickname before they fell into a comfortable rhythm and forgot to add the extra layer of caution.

Her ankle itched fiercely, the stem of a larkspur wriggling underneath her stocking and scratching at her skin. They needed a room, a private one, and fast, so she could dispose of the poison growing out of her skin.

"What?" Flora asked, sidling up to Anise against the bar.

"It's one gold coin for a night, and two for three nights. How long do you think we need?" Anise asked, jerking her thumb at the grisly man.

Flora's heart kickstarted in her chest and she hastily swallowed her nerves and said softly to Anise, "One."

"We'll take just one night, please," Anise said, slapping a single gold coin on the scuffed bar. The man grunted but accepted her coin as he exchanged it for a brass skeleton key.

"Your room is up the stairs and the second door on the right," he said, voice harsh. "Dinner is included in your fee."

"Excellent! We'll take two plates then," Anise said, grinning at Flora as she gave Anise a half-hearted smile in return.

The man disappeared behind a swinging wooden door, before appearing a second later holding two plates. Flora could make out a hunk of something that resembled charred meat and steamed vegetables.

"Thank you," Anise said, and Flora muttered the same under her breath.

The two girls sat down at a rickety oak table, the only one in the room without crumbs or sticky substances left over from previous patrons. The food wasn't as bad as it looked. There was exploding flavor on their tongues, and it properly filled their empty bellies from a day of wandering around a maze of a city.

"Do you really think we can find it in a day?" Anise asked, scraping her plate clean.

"We've already spent a couple days traveling here. If we don't move fast, we won't make it by the end of the month," Flora said softly and pointedly, trying to get Anise to lower her own voice. Flora's stomach roiled at the truth behind her words. They needed to move faster, so the one-day time limit would have to do.

"I wish we had a map or something. This city just goes on forever. Like, it didn't look *that* huge outside the city walls, but it seems bigger inside," Anise grumbled, dropping her chin into her waiting hand.

"Excuse me," a masculine voice that sounded like velvet and smooth whiskey said behind them.

Flora turned to the voice and found the hooded figure leaning across his table a few inches from them. He had dropped his hood to reveal cropped wavy hair artfully styled against the brown walnut-hued skin of his forehead. A smirk rested on his full, pink lips as he stared at the two girls, dimple popping on his cheek. Her breath caught in her throat at the sculpted features, her stomach heaving lightly, his beauty causing a visceral reaction, like it had punched her.

"Yes? Can we help you?" Anise asked, narrowing her eyes. She was used to attention from men, usually unwanted, and she loathed when they interrupted her scheming. She liked attention on her terms. And more importantly, she didn't like when they approached her without any warning.

"I couldn't help but overhear your struggles with the city," he said, his voice sounding like music to Flora's ears.

Her cheeks flushed as she realized she had been staring at him too long. But she couldn't help it—he was captivatingly beautiful. His face was like a magnet. She hastily shot her gaze away from him, scolding herself. She had never had such a visceral reaction to a boy before. Sure, there were some cute boys in her village, but her eye usually caught on the girls. But something about this boy grabbed her gaze and refused to let it go.

"And?" Anise asked, her hostile glare slipping as a coy smirk slid onto her lips.

Flora dropped her gaze to her empty plate, her cheeks burning red, no longer from embarrassment, but jealousy. Of course, she may have thought the boy beautiful, but he would want Anise and Anise would want him. No one would ever be allowed to want Flora. An angry green wave washed over her as Anise gave him a flirty twirl of her fingers. She always got everything. Flora tried to shake the thought away. She loved Anise, and unless she wanted to talk about her issues, she needed to let them go. Flora hated confrontation and would rather take her grievances to the grave.

But to Flora's surprise, the boy barely cast Anise a second glance, instead focusing on Flora. He watched her with a burning gaze, his eyes smoldering as he looked her over. Flora jerked against her chair in surprise and her cheeks flushed even deeper. She was sure she had to look like an overripe tomato at this point.

"I can help you. I know the city well—I can be your guide," he said, and Anise pursed her lips as Flora's ears perked.

Anise scoffed. "I don't think so. We don't know you and we can do fine on our own."

"Anise," Flora whispered, tugging her sleeve. Anise glanced back at Flora, eyebrows furrowed. If either of them should want the boy to scram and leave them be, it would be Flora, not Anise. But something about him made her want to stick around and see what could happen. She almost wanted to get to know him, which was a ridiculous notion for her. But she knew herself, and even if she *wanted* to see him more, her mind would never allow her to actually act on her desires in full. The only thing she could do was extend their time together by letting him guide them around the city while she cowered behind Anise. It wasn't perfect, but Flora would take it.

"What's up?" Anise asked, concern dotting her brow.

"I think we should take him up on his offer."

"*What*? We don't know him—he could be a killer!" Anise whispered harshly and the boy scoffed.

"You know I can hear you, right?" he said, his incessant smirk still playing on his lips, showing off the little cleft in his cheek.

"We wandered around this city all day without even realizing it! We didn't accomplish *anything*. We need help," Flora said, body turned from the boy and voice low. "This city doesn't *feel* right."

"But, *Flo,* we don't know if he can even help us."

"I am an expert on all things Vale Centre," the boy interjected. "I know how to trick it instead of letting it trick you. Please, let me help."

"What do you want?" Anise asked, jaw tight.

"Pardon me?"

"To help us—what do you want?"

A smile fell on his smirking lips, revealing a row of straight, pearly white teeth with sharp canines. He replied, "I don't want anything."

"Please," Anise scoffed, crossing her arms over her chest.

"Truly, I don't want anything—just the opportunity to help two girls in this cruel city is payment enough," he said, eyes twinkling as he pressed his hand over his heart.

"Why?" Flora whispered, pushing over her anxiety at speaking to this gorgeous stranger.

"What? I can't just be a kind stranger, with a good heart?" he asked, pouting.

"Seriously, I don't like this game," Anise muttered, glaring daggers. "If we accept your help, you get nothing. And if you rob us or screw us over, we will come after you."

"Then I guess I'd better be on my best behavior," he said, smirking again.

"We accept your offer. We would really appreciate the help around the city," Flora said, her tongue and throat dry. But she was proud of herself, and she knew Anise was too by the light squeeze on her arm.

"Excellent. Let's meet here tomorrow morning?"

"Bright and early. I'm Flora, by the way, and this is Anise," Flora replied, as a grin cracked open on the boy's face. She decided to forgo the ruse since they were going to spend a lot of time together. She didn't pass *that* well, and usually forgot to deepen her voice as her disguise was for first glance only. He would find out eventually, if he didn't already know, and judging by the lack of surprise emitting from him—he did. "What's your name?"

Two velvety melodic notes hit her ears as he said, "Kaanan."

Chapter Seven

Once upon a time, stone giants roamed the world.
They were happy and content to live as they pleased.
Until small living beings appeared: humans. The giants
were overjoyed to have such tiny pets to play with. They
showered them in attention and love, but it was never
human nature to be at the bottom of the food chain.

One brave soul found something special, something
magical, and created an all-consuming disaster for
their world. The ground started shaking, and the ocean
crashed in fury, because of the human. The giants were
unaware of why their world was retaliating. All they
knew was their pets were weak and fragile. So, they
gave their stone lives to the humans. Their bodies
created a base for their city, and the pets lived happily
ever after...for a short time.

-The Incomplete Tales and Folklore of Woodvale

Birds chirping behind the murky window woke
Flora up before dawn. The sun was just starting to rise
in the sky, a pastel pink horizon meeting her gaze. Flora
yawned before crawling out of bed, leaving Anise
behind. She was still fast asleep, limbs thrown wild in
the double bed they shared.

The bed was surprisingly comfortable, a thick
mattress with a duvet of feathers. The room itself was
even cleaner than the bar. Everything was dusted to
perfection, and only a few small stains marred the

surfaces. It was tiny, resembling Flora's room back home, but it had a lock and a bed—the most important things on a journey where she was out of her element and comfort zone.

Flora was surprised with how deeply she slept. From her guidebook, she thought she might have been up all night, tossing and turning. Vale Centre rarely slept. Bars and clubs were open all night, patrons staying until their pockets and tankards were empty. But their room was on a rare quiet street, and the two girls slept deeply in their dark room as the moon was covered behind a cloud.

Flora packed up their belongings and chose to let Anise rest longer. She wanted to wait, take Anise with her, but Flora woke up on a new side of the bed. She wanted to try something new, to try to work on herself. If she was going to finish this quest, she needed to stop letting herself stay in her bubble; she had to leave it sometimes. And this morning was the perfect opportunity.

Her heart in her throat, she descended the creaking stairs into the barroom below. The grisly owner was missing behind the bar, but a familiar figure in black leather trousers and a black as tar cloak sat on a stool, scooping what looked like porridge into his mouth.

Kaanan.

The thought of his name sent butterflies fluttering around her stomach. She was frozen on the stairs, watching him like a peeping Tom. A rosy-pink tinge colored her cheeks in the pale morning light as she shook herself out of her stupor and cleared the rest of the steps. A particularly loud creak gave her away, and Kaanan's head whipped toward her, foot hovering over the last step.

His face split into a charming grin when he saw her. He said, voice still husky from sleep, "Good morning, Flora."

Flora's mouth was dry as a bone in a desert baking under the hot sun. She swallowed thickly, begging saliva to bless her tongue. She cleared her throat before saying quietly, "Good morning. How did you sleep?"

Ugh—*how did you sleep*? Flora fumed internally. Did that sound stupid? Maybe she shouldn't have asked. It wasn't any of her business. She was trying to be polite, but she wasn't sure why she bothered.

"It was excellent. How was yours?" he asked, smile blindingly molten in the early morning light.

"It was good, very quiet, like home," she said, taking a seat beside him at the bar, her mint green skirt fanning around her.

She had decided to wear one of the few skirts she packed as they would be traveling with Kaanan and he seemed like the type to ensure both girls were unharmed. Unless she was reading him wrong, and he was in fact a con artist who wanted their coins or worse. But she tried to shake her doubts away. She would keep her guard up but trust him an inch. Maybe.

"Yes, it was quiet. I'm glad you slept well," he said, smiling. "You said like home? Where are you from, Flora?"

"Why?" she asked slowly, lips tightening as uneasiness bloomed. Rosie had always harped on Flora to share little and refrain from talking to strangers—a warning that fell in line with her usual behavior.

"Because we can't be friends if we don't know anything about each other."

"You want to be friends?"

"Of course! I'm your tour guide, but where's the fun in just that? Being friends is much more enjoyable," he said, smirking again.

The shadows falling on his face made his smirk less kind and more…threatening. Flora squirmed in her seat, the hairs on the back of her neck rising before they fell silent almost instantly. The shadows were cast away as the sun flared to life in the window behind them. A warm, orange glow cascaded against their faces, and Flora couldn't help but notice how beautiful he looked in the radiant light.

He cleared his throat, shying away from the light and into the shadows beside him. Flora frowned, narrowing her eyes, but let it go as the sun cut into her pupil. She cursed in her head as she shielded her eyes, scanning for a curtain, but there was none.

"Let's move down the bar," he suggested and the two slipped into the shadows.

"Where did you get that?" Flora asked, mouth salivating at the porridge.

It wasn't that it looked particularly appetizing. She was just starving. Her mind conjured up images of her mother's baking, and a pang hit her hollow stomach. She had a couple of rolls left in her pack, but she wanted to savor them as long as she could. The smell of them alone gave her such deep comfort, she couldn't bear eating them.

With another bright grin in her direction, he vanished into the swinging door behind the bar, only to appear a second later with another bowl. He placed the chipped ceramic in front of her and returned to his perch. The porridge really didn't look *good*, but her stomach was empty, and she figured it would be a long day ahead of them.

"Thank you," she said softly.

"It was my pleasure."

She devoured the tasteless porridge. Apparently, spices or syrups or fruits were nowhere to be found in the kitchen. Only after finishing half the bowl did she finally answer Kaanan's question. "I live in Sanarbre."

"Ah, that would explain it then."

"Explain what?" she asked, sharply—sharper than she intended, but his comment unnerved her. She eyed him warily and he grinned while raising his hands in a placating gesture.

"You. Yesterday you were looking at the painting of Sanarbre so intently. This just explains it," he said, gesturing to the painting splashed against the wall behind them. "Plus, it explains your...*look*."

"My look?"

"Yeah, I mean you're clearly not from Vale Centre. Your clothes are too plain."

"Right," Flora muttered. She had noticed that yesterday, too. The city was far more vibrant than Flora and Anise dressed.

"It's not a bad thing," he assured, and she nodded. She already knew that.

Flora liked the way she dressed, in muted and pastel colors, in trousers and skirts her mother made her. She didn't understand the attire the city folk wore—it was too flashy and looked so uncomfortable and *tight*. She couldn't wait to finish this leg of the quest and retreat back into the farmland and villages where people cared more about keeping their families healthy, and less about extravagant fashion.

"Where are you from?" Flora asked, scraping the sides of her bowl in an attempt to get every single ounce of nutrients from her breakfast.

"I'm from the great province of Myrkurden," he said, leaning back in his chair as he quirked his eyebrows.

"Myrkurden?" She pondered. "I suppose you fit."

"Born and raised."

"What's it like there?" she asked, leaning her chin on her hand. Her stomach still danced in her belly, butterflies and anxiety battling, but she kept sitting there. Her legs quivered, wanting to run to safety, but she held strong.

"It's nice, I suppose. It'd be nicer if the land wasn't empty and dying, but that's everywhere."

"But...it borders the Pitch Woods, right?" she asked, whispering the last part, like saying the words too loudly would summon the Pitch King.

She cursed herself for playing into the superstition, but it couldn't be helped. She may have feared the Sage Witch before, but now she was terrified of her. However, Flora had always been scared of the Pitch King—everyone was. He was the one who starred in nightmares and Flora couldn't even comprehend what it would be like to make an enemy out of him.

Kaanan chuckled, throaty and deep as he said, "Yes, it does. But there's nothing to be scared of. It's just a forest, albeit a dark one."

"What do you mean 'nothing to be scared of'? It's the *Pitch Woods where the Pitch King lives*. You know, slayer of mortals who sics his pet monsters on anyone who dares enter?" Flora gasped, and then promptly shut her mouth, the fear of the Pitch King potentially hearing her taking hold of her stuttering heart. She knew it was ridiculous, but he was a phantom and all-magical and Flora didn't want to tempt fate and anger him even when it was impossible for him to hear her. There was a deep-rooted paranoia that speaking about him would bring about darkness and death.

A queasy feeling settled over her at exposing herself so much. She shouldn't have come down here, should have waited for Anise. Now, this stranger knew a weakness of hers, and she had too many. She was an easy target—she couldn't let people see how simple it was to break her into a million pieces, to bend her to their will.

"Pfft. I don't think he's all bad. I'm sure it's mostly talk—I grew up there. No one even goes inside anymore. Maybe he's even dead."

"Do you really think that?"

"Sometimes, but other times I'm like you—scared witless of stepping too close, lest a bloodthirsty, growling monster tear me limb from limb," he said, backtracking. Flora couldn't tell if he was serious or if he was teasing her—his face was too impassive.

Thankfully, she was saved from having to respond, from having to decide if she wanted to confront him for teasing her. Anise thumped down the stairs, rucksack slamming on her shoulder blades as she yawned loudly. She groaned as she collapsed into the chair beside Flora.

"Ugh, I'm so tired," she moaned, pouting. "How did you sleep?"

"Good, did you not?" Flora asked, concern growing for her sleepy friend.

"No, it was good—too good. I wanted to stay

asleep forever," Anise said and then stiffened when she saw Kaanan. Her eyes darted between Flora and the boy, and she raised a questioning eyebrow. "Well, well, well. What do we have here?"

"We were just chatting about our childhoods, swapping stories, becoming best friends. Isn't that right, Flora?" He grinned, and Flora glowered.

"Sorry, but that position's already taken," Anise sneered.

"We were just talking," Flora said.

"You were?" Anise raised her eyebrows.

"Yes," Flora said, and then whispered to her friend, "I'm trying to improve."

An indecipherable look crossed Anise's face at the words, but before Flora could question her, she said, "Okay. Well, I just need some breakfast and then we can leave."

"Excellent! Your options are bland porridge or flavorless porridge," Kaanan said, gesturing to the kitchen.

Anise sighed through her nose, disappointment clear in the grooves on her normally unmarred face. It was a meal she was used to. In the village, most families had some sort of porridge for most meals. It was cheap and one of the few things they could still grow ingredients for, at least for now.

Flora watched Anise waltz into the kitchen, leaving her and Kaanan alone once more. She glanced at him to find him staring at her with a broad smile on his perfect face.

"What?" she asked, eyes darting away from his deep and dark orbs.

"Nothing," he said, softly. Then he cleared his

throat before asking, "Where exactly am I guiding you two? Is there anything in specific or did you just want the safe passage guaranteed with a tour guide?"

"Um, we're, um…we're just needing a tour guide for protection," she said, settling on that option. She couldn't just say they were looking for something when she had no clue what she was looking for. Her ankle hummed, the warmth a steady reminder she needed to speed things along.

"All right. Is there anywhere specific you want to start?"

"Can we just wander around maybe? See where the day takes us?"

"Of course. I'll keep track of things to make sure the city doesn't swallow us whole," he assured, and she nodded shakily—she wasn't aware that was a possibility. Their eyes connected, his dark pits to her white oblivion, and Flora felt a tug in her navel.

Anise burst into the room, the swinging door clanging behind her loudly, a jarring sound in the calm and peaceful morning. Kaanan and Flora broke eye contact, a flush rising in her cheeks and Anise dropped her belongings roughly onto the bar.

Flora watched her friend eat, patiently waiting as she tried to ignore the warm and darkly alluring presence beside her. She could feel his gaze burning a hole in her cheek, and in that moment, she prayed to any of the old Gods who would listen to keep her, her mother, her friend, and her heart safe.

Chapter Eight

Arriving in Vale Centre is a dream—easy and languid.

Leaving is a nightmare maze shrouded in shadow and mystery.

I warn you, fair traveler, keep your wits about you—Vale Centre will hook its sharp claws into you, and never let you go if you let it.

If you want to leave, and the city won't let you, follow the golden larkspur.

-Proverb

The city was a cacophony of peddlers and tourists and city-dwellers, all trying to buy their morning breakfast and goods in seemingly every single store. Each store they passed housed a plethora of people, all engaged in trade. The clank and jingle of coin hitting stone and wood hurt Flora's ears, which were accustomed to the quiet peace of the countryside.

Kaanan and his flowing obsidian cloak guided them through the gilded city streets. Flora's ankle hummed, and she desperately tried to decipher where it wanted her to go. She cursed the *Króna* repeatedly for her vague instructions. "Your birthmark will tell you where to go." *Please.* The only thing it did was thrum under her skin and create a pool of sweat in her boot.

When the sun fully rose, letting loose a sky of pure blue, Flora's nerves grew taut. While the day was going somewhat better—as in, it hadn't passed them by without notice—it could've been excellent. They could have found the shard instantaneously, which was highly unlikely, but would have made Flora's life so much easier. Flora sighed as Kaanan turned down another street, glancing back at her and Anise as they walked arm in arm. He kept looking back, with a questioning gaze of *"where to now?"* But she kept shaking her head, and he led them down rainbow streets full of gold and brass and pointed out beautiful landmarks.

There were so many statues and sculptures in addition to endless shops and gambling dens. Her favorite was the one that told the tale of the giants and the Svart Sea Serpent. They were gorgeously crafted, with immense detail she knew would have taken months if not years to perfect.

As the sun neared its peak, her ankle finally let loose from its cage and a stem began poking through her skin as her eyes caught on something strange.

A larkspur.

There it was, in plain daylight—a gilded larkspur was carved into one of the streetlamps. The sun hit it at the perfect angle, sending an arc of light reaching to the left, down a tucked-away alley off the main thoroughfare. She let loose a breathy gasp, and both Anise and Kaanan looked at her sharply before scanning the area for a threat as her eyes widened and body tensed. Their confusion reigned when no threats were found, and Flora confidently curved her spine to its full height.

"I want to go down there," she said, pointing her finger down the alleyway.

The alley itself was shrouded in shadows as the

two buildings anchoring were taller than most and blotted out much of the natural sunlight. Flora moved without waiting for Anise and Kaanan, fingers trailing along the brickwork of the building, a musty, almost rotten smell of decay worming into her nose. The alley was filthy, but she couldn't bring herself to care. Finally, at the crest of the beam of light was another larkspur. But this time it wasn't attached to a lamppost. It was painted in a mural, so tiny and obscure she almost missed it. She would have, if her eyes weren't searching for even a hint of her birthmark.

"What's down here?" Kaanan asked, silky voice startling her out of her trance as he glided to stand beside her.

"I...don't know. It just looked interesting," she stuttered, at a loss for words.

Anise elbowed her way forward, slipping her arm through Flora's as she forced the three to walk shoulder to shoulder in the tight alley. "It's none of your business. You're our guide, not our interrogator," she huffed.

Kaanan frowned at her. "If I'm your guide, shouldn't I know where we're going and what we're doing?"

Anise hesitated, pursing her lips before replying, "You just need to keep us on track, and help us leave later."

"Yes, please," Flora interjected as Kaanan straightened at her words. "We would appreciate your help getting out of here later—this place is like a maze."

"All right," he murmured, and hooked his arm through Flora's available one.

Flora jolted and almost tripped on a loose cobblestone. Anise and Kaanan's arms were the only things keeping her upright. Her cheeks flared crimson, and her heart sped up like she was running a marathon.

Breathe, she told herself. *Just breathe.*

It had been a long time since someone other than her mother or Anise had touched her, especially such prolonged contact. She usually kept to herself in her village, and since she mostly spent time with Anise and trees, she never had any excuse for others to touch her. His arm through hers warmed and soothed her more than she would've expected. And after walking a couple of blocks, she decided she liked it—it was surprisingly nice.

But she needed to focus. There were more important matters at hand. So, she continued scanning the walls and lampposts and windows for larkspurs, every square inch of the alley. She thought she must have missed it and almost asked them to turn around before she saw one again.

This time, it was straight ahead, a part of a stained-glass mural display—attached to a church.

The church spire towered over them, shooting up into the sky like the stem of a flower. It was small in width, the same as all the shops lining each side, but instead of hugging the street, it was set back a beat with what should have held a garden before the carved mahogany doors. Flora could imagine it in all its glory. But the illusion was cast away when the wind caused dust to twirl into the air.

She had never gone to church. There was one in the neighboring village a lot of families went to, but she and Rosie never did. They didn't believe in the King's religion, and instead chose to have faith in the old Gods and the folklore surrounding Woodvale—not that some random man created their world. Flora couldn't tell *what* religion the church housed, as there were others she only knew in name, but she didn't believe it could be a coincidence that the stained glass held larkspurs. They were tiny, and again, blended in so subtly only a trained eye could make them out. But they were there— in hues of purple, pink, blue, and white—acting as a beacon of support to Flora.

"In there," she breathed. "I want to go in there."

"A church?" Anise asked, wrinkling her nose—her family practiced no religion and barely even read the old tales. Anise liked them, though, as they were full of heroes and villains, and adventures and quests.

"A church," Kaanan murmured, eyes darting over the glass as a small smirk rested on his lips. "Let's go in."

The mouth of the alley spat out into a busy street, throngs of people milling about, and the three ruthlessly cut through the crowd as their arms remained linked. Flora felt unusually comfortable being surrounded with a person on each arm, and it provided solace she hadn't expected. She almost hoped it would last, that Kaanan would come with them later. But she released the thought to the wild quickly, quashing it instantly because they barely knew him. He may have fascinated her, and she may have been starstruck looking at him, but he was a stranger and she needed to remember that.

The mahogany door of the church was heavy and creaked fiercely when they tugged it open. Inside, the entryway was shrouded in shadow, but a step beyond the concave room opened to a rainbow of colors from the floor-to-ceiling stained-glass pane windows. Wooden pews passed row by row as Flora walked down the aisle to the raised platform that held a statue of a Larkspur Lady. Flora couldn't tell which one it was, but there was no mistaking the larkspur on the thrust-out ankle of the woman.

Beside the statue was an area to light candles, and a box with a heavy, velvet curtain. A confessional. Flora's ankle burned as she looked at the confessional and the statue. She felt a tug in her navel, coaxing her toward the Larkspur Lady as her heartbeat roared in her ears.

"Do you feel something?" Anise whispered as she slid up behind Flora, startling her out of her reverie.

"Yes, but I don't know what I'm supposed to do," Flora admitted, casting a sheepish look to Anise as Kaanan leaned against the first pew with his arms crossed over his chest, watching Flora intently.

"Well, let's think about it. That statue has a larkspur, and we're in a church," Anise reiterated, as frustration rose in Flora.

Flora glared at the statue, willing for something to be made clear. Almost as if it heard her request, the stone lady rose taller, looming gigantically over her as it shimmered and sparkled as the light hit it, turning her face a shade of violet, and something invisible struck Flora's mind.

A single booming word wormed into her thoughts. *Confess.*

"Confess," Flora whispered, and Anise shot her a confused glance, her eyebrows turned down.

"What?"

"I have to confess."

"Confess what?" Anise asked, trying to keep her voice quiet as she glanced back at Kaanan. "Can we get some privacy please?"

"Why?"

"Because we are here to…pray, and we don't want an audience. Just, wait for us outside. We'll be out soon," Anise lied, and with one last glance at Flora, Kaanan slipped from the church, and finally, they were alone.

"Okay, Lady Larkspur—confess what?" Flora asked aloud, mentally willing something more to release from the stone lady frozen in time.

"Maybe just confess anything, see if something happens," Anise suggested.

Flora gulped thickly as her stomach heaved. She and Anise may have been best friends, but there were thoughts and feelings Flora shared with no one—not even her mother. She wished in that moment Anise had left with Kaanan, but if Flora told her to leave now, Anise would throw a hissy fit and give her the cold shoulder for being excluded from their quest.

So, Flora squared her shoulders, breathed in and pushed down her worries and fears, and let a secret loose from her lips.

"I hate my biological mother sometimes," she whispered, and a shiver ran down her spine as a trail of something caressed her mind. Magic. She instinctively knew what it was—there was no doubt in her mind and no other explanation for the sensation spreading through her veins.

More.

"More?" Flora squeaked. She had hoped it would be a one-and-done kind of thing.

Something deeper.

"Something deeper?"

"Do me," Anise said, causing Flora's cheeks to flush.

"What?"

"Confess a secret about me—you have to have one. Not everyone is honest all the time," Anise said, and a thorn of worry stabbed into Flora. What was Anise hiding from her? Was it the same thing Flora was hiding?

"But I don't want it to change our friendship."

"Flora, nothing you say will change it. We won't let it. But if the magic wants you to dig deeper, than dig deep. Tell it something you've never told me."

"Fine," Flora said, and took a deep breath, before releasing it slowly. Only one thought popped into her head and circled until she accepted it was the only secret she felt even remotely comfortable starting with. "I used to have a crush on Anise."

The words hovered in midair before Anise let loose a sharp laugh. "Flora, I already knew that."

"*What?*" Flora screeched, mouth dropping open, appalled her best friend already knew. It was a long time ago that Flora found herself looking at Anise differently. It was when they were fifteen, and just starting to notice others in a romantic sense. Flora realized she liked both boys and girls, and vowed to get over the idiotic crush because she knew Anise would never feel that way about her. And she was too valuable of a friend to let a silly fancy ruin their friendship.

"You're not the most subtle person. I knew. I just didn't want to say anything because I knew how awkward you'd get," Anise said. "Don't be mad and don't feel weird about it. We're good."

"I don't feel that way *now*. You know that, right?"

"Yes, Flora. I'm aware," Anise said dryly.

"Was that enough?" Flora asked, turning back to the Larkspur Lady.

No.

"Shit. Okay, um, sometimes I hate Anise," Flora said and froze, wishing she could take the words back as Anise's face fell, crushed. The words fell from Flora's lips without warning, without filter. "I didn't mean that. I'm sorry."

"It's okay," Anise said, looking anywhere but Flora.

"It's just stupid stuff, dumb jealousy I don't really mean. I love you. You're my best friend. Sometimes I'm just having a bad day and it's not your fault. It's mine, and I really truly don't mean that I hate you," Flora rambled, cheeks burning and eyes watering.

"Flora, I get it, okay?" Anise said, flatly. "It's just not…nice to hear. I'll get over it."

"But—"

"Just focus on the statue." Her words were sharp as the blade of a knife, and though Flora knew Anise would be okay, she still felt a crack snap her heart as guilt and sorrow threatened to shove her down. However, Flora was used to taking direction from her friend and she turned back to the statue, but it remained impassive.

No.

Flora looked inward, searching and clawing for something to confess. But she was boring and didn't have many secrets, or anything the statue would be impressed with. Flora already felt like she was going to throw up—she couldn't take being in the church much longer. The magic from the statue was cloying, and suffocating. But what did it want?

There was only one thought that danced into her mind that stuck, that sounded right and wrong, like something she needed to confess.

"I...I don't think I want magic." The second the words escaped Flora's rosy lips, a sparkling peony-colored quartz in the shape of a larkspur petal sat in her palm.

A gasp fell from Flora's lips as a wave of magic washed over her. Her ankle burned with the intensity of an inferno as her fingers unconsciously closed around the shard. An intoxicatingly dizzy feeling rolled in as tendrils of almost invisible pink beams wrapped around her, and then burst into a shattering of light, seeping into her skin.

A pink larkspur shot from her ankle, releasing a jolt of electric magic inside her, and broke off, landing on the floor in a patch of sunlight. *Use it wisely*, the voice told her, and then the statue returned to normal, pure stone and appearing less magical by the second. Whatever was keeping the shard there was leeched out of it and into Flora, filling her with a pink haze.

Flora could barely breathe with how the magic twirled inside her. She couldn't quite get a grasp on it, but she *felt it*. It was there, inside her, no longer dormant, but not quite graspable either. But it was there. She had gotten the first shard—she had done it. She stood taller, a rare dose of confidence boosting her up. A grin grew on her face and Anise flung her arms around her.

"Good job!" she cheered, and Flora squeezed her

friend tight.

Flora was worried she had damaged their friendship, that soon enough they would part ways forever, and Anise would hate her. She tried to shove those thoughts away, and focus on the present, where a sharp shard of quartz dug into her palm.

"I can feel the magic."

"That's great! We're really on our way now."

Flora's eye fell to the pink larkspur, her stomach twisting—her larkspur was always purple. She didn't know what it meant, but she nearly screamed when Anise went to grab it. Her hand shot out and wrapped around Anise's wrist tightly. "Don't touch it—it's poisonous."

"Jeez. Sorry," Anise said, rubbing her wrist when Flora released her.

Flora snatched up the fallen larkspur and shoved it into her rucksack. Then, she pulled a length of string holding her bread together and tied it tight around the shard. Flora hung the ensemble around her neck, a peaceful sensation washing over her as the quartz kissed the skin of her chest, tucked safely under her flowing shirt.

The second the shard was secured and hidden away, the church door burst open, revealing a shadowed Kaanan. He stepped forward, a beam of light cutting into his charming face and said, "You ladies ready to go?"

His face held a kind smile, and Flora's navel tugged toward him again. Her crush on Anise had definitely died a long time ago and was never revived by anyone else—until now. Now her heart was creating a flickering flame for a boy she barely knew but felt drawn to all the same. There was something so inherently *right* about him, something that drew her forward like a magnet and though she knew it was just a simple case of infatuation with someone so gorgeous, she couldn't help but let a small, miniscule part of her long for something more.

Flora smiled at him, her face bright, but pale. Acquiring the shard didn't return any color to her. She was still washed out, and fading away, but in that moment, Flora didn't care. She was exhilarated, the quartz humming against her skin as her ankle cooled down in contentment and distance from the next shard. She knew going forward things might still be challenging, but she got one already—how hard could the others be?

Chapter Nine

Pink shard properties: fickleness, contrariness, and affection.

(*A difficult shard to wield, this will fill you with opposing opinions and ideas. Good luck picking one. But, if you're around someone you care about—it's easier.*)

The budding confidence Flora felt was crushed quickly by her anxiety-ridden mind. Her good mood from finding the first shard died as the sun started sinking, the sky bruising, and seeing the city guards inspect people as they left.

Everything slotted into place. She was no longer confused why getting into the city was so easy. It was littered with guards, so the King was always safe. And the entire city was a maze—no one left unless they were lucky or the guards forced them out. So, of course, they would check people on their way out. They could look for the Lost Larkspur easily, because if she had wandered past their gates, she could never leave without being checked.

"*Shit,*" Flora muttered under her breath as they hovered in the stable entrance.

Kaanan had easily walked them back to the stable where they housed their horses. Whatever caused the city to mess with people's heads, he was apparently immune to it. Flora had never so much as seen him look

98

confused for a millisecond—he always knew exactly where he was going.

Her quartz buzzed under her shirt, but even if she wanted to expose herself and perform magic to get out, she had no idea how. And she wanted to practice in a safe place before experimenting in public. She didn't want to alert everyone to her presence or hurt anyone by accident. She wasn't even sure how much magic she could do with one shard. According to the *Króna*, she needed all four to unlock her full magical potential.

"What do we do?" Anise asked, clutching Flora's forearm. Both girls were stiff, with straight spines and limbs, fear and nerves thrumming under their skin.

If the guards inspected Flora, she would be caught—there was no doubt in her mind. And then everything would be ruined.

"You know, I can't help but get the impression you don't want to participate in the involuntary inspection?" Kaanan drawled, leaning against the doorframe post, obsidian cloak artfully drawn around him so he looked like a regal painting.

"Is it always mandatory?" Flora asked, wringing her hands.

"Yup," he said, popping the "p". "Haven't you provincial girls heard of the missing Larkspur Lady? Our savior?"

Anise shot him a withering glare and said, "Of course we have."

"So, what's the issue? Why can't you two be inspected? Are you, perhaps, the missing Larkspur?" he asked, grinning as he looked them both over.

"Don't be ridiculous," Anise said, a flush rising up her neck. "We just don't want to be inspected. It's inhumane."

"Right," he said, drawing out the word as he continued to watch them with narrowed eyes, trying to figure out who they were and what they were up to.

Flora wrapped her arms around herself, her ankle itching as her throat closed. She couldn't be discovered. It would ruin everything. They had barely even started their quest! And to be caught after gaining an ounce of her magic would be soul-crushing.

"Kaanan," Flora said, spinning to face him directly. Their eyes locked—his dark to her light. "Can you get us out of here without going through the inspection?"

He watched her, cocking his head to the side as his gaze darted over her face. She kept her features stern and flat, eyebrows drawn, and lips pursed in a line as her eyes narrowed. A strange feeling crept up on Flora, her magic dancing in her veins, drawing her closer— like the magic wanted to be closer to him. Flora took a deep breath. Her gut, and her magic, were saying to look to him, this intriguing stranger with such an air of confidence and ease. He had to have something up his sleeve to help them.

"Maybe. What's in it for me?" he asked, shrewd eyes narrowing.

"What do you want?"

"Flora!" Anise hissed, grabbing her arm. "That's the worst thing you can say in a negotiation. *Shut up!*" She stepped in front of Flora, shielding her from view of Kaanan. "We can offer you payment for providing us safe passage through the checkpoint."

Kaanan clucked his tongue, shaking his head. "I wasn't talking to you. I believe Flora and I were making negotiations—beat it."

Anise let out of gasp of indignation, her mouth falling open at the forceful exclusion. It was not something she was used to. Flora grabbed her arm, tugging her backward so they stood in line with one another. With a reassuring smile at her friend, she said, "I got this."

"But—"

"Anise. Trust me, I can handle him," Flora said, a white lie, but her tone was convincing enough. Although Anise did watch her for a minute before relenting.

"*Fine*," she huffed, arms crossing over her chest, accentuating her cleavage in her sweetheart neckline, peach-colored dress. She glared daggers at Kaanan as she lifted her chin higher.

"Kaanan—what do you want?" Flora asked again. She was aware Anise had a point—it was a rookie move to ask someone what they wanted in a negotiation rather than give them options. But she needed help to escape the city, and her desperation had a clawed grip on her throat that kept tightening. So, she would play a game with him, would let herself be a pawn to ultimately get what she wanted.

"Ah," he sighed, a pleased grin growing on his face, "that sounds like music to my ears. What do I want? Oh, Flora, I want what everyone wants."

"And what is that?" she asked, teeth gritted.

"I think it would be better discussed *outside* of the city. How about we agree you owe me a favor of my choosing in exchange for me getting you two out?"

Flora scoffed, "A favor? No. Not unless you tell me what it is first."

"All right, good luck getting out," he said, saluting

them as he rose and turned away, spinning on his heel dramatically.

"Wait!" Flora exclaimed, lunging forward until her fingers touched the edge of his cloak. It was such an inky black it looked like it swallowed her fingers whole. A zap of energy tingled her fingertips where they touched and she swallowed a gasp as she looked him in the eye—pretending to be brave when in reality, her heart pounded wildly in her ears.

"Please, just wait," Flora said, and released a breath as she said words she knew she might regret soon. "Fine. I will owe you a favor if you get us out without being detected—both of us."

"Deal," he said, grinning deeply, but it went from intoxicating to sinister in seconds.

Flora gulped, drawing away from him, and asked, "So how do we get out?"

"We wait for nightfall."

****

When the burning sky died, leaving a sea of black in its wake, Kaanan rose from the stable floor, shadows curling around him as he strode toward the door. Flora and Anise hung back, as instructed, and finally had a moment alone. They had spent the past few hours making idle conversation with Kaanan. All the while Flora wished they could discuss the quartz burning a hole in her dress and the larkspur itching her ankle.

"What was that earlier?" Anise hissed, eyes darting to where Kaanan scoped the darkened but lively street outside, partiers cheering drunkenly under the stars.

"What?"

"The negotiation—I was trying to *help* you," Anise scoffed, arms crossed over her chest again. Flora's stomach sank and guilt crept up as she realized Anise was more hurt than she had originally thought.

"I wasn't trying to cut you out, or hurt you, I just...we need to get out of here, and it's my cross to bear not yours."

"We're a team. It's both of our crosses, and you just gave him *all* the power. He could ask for anything he wants and you have to do it, unless you can magic a sword and we somehow take him down."

Flora's stomach heaved, and she cursed her tongue and her idiotically naive thoughts. She never should have spoken, should have kept her opinions bottled up to herself and let Anise take the lead, as she always did. Anise never let anything too terribly tragic happen to them, and she was right about this—Flora had placed them in the palm of Kaanan's hand. As much as she was intoxicated by his beauty, and his unwavering attention on her, she didn't know him. He could be a killer or a rapist or he could work for the King or the Sage Witch. Maybe that was why he helped them—because the Witch put him up to it. Or maybe it was the Pitch King.

The thought struck Flora's core deeply, a gashed wound splashing open, a quiver of fear pulsing through her veins as she watched him with a new idea in mind. He wanted to wait until dark, like the Pitch Woods, and he wore *all black*, the color of the Pitch Woods. The sinking pit in her stomach grew, nausea rising in her throat. They were doomed. He had to be working for one of them—probably the Pitch King—and when they left the city, he would have monsters and ghouls there to take them away to be eaten and tortured—

"*Flora*," Anise whispered harshly, her hand a stone

grip around Flora's, drawing her out of her spiraling thoughts and back to reality. "Get out of your head. I'm sorry for being harsh. I'm just worried."

"It's my fault," Flora whimpered, her eyebrows pinching together.

"Sort of, but we'll be fine. As long as we're together we can deal with whatever he throws at us," Anise said, nodding with a firm tone that had Flora nodding along as well. They could do it if they were together.

"Okay," Flora said, breathing through her panic. "Wait. One more thing—we need a plan in case we get separated. I don't know what his plan will entail but we need a contingency."

"Which shard are we going for next? We can plan it that way—if we get separated, we just head for the next location."

"The Svart Sea is closest. We can go there."

The girls agreed on their plan just as Kaanan returned, shadowy cloak sweeping around his feet and the loose hay on the floor. He held out his hand to Flora and helped her rise to her feet as Anise glared when he ignored her.

"Follow me and my lead, and we'll be out of this Godsforsaken city in no time."

"Got any more details there?" Anise asked, dryly.

Kaanan grinned at her darkly, dimple popping, as he said, "If you insist—it's really quite simple. I will provide a distraction, and then you will ride through the gates as fast as you can."

"And where will you be?"

"Flora and I will ride together," he said, sending Flora a kind smile. "That is, if you'll let me?"

"Flora," Anise warned as she read the look on her friend's face.

"Sure," Flora said slowly, unable to resist.

"Excellent! Let's go, ladies. We need to get moving."

Anise got on her horse, grumbling the entire time, while Kaanan gently helped Flora up and onto the saddle before deftly swinging up behind her. Flora's cheeks were a deep, rosy blush at the feeling of Kaanan pressed flush against her back. Her face burned as she struggled to keep her composure. Part of her was very...pleased at the position, while part of her felt hopelessly awkward and out of place. This was all too new to her. But Kaanan was the perfect gentleman and only guided their horse onto the street, Anise a hoofbeat behind.

The street was brighter than Flora would have thought. The lampposts burned bright and far, and many bars and taverns were still open, patrons spilling out onto the cobblestones. The night here was full of life, mindless chatter, and lilting music, unlike back home where it was lights out when the sun went down, everyone safely tucked in their beds.

"You ready?" Kaanan murmured in her ear, sending shivers down her spine at the rumbling, silky voice against her back.

Flora nodded and Kaanan took the reins from her hands, guiding them down the sloping street toward the golden gate, guards chatting aimlessly as they waited for travelers.

"Hold tight," he whispered to Flora, and then to the both of them he said, "Remember to keep moving—no matter what you see. This is a one-time opportunity. If we fail to get out—we will not get out. This place will be under lockdown for weeks."

"Okay," Flora whispered as her palms began to sweat.

"Got it," Anise said, rising taller in her saddle.

"We'll be fine," Kaanan said to Flora, grabbing her hand briefly. Her cheeks burned hotter and then the flame died out as he dropped her hand and forced the horse into a canter.

As they rode toward the gate, hooves echoed on the cobblestones loudly, alerting the guards to their rapidly approaching presence. Shouts rang through the night as the light dimmed. Sparks flew as the lampposts burst and popped, cloaking the street in shadows.

In seconds, the shadows appeared to come alive. They writhed against the ground and drew up into a cyclone around the two horses. Flora's heart was in her throat at the sight. A whispering hit her ears from behind her, but she couldn't make out the words—if they were even words.

In the blink of an eye, the entire world went dark, cast in thick as tar shadows. Flora couldn't make out an inch in front of her. But still, the horses kept beating against the stones, moving downhill, and she knew they must be nearing the gate. Shouts from the guards clawed her eardrums as shots started ringing out.

"Kaanan!" Flora screeched, hands flying in front of her face. Oh Gods, she had no eyes on Anise either. Flora didn't think the guards would shoot—they were on the lookout for her and she was no use to anyone if she were dead.

A sharp, agonized cry rang out that sounded like Anise. Flora almost flung herself from the horse and into the shadowy beyond, but Kaanan hooked a muscled arm around her waist, forcing her to remain in the saddle. Flora's vision became spotty, her head pounding and breath coming out in short gasps. And then, the shadows seeped away, revealing a dirt road and dust kicking up.

"Anise!" Flora called, twisting in the saddle, trying to make out her friend. But only silence answered.

As the last of the shadows fell away, the night was revealed. They were racing off the main road and into the valleys beyond, while guards scrambled to chase them in the distance. But they were too slow and too late.

The air around them was empty, and Flora could only hear one set of hoofbeats.

"Anise," Flora whimpered, desperately casting her gaze around her, begging the Gods to show her friend.

But it was to no avail. Kaanan's arm was still tight around her middle, as he forced the horse to take them farther away from the toxic city. Tears burned Flora's eyes as she begged and prayed to every God she knew to save her friend and return her to Flora unharmed and fast.

"I'll find you, Anise," Flora vowed, her hand closing around the quartz shard under her shirt. She would find her friend. She had to—she couldn't do this without her.

Chapter Ten

No one seems to realize I have limitations—that there are rules I must follow. No, they all just ask for more and more, but I can't give it to them. It is so tempting, though. Maybe I should just let loose, please everyone.

I don't know. I need guidance.

At least Desmond is by my side, helping me through it all. I couldn't do this without him, or Jeremiah.

-Diary entry by Anneliese Larkspur

Kaanan finally stopped the horse after an hour of steady, breakneck riding. They were far from the city, and well on their way into Whaelmere and toward the Svart Sea. The landscape turned from a dusty, flat desert to rolling hills quickly, with small copses of trees cropping up in addition to desolate rice fields. Flora discerned they were still a ways from the ocean as it was yet to even become a speck on the horizon.

The horse slowed to canter and then stopped completely. Kaanan's grip on Flora's waist loosened and she immediately leapt from the horse, harshly colliding with the dry grass and hard earth. Pain shot through her body as she landed poorly, her breath coming out in pants and gasps as her heart wouldn't calm down. Her lungs heaved and burned from screaming at Kaanan and her hands were raw from yanking on the horse's lead to no avail. She had barely even been able to shift in the saddle to shove Kaanan off the horse before he closed his arms tightly around her, cinching his biceps against hers so she couldn't move. And then, pathetically, like a weak little duckling, she had given up, had gone slack against him as she forfeited the fight and wallowed in self-loathing and fear. She had spent the last hour or so in a state of intense panic, her lungs seizing and her heart hammering, her grip loose and damp.

She had left Anise behind. She was despicable, disgusting.

Was Anise wounded? Was she dead? Did she escape too? Flora didn't know the answer to any of her questions, and it killed her. A knife had been stabbed in her back, and she sat centimeters away from the man who tore them asunder.

Kaanan was a black mark against the darkened sky. He watched her, face unreadable in the low lighting as he absently petted the horse. Flora could barely think—her brain felt like it was melting in a fiery inferno of rage. His stare only fueled the fire burning inside, but something had clamped down on her tongue. The words were there, swirling in her mind, but she couldn't get them past her lips. She shrunk against the ground, lip starting to quiver as he just *stared*.

Her tongue felt like it was wrapped in a stem full of rose thorns, her acrid, tangy blood pooling until her mouth had no choice but to bleed, bursting at the seams. Rivulets of blood gushing past her sewn lips and down her chin, dripping farther until it watered the earth under her feet.

She couldn't speak, couldn't move, and Flora truly

hated herself in that moment, despised that she was unable to scream or fight him. She hated that her stomach was queasy with anxiety and her throat wouldn't let her speak. The worst part was that as much as she wanted to yell at him, she also didn't. She didn't know what the consequences of her words would be, or what he would say—it was almost better to say nothing at all, let the moment pass into oblivion. But what would that accomplish?

Flora wanted to tear her hair out as she dug her palms into the rocky earth, the pain keeping her focused on the situation and not retreating into her mind.

All the while, Kaanan stared. His head cocked as he watched her, and she could imagine the smirk on his full lips highlighting his eye-catching dimple, and then he started to approach. Just one step closer to close the small gap between them, and that was all it took for Flora's unbidden voice to cry out and overpower her anxiety.

"Stay away from me!" she shouted, her voice loud in the quiet of the isolated, abandoned farmland.

She had no idea how close the nearest people were, so she bit her tongue harder. The last thing they needed was more attention. She didn't even know if the guards had given up. They could be chasing them down that very moment with their sharp swords and their thunderous guns with deft bullets that could kill instantly. The ruthless weapons were largely underproduced in Woodvale and most people used blades or arrows. But the guards showed no mercy with their barbaric guns and Flora needed to stay far, far away.

Flora's chest clenched as she thought about the

guards. She knew they must still be on their way and they were just sitting there like nothing was happening. They were coming and they would bring death and destruction with them, or she would be captured and oh Gods, she would rather *die*.

A wheezing gasp left Flora's lips as her hand clutched her chest. She couldn't breathe. It was too much. Her lungs were so tight it felt like they would explode from the pressure, and then she would never get to save her mother or her country. Either way she was doomed—destined for death, just like the poisonous birthmark marring her ankle, a prophecy incarnate.

"*Flora*, breathe with me," Kaanan commanded, kneeling in front of her. She hadn't noticed him moving closer, but she was eternally grateful to have something real and solid to focus on.

"Breathe—in and out. That's it now," he said, breathing with her as his hands rested on his knees, twitching like he wanted to hold her. Finally, after what felt like an eternity, her breathing steadied, and sounded less cloying. Her head felt better—she could think properly again with oxygen floating around in her lungs. Kaanan daintily lifted her chin slightly with the tip of his finger, ever-so warm and grounding, so their eyes would collide, and asked softly, "How do you feel?"

"Don't touch me," Flora whimpered, whacking his hand away with hers, a stinging sensation following at the skin-to-skin contact.

"Flora." Kaanan sighed, leaning back on his heels. She just stared at him, eyes raking over his features.

He looked tired—from what she could tell as her

eyes adjusted to the dark lighting. There were bags under his eyes and his skin was sallow. Gone was the charismatic, youthful guide, and in his place was a tired young man in need of a break. Flora hated the way butterflies still roamed her stomach, how her chin tingled from where he touched her, and how even at this low point for him, she was still attracted to him, still wanted something more with him. But that wouldn't be possible now—he had broken her trust. He was something else, tainted and terrible, his actions loathsome.

"Who are you?" Flora asked, voice quiet and shaking. Fear had a death grip on her heart at the sinking realization that she didn't know him or what he was capable of. His beauty couldn't mask his ugly heart for long. He had *left her*. Before he could answer her question, she cried, "Where is Anise?"

"Flora," he said, starting again, but her words were like a floodgate—now that her lips were loose, she couldn't stop them from spilling from her throat.

"What was that back there? With the shadows? Was Anise shot? Do you think she made it? Why didn't you help her!" she yelled, her eyes wild as she scrambled from her cowering position and rounded on him.

The two stood, wind blowing Flora's almost white hair behind her as Kaanan's pitch cloak flurried around his strong legs. He stood a head taller than her, but she didn't care in that moment. Her fury thrust her taller, so they looked eye level to her. She narrowed her eyes at him, nostrils flaring. His dark eyes met her light ones, and a smirk grew on his lips.

"Stop smiling! This is serious! Anise could be *hurt*

and she's *alone*. I can't do this without her," Flora said, voice caught between crying and yelling as her eyes started to burn with unshed tears.

His eyes sharpened as he said with a voice of steel, "You don't *need* her—you don't need anyone except yourself."

Her lips parted as she jerked back in surprise. Her heart warmed behind her ribcage, and she moved an inch closer, forgoing her instinct to move away from him, cast under a spell by his words before she shook herself out of it.

"Who. Are. You." Her eyes were daggers, and her voice was cold as a flurrying blizzard.

"Don't you know already? Can't you feel it? Aren't you smarter than this?" he asked, staring her down, eyes burning holes into hers.

"You can't be—it's impossible," she murmured, and he shrugged.

"Then I'm probably not."

"Just tell me," she said, exasperated, as she threw her hands up in the air.

He hesitated, eyes darting over her face as if he were contemplating his answer. But all she wanted was the truth. In that moment, she didn't care if her worst fears became true. She just *needed* to know the truth.

"You have to promise not to run—it's not safe for you to go off on your own. And while I would catch you with ease, I'm not in the mood to chase you right now. I'm tired too—that took a lot out of me." Even with the soft confession that mirrored her own battered and bruised and exhausted body, Flora held no sympathy for him.

Flora crossed her arms over her chest, narrowing

her eyes. She let out a huff of air from her nose before complying. "Fine."

"I work for the Pitch King. An apprentice of sorts, his jack of all trades," he said, grinning in the dark as Flora's stomach sank, but not as deep as it could have.

"What?" she whispered, her voice as loud as she could dare it.

She had assumed he was the *Pitch King*. In her darkest fears she questioned that possibility as it made sense to her with his use of the shadows—because there was no way that occurred naturally. She prayed he wasn't the Pitch King, not because of the danger, but because if he were the Pitch King, she didn't think she could survive such a betrayal. His features were widely unknown, but there was a reason for that—he couldn't permanently reside anywhere but the Pitch Woods, same as the Sage Witch. They were bound to their domains. At least, that was the general consensus she and Anise gleaned from eavesdropping during their travels and their own theories. No one knew *why*, but everyone took comfort in that fact.

Still, a small niggling remained, that he was lying, and he was in fact the Pitch King in all his dark glory. But, she supposed, *working* for him was just as bad. She had no idea what to do with the information, how she should act or what she should say. She was at a complete loss—cast adrift in her worries and fears.

Flora found her voice again and demanded, "Explain more, please. Why are you here? Why did you help me? Where is Anise?"

"It's precisely like I said. I work for him, and he wants to…keep an eye on you. You're the last-surviving Larkspur Lady with a boon of world-altering magic from the Sage Witch, are you not?" he asked, eyes seeming to twinkle in the starlight. "If I lift your skirt, will I not find a birthmark of a larkspur? And under your shirt—you found one of the shards earlier, didn't you?"

"How do you know all of this?"

"Because it's my job. You're Flora Larkspur, the girl I need to watch and you know, etcetera—more things I can't say now," he said. "But don't fear, Flora. I'm here to protect you. My boss and I *want* you to get your magic back."

"Why? So you can use me, too?" she huffed, arms crossing over her chest as she shied away from him. A caw from a crow sounded overhead, making her jump while Kaanan didn't even flinch.

"Maybe, maybe not—time will tell. I don't know exactly what he wants from you yet. But for now, you and I are partners in this little quest of yours. What you need, I will gladly give. I promise to help in any way I can," he vowed with a grin eating up his face.

Flora didn't know what to say. She was at a loss for words again, but this time because she was frozen. Everything was becoming so complicated and convoluted. She could barely string together enough thoughts to form a basic opinion. She needed a good night's sleep and a breather from the threats on her life and then she could puzzle this all out. She could figure out what to do about Kaanan, apprentice to the Pitch King. Oh Gods, even the thought sounded so ridiculous—that she was even entertaining the idea of his help—because how could she ever trust him? He worked for *the Pitch King*—killer of humans, master of monsters and beasts, and ruler of shadows.

"What if I don't want your help?"

"Then I follow from a distance. You can do it with or without me. It's just, if I help, we might finish faster and that way I don't get myself killed if someone or something catches you."

She swallowed thickly, because there were those words again, that stark belief in her that Flora herself didn't feel. "How can you think I can do this alone? I can barely do...anything by myself."

"Flora, you can do lots by yourself. You just haven't had the chance with that leech and anchor hooked around your ankle," he muttered, darkly.

"What are you talking about? Anise? She's my best friend—she's only ever helped me." Flora's words were harsh in the quiet, cutting deep as her eyes blazed and her lips pursed.

"Never mind, then. Just an opinion from an observing stranger—I may be wrong." He smiled, and Flora recoiled again.

"Where is Anise? Do you think she's okay?" Flora asked, her heart racing as guilt ate away at her insides. She should have done more to ensure they remained together. Now Anise was lost and alone and potentially wounded. Flora was a despicable friend.

"How should I know?" he asked with a laugh, causing Flora's heart to drop.

"But...you were the one leading us! And you clearly have magic! Didn't you think to check on her? She could have been shot!"

"Flora, my priority is *you* and you alone. Anise was deadweight—and yes, I would leave her to be shot and killed because *you* were in danger. You are the important one here, Flora. She doesn't matter—you

116

do," he said, driving his point home as it stabbed the knife into her deeper. "Look—she'll be fine, okay? Weren't you two whispering about a meeting spot? Didn't you set one?"

"Well...*yes*, but I don't know if she's capable of meeting me anymore. They were *shooting at us*, and she screamed," Flora grumbled, her arms crossing over her chest as she frowned.

"Well, we can't go back—we can only move forward. You just have to have faith in your friend, bleeding out or not."

"That's not comforting," she huffed as he raised his perfectly sculpted eyebrows at her.

"I'm sorry? Is it my job to comfort you?" he scoffed, and narrowed his eyes. "You're what, eighteen? I've been self-reliant for four years—ever since I turned fifteen and my father died. I've worked through it so don't go pitying me—life goes on. You need to learn to comfort yourself—stop relying on others so much."

A pang of sympathy stabbed at her middle at the information, but his burning glare had it disintegrating just as quickly. Flora glowered at him, her lip wobbling, and she hated to admit, even in her mind, he had a point. She did lean heavily on Anise and her mother for everything. She was eighteen now, technically an adult, and needed to grow up. Things were only going to get worse before they got better. She needed to work on herself, and she had to do it on her own.

Kaanan was at least still with her, and she wanted to lean on him, forget all the lies and who he worked for and just glom onto him—be a barnacle on his ship while he carried her through her quest. But she couldn't, for numerous reasons: the most important one being that she couldn't trust him. He was a liar and he worked for the Pitch King. She needed to hate him, needed to look past her rose-colored glasses and see him for what he was: another one of the Pitch King's monsters.

Chapter Eleven

King Desmond was a fool. The question, however, is this:

Was he just a fool? A man who wanted the best for his people and land, who put his hopes and dreams for his people in a woman untested?

Or was he a fool in love? Did he give his cards to a seductress, or a simple girl who caught his eye?

-The Age of Larkspur by Cassius Muscari, IV

Fire crackled and flared, burning bright against the inky pool of the night.

Flora had heavily protested starting a fire, even though the temperature was dropping, and the darkness was making it impossible to think. She liked the nighttime, and the peace it offered, but combined with the dry landscape and lack of vegetation, she couldn't bear it. She needed plants like she needed to breathe, and doubled with the suffocating darkness, her pulse spiking with every crackle and snap of the unknown, she needed light.

"Won't they see us? This place is flat and the fire would be a beacon to them! We're exposed out here," Flora protested at Kaanan's suggestion for a flame.

"It's only going to get colder. It'll be a long night ahead of us and unless you want to cuddle—which I am more than happy to do—we need a fire," he said, smirking.

She was glad for the dark in that moment, as her cheeks flushed, and her face filled with longing. She shook herself out of it and sighed. "But they could see it."

"I can wrap us in shadows—they won't see a thing."

And so, she let him, even though her skin crawled at the dome of whispering and slithering shadows surrounding them. The dome was impenetrable, the outside world a distant land where they would have no idea if someone snuck up on them in the night.

"What does it mean to be the Pitch King's apprentice?" she asked, picking at the skin around her nails as she stared into the fire.

"It means I work for him. I do what he tells me when he tells me in exchange for magic lessons," he said with a flat tone.

"How could you apprentice for him?"

Kaanan glanced across the fire at her, his intense gaze burning her soul. She breathed in an expectant breath, hoping and waiting for him to redeem himself in her eyes. But for the hundredth time that night, he only disappointed her.

"Get some sleep. It's going to be a long day tomorrow," he said, eyes glowing molten golden in the firelight, drawing her in.

She wanted to fight him, tell him she could do what she pleased and she wasn't tired yet. But she had been swallowing yawns for the past twenty minutes and sleep sounded delightful—even if it wasn't in a soft, downy bed.

He kept watching her, an indiscernible look in his eyes, one Flora couldn't quite decipher. He was a treacherous river, murky and beautiful, hiding sharp rocks and beasts with teeth under the navy surface, and she was an innocent forest creature who slid on the slippery bank, trapped in the cutting waves until someone helped her. Or she helped herself. But the currents were strong and kept dragging her down, and she didn't know how to stop herself from drowning.

****

Tweeting, melodic chirps caused Flora to stir the next morning. When her eyes opened, she was met with darkness and a glowing face. She gasped startingly loud in the quiet of the morning. Flora scrambled backward, causing dirt to crust into her already filthy clothes and hard patches of earth to scratch her skin.

A dark eye cracked open, the boy's face illuminated by the dying embers, casting his beauty in complementary lighting. He sighed as he closed his eye, a soft, content look settling over his features.

Meanwhile, Flora's heart felt like it was going to jump out of her chest. Her eyes were wild and her head spun as she took in her surroundings. They had gotten closer in the night. The thought caused her eyes to narrow at the cherub-faced boy sleeping peacefully beside her. When she fell asleep, he was on the other side of the fire, nowhere near her. But now? He had been inches from her. The warmth his body heat provided still lingered.

"I can feel you staring at me," he said out of the corner of his rosy mouth, voice deep and thick with sleep. "What have I done now?"

"You...you're right beside me! I distinctly remember going to sleep on *separate* sides of the fire," Flora said, her voice sounding loud and a bit shrill to her ears. The birds still chirped, making her head hurt at the notion.

"It was cold."

"But—"

"Flora, you were shivering when the fire started dying, and so was I. It was the only way to not perish from frostbite."

"It's not that cold!"

"Fine, maybe not perish," he mumbled, snuggling into his cloak, "but it was the only way to have a comfortable sleep."

The birds chirped louder and she nearly tore her head off. It was still pitch black, the only light from the dying embers, but the birds and her internal clock knew it was morning beyond the impenetrable wall of shadows. She did wonder just how powerful he was to hold the shadow dome overnight while they slept. She hadn't heard of any apprentices to the sorcerers in the land, but she supposed it wasn't a completely outrageous thought. She briefly wished she had found the Sage Witch's apprentice, until she remembered the Sage Witch had a wicked, maleficent side.

Any other magic apprentice in the land would do, but magic was as dry as the land and rare as green grass fields. Flora only knew of five magic wielders: the Pitch King, the Sage Witch, the *Króna,* herself, and the Larkspur Ladies—and now a sixth: Kaanan.

"Can you bring down the dome? Please?"

He didn't respond, just let the shadows melt away to reveal an orange horizon and brightened landscape. They were in the nook of a valley, rocks and dead crop fields surrounding them. There were no houses or villages in sight, but Flora assumed they were over some of the hills encasing them.

Even dying and desolate, it was beautiful. Her eyes drank in the new scenery, and she could picture it so clearly in its glory, with blooming flowers and crops, people working the rice fields as greenery exploded around them. She inhaled sharply when her chest warmed—the shard was burning against her skin. She peered down, amazed at the quartz as it brightened, emitting a soft glow.

"Wow," she breathed, fascinated at the sight.

It must have been her magic coming through. Or maybe her longing and imagination conjured some aspect of her magic. The thought comforted her, that maybe this whole ordeal was manageable and accessible. But when she tried chasing the warm threads in her mind and body, they slipped through her mental fingers. Frustration rose as she pressed her hands and feet harder into the ground, rocks cutting into her skin. A couple of beads of blood bloomed, and she sighed as she wiped them on her filthy skirt.

She ignored the shard and focused on the land again, looking past the overhead layer of deadened landscape, and underneath, the scenery she knew was there, just waiting to be saved and blooming again.

She glanced down, chest warm again, and startled when her eyes caught on the ground beside her bleeding hand. It was beautiful, magnificent, and perfectly healthy. A blade of grass split through the packed earth and swayed in the faint breeze as a smile burst onto Flora's face.

Flora sighed with her whole body, pure joy spreading through each limb and organ. She couldn't believe she had done that—had created life from dead earth. Her eyes welled as her smile threatened to split her face open.

She glanced at her companion and jerked back when her eyes met his. He was staring at her, eyes gleaming and smile wide, his dimple deep in his cheek as his eyes flicked down to the blade of grass.

"Well done," he said, grin continuing to grow wider.

Flora hesitated, unsure what to say or feel. Was it good he saw? Now he knew she could access her magic, even faintly. As their eyes connected, she was reminded of the secrets he revealed last night. A hard coating grew over her limbs and mind—she needed to hate him. Or at the very least, not trust him. She had to keep her distance, and that doubled for the butterflies dancing around her stomach. He was working for the scariest and darkest man known to Woodvale—he was not to be trusted or liked.

"We should head out," she said, ignoring his compliment as she dropped any emotion from her features.

His eyes flashed as the smile fell off his face. He rose from the ground in one swift motion, swinging his cloak around his broad shoulders, and extended a hand toward her perch on the ground.

Her hand almost crept into his, *almost*, but she restrained herself and flung her body off the ground and away from him, not even remotely as graceful. When she looked back, his head hung for a second, hand still extended, before he closed himself off and made for the horse.

Kaanan mounted the mare with ease, stroking the animal tenderly before turning in the saddle to face

Flora. She stood beside them, holding her rucksack in a white-knuckled grip. His eyes were narrowed as he cast his gaze on her, and she shrunk away from his piercing stare.

He cocked an eyebrow, hands resting on his thighs and asked, "Can I help you up this time? Or can you do it on your own?"

She glowered at him. "Weren't you the one saying I could do anything, even by myself?"

"Touché," he said, smirking rising, "but I was really just trying to be helpful…no! Chivalrous."

He grinned at her, and she rolled her eyes internally. Externally, she gave no reaction save for grabbing the edge of the saddle and sticking her foot in the stirrup. She could hear her heartbeat in her ears as her body lifted far from the ground.

It was all going fine. She was almost able to swing herself over and up onto the horse, but her sweating palms caused her to slip. Before she could collide with the ground, Kaanan's strong arm shot out, grabbing her waist and hauling her onto the saddle in front of him. He was pressed against her, thigh to thigh and back to chest. Flora's cheeks glowed at the warmth encasing her. How could she distance herself when they were literally snuggling up against one another and her heart fluttered and belly was full of lively butterflies, when she melted into his arms? She was doomed.

****

Flora wanted to push Kaanan off the horse. The longer they traveled through the province of Whaelmere, the more irritable and sour she grew. The breakneck speed he forced on them made her veins lust for revenge. It made her wrath toward him fester and blossom into a vengeful weed. She glared daggers at the horizon, wishing she sat behind him so he would at least feel her stare. Nevertheless, she envisioned her knives cutting through the air and circling back toward him.

Her thighs and backside ached fiercely. Each jolt from the horse's hooves hitting the earth shot agony through her limbs. The sun bore down on them, its rays fiercer in Whaelmere than in Sanarbre. Her sensitive color-leeched skin was reddening and blistering with each passing hour under the burning sun. But still, Kaanan set an unyielding pace.

The horizon teased them multiple times, a mirage of the oncoming ocean she knew would eventually appear lingering until they passed it. It was an endless cycle. Flora wasn't aware how much bigger Whaelmere was than Sanarbre. It looked the same on the few maps she had studied, but the maps were created by bold liars. She concurred Whaelmere must be twice the size of Sanarbre, filled with small towns and dusty, never-ending fields.

Kaanan refused to stop, even with Flora's begging and pleading. But each word out of her mouth was stolen by the wind. They never stopped at the towns they passed. Kaanan would pull shadows around them and give the towns a wide berth. They teased and toyed with her senses. Even though most were specks on the horizon, some were closer, and she could make out details on buildings and she could smell food on the wind. With each flare of her nostrils, her stomach cramped harder, and she longed for her mother's cooking.

Finally, instead of veering away from the

oncoming town, Kaanan urged them toward it. The sun was about to begin its descent from the sky, almost giving way to a burning orange and pink, but not quite—the blue held true for a while longer. Kaanan whisked them into a town and stopped at the stable.

He, once again, gracefully dropped from the horse, and this time, instead of fighting him, Flora let him help her down. She was exhausted and sore and wasn't interested in putting up a fight again for something so trivial.

"We just need some supplies, so stay close and don't talk to anyone," he instructed, causing Flora to frown.

"Can't I stay here?"

He startled and quirked an eyebrow at her. "You want to stay? Why? I thought you would be dying to see a new town."

"Well, I am, but I'm tired and aren't we staying here for the night?"

"No, we're not staying here for the night—we need to keep moving," he said as Flora pouted, scrunching up her nose. "I'm sorry to say, but I need you in my sights here. I can't go shopping while worrying someone might have spotted you and snatched you up while I'm none the wiser."

Flora shrugged and nodded, ceding to his desires. She really did want to take a nap, even on the hay strewn floor, but she understood where he was coming from. Kaanan nodded once at her and then rustled through the saddlebag. He produced a piece of cloth and extended it toward her. "Here, wrap your hair in this."

"What? Why?"

"Because if anyone is looking for us, your hair is a dead giveaway. It's even brighter and paler than when we left," he said, and his features tightened. "Are you okay? Are you feeling all right?"

"I'm fine." She waved him off, her exhaustion overpowering her desire to complain. "Just sore and tired."

He gave her a dubious look, with pinched lips and narrowed eyes, but relented. "Fine, but please, do tell me if you're not feeling well or if something is going on. I'm here to help you."

"Whatever," she mumbled, turning away from him so he couldn't see the pink starting to color her pale cheeks.

She snatched the cloth from his hands and wrapped her bright locks neatly underneath the cloth. She wished there was a mirror in the barn as she was sure she looked like a housewife or old lady out shopping in the sun. Kaanan snickered when he turned to her, and she glowered at him.

"What?" she said, voice dull and emotionless.

"Nothing! You just look like a mother of unruly kids," he said, a broad grin on his face. "You look cute. But don't let the fact that this is cute go to your head." He paused, a contemplative look settling on his face. "Although, I do prefer your normal look."

"Hey—"

"Scratch that," he said, waving her off. "It doesn't matter what I think. Dress how you want, Flora."

Flora pursed her lips, and turned away from him, pretending to rustle through her rucksack so she didn't have to respond to his comment and so he couldn't see the smile threatening to bloom on her lips. She liked how he spoke to her—it bolstered her instead of tearing her down. He actively went against her anxieties and didn't let her use them as an excuse. Because while she did truly find some situations insurmountable, sometimes she was just being a coward.

But he was the enemy—she needed to remember that, remember who he worked for and all of the nightmarish stories she had heard.

A tickling sensation flitted against her ankle, and she sighed. The flower furiously itched against her stockings and skin. Her ankle had left her alone for the day, just staying her body temperature. As much as it disappointed her, since the second shard clearly wasn't anywhere near her, she hoped they were at least going in the right direction since her ankle wasn't telling her. But ultimately, she was okay with the dormant birthmark. Aside from the general stress it caused her, as the flower was poisonous, if anyone saw it, she would be hunted and strung up.

"Let's go," he said and turned to the stable entrance, leaving their neighing horse to rest.

Kaanan and Flora slipped out of the stable and onto the moderately busy street. The roads were gravel, and only held foot traffic of robust and stocky people, skin tones varying per person, but all sporting some degree of tan. Their skin was more weathered than the people in Sanarbre, the sun fiercer in Whaelmere. Flora could attest to that with the blister currently forming on her ear—it had somehow gotten exposed during their trek, and now it scraped against the cloth painfully. Flora envied each person who wasn't burnt to a crisp. Her skin was on fire, but her legs had been covered. It was just her face and arms that bore the brunt of the harsh sun.

"What are we looking for?" Flora asked, elongating her stride so she matched pace with Kaanan, who was currently darting through the crowds on the tight street.

"Supplies," he said and grabbed her hand.

His calloused fingers closed around hers, causing Flora to gasp from surprise. She could feel her cheeks burning and she hoped it was mostly masked by the sunburn. He tugged her to his side and dragged her along, barely putting pressure on her arm socket, just guiding her and keeping her close.

The street let out into a big open marketplace, full of stalls of everything and anything, peddlers calling loudly to passersby, trying to entice anyone with a pocket of coin to spend.

"Stay close," Kaanan said into Flora's ear, leaning down to reach her.

They moved through the market together, and Flora watched as Kaanan made his purchases. He bought mostly dried food, medicine, rope and other survival items, and a set of sharp knives. Flora eyed him suspiciously as he purchased the wicked, gleaming blades. He quirked his eyebrows at her questioning gaze and then threw a sword onto the bundle of knives. The blade gleamed against the light and looked razor-sharp. Flora could almost feel the cut of the blade just looking at it.

Flora was concerned with the purchase, as she didn't know *who* it was going to be used against. She hoped someone other than herself and Anise, if she could reconnect with her that is. She was also reassured at the purchase. It was an added layer of protection she may need, especially after the high stakes exit of Vale Centre.

Kaanan did one thing that confused and flustered Flora again at his thoughtfulness. She wished he would stop and be the Pitch King's apprentice—dark and cold, menacing and ruthless—it would be easier that way. But, without being prompted, he purchased a pot of cream mixed with *Aloe vera*—an expensive gift with the dwindling supply of coin.

"Thank you," Flora said, tugging on his hand still tightly, but comfortably clasped around hers.

"Anytime," he said, shooting her a grin as the moved onto the next stall. "I mean that."

Before Flora could return his smile with one of her own, a scream pierced the dusky air, causing Flora's heart and stomach to drop and Kaanan's hand to yank against hers, tugging her into the confines of his thick cloak.

What's going on? Flora thought, the words dying in her throat before her tongue could form them. She scanned the crowd and easily found what she was looking for: a thief and a guard, an apple and a broadsword.

"We need to leave," Kaanan said, and whisked her away, out of the market with ducked heads and back to the stable where their horse was waiting. Flora hesitated for a fraction of a second, caught with wanting to help the poor, hungry person. But she let herself be led away. It would do more damage to herself and others if she got caught. Guilt ate away at her stomach as she realized Kaanan may be powerful enough to help the thief. And yet, she kept her lips sealed and followed her protector away from the horrific spectacle forming.

In record time, they put away their supplies and mounted their steed. They chased the dying embers in the sky, racing through the blackening world and a little bit closer toward their destination.

Chapter Twelve

My darling,
We must be careful—people are starting to talk.
The whispers keep chasing me when I leave the
palace—it's driving me insane.
I need you now more than ever. Promise me you'll
always be there for me—I can't do this without you. I
miss you so much, even when we spend an hour apart. I
am dying for some alone time, my love.
Meet me at our spot—midnight, sharp.
I'll be waiting impatiently,
Your larkspur forever,
Anneliese
-Letter found in the ruins of Anneliese's chambers

Dust kicked up into the darkening air behind them.
Each jolt of hooves hitting the hard ground sent pain
ringing up Flora's spine, and her and Kaanan pressing
closer together. Her eyes were drooping, her body
slackening against the solid wall behind her, exhaustion
creeping and crawling up through her body. She would
kill for a bed—even a soft patch of earth would do.
Anything but the saddle and jarring movement of
horseback riding.

The hills and valleys dipped and rose, each one
looking identical to the last. Except, in the distance,
Flora's eyes caught on a haven. A sharp gasp escaped
her lips, and she tugged on the reins, jerking them off

course toward the sight she was intently focused on.

Her eyes were wide as she stared at the beauty before her. Because there it was, a perfect, and lovely, green escape. A copse of trees, healthy and small, but there all the same, calling her name in a chant that reverberated with the hoofbeats.

"What do you think you're doing?" Kaanan asked in her ear, trying to jerk the reins from her white-knuckled grip, but Flora held on for her life—she was a force to be reckoned with when it came to plants.

"We're stopping there for the night!" Flora yelled back to him, voice carrying on the wind whipping against her face and causing her whitening hair to fly wild.

"Fine," he muttered, unknowingly giving into her deep desire for the trees and the protection they offered her.

The horse had barely stopped when Flora lunged off and bolted into the trees.

"Hey!" Kaanan yelled, and she could hear him scrambling to catch up with her. He spewed curses and more at her back, but she didn't care—she was in the trees and the wild freedom they afforded.

Flora breathed her deepest breath in days. She inhaled the earthy smells and let the greenery rejuvenate her body and soul. She had terribly missed her copse back home, and being in this new one showed her how much. Her eyes watered as she delved deeper into the shadowy trees.

She trailed her fingers along the bark and leaves and the bushes and moss coating every surface. Pine needles littered the ground, and she inhaled the rich scent, a calmness washing over her entire body as she sank to the forest floor in an open patch wide enough for sleeping. Her knees were protected from roots by needles and moss, and she closed her eyes, hands gripping the earth around her.

That was how Kaanan found her, sitting in the woods, her pale hair and body casting an ethereal glow in the night-shrouded woods. Flora's face was soft, and her body was relaxed as a wave of contentment swept through her. But the moment was cast adrift when the snap of a twig echoed through the quiet forest. Flora flinched, eyes wild as she searched for the sound only to find Kaanan staring at her intently. A blush bloomed on her cheeks as she wondered how long he had been standing there, just watching her quietly with an unreadable look in his eyes.

"It's just me," Kaanan said, coming closer and putting their packs down.

"Where's the horse?" she asked, grabbing her rucksack.

"She's tied to a tree nearby. The thicket is too dense for her to come any closer," Kaanan explained, rummaging through his pack.

"Thank you for letting us stop here," Flora said, ducking her head as she tried to hide her pleased grin.

"We had to stop eventually. Might as well pick a place no one would dare enter," Kaanan said, shrugging.

The living and breathing, healthy greenery rejuvenated Flora, energizing her as the life from the plants coursed through her veins. She felt the most like her usual self in days, the side of her she only shared with the trees. Even though she shared it with Kaanan, when she usually kept the woods to herself, he didn't dampen the energy the thick, green trees and plants provided.

"So, I have a question," Flora said, tucking her loose hair behind her burnt ears as she shyly cast her gaze on Kaanan.

Kaanan startled, jerking his head to her, his hands falling out of his pack as he quirked his thick eyebrow and prompted, "Shoot."

Her tongue was loose, and while her anxiety had a healthy grip on her throat and heart, the forest emboldened her, allowing her to speak her mind. She could worry about the repercussions and spiraling replays later. The branches and pine needles urged her on, creating a safe halo of space for them to talk.

"*Why* are you apprenticing for the Pitch King?"

"Why? Well, why not?" he asked, raising his eyebrows at her as she sighed.

"Seriously, Kaanan. *Why*? He's a monster."

His face shuttered, closing off entirely before he cast her an appraising look. "So what?"

"You're just so…nice and not cruel."

"You barely know me. Maybe I'm hiding my cruelty to get close to you."

"If you were, then you wouldn't say that. You're not him, and I want to know why you're working with him. Doing his monstrous bidding?"

"Because I want to," he said, tensing his jaw. "Look, you're not going to get a different answer out of me—it's not some big reason why I'm his apprentice. He needed one and I was there to fill the spot. I wanted magic. Simple as that."

"Really?"

"Yes, really. But, Flora, I have one thing for you to

think about—how do you know the Pitch King is monstrous and cruel? Have you ever met him?" he asked, leaning his elbows forward on his criss-crossed knees.

"Everyone knows he's ruthless and…evil. He literally represents darkness," Flora said, shaking her head in confusion at his words.

She supposed maybe the Pitch King wasn't *exactly* like the rumors promised—it wasn't *impossible*. But there were too many stories, too many accounts of his cruelty for Flora's opinions to be swayed. The forest was literally said to leech crawling darkness, shadowy tendrils extending from the treeline, searching for prey. And there were too many eyewitnesses to monsters, terrifying beasts that sucked the blood and marrow from bones, the lifeless husks found on the treeline in Myrkurden.

"Fair enough," Kaanan said, shrugging his broad shoulders. "But everyone's entitled to their own opinion and choices. My choice and allegiance is with the Pitch King. Is that going to be a problem?"

"Are you going to give me to him?" Flora shot back.

"I don't know yet," he said, an air of truth dripping from his words. "We'll see what he says."

"Then I don't know if it's going to be a problem—time will tell."

Kaanan nodded, jaw still tight and flexing as Flora sighed. She wanted more information from this conversation, but Kaanan was locked up tight, unwilling to share more than the basics.

"What about you, Flora?"

"What about me?"

"Your larkspur powers, that shard you found. Care to share more about that?" he asked, quirking his eyebrows with a snide smirk.

"Are you going to share what I say with your boss? If so, not particularly," she said, crossing her arms over her chest, the sleeves stiff from dirt, dust, and dried cream.

"Not so easy sharing, is it? Especially around mixed company?" he teased, a wicked glint in his eye.

The moon was high over their heads now, casting its eerie, silver glow into the small gaps of the trees. Kaanan and Flora each sat in a patch, their faces illuminated as they basked for different reasons. Flora was still in awe of the thicket, twirling her fingers over the grass and dirt, in ecstasy at being around living, breathing plant life again. Kaanan was basking in the dark, the shadows, the different air that appeared at night, when all was quiet in the world save for a rare few who thrived on moonlight and night. He appeared to prefer this time of day, and with the trees growing and towering around him, Flora could only assume he missed the Pitch Woods terribly. His lips were parted slightly, a wistful lilt to his eyebrows that softened Flora's defenses and endeared her even more.

"If you could do anything, no restrictions—just your imagination and desires—what would you do?" Kaanan asked, leaning back on his hands as he kicked his long legs out in front of him.

"Anything?" Flora pondered, pursing her lips as she contemplated her response and wondered what game he was playing. As much as she feared her words would reach the Pitch King, and he would somehow exploit her, she wasn't even a lick tired, and the comforting trees bubbled words to her mouth, unbidden and unrestricted by anxiety. "I would make a home, a real one, where I didn't have to worry about anyone finding me and kidnapping me for my magic. And save Woodvale. I want to see it in its glory, with blooming plants and healthy crops and happy people."

Kaanan nodded, a soft smirk on his lips as he listened to her response. "That's a predictable answer."

"What do you mean?"

"Well, you're the child of the woman who destroyed the country, and you were raised by her handmaiden, yes?" Flora nodded. "Then it's an obvious answer. She would've had to have been a good person to raise you with so many people after you—people who would kill to have the savior in their clutches. She directed all her goodness on you, and from what I've seen so far, you're kind and trying to make the 'good' choices. The 'good' person's answer to my question was your answer to a T, but that's not what I meant when I asked."

"What are you, omniscient?" She scoffed, "How do you know all that?"

He shrugged, a devious glint in his eye. "Call it a hunch, or maybe I'm just that observant and clever or maybe my mentor discovered a lot more about your circumstances than you might've thought."

Flora pursed her lips, tempted to pick apart his story more, figure out how Kaanan or the Pitch King found out so much about Rosie and her. She sighed and instead focused on what he said previously. "What did you mean, then? About the question?" Flora asked, her eyebrows furrowing as she tucked her knees under her chin.

"Forget being selfless. Be *selfish*—what do you want from this life? What do you want to do, experience?"

"I…" Flora trailed off, unsure what she wanted. While he may not have liked her previous answer, it was the truth. But she also knew she wanted more. She wanted to see Woodvale in all its glory, and travel and eat, trying each and every fruit and vegetable from each province and sitting in each field and valley of green. But after that? She didn't know. She wanted a home, but she didn't know where that was, and after traveling, she had no idea what she wanted from her life. The only thing she knew was she wanted to spend it with her loved ones.

"You don't have to answer now, just…just think about it, all right? I think it would do you some good to not care about good and bad and just…be. Figure out what *you* want, not what the country wants," Kaanan said, igniting a flame in Flora's heart.

Why, oh why, did he have to be so *nice* to her? Her flickering and blossoming flame for him would be snuffed out if he could be who he was supposed to be— a monster's apprentice. But no, he had to be sweet and charming, and force her to look at her life. It wasn't fair and she had never missed Anise more. She missed the stagnancy, predictability, and safety net Anise provided. And on top of that, it made her miss her mom. That was when she needed her most, when Flora's head was spinning, and her world had been tipped on its axis.

"What about you, Kaanan? What would you do with freedom?"

"Me? I would find a way out of Woodvale."

"What! But that's impossible—people have *died* trying to leave! The Pitch Woods and Sage Woods go on for eternity, the mountains are too high and treacherous, and the ocean is never-ending and full of Gods-know-what," Flora protested, mouth agape as she stared at him.

"That's what we're told, but I would like to try for myself—see if there's another world out there, because honestly, Flora, this can't be it. This one small country? We can't be the only ones out there, because then how did we begin? What are our origins, where did magic come from, and the *folklore*? There's more out there, I know it," Kaanan said, voice so sure and strong it almost convinced Flora.

It was a nice tale, and it sounded appetizing. It was a story she would love to sink her teeth into, but that's all it sounded like to Flora—a story. If it were true, then maybe that was what she would do after she saved Woodvale, if she could manage it. But no, it sounded daunting, and everyone had died or never returned, and Flora couldn't imagine her life becoming that—a cautionary tale to young adventurers who set their sights too high.

"What folklore are you reading?" Flora asked lightly, her stomach a bit queasy at the implications of his theories.

"There's a book, in the Pitch King's castle, that details folklore that doesn't exist in the provinces or in Vale Centre—I've checked."

"What about the King's palace?"

"It's not there either."

"How did you get into the King's palace?" Flora sputtered and Kaanan laughed.

"I have my ways, but they're not for you to know yet," he said, smirking as Flora pouted in jest.

"Well, I would love to read the folklore book. I love the old tales of the creatures and Gods," Flora gushed, her eyes lighting up at the shift in topic.

She had the strongest desire to read the book, to see what folklore he had read that made him think there was a whole world outside of Woodvale. She needed to know; the desire was burning hot, scalding her insides. Even if it didn't give her the same truths it gave him, her thirst for knowledge and stories was like a vise around her mind—she needed to read it, to consume the words and have her world and imagination expanded.

"Do you have any plans on going to the Pitch Woods?" he asked.

"That's where one of the shards is," Flora said, and his eyes bugged as he bolted himself into an upright sitting position.

"I beg your pardon?"

"One of the shards is in the Pitch Woods," she said, shying away from his wild energy.

He sputtered, at a complete loss for words before uttering, "That can't be. I would know if one were in the Woods."

"Well, it's probably hidden, or maybe the Pitch King knows and he didn't tell you," Flora said and he vigorously shook his head.

"It makes no sense. The shard's magic and energy should be like a...disruption to the entire *structure* of the Pitch Woods," he said, voice soft as he was no longer talking to Flora. "I can't believe it."

"Well, unless my intel was wrong, it's there and I'm going there after the Svart Sea, assuming I can get this next shard."

He nodded but didn't speak again. As a wave of exhaustion crashed into Flora, she hunkered down in the soft moss and pine needles to sleep. She used her rucksack for a pillow and could practically *hear* his thoughts turning and racing from their short distance.

"Go to sleep, Kaanan. It'll be a long day tomorrow and any thinking tonight won't change anything," Flora said, her back to him. "Sleep."

"Okay," he whispered, and she heard him ruffle his cloak and sink onto the forest floor several centimeters from her.

Flora waited until he stopped moving and then whispered, "Goodnight."

"Sweet dreams, Flora," Kaanan said, and the two drifted off to sleep in the dark woods, the trees offering much needed protection, comfort, and energy for both. Each knew in their very marrow it would be another long day tomorrow.

Chapter Thirteen

This can't be happening. I refuse to believe it.
When I wake up tomorrow, everything will be fine and
back to normal.

He couldn't do this to me, it's not possible—he
loves *me.*

What do I do if I can't have him? What am I then?
A doll who does tricks? A show pony?

No.

I would rather the world burn than be the girl they
all want me to be.

-Diary entry by Anneliese Larkspur

Flora dragged her heels as they left the copse of
trees the next morning. A hazy orange glow cut through
the branches, causing Flora to squint and throw her
hand up to block the blazing sun. She kept turning
around, glancing back at each and every flora and
greenery, internally begging Kaanan to let them stay
just a minute longer. But even without Kaanan's
eagerness to head out, time was ticking, and traveling
was taking longer than she thought.

A pit of worry was lodged in her stomach, growing
by the hour, as she was beginning to lose track of time
as to *when* the meeting would take place. The days of
traveling and the odd air in Vale Centre muddled her
mind. She tried to reassure herself she still had time—
there was still over half of the pearlescent moon left in

the sky.

Kaanan was a pace ahead of her when Flora's ankle burst to life after a dormant day. She lifted her trouser leg and watched the pale skin crack open. A fern-colored stem shot up from Flora's ankle, breaking through skin and sinew as it grew a couple of leaves, dancing in the morning breeze, straining to get closer to the green covered earth.

"That's a neat trick," Kaanan said. He had come closer without her realizing as she was too wrapped up in the larkspur. She was always so intoxicated by the flower, how it grew from her flesh in flawless shades and strength, all because of her and her blood.

"Thanks," she muttered, and snapped the stem off at the root, the remainder of the stem crumbling to dust and falling to the forest floor below.

Flora held the flower up to the orange glow, the petals a never-ending sea of purple streaked with indigo. It was beautiful, pretty and poisonous, like most things were, and Flora couldn't wrap her head around how she felt about it. It was mostly an annoyance, a flower growing out of her ankle, but it was also maddening it was a poisonous flower no one could touch. She didn't understand *why* the Sage Witch chose this. Besides her ancestors' last name, why have them represented by poison if their gift was capable of making Woodvale thrive and healthy? But part of her also liked it, was infatuated with the power that zinged through her veins, the possibility of all the things she could do with it.

"Can I see?" Kaanan asked, snapping her out of her thoughts.

"No!" Flora exclaimed, shielding the larkspur from

his extended hand. "It's poison, Kaanan—it'll hurt you."

He raised an eyebrow as he puffed his chest out and a grin blossomed as he rummaged through his bag. He produced a pair of black leather gloves and snapped them on in one swift movement, dark fingers enclosed in even darker supple coating.

"Now may I?" he asked, wiggling his fingers at her expectantly.

"Fine." Flora sighed, as she reluctantly placed the larkspur in his waiting palm.

She watched him intently, waiting for the leather to not be enough protection, or the magic that created the larkspur to riot as it had only ever been touched by Flora. Rosie had crushed it with a mortar and pestle, the poisonous beauty never touching her skin. But nothing happened. It remained docile as he twirled the stem in his fingertips, petals shining in the dewy morning light.

"It's beautiful. I've never seen a larkspur in person before, just in books," Kaanan murmured, dark eyes focused intently on the flower.

"Thanks," she said, tone unsure as she wrung her hands.

He shot her a brilliantly bright grin and asked, "May I keep this?"

Flora bit her lip, toying with the skin as she sucked in a deep breath in contemplation. Her gut was saying no, but she couldn't see what he could possibly do with it. It was a flower, and she was safe from the effects of its poison. She supposed he could use it against someone unassuming. But he was the apprentice of a monstrous sorcerer—if he wanted to hurt someone, he had an arsenal of options, and she found the idea of him choosing the larkspur unlikely.

"Sure," she said, slowly, elongating the singular word.

He flashed her another grin and carefully tucked the flower in his bag, removing the gloves when he was done. He extended his hand to her and said, "We need to get moving."

Flora wasn't going to accept his hand. She really wasn't—honest—it was the trees that did it. A stray root cropped up in front of her toe. She collided with it, stumbling forward, and as she didn't want to eat dirt, she grabbed onto the one thing that offered a safer option—his hand. Her fingers connected with his and he held on tight, keeping her upright. Kaanan directed her hand into the crook of his elbow and the two cleared the remainder of the forest in record time as Flora desperately tried to push the flustered rush away. Kaanan guided them toward their waiting horse tied to a tree. The animal was far less disgruntled than Flora would have been if she had been left alone all night with no protection. She brushed her hand against the creature, coat roughly smooth against her skin as she murmured a soft apology.

The world basked in the warm and gentle orange glow, villagers just starting to rise and begin their challenging day of scraping together meager coin and trying in earnest to find happy moments amidst the slow death surrounding them. With a heavy heart and roiling stomach for Flora, the two set off toward the Svart Sea.

****

Flora realized she didn't need to worry so much. After two brutally long days, the sea rose on the horizon, an endless blue extending out as far as the eye could see. Flora began to notice the change in the air, the salt content rising, and her heart was full at the smell. Flora wished they could stay longer, take their time to explore the new towns and observe how sea-folk lived their daily lives.

According to Kaanan, most of Whaelmere's population lived close to the sea. They only cut through a small swath of the province, but from what she had seen, she believed it. The closer they got to the ocean, the more quaint cottages surfaced. Flora could get used to this province. It was vast and beautiful, full of rolling hills and an unimaginably infinite ocean, full of unexplored life and plants. She loved Sanarbre, in the way one loved their childhood home, but the more she saw of Woodvale, the more she wasn't convinced Sanarbre was where she would eventually put down her roots.

"Nice, isn't it?" Kaanan yelled from behind her and Flora nodded vigorously, eyes glued to the ocean.

The one thing Flora still hadn't gotten used to on this journey was sitting so close to Kaanan—really just sitting so close to another person, especially one she didn't know all that well. Anise was somewhat touchy, but it was a touch Flora was used to, and she had never spent so many hours pressed against someone else. She didn't hate it, and though her blush was never as deep anymore, she just wasn't used to it yet.

The sea bloomed before her eyes, the large expanse making her chest tight. The closer they got, the closer she was to finding another shard. She just hoped she would get lucky and could just pluck it from a pedestal and run—no confessions, no awkwardness, no danger.

Her ankle had been lukewarm all morning, and now in the ferocious afternoon sun, hours from the Svart Sea, it was burning.

Flora was also desperately worried about Anise. But there was nothing she could do except push forward and dream in delusion. She inspected each person they passed, and she found herself craning her neck to catch a glimpse of her friend in the desolation only to fail each time. She was chasing shadows and masked faces, and they apparently didn't want to be caught. She just had to keep on believing there was a "yet" at the end of that sentence. All the chasing made her appreciate the domestic bliss of her life with Anise back home. She just hoped Anise would somehow be waiting for them when they reached the sea.

****

They reached the endless obsidian waters by dusk, the world cast in shadow, the only light coming from the reflection of the pearlescent moon. Kaanan and Flora chose the quaint town of Port Lagar, which housed mostly fishermen and women, and was covered in dustings of sand as the buildings hugged the ocean. The salt air rusted metal and the sun's constant fierce rays weathered skin.

Flora was amazed. She walked with Kaanan to the inn, wide-eyed with excitement buzzing through her veins. An intricate gold bull statue rose in the town square, and she faintly recalled a story of a bull protecting the land from the raging ocean as it attempted to wash away a seaside town.

Her ankle was roasting, and she breathed easier at the confirmation they were in the right area. The next battle would be figuring out the exact location. She assumed the town's church would be unlikely as her gut told her this was all more complicated and convoluted than she would have preferred. But that was tomorrow's problem. Tonight, her limbs ached down to the bone, and her back begged for a bed. So, the two rented a room for a night.

Flora was going to protest at the one-room scenario, but Kaanan shot her a withering look when she went to whisper-argue with him as she didn't feel comfortable speaking loud enough for the innkeeper to hear. When they were alone, Kaanan explained he didn't trust the town's people for her to have a room to herself. She argued that with a locked door, she wasn't sure what they could possibly do, but at Kaanan's dark look, she let the fight drain out of her.

Flora had seen no sign of Anise, and she wasn't sure how she could sleep with her stomach tangled in knots. But even though her body was humming with worry, her muscles were exhausted, and the fluffy duvet on the bed looked like heaven to her weary bones.

"Look, I would love to be chivalrous and gentlemanly, but honestly, I'm too tired and sore to sleep on the floor," Kaanan said, and held up a hand when she opened her mouth. "If you're uncomfortable with it, the floor is all yours, or we can put the pillows between us—but I am sleeping on that bed tonight, and any night we're here."

Flora's cheeks burned as she shifted away from him. The bed was in the center of the wall, and the room was in swaths of seafoam and beige, an idyllic oceanside pattern with seashells and ceramic fish littering the room. There was even a sea serpent figurine on the dresser, reminding Flora of a folktale about the ocean creature from her book.

Taking a deep breath, she turned to Kaanan and said, "It's fine—we can share." Flora felt like bars came down around her, like with those five words, she sealed her fate somehow.

Flora was a bit uncomfortable with the idea of sharing a bed with Kaanan, but they did spend hours in closer quarters on a horse. Besides, she was tired, and she couldn't bear the thought of sleeping on the floor either. It was just a bed, and it was just for one night, hopefully. *It'll be fine*, she reassured herself—there was nothing to worry about or fear from this scenario.

Flora snuck into the attached bathroom and was shocked to find running water in the chipped porcelain sink and bathtub. Unable to resist the appeal of a clean body, she quickly left and returned with her rucksack and got to work.

Flora cleaned all her clothes and hung them to dry before she sank into the almost boiling hot water, her sore muscles and limbs breathing a sigh of relief at the feeling. Flora soaked for what felt like hours, until the water turned cold, and her skin was pruned, but she had never felt better. The bath rejuvenated her even more than the night in the thicket had. Her mind cleared, and her body and muscles were loose, and she longed for the simplicity of her life before. She missed her mom, her best friend, and her quiet village where nothing changed, and she was left alone.

When Flora exited the bathroom, she was surprised to find Kaanan clean as well, sporting damp, curly hair. He was leaning against the headboard, gaze to the ceiling. He wasn't under the covers yet, and at the click of the bathroom door, his gaze shot to hers.

"Is there another bathroom?" Flora asked, wringing her hands as she shuffled to the other side of the bed. "I'm sorry I took so long."

"It's all right. There's another bathroom downstairs the innkeeper let me use. She said she felt sorry for us and our filthy clothes."

Flora daintily climbed into the bed, springs creaking under her weight and blankets shuffling loudly in the small space. Kaanan watched her the entire time, eyes tracking her body as she got comfortable under the covers, her back facing him when she finally settled. He slipped under the covers as well, seemingly hovering between facing her and facing the wall. He ended up choosing the wall and said, "Goodnight, Flora. Sweet dreams."

"Goodnight, Kaanan," Flora whispered, and though her mind was wildly alive with worry, she fell asleep in a matter of minutes, exhaustion overpowering her worries.

****

Flora woke with a start, a cold sweat breaking out on her skin, goosebumps pebbling as a faint breeze snaked in through the window, icing her down to her bones. A wheezing gasp escaped her lips as she flung her legs over the side of the bed, planting them on the cold floorboards and staggering to her feet. The room was engulfed in shadows with only the faint glow of the moon to navigate her way. She unwittingly walked toward the door, a tug in her navel drawing her into the hall and down the stairs. Her hand trailed on the railing as the wood creaked and groaned, a gusting breeze slashing through her as she stepped into the barroom. The door was flung open, clanking against the wall as a funnel of wind whirled inside, haloing Flora's hair. Her stomach sank and pitched to the floor.

"Hello?" she called softly, as she delved toward the open door, her curiosity burning a flame in her core.

Flora's heart was in her throat as she stepped outside, the street empty, all light extinguished as every other soul lay in their beds sound asleep. She walked barefoot down the road, the gritty sand clinging to her toes as a howl tore through the night, unnatural and ferocious. She gasped and she whirled around, searching for the sound as a guttural grunt echoed from the alley near her.

Flora.

Her name, whispered with the wind, coaxed her into the auspicious alley. Her stomach tilted, her heart hammering as her foot crossed into the shadowy lane and in the blink of an eye, a figure popped to life inches from her face.

A scream tore free from her throat as she threw herself backward, tripping on her own feet and crashing to the ground, skin bursting and pain fluttering to life where she collided.

"Flora," Anise said, voice breathlessly agonized.

A cracking bolt of lightning smashed into the ground beyond them, the bright light illuminating the shadowy alleyway and highlighting her best friend, torn to pieces. Flora gazed in horror, her lips parted, and eyes blown wide at the sight. Anise was covered in matted crimson from head to toe, the viscous substance dripping drops to the stones below her. A gashed wound tore through her shoulder, the arm attached hanging limp and lifeless. But that was nothing in comparison to the gaping hole where her torso should be.

"Help me," Anise begged, her teeth stained maroon, scratches marring her once perfect face.

"Anise," Flora breathed before her breath escaped her and her lungs stopped working. Flora could only stare at her best friend, bloody and broken like a doll played with too roughly, and all she could imagine were the horrific scenes that would bring Anise to such a state. And with those images burned into her brain, a wave of black dropped over her, and Flora fainted to the ground.

****

A noise Flora had never been so lucky to experience before woke her as dawn crested over the horizon, the sound she only knew from tales. Seagulls cawed and cried outside the inn's window, causing Flora to wake slowly with a content energy buzzing through her body. The gull's sound was music to her ears. But it was gone in an instant when flashes of her nightmare weaseled into her wakening mind.

Her breath escaped her again, her lungs seizing as she slammed her eyes shut and tried to regulate her stuttering breathing. She desperately tried to erase the images from her mind, the horrors she had envisioned Anise succumbing to all because Flora left her behind. She was a horrible person, loathsome and awful. She didn't deserve to bask in the seagull's music.

Flora wallowed for several minutes, earnestly trying to overwrite her nightmare with happy thoughts and hopeful imaginings that she would find Anise easily and in one piece. She knew there was little else that could be done now. What had happened was in the past, but she would not truly be calm until she reunited with Anise.

With great effort, Flora pulled herself out of her guilty wallowing and let the seagulls soothe her back to life. The novelty of the birds was so intoxicating she was beginning to fall in love with traveling and experiencing new things. Of course, with some exceptions and a fair dose of anxiety tied to it. But travelling with Kaanan was helping her. Flora's mind wasn't spiralling as much because she was so focused on the landscape and scenery she hadn't fallen down many mental holes since leaving Vale Centre. However, she knew the peace would be shattered as she needed to search for the second shard and Anise.

Flora was so warm and comfortable it took her a minute before realizing why she was so fluffy and content. An arm caged her waist and her cheek rested on a firm, heated body. Flora's eyes fluttered open to find Kaanan's face inches from hers. Every detail, rise, and swell of his face was in perfect view. Flora gawked as her face burned. His arm was a heavy weight holding her against him as he slumbered on. Flora couldn't tear her eyes from his exquisitely crafted features. His breath warmed her face, and before she caught on to what she was doing, she snuggled closer to him, his heat warming every inch of her body.

A particularly loud gull cried outside their closed window and Kaanan jolted awake. His arm tightened on her waist and he half-rose, frantically searching around the room for a threat. When he came up empty, he relaxed and sank down into the fluffy mattress beside Flora. His gaze caught on hers and a blinding grin bloomed on his face, the eye-catching dimple drawing Flora's gaze.

"Good morning," he said, voice as deep and rough as the bottom of the ocean.

"Hi," Flora squeaked, causing Kaanan to chuckle breathily. She stuttered saying, "We should, um, should, um…get going, right?"

Kaanan sighed through his nose, eyes fliting over her face as he brushed a stray lock of hair behind her ear. His smile was soft and kind, and Flora hated every second of it, because it went against the rules. He wasn't supposed to be sweet or charming. He wasn't supposed to give her butterflies and a heartbeat that skipped—he was supposed to be mean and ruthless and grim, causing her skin to crawl and body to shy away from him. Flora could barely take it anymore, her bottled up feelings begging for a release, begging for her to yell at him and run away. She was at a loss about what to do. All she knew was staring into his eyes, so deep she felt like she was sinking into them, wasn't helping at all.

"That we should," Kaanan said, and rolled out of bed, grabbing his clothes and retreating into the bathroom.

The second the door clicked shut, Flora leapt from the bed, her heartbeat roaring in her ears. With haste, so Kaanan couldn't catch her in a state of undress, Flora donned her stockings, skirt, and Rosie's knit top ensemble. When Kaanan exited from the bathroom, in his all-black attire, he donned his coat and the two went downstairs for breakfast, silence and unspoken words accompanying them.

The inn was quiet save for the clanking of dishes being cleaned from the breakfast rush of fishers getting an early start to the day. Flora inhaled deeply, sugary-sweet aromas and roasting oils making her mouth water as they entered the barroom.

Flora had barely left the confines of the stairwell alcove when a familiar feminine voice screeched her name. A flurry of bright fabrics and dark hair flew at Flora's face, and she only just forced herself not to flinch as a body collided with hers. Arms wrapped tight around Flora's waist, squeezing her as laughter she had grown up with hit her ears.

"Anise?" Flora whispered, her body close against the other one, as her heart squeezed. It felt too good to be true, that her best friend had found her, in the same inn they were staying at even. Flora pulled away from the grinning girl and inspected her face. It was tanned and flaking from the boiling sun, and thinner than it had been, but there was no mistaking those features and bright smile that always exuberated bubbliness. "Is it really, truly you?"

"Oh, Flora! You silly goose, of course it's me! I missed you so much," Anise cried, clinging to Flora again.

"Are you okay? Are you hurt? What happened to you?" The words flew out of Flora's mouth faster than she could process them. The worry and fear she had been harboring rose to the surface, lodging in her throat, and tears burned her eyes. Flora glued her eyes to her best friend's form in front of her at long last, whole and healthy, unable to believe the sight.

"Well, do I have a story for you," Anise said with a broad grin.

Chapter Fourteen

Woodvale is boxed in by mountains and forests, impenetrable and never-ending. They were two features the citizens of Woodvale either revered or feared. There was one forgotten constantly, its stories and lore sinking to the bottom of it, waiting to be found and to have the same grandiose opinions expressed about it.

The Svart Sea.

Its obsidian waves went on in the distance as far as the eye could see and went deeper than any explorers have been able to determine. The waves were usually kind to those who lived on its edge, never cresting too far onto land and providing citizens with food and respect—but the same respect was never returned.

Creatures roam the ocean we haven't discovered yet, and some we probably never will. The one creature that has never been truly forgotten, the one that is still seen on occasion is the Sormurinn, the sea serpent or sea worm, depending on your persuasion.

The Sormurinn is said to relish gold and treasures, and spew poison at trespassers who dare venture too close.

Be warned, fair traveler. If you venture to the Svart Sea, travel with little gold or be prepared to give it away, lest you wish to have the skin melted from your bones at the hands of a godly, mythical monster.

-An Adventurer's Guide to Woodvale: The Svart

Sea by Gísli

"...and then I found someone coming here, and I figured it must be the same town you're going to since it's the only one practically *on* the sea." Anise had been telling her tale of adventure and woe, her arduous struggles to reconnect with Flora for the past hour, a permanent grin on her face at the undivided attention and reunion. The sky had burned away the orange and replaced it with streaks of blue and yellow littered with puffy clouds.

Flora could barely tear her eyes away from her friend when she recounted her adventure. Anise described such horrors and terrifying situations, Flora's chest was clenching, and she gasped on several occasions.

According to Anise, when the city guards started shooting, and, in her words, she was "abandoned and left to her own devices," she was shot. At Flora's eyes bugging out of her head and her frantic questions of where she was shot and how she was healing, Anise revealed it was only a graze. The silver bullet had grazed her upper arm, and while it felt like she was dying and bleeding out from the wound—she wasn't. Anise was fine once she got far enough away from the guards and tightly wrapped her arm in cloth. And then she found kindness in strangers, who sewed her wound and covered it in salve.

Then, Anise and her horse hustled through the province at breakneck speed like Kaanan and Flora, but she took less stops, and tired her horse out too much for it to continue. She quickly became landlocked in a small village, waiting for someone to take her farther as her meager coin could not buy a new horse. Anise didn't have to wait too long and arrived in the dead of night just after Kaanan and Flora.

Anise spoke of terrifying people who sneered at her, and wild animals crying in the night, hungry for her flesh and marrow, but she was unharmed in the inn. Regardless of her relatively healthy self, Flora could see the ragged state of her friend, and a bottomless pit of guilt opened inside of her. Flora wished she had done more to find her friend, instead of just *leaving* her.

"But enough about me. How are you, Flora? I can't imagine how difficult it's been for you without me," Anise said, clasping her friend's hand in hers as their empty plates of breakfast littered the table.

"She's been excellent, actually," Kaanan interjected. He had kept quiet throughout Anise's tale, only raising an eyebrow or uttering a small scoff at certain points, but he didn't contradict or berate her. "Really, Flora has done remarkable without you. She's been a huge asset to our travels."

Flora's face flushed crimson at the words and she was quick to say, "No! I wasn't, I was a mess without you, Anise. It's been so hard."

The words escaped Flora's lips and it wasn't until the air captured them that she questioned how true they were. Yes, she needed Anise. She loved her and her support as her best friend was lovely. But she had been okay with Kaanan. She had held her own and didn't spiral into oblivion like she thought she would. She had even grown more comfortable speaking to him without mincing her words and rehashing the conversation later. Everything was slowly changing for Flora. Either she was growing or there was something about Kaanan that started to slowly bring out her confidence.

"Oh, you poor thing," Anise cooed, ignoring Kaanan's sharp glare. "We're together again. It'll all be fine now."

****

After a tense breakfast of glares and cutting stares, the three set off in a silence filled with awkward tension and unspoken words. Flora and Anise walked together, arm in arm, while Kaanan trailed behind, his black cloak billowing in the lacerating ocean wind.

As they walked through the sandy streets, seafoam blues and greens and pastel yellows and pinks littering the town, Flora's ankle warmed to an almost uncomfortable level. The scalding sensation heightened as they walked farther out of town on the boardwalk, and toward the hill with cliffs and caves hugging the ocean.

Flora couldn't take her eyes off the glittering ocean waves under the sun, the waves magnificently obsidian and so crisp she longed to dive in and experience swimming in the ocean. She had swum in a river before, but the ocean waves and currents looked deathly frightening to her. Flora swore she saw a head of a creature pop up, but it disappeared before she could get a good look.

Her ankle burned like an inferno as they neared the cliff. Up to the left was the rise of a deadened grassy hill, and to the right was a narrow strip of stone with a wall of sharp rocks. Flora was about to turn left when a glistening carving in the jutting rock caught her eye. Just as in Vale Centre, glittering in the sun was a carving of a larkspur.

"This way," she breathed to her companions, a burning excitement sparking to life.

"Why?" Anise asked, her eyebrows furrowed as she gazed at the rough path.

"Can't you see it?"

"See what?"

"The larkspur," Flora said and pointed to the carving, but she was met with frowns and confused glances.

"It must be appearing to your magic," Kaanan said, and Anise shot Flora a confused look as she realized Flora had divulged sensitive information to him. Before Anise could question her, Flora nodded to Kaanan and set off onto the treacherous rocks, leaving the other two to follow.

The cropping of rocks and minerals was a mix of smooth and sharp, rising tall above their heads as the waves rolled into the small patch of shore, dampening their shoes. Flora inhaled deeply, wishing to commit the salt air to memory.

The larkspur was carved into a glimmering rock littered with minerals. Flora trailed her finger down the larkspur, no longer needing to hide from Kaanan or any onlookers. She gazed ahead, trying to find another one, and when she came up empty, she kept going forward. The trio walked for a few minutes, stumbling on rocks and sand and crashing waves.

Eventually, Flora found the next larkspur.

Up ahead after a bend was a larger carved larkspur on the edge of a deep-sea cave. The ocean water rushed into the cave in a killing current, blocking off the continuing path of beach. Flora gently touched the larkspur on the wall, her ankle burning in a searing pain so intense she almost doubled over. Beside the larkspur was a series of drawings she couldn't make sense of.

One was a squiggly line that turned into two, and then they connected in a never-ending circle like a double ouroboros.

A gong sounded in Flora's head as a memory flickered to life. She hastily rummaged through her rucksack as Anise and Kaanan watched as she pulled out her book of folklore. The book was thick and weathered with age, and had seen better days, but it was well-loved and held multiple dogears. Flora flipped through, eyes scanning so fast her vision turned blurry, but she found what she was looking for:

The Sormurinn

Once upon a time, a little girl with a curious mind and open heart lived in an isolated cottage on the seashore. She was all alone and made do with gifts and treasures from the sea and its creatures.

One day, the girl found a worm, writhing in the sand as it tried to get to a gold coin that washed to shore. The girl was fascinated and loved meeting new creatures. So, she picked up the worm and deposited it on the coin. The worm swallowed it whole and then raced back to the ocean waves. The girl was sad, as she believed she would never see the worm again.

But the next day, farther up the beach, the worm was back, a bit bigger now, and was hungering after a gold nugget. The girl was curious and wanted to help, so she scooped up the nugget and tossed it at the worm. The worm swallowed it whole and darted back to the safety of the waves.

This continued for several days. Each time the girl saw the seaworm, it was bigger and hungrier, drool foaming from its mouth at the sight of treasure. Concern rising, the girl went into town and inquired after the worm, curious if any townsfolk had encountered it. The townsfolk were horrified to hear of the creature—their grandmothers had told them tales of such a creature, who ate gold and treasures until it was bigger than the ocean itself, swallowing towns and people whole as its stomach grew ravenous, billowing with poison and acid-spewing saliva.

The townsfolk decided they had to do something, much to the girl's dismay. She wanted to talk to the seaworm, explain that while it may consume treasure, it couldn't be greedy. But the townsfolk beat the girl to it and hired a sea witch to destroy the seaworm.

When the sea witch attempted to rid the poisonous creature, she found a second worm with the first, a mated pair. The first one shared the little girl's treasure with its mate, protecting and feeding what it loved as the two creatures grew hungrier for everything. They were too powerful for the witch to destroy, so she cast a spell and tied them together into a never-ending circle using a rope of magic around their tails and heads. A double ouroboros of avarice and adoration.

No longer able to eat properly, or swim, the seaworms remained captive to the ocean for eternity, only occasionally rising to the surface, to warn villagers of their eternal presence, that humans were not alone in their world.

Flora's eyes drank in the words hungrily, eyes raking over the page and the drawing of the Sormurinn beside it. She didn't know how to process it, or if it was relevant, but the drawing in her book mirrored the drawing on the cave wall.

"I think I found something," Flora said, turning to Anise and Kaanan. She thrust the book in their direction, and they leaned in to read the tale.

"So what does it mean?" Anise asked, her face taut with confusion. "Is your birthmark hinting at anything?"

"Try using the shard. See if it calls to the second one," Kaanan suggested, dark eyes centered wholly on her.

Flora briefly caught Anise's withering glare at Kaanan before she ignored them and focused on the magic pulsing through her veins. She gripped the shard, pulling it out into the sunlight, and closed her eyes.

Flora swore her veins turned green as the plants she loved mixed with brilliant shades of rainbow colors, magic singing through her. A breathy gasp escaped her parted lips as the magic tugged her toward the churning sea. A strong hand encasing her bicep stopped her from stepping into the current as a vivid image sparked to life inside her mind.

Flora saw the mated seaworms, the Sormurinn, floating at the bottom of the sea-cave, living their life with a diminishing pile of jewels. They were smaller than she thought, but they were exactly as described in the tale. They were tied together with glittering strings of magic, trapped in an endless circle, just like the sea witch planned. The image shifted and Flora saw inside the hungry maw of one, and there in the pit of a darkened stomach, a petal-shaped shard of brightly burning blue rested.

The vision abandoned Flora as quickly as it pulled her in and she gasped to life, turning to her friends, eyes wide and heart racing. "It's in the Sormurinn," Flora said, voice soft but sure.

The magic from the shard still sung in her veins,

and an overwhelming urge to *grow* something erupted in her. At her feet, seaweed grew in long tangles, twisting around her ankles and dragging her into the sea. Before Flora or Kaanan or Anise could process what was happening, the seaweed thrust her into the writhing waves.

Icy water sloshed over Flora's head as her back collided painfully with the ocean. Water filled her nostrils and lungs as the current almost instantly whisked her away into the deep, echoing cavern. Flora was thrust against a solid rock wall, scrapes and bruises bursting to life as blood bloomed around her. Her eyes burned as her fingers dug into a divot in the rock, and she held on for dear life, clinging to rock as the sea raged behind her.

Her lungs screamed from lack of air, and as spots clouded her vision, she kicked her legs in a swift arc up, toward the dark shadows of the cavern. A particularly strong current bashed her head into rocks, and a searing pain lit a fire in her skull. Blood clouded the water and her vision fogged and blackened, but still, she swam up, kicking faster and faster as her lungs seized.

Finally, her head crested out of the water, and she breathed deep, gasping breaths as she clung to the rock wall, blood running in rivulets down her face and arms. She heard cries of her name, and she shakily looked their way. Anise was perched on the edge of the water, waves lapping against her feet as her ashen face drained of every ounce of blood. Her hands were clasped over her heart, and Flora shook her head at her when Anise stepped closer—Anise couldn't swim well, and Flora couldn't have her friend die because of her.

At that thought, she clued into who was missing

from the scene. She screamed over the roaring waves, "Where's Kaanan?"

A loud gasp broke through the water behind her, and Kaanan appeared, swiftly swimming through the currents to her spot on the wall. He sidled up beside her, hands clasping the rocks, and the waves bumped their soggy bodies together.

"Are you okay?" he asked, breathless and ashen, jaw taut as his eyes raked over her. His hand came to her face, and he wiped the blood from her head, searching for the source.

"Fine," she said with a cough. Her heart was roaring like a lion in her ears, deafening any noise around her.

Kaanan's eyes were frantic, and doubled with Anise's cries of concern, Flora couldn't take it. She was already petrified and desperately needed out of the cave. She could imagine her fingers slipping, the current thrusting her roughly into the stone, and she would pass out and then water would fill her lungs so deep she would sink to the seafloor and die an agonizing death from lack of air and—

"Flora, focus," Kaanan said, moving closer to her so their faces were inches apart. "Focus on me—we need to get out of here. Forget the shard. We can try again another day."

"No," Flora said, shocking herself, but the word felt right. They couldn't leave and come back—she was already in the Svart Sea, and she refused to leave before accomplishing what she came for. "I am getting that shard—today."

Kaanan sighed, and then said, "Fine. I brought the sword and a knife. They're in a sheath at my waist.

Which one do you want?"

Flora blanched. The idea of handling a knife in the raging sea didn't bode well with her, and she didn't know if they needed to *kill* the seaworms to get the shard. Maybe they could ask nicely?

"Flora. Which. One," he said, nostrils flaring. "You're not leaving here without a weapon."

"The knife," she said, and he nodded, clinging to the rock with one hand as his other slipped the sheathed knife into her waistband. His palm lingered on her hip, molten and burning as it was reassuring in its pressure. The sensation shot crimson to color her cheeks, warmth spreading through her freezing body as he nodded encouragingly. Flora ignored the flushed haze and quickly said, "What now?"

"Where exactly is the shard?"

"It's inside one of the seaworms—the shard's magic sent me a vision. They're at the bottom of this cavern."

"Stay close to me. And while I loathe to have you use your magic when it pushed you into the ocean, can you grow something to light our path?" Kaanan asked and his words sparked an image of bioluminescent bacteria clinging to rock walls. Her magic flared to life like a small flame, and she longed for it to burn like a raging wildfire. The shard sparked against her chest as her magic seeped into the water below. Looking down, she could just make out faint trails of glowing light underneath the surface. "Excellent. Let's go."

The two slipped below the waves, Anise's piercing cry the last thing they heard before water dipped into their ears, muffling any sounds. Flora's magic had worked, but not in the way she imagined. The fungi didn't cling to the walls—it hung midwater, a trail of starlight trickling down to the bottom of the seabed. She was proud of herself, that her power had done something, but disappointed all the same. She had little control over it to the point where she was unsure she could reliably put her faith in it for such dangerous missions.

Regardless of her worries, the bioluminescent glow did exactly what she needed it to. It sparked against a pile of gold and treasure and highlighted the twined circular bodies of seaworms—the Sormurinn in the flesh.

Chapter Fifteen

Blue shard properties: trust, support, dignity, and grace.

(An easier shard to wield than pink, this shard works best when you're sure, when you trust yourself or trust another.)

The obsidian water was alight with stars as Flora and Kaanan drifted deeper toward the slumbering seaworms. Effervesce of air bubbled out of their nostrils and Flora's lungs burned fiercely until darkness clouded her vision. Writhing and murky shadows encased her head before a slit appeared before her eyes, highlighting Kaanan. As water dripped away from her face, clearing her vision completely, a pocket of air formed before her eyes.

He gestured around his head, an identical bubble of black shadows, and Flora understood his basic miming. He had somehow used his magic to encase them in a bubble of air, and as he tapped his wrist, she knew they had a limited amount of time.

The two swam deeper, the air circling their lungs emboldening their strides. They hit the seabed in no time, twining seaweed dancing in the waves as they kicked up silt when their hands brushed against the bottom. Kaanan and Flora hovered inches from the sleeping seaworms, their bodies rolling in the water in a mesmerizing circle of iridescent scales of every shade of blue, almost melding into the water itself if not for the glow sparking against the shimmering scales.

Flora's stomach dropped with how close they were and with how big the seaworms were up close. Terror had a death-grip of sharp, searing claws on her heart and throat. Her breath came out in gasps and her lungs felt like they were full of water. But before she could cut off her air supply or spiral down a deep chasm of anxiety, Kaanan wrapped her hand in his, grounding her, as he shifted into her small line of vision and nodded reassuringly. Flora felt warm tendrils of support and trust twirl up her limbs as her breathing regulated.

Kaanan unsheathed the sword from his hip, the silver blade shining in the glow, reflecting jarringly into Flora's eyes. The light flicked toward the seaworms as Kaanan shifted the blade and in the murky black, a glowing eye with a slit pupil snapped open. Flora and Kaanan froze, terror building in a crescendo so pure it almost hurt.

The twined seaworm wriggled away from the frozen Flora and Kaanan, and hovered over their treasure stash, spinning in an endless, dizzying circle as each worm watched them with slitted eyes. Flora was amazed at the sight—they were beautiful and elegant, power incarnate, but forced into a prison made by humans who couldn't grasp the concept of conversation before destruction. Flora wanted to help them, wanted to untie them, somehow let them live their lives without causing endless chaos, letting them be free. They were shackled to a cave, cowering above their jewels, just like she was. Flora was shackled to her magic and responsibility to fix her biological mother's mistakes, and save Rosie, but had to hide her treasure at every turn lest the wrong person see.

She waved Kaanan's sword away and he shot her a murderous look, eyes dark and glaring, but she persisted. They pantomimed an argument, Kaanan wanting to use his sword as protection, while Flora begged him to understand her desire to get the shard peacefully. They were just a creature and had been locked up for so many years. Flora didn't think it was fair to judge them so harshly without more information.

Flora mouthed "please, trust me," and Kaanan nodded. She knew in her gut she was right, she had to be, her magic was all about life and providing help to others—it wasn't about death and destruction. Kaanan dropped the tip of his sword, and Flora shot him a thankful look as she turned her attention to the Sormurinn.

Flora stared at the seaworms, begging and willing with her eyes for them to understand her, that she meant no harm and wanted to *help* them. She held her hands out in front of her, palms facing out and backed up an inch, tipping her head respectfully. When she glanced up, she found the worms eyeing her, but then they shied away, and she didn't know why until she glanced down. The pink shard was glowing brightly under her shirt—like calling to like—as it felt its sibling nearby, sitting in one of the seaworm's stomachs.

Flora swam closer, silt clouding her vision as her feet kicked against the seabed. At her movement, the seaworms reared backward, glowing eyes narrowing threateningly to protect their treasure. Her heart in her throat, Flora continued closer, palms out, trying to mentally connect with them so they knew she meant no harm. Her shard flared against her chest and magic spun through her veins.

My treasure. Stay away, witch, a voice hissed in Flora's mind causing her skull to ache and throb so intensely she grabbed her head in both palms. She felt Kaanan move closer to her, but she waved him way, lest they scare the Sormurinn any more.

It was like a channel had opened between them. Flora could feel a tunnel in her mind, one that entered a void of something unique. She could feel the sorrow of the seaworms, the gnawing hunger, and the hatred of humans and witches alike. Flora felt the void have two separate entities, both seaworms occupying the same mental plane they now shared with her.

"I'm here to help," Flora thought, projecting her voice through the tunnel of shimmering scales in her mind.

For what price, witch?

"I need something inside of you."

My treasure, the Sormurinn hissed, venom spewing and teeth snarling.

"Please, I need it. I can help release you," Flora projected, coating her words in desperation. She wasn't sure if she could actually save them. The bonds of magic encasing them were complicated, tangled and tussled, and Flora was only going off of instinct. But she needed the shard, and a little lie never hurt anyone if she could get what she wanted in the end. Because she would at least *try* to untangle them, and that was what mattered.

How? the Sormurinn asked, their bodies spinning faster in their endless circle.

"I have magic, and with the shard inside you, I can have more—I can help you. You shouldn't have been punished like this."

Silence reigned in response.

"*Please*, I need it," Flora begged and the seaworms cast an appraising slitted eye over her.

Come closer.

"Why?"

If you want to help, if you want our treasure, come closer, the Sormurinn demanded in a freezing tone, ice shooting down Flora's spine, her skin erupting in shivering goosebumps.

She had no choice but to obey. Flora moved closer, inch by inch, and just as she was close enough to touch, crashing bubbles clouded her vision, the water churning violently around her.

A flash of tan limbs appeared before Flora's eyes, and she startled backward, kicking up silt, seaweed stalks tangling in her limbs and untied hair. Flora collided with a hard, familiar body as what looked like Anise lunged toward them. But it couldn't be her. Anise wouldn't be so stupid. She wouldn't jump into this risky situation like this when she was unconfident at swimming. Flora was adamantly shaking her head, eyes widening with horror as Anise's flushed face flashed into view. Flora could almost feel how her lungs must have been burning. Her confident strokes flabbergasted Flora, but she supposed Anise had gone crazy waiting above them with no word or sign they were even alive. Desperate people did desperate things and Anise was no better.

In a swift movement, Anise grabbed the sword from Kaanan's slackened grip and turned. Flora's stomach clenched and her heart dropped as she lunged forward, chasing Anise until the bitter end because she couldn't let this happen, couldn't let her best friend commit such an atrocity without even *discussing* it first. The Sormurinn were going to help her—they were cooperating. They didn't deserve to be cut down at her hands when they had done nothing to earn such blatant disrespect and cruelty.

Flora tried her best. She threw her body through the churning water, her body cutting through it, but Anise was faster. Before Flora could stop her, Anise slashed the Sormurinn in two. The ring was broken, and screams of mutilated animals' muffled pain hit her ears as Anise slashed again, turning the two halved seaworms into four floating pieces in the water.

Crimson blood swirled, blooming in bursts of scarlet in Flora's vision. The water was more red than blue when Anise dropped the sword and kicked herself up to the surface. Meanwhile, Flora was frozen in time, her mind replaying the scene, displaying different outcomes, things she could have done had she been faster, been *better*.

The pieces of the Sormurinn floated toward Flora in a haze of maroon, their scales shimmering and their dead eyes meeting hers. The sight would haunt her forever. It pierced her soul so deep she would never forget.

A flurry of movement jolted her out of her trance, sending one of the seaworm pieces directly at her. Wet, slimy skin met her outstretched arms, and she could feel the congealing blood cling to her skin. She gagged in her shadow bubble, her stomach a mess of tangling intestines and nausea. Bile burned the back of her throat as she swatted away the pieces, trying to keep the current from making the others touch her and contaminating her limbs with blood and gore and tragedy.

A swath of dark floated past her vision, and Flora breathed a sigh of relief when she realized it was Kaanan. He landed in front of her, holding her biceps and connecting their gazes. His eyes were soft and wide, and Flora knew the look he was giving her. She could feel the concern and question of "are you okay" radiating off him. Flora tried to send him an unspoken message back, but her face felt frozen and awkward, so she simply nodded.

Kaanan jerked his head back, gesturing to the pieces of the Sormurinn. They needed to hurry up, to get the shard from the mess of blood and guts, or else their death would be for nothing. Kaanan took the lead, darting toward the floating pieces, while Flora went after the one that assaulted her.

Flora could feel a pull, a tug in her navel, to the one piece of the Sormurinn that drifted away from the others. She knew where the shard was—she could feel it. With a roiling stomach and bile-coated throat, she latched her fingers on the serpentine body. She gagged again when her fingers touched the slimy, scaly flesh. Her stomach heaved as she took a deep breath, closed her eyes, and stuck her hand in the opening Anise's sword-work had created.

Flora's skin crawled and a shiver ran up her spine, ricocheting throughout her entire form, her body jerking at the sensation. She tried her best to ignore it and rummaged in the slippery and squishy yet hard innards of the seaworm. It took a minute or two of searching, but her fingers finally shot to the shard like a magnet. Flora yanked the shard out. The second it hit open water, it sent a jolt of energy so cutting she almost dropped it to the weedy dark below. When she was confident it wouldn't play more tricks on her, she kicked away from the dead body, swimming over to where Kaanan was searching. She tapped him on the shoulder and held up the shard, and with a smile that reached his eyes, he grabbed his sword and the two raced up to the surface. About an inch from the water's end, the shadow burst. Water hit her face and, in the shock, she opened her mouth.

Salt water flooded her mouth and lungs, and she swam faster to the surface. She broke through the ocean waves, spewing water and coughing from deep in her lungs as she crawled to the wall. Flora clung to the rocky seawall, her body weak as her lungs and throat burned from the assault.

Kaanan burst out of the water behind her with a loud gasp as he made his way over to her clinging position. "Hi," she said, weakly, her voice shaky.

"Are you okay?" Kaanan asked, voice deep as the ocean they were treading water in.

"Yeah, you?" Flora asked and Kaanan nodded. He extended his hand, and she placed hers in his and let him guide her to shore. They mostly used the rock wall, the current still too strong against their water-logged bodies without help. Although the raging ocean had calmed slightly, like it felt the death of a magical creature in its waters, a dose of sorrow lapping through the slightly less violent current.

After what felt like an eternity, the mouth of the cavern came into view, and with it, Anise. She sat on the sand, clothes soaked and sticking to her skin as her drenched hair dripped drops onto the patch of shore.

She was playing with the ends of her hair, a pout gracing her lips before her face brightened when she caught sight of Flora.

"You're all right! I was so worried," she gushed, flying to her feet.

Kaanan pulled Flora ahead of him, and with Anise grabbing her hands, the two pushed Flora to shore, beautifully solid land under her limbs. Flora wanted to bask in the firmness under her feet, but she wanted to ensure Kaanan got out all right. And with that thought, she really did know that as much as she wanted to, and as much as she tried, she couldn't not have her feelings grow for him. After traveling with him for days, and not once showing an ounce of the brutality within his master's monstrous legends, Flora couldn't help but nourish her budding care and affection.

Kaanan, however, needed no help. With the sleeves of his black shirt pushed up his arms, he pulled himself out of the water, strong forearms flexing deliciously in the sun as flecks of water dripped to the ground, creating a mottled pattern. A crimson blush spread across Flora's cheeks, and she couldn't turn away in time—their gaze collided, and his eyes flicked down and lingered on her blush before she turned away.

With a fluttering filling her previously roiling stomach, she rounded on Anise, the events under the sea coming back to her tenfold as she stared at her friend. Flora's nostrils flared, and her lip wobbled as furious words sprung to life from the depths of her soul—but she couldn't spit them out. The cruel words she wanted to spew couldn't move past her tongue. Flora knew whatever she said now, she couldn't take back, but she wasn't sure if she cared. Her emotions were a convoluted mess, all tangled and knotted. While she wanted to cower, wanted to run away from the confrontation she knew needed to happen, she couldn't—she had to stand up for herself.

"How *could you?*" Flora cried, the words shrill to her ears as Anise jerked back. Kaanan moved to stand beside Flora, a united front that set Anise on edge, her jaw clenching and teeth grinding as her eyes flashed. Flora knew she wasn't supposed to be standing with *him*. She should be standing with Anise. But Anise had gone too far this time.

Her heart pounded in her ears as Anise's eyes watered, her face falling in front of Flora's eyes. "What are you talking about? I helped you!" Anise cried, clasping Flora's hand.

But Flora yanked it out of her grasp, Anise's mouth gaping, and said, "I didn't want you to kill it! You were supposed to stay on the shore, where it's safe. What if you got hurt, too?"

"I'm fine! And what were you planning, Flora? *Asking* it to help you?" she scoffed, tone cruel. "It was a *monster*. It would have killed you if I hadn't shown up."

"It wasn't a monster! It was a living thing, and it deserved respect, and at the very least, to die with dignity—not be slashed up by someone who isn't even a part of this," Flora spat, chest heaving. Her brain was telling her to shut up, her stomach spasming, and she desperately tried to wash away the anxiety with anger.

"Flora's right. We were trying a peaceful approach," Kaanan interjected, squeezing her bicep as he hefted the glinting sword into the scene, tip dangerously close to pointing at Anise. Diluted bloody droplets rolled and dripped onto the sand below. The sight caused Flora's stomach to clench, and she was seconds away from reprimanding him too when Anise jerked her attention back to her.

"Flora, you know I'm right. I didn't want you to get hurt. You were taking so long, and then I get down there and the monster was holding you hostage!" Anise cried, tears streaming down her face. "I was so worried, and I couldn't breathe underwater like you two apparently can."

Flora paused, her eyebrows furrowed as her lips turned down. She knew Anise wasn't a particularly violent person, and she seemed remorseful now. While Flora wanted to help the Sormurinn—at least talk to it more and scope out her options, like the little girl from the tale—the deed was done, and the shard was in her possession. A life was lost, but she gained from it all the same. And dwelling on it, letting it taint her relationship with Anise, would only hurt Flora more.

"The story said it was a poison-spewing, greedy monster—I couldn't let anything happen to you. I love you—you're my best friend." Anise's words convinced Flora, cut through her anger and filled her with begrudging warmth.

"Okay," Flora said, and Kaanan's hand dropped from her arm like it was on fire.

"So, you got the shard, right? Can you feel it? The different magic?"

Flora had almost forgotten about the shard in her hand as, aside from the initial shock, it had laid dormant in her clenched fist. She uncurled her hand, and a beautifully deep blue appeared before her in the shape of a larkspur petal. It wasn't pulsating like the pink one under her shirt, and while Flora could feel the two begging to be closer together, the magic like magnets, the shard felt...quiescent.

"Something's wrong with it," Flora said, frowning at the blue in her palm.

Kaanan stepped in front of her, beside Anise and said, "You must have done it wrong."

"What do you mean?"

"Your other one. You may have had help, but ultimately you did it by yourself—you earned it," Kaanan said. "Magic is fickle, and has a million, confusing rules, but it always requires it to be deserved, to be earned. Not everyone can have magic because few respect it enough to listen to it, to follow the rules and understand it."

"But I barely understood my magic before all of this," Flora protested, a sinking pit forming in her stomach.

"Yes, but you deserved it, respected it, and were punished for mistakes, even if they weren't your own. This whole thing is a test, right? To prove you can harbor magic. To prove you can honor it and be worthy, unlike your mother," Kaanan said, and Flora's face dropped as she took in his words, how true they sounded. "Magic is a mercurial mistress, and this has clearly gone against her rules. Know them or not, she doesn't care—you broke them—that's why it's not working."

"But how am I supposed to *earn* it when I already have it?" Flora asked, her mind spinning as she gnawed on her lip. Her thoughts were circling in a spiral, down a drain of despair and worry. Everything was a mess and she still had two shards to get.

"I don't know. Like I said, magic is fickle. You have to figure it out. Just...try to see if you can feel what it wants, what it's asking for."

"Does magic really work like that?'

"Yes, it's not necessarily a give and take or balance—its all about respect and following its wishes, and it varies per person and thread of magic," Kaanan said, and Flora tried to make sense of it.

She knew very little about her powers, only that the Sage Witch granted her ancestor a boon of magic to grow and heal the land, tying her and her descendants to plants for eternity. With that, and Kaanan's information, Flora assumed it meant she needed to have a healthy respect for the land, which she did, and somehow, she could heal it and grow things. Flora sighed, the task sounding so daunting and unattainable. She wondered how Kaanan's magic worked, what his rules were, and how his thread differed from hers.

"How do you know all this?" Anise asked, arms crossed over her chest as she narrowed her eyes at him and interrupted Flora's contemplation.

Flora darted her gaze to Kaanan, eyes wide as he shrugged. "My parents were big fans—they have an extensive library."

Flora reared back but quickly tried to mask her shock. Anise hummed, eyes still narrowed like she didn't believe a word out of his mouth, and then her eyes lit up. "You liar! You did that weird smoke thing at Vale Centre!"

"It was just a smoke bomb," Kaanan said, shrugging.

"I don't think so. I saw it—it followed you two," Anise argued, eyes blazing.

"Fine, you caught me—it was a *magic* smoke bomb."

"How did you get it?"

"I bought it. You'd be surprised how many stalls in Vale Centre sell magic potions or tricks. They have it all—underwater breathing, smoke bombs, whatever your imagination can conjure within reason," Kaanan said with a shrug.

"But who makes them?"

Kaanan barked a harsh laugh before grinning. "How should I know? I don't question good things when they appear. All I know is the magic I've bought has worked. Maybe the Pitch King or Sage Witch has a side hustle. Or maybe there's more magic wielders than we know. Either way, as long as their potions and tricks work, I don't care where they come from."

Anise held him in a narrowed gaze, her lips pursed and nostrils flaring like she wanted to call him out further, but she said nothing more and let the contentious subject drop, much to Flora's relief.

With Anise dropping the subject, the three decided it was best to head back to town, to get a good night's rest and leave the blood and folktales behind for the day. The sword was sheathed and not a comment was made on its presence in their heated discussion. It was a fact Flora was concerned about bubbling up later—but like with most things that were too daunting to deal with, she pushed it aside for another day.

She was surprised Kaanan lied to Anise, but she knew he didn't trust Anise, and with her stunt, Flora didn't blame him for hiding his secret. And really, his secret wasn't a good one. He was working for the bad side, for a monster—Flora really needed to get that through her thick skull and bleeding heart.

Chapter Sixteen

By order of the great King Desmond:
A girl of 18 years was spotted with a man dressed in all black fleeing Vale Centre. She could be in any province, but she was spotted fleeing into Whaelmere. There is reason to believe this girl is the lost Larkspur Lady, our savior.

Any information is to be told to an official: your local governing bodies or guards.

Rewards will be presented to those with accurate information.

We urge everyone in our great country of Woodvale—find her so she can save us all.

-Notice distributed to every town in Woodvale

"Flora, are you sure we can trust him? I think he's lying!" Anise hissed, fingers in a clawed grip around Flora's arm as she dragged her to the corner of the bar, far away from where Kaanan was ordering their food.

Pain sparked and fizzed in Flora's arm as Anise dug her nails harder. She tried to ignore the discomfort and asked, "What are you talking about?"

Flora's eyebrows were furrowed as she stared at her friend. She was incredibly lost in the conversation. They had just arrived at the inn after an hour of walking in the burning sunrays, almost immediately drying their clothes and sparking red, angry burns on Flora's exposed skin. The walk back was tense, but beautiful.

The sea glimmered and gleamed from the afternoon light reflecting off the obsidian surface. Flora had been transfixed by the sight, and the other two were too distracted in their annoyance to provide a distraction for Flora. So, the glistening sea it was.

"What am *I* talking about? *Flora*, focus," Anise cried under her breath, hastily looking at where Kaanan was—still talking to the innkeeper. " 'Magic smoke bomb?' Come on, he has to be lying—there's no such thing! Witches and sorcerers don't *sell* their magic."

"Well, they don't in Sanarbre, but who knows about Vale Centre—it's filled with grandeur, rich people obsessed with money and showing it off."

"Are you defending him? Seriously?" Anise said, voice hard as rock, and eyes not far behind.

"I'm not defending him," Flora protested, "but there's lots we don't know about magic. He's helped me get here, helped keep me alive, so I don't know, I somewhat trust him?"

Flora cringed, shying away from Anise's bewildered stare. Flora did partially trust Kaanan. He had proven to help her, not hinder her—not like Anise had just done, destroying her plan without thought, without concern for Flora, without consulting her. The thought sent a wave of freezing cold through her veins—she couldn't think like that. She didn't want to. Anise was her best friend and while she made a mistake, nothing could change that. At least, Flora had always thought so. But doubt was worming its way into her mind, festering like an untended wound. She didn't know what to feel anymore.

"We can't trust him—we don't know him. He may have helped you, but he separated us in the first place!

He's manipulating you, mark my words," Anise insisted, and Flora frowned—Anise had a point.

Doubt was a dangerous plant, able to grow wild and crazed in a matter of moments, destroying trust and prompting delirious actions. Flora gnawed on her lip, her stomach clenching painfully. This was not what she needed right now. She needed to focus on the dormant shard, fix what was done, not be cast in doubt about her companions.

"I don't know what you want me to say," Flora said. "He's been helpful, and maybe we can't trust him, but I think he can help me get the other shards."

Flora needed Kaanan for the next shard hidden in the Pitch Woods. The domain of darkness, monsters, and terror. The domain where Kaanan resided, where he was studying, where he had intel no one else in Woodvale did.

"But we can do it ourselves; I know we can. We don't need him."

"Anise, I think he'll be helpful in the Pitch Woods. He knows about magic, and the Pitch Woods are full of it, and beasts and monsters. We need that advantage."

Anise pouted, her full lips dropping as she scrunched her nose delicately. "Fine—we work with him for now, but the second we don't need him, we ditch him. Deal?"

"Deal," Flora said, the lie dropping from her tongue easier than she would have thought.

Flora had no intention of ditching Kaanan. Nor did she have any desire to ditch Anise, despite her mistake earlier. Unless one did something so dastardly she couldn't reconcile with it, Flora would cling to the two for as long as she could. Trust was rare for her, and when it cemented, even a little, Flora never wanted to let it go.

****

Flora woke with a start, her heart racing and breath panting as the last tendrils of her nightmare washed away as quick as a wave rolling out into the ocean. Her ankle throbbed, releasing a dull ache that sent her fingers flying to the location. She glanced over at Anise and found her still fast asleep. The curtains were drawn, not letting a lick of light in, even though Flora could see the world beginning to brighten.

Flora's fingers found her ankle, and she gasped, her stomach dropping. A thick, hard stem met her fingers, the fuzzy coated outside soft. But it wasn't what made her gasp. She didn't just find one stem, but two twin stalks twining up her calf. Flora tugged her skirt over her knee, and her heart dropped out of her chest. The twin stems had split into a bushel of deep indigo larkspurs, their petals a magnificently vibrant hue.

Her leg and hand were starkly pale, the faint color she had leeching away from her. The words of the dream she had came back to her in rushing force: *When your birthmark has reached its potency, and the color has been fully leeched from your body—your time will be up. You will join the other Larkspur Ladies, like pretty dolls on a shelf.* She didn't want to be a doll, or a decoration. She only had so much time to get her magic back and fix things before her curse would sap away at her until she was a lifeless husk.

Flora's throat was tight and her chest clenched. Her hand clambered to the string around her neck that harbored her two shards. They clacked together, and while the pink warmed in her hand, the blue stayed cool.

A low groan from Anise had Flora jumping in alarm. She looked down at the larkspur-covered bed as the blood drained from her face. Flora frantically ripped the bedsheet covering her leg off and stared in horror as a petal brushed against Anise's skin. A red welt grew on Anise's leg and Flora yanked away the flower, ripping the stems out of her skin and racing to the bathroom with her rucksack.

She deposited the larkspur in the bathtub, breathing heavily as she sank to the floor, her head in her hands as she rested against the cool porcelain. Flora didn't know what to do anymore. Her birthmark was getting out of control, and she could feel her body simultaneously weakening from the leech but growing stronger from the shards.

"Help me, please. Tell me how to fix this," Flora begged, clutching the blue shard tightly in her palm.

Who says you can fix it? An inky voice said in her mind. Flora jolted, back hitting the wall as her eyes widened.

"Who are you?" she whispered to the dead air in front of her.

I am the shard.

"Magic is...sentient?"

Some is, if it's powerful enough.

"Well, how can I fix it? I tried following the rules. It wasn't my fault."

Maybe start with taking some responsibility, the voice snapped.

"I'm sorry," Flora whispered. "It was my fault everything didn't go as I wanted. I should have...led better?"

You should have, the voice coaxed, and Flora nodded.

"But what can I do now? To prove myself?" Anticipation hummed through Flora's veins, and she waited with bated breath for the voice to speak again.

You don't. You wait, you think about the task laid out before you in that cave, and figure it out. I cannot help you—you must do this on your own.

Flora wanted to tear her hair out, and she nearly did—her fingers were gripping her skull so tightly. It was all so complicated. Was it too much to ask for something to be easy? Flora sighed, longing for her simplistic childhood of carefree fun in the sun. Everything now had this dark, sinister undertone to the world as Flora saw shades she had never seen before.

A soft knock sounded at the door, causing Flora to fling her back roughly against the wall behind her. Pain shot down her spine and she groaned under her breath.

"Everything all right?" Anise's voice called out, soft from sleep.

"I'm okay! I'll be out in a second."

Flora bit her lip, and then hastily mashed and crushed the larkspur under her palms. The bathtub looked like a purple murder had been committed, petals and stems a mess of tiny pieces and smeared substance. Thankfully, evidence of her uncontrollable birthmark washed away under the spray of tepid water.

When she was done, and the tub was unstained and unharmed, Flora exited the bathroom to find Anise dressed and ready to go.

"Are we leaving already?" Flora asked, rushing to pull out a pair of clean clothes.

"Yup," Anise chirped, her foot scratching at her leg, but she said nothing and didn't seem bothered by the itch. Before something could come from it, Flora made haste to get herself dressed in record time.

The two exited their room, and Flora glanced down the darkened hallway to Kaanan's room at the end. The rest of the hall was silent and still, most guests sleeping, so they went downstairs. Breakfast wasn't officially being served yet, but a tray of bread and butter was laid out for early risers.

"Ugh." Anise groaned and Flora jumped. "I think I got bit or something gross touched me yesterday. My leg is so itchy." Anise pouted, furiously yet absently scratching at her leg under the table as Flora blanched. She had hoped Anise wouldn't notice more, and she could sweep it under the rug.

Should she tell her? Should she admit to her larkspur brushing against her, that it was Flora causing her discomfort and infection? No, she couldn't—she didn't do it on purpose and admitting to it was too…scary. If she told Anise, then she would blame Flora, and rightfully so. Their relationship was already rocky, fracturing and splintering, and Flora didn't want to add any more fuel to the fire.

"That's awful. I'm sorry," Flora said, desperately trying to sound and act casual as she munched on her breakfast, a coil of guilt unfurling in her stomach.

"Thanks, I'm sure it'll go away soon," Anise said, smiling. "How are your burns?"

"They're okay," Flora said, absently touching the red skin. She looked dreadful in the bathroom mirror, like some pale zombie with a burning scarlet rash.

"That's good. Now, eat up. We have a long day

ahead of us."

"Did you speak with Kaanan?" Flora asked, craning her neck to look around the empty barroom. They were the only two dining so early. The amber rays of the rising sun streamed through the open windows, and Flora smiled as the seagulls sang.

"He popped in when you were in the bathroom. He's getting a few last-minute supplies," Anise said, with a smile, as Flora frowned slightly.

"Okay," she said slowly, her gut clenching a warning, but she wasn't sure how to decipher it.

She trusted Anise. Mostly. Trust could shatter like glass in the blink of an eye, in one swift move, and after her stunt, Flora felt like she was gazing at Anise with cracked lenses, her vision distorted and hard to make sense of. But it was Anise, the girl Flora had grown up with, and no matter how uneasy Flora may have been feeling, she couldn't throw away years of friendship over a mistake. She had to get over it or she would lose her cherished friendship forever.

When the two were done eating, Anise ushered them out the door and into the crisp morning air. The rising sun cast amber rays along the street, blinding Flora's eyes as she scanned for Kaanan. He was nowhere to be found, but she wasn't allowed to look too long—Anise grasped her hand and tugged her down the street swiftly. They followed the entirety of the main street before stopping at the last shop before the town ended—a stable. A grisly man and smiling woman greeted them.

"Anise! Lovely to see you again," the woman cooed, clasping her in a hug and Flora recoiled. "This must be Flora, yes?"

Flora hesitated before nodding, hiding behind Anise lest the woman try to hug her too. But she only sent her a soft smile.

"Are you all ready to go? It'll be a long day ahead of us."

"We're all good!" Anise said brightly. The man went into the stable and a minute later came out with a horse and large wagon. He rode at the seat and told them to get in the back as the woman leaped up to sit with him.

Anise guided Flora onto the wagon, the oak wood worn from use, silky smooth against her hands. They weren't the only ones using the wagon as it held multiple crates of sealed goods, but there was enough room for them to stretch out.

"What about Kaanan?" Flora asked, frantically searching the area for that black cloak or thick dark hair, the dimpled smirk and glorious eyes.

"He's meeting us here. Just get comfy, Flora," Anise said, but Flora didn't listen.

Flora sat stiff as a board, waiting for Kaanan to appear, while Anise sighed behind her. She couldn't take her eyes off the open hatch, waiting for that face she longed to gaze upon to appear. She needed him— she couldn't go to the Pitch Woods without him, and she desperately needed his information about magic.

"Where is he?" Flora said under her breath, her knuckles white from how tightly she was clutching her skirt.

"I'm sorry about this, Flora," Anise said from behind her and before Flora could turn, could ask what she was talking about, why she would be sorry, a scorching pain erupted on the back of Flora's skull. She dropped forward like a sack of potatoes, her forehead banging against the wood, splitting open the cut from yesterday. Just as she was swept away in the oblivion, she swore she heard a familiar deep voice scream her name.

Chapter Seventeen

Everything feels wrong.

My daughter was born last night, her father by my side, and he loves her, I can see it in his eyes. But when I look at her, at the innocent babe, a tuft of blonde hair and doe eyes, I feel nothing.

I don't know what's wrong with me. She's my daughter, my legacy, and yet, I am empty inside.

He *ruined her for me. He destroyed me, my magic, took so much without a care, and now my life is over. I can feel it, festering and rotting beneath my skin.*

I don't have long left. I need to do it soon, tomorrow maybe, or it will be too late, and I refuse for that to happen.

I will get what I want, what I deserve, if it's the last thing I do.

-Diary entry by Anneliese Larkspur

"Flora?" Anise asked, her voice soft. It sounded far away to Flora, like they were separated by water or glass. "Flora, wake up."

The words stirred something in Flora, made the fuzzy fog in her brain dissipate, helped coax her from her sleep and to the land of the living. Her eyes fluttered open. Pale blue and fluffy clouds met her distorted vision. Her eyes wouldn't focus, and everything swayed as she squinted. A searing pain gnawed at the back of her skull, and Flora moaned in agony, her hand flying to the wound, only to find soft fabric and something squishy.

"I'm so sorry," Anise said, and Flora could read her tone like a book. It was a rare sound for Anise, apologizing so sincerely, her voice clouded with guilt and anguish.

Anise's obvious discomfort and guilt over her actions made Flora feel a bit better about the situation as the morning's events came flooding back to her. An inferno sparked to life in her veins, blazing her body in a singe of fury. Flora practically vibrated from the anger coursing through her limbs, but she tried her best to stifle it down. Flora knew Anise wouldn't take well to be yelled at, and Flora wasn't all that comfortable screaming at her friend. Her tongue was tied and her stomach ached at the thought.

Flora did the sensible thing for herself. She released a withering breath, and flicked her eyes up, catching sight of Anise. Flora's head was pillowed on Anise's soft thigh, and her hands cradled Flora's head lightly. Anise stared down at Flora with watery eyes and a wobbling lip, like she would burst into tears at any moment.

"Why?" Flora croaked, her own eyes watering as the two girls' gazes connected.

"I'm so sorry. I had to get us away from him. I don't trust him, and I don't like how he wormed his way into *our* quest, *our* friendship," Anise said, her face contorted in agony. "Please understand—I regret hitting you, I do. I regretted it the moment you fell, but I didn't know another way around ditching him."

"I see," Flora murmured, her eyebrows furrowed.

"I am truly, eternally, sorry."

The high road, Flora thought. She needed to take the high road, forgive Anise, not forget—she wasn't capable of *that* much forgiveness—but she had to somehow move past this. What Anise had done was not okay. She had willingly hurt her. Flora was starting to see her friend in a new light, and it was not good. She had always known Anise to have some faults, to be brash and commanding and controlling, but this was on a whole new level. Except there was little she could do in their current predicament. She had to let her anger and suspicion sleep so she could continue on their journey. Her end goals were more important than fighting with Anise. She had to succumb to Anise's ministrations, at least until she got her shards and mother back. After, they could talk, and truly move past the grievances plaguing Flora because something would need to change if their friendship wanted to survive.

"Okay," Flora said. "I understand why you did it, and I...forgive you." The words were like honey coming out of her mouth, sweet sounding, but sticking to every surface and impossible to remove.

"Thank you!" Anise cried, planting a kiss on Flora's forehead.

"Where is Kaanan? I thought I heard him before I...well, you know," Flora asked, and Anise's cheeks flushed in a rosy pink as she scowled.

"You imagined that Flora," Anise said, her tone sure and eyes serene as she gazed down at Flora. "I don't know where he is, probably back at the inn. Don't worry about him, forget him—it's you and me now, okay?"

Those words once would have filled Flora with warmth and covered her eyes in a rose haze, everything pink-hued and sugary sweet. The reassurance that Anise would always be with Flora, always stand by her because they were best friends. It was confirmation Anise hadn't grown bored of Flora, or found someone better, because Flora was constantly fearing she wasn't good enough, wasn't entertaining enough. It had taken months of constant outings for Flora to finally admit comfortably to herself that she and Anise were friends. Prior to that she would flush and skirt around the question, preferring to call her an acquaintance in her head. So, whenever Anise said or did things to reiterate that they were friends—best friends—Flora was high as a kite with joy.

But not now. Now, the words were *too* sweet, the sugar doused so much Flora felt sick to her stomach. It was almost cloying to her senses. There was an underlying nefarious substance to the words, even though they sounded the same as they always had. Flora's stomach dropped at the realization. Her years of progress with Anise were being assaulted, disintegrating before her eyes in tandem with herself. While her birthmark was growing more potent each day.

Flora swallowed thickly, trying to push away the thoughts, the fears, and pretend like everything was okay. It was all normal, it was her and Anise, and they were good, they were great even—they were on an adventure. They were on the road and would travel for a few days and then arrive in the Pitch Woods where the next shard was…without her second shard working and without Kaanan, apprentice to the Pitch King and the only person she knew with genuinely helpful information. Oh Gods, they were going to perish in the

Woods, they would be eaten alive by bloodthirsty monsters, and their blood would be drained until they were husks and their skin would be peeled from their bones, before they were torn limb from limb, spattering the Woods with blood and sinew and gooey substances.

Stop, a voice hissed at Flora, like the one in the bathroom—deep as the ocean and she startled, exiting from her spiral like she had been pushed as her eyes widened and breathing quickened.

No, keep going, a different voice crooned, this one delicately feminine, coy as a fox.

Flora blinked, her emotions and thoughts in a game of tug of war before she pushed both aside, throwing a blanket on the feelings. Hearing voices in your head was never a good thing, and it had been happening too much recently for Flora to remain calm.

What is happening? She thought and a trinkle of laughter echoed.

Magic, the feminine voice said in a croon and Flora gasped lightly as the information sank in.

If magic really was sentient, and the blue shard spoke to her, then the pink one must speak as well. Gods, she was losing her mind. She genuinely believed the magical shards were talking to her—but that *must* be impossible. Once again, a deep longing filled her, casting her adrift in the feeling as she wished she could ask her biological mother questions and have grown up with her so she wouldn't be shoved off a cliff without a parachute like this. Although she would have still wanted to be partially raised by Rosie—she loved and adored her too much.

"Flora, is everything all right? Is your head okay?" Anise asked, drawing Flora out of her head.

"I'm fine," she assured, sitting up and gazing around at the scenery as the buggy rocked them back and forth in a steady motion, kicking up dust and dirt. "Where are we now?"

"They said we were just nearing the Whaelmere and Myrkurden border."

Flora nodded, watching the rise and swell of the rolling hills littered with small farms and massive dead crops begin to fade from view. Her lips tugged down as she didn't catch sight of the oceanside town they stayed in, where Kaanan most likely still was. Unless Anise was lying of course. Though at that point, Flora wasn't really sure who she could trust completely besides herself—sort of—and Rosie.

****

The sun turned into a burning ball of flame, oranges and reds cascading across the horizon, before letting a dark navy loose to blanket the world in night. Stars blinked awake and as Flora watched the moon rise, her countdown kept ticking. She wondered where her mother was now, and if she was okay, if she was warm and well-fed. She prayed to the Gods who would listen that she accomplished her mission in time for the Sage Witch's deadline. Especially when the deadline from her ankle had a mind of its own and she had no idea how close the sand was to running out on that hourglass.

The rocking of the buggy on the worn dirt paths was soothing to Flora. She spent most of the day resting against Anise, watching the path extend out behind them, hoping for a certain dark clothed figure on a horse to appear. Yet, there was none to be found. Flora was disappointed. She had thought Kaanan would be racing after her, if not for the budding friendship blooming, then for his boss—Kaanan had said the Pitch King sent him. She hoped Kaanan would show up again, preferably *before* they reached the Pitch Woods. She had little faith she and Anise could tackle the Pitch Woods on their own—the Woods were too grim and dangerous.

The couple driving them were quiet for the majority of the day, until the sun went down, when they called that they would be stopping for the night at the next valley. They had just passed a copse of trees Flora thought would have been a perfect place to rest for the night—it looked just like the one Kaanan and her stayed in—but they gave the trees a wide berth like the Sage Witch would pop out when they were at least a week or two and many kilometers away from the Sage Woods.

The couple pulled the buggy and horse to stop in the fall of a dry valley, and Anise and Flora crawled out, stretching their stiff limbs.

"You okay?" she asked Flora.

"I'm fine, are you?" Flora said and Anise nodded. "You should ask whereabouts we are."

Anise nodded and ventured over to the couple who were erecting a canvas tent that looked big enough for two. Flora sighed and shot a contemplative glance at her meager rucksack. That was another reason why she needed Kaanan—he was well equipped to travel under the stars.

Flora heard Anise ask where they were and she got a reply of, "Just around the border between Myrkurden and Whaelmere, dear."

Flora narrowed her eyes at the conversation taking

place and glanced around at the landscape. While she had never been to Myrkurden, she had traveled through Whaelmere, and the landscape looked *so* familiar. She knew all of Woodvale looked mostly the same in its current desolate predicament, but a niggling feeling in Flora's gut refused to be displaced. A finger of cold ran down her spine, her skin erupting in goosebumps. The air tasted off to Flora—everything was turning a shade of wrong; Flora could *feel* it. Maybe she was just being paranoid, but Flora couldn't shake the feeling she was missing something.

Anise came traipsing back and the two laid down their rucksacks and waited while the couple began to start a fire. Flora's skin crawled as she watched the two strangers, their skin weathered from age and sun. They looked harmless, but the vibe they gave off made Flora wriggle in the dirt. While Anise began to make conversation with the couple, Flora's eyes wandered over to the copse of trees, the dense thicket calling her name and drawing her eyes magnetically. Flora wished she had better night vision so she could see the trees clearer in the dark. Despite the night air and shadows cast from the fire, the longer she looked, the more she could make out details.

Her ankle itched fiercely, but she ignored it as her shard warmed her skin. Her eyes finally raked over the right spot, a spot that caused her stomach to drop and breathing to halt. The edges of the trees and bushes were trampled, a deep depression in the otherwise pristine treeline. Her only thought was that it was made by a large animal tied to a tree by a certain man she couldn't get out of her head. It was the copse she and Kaanan stayed in. The thought felt right to her, and even if it sounded ridiculous and she was wrong, she couldn't shake it.

It had to be the trees where she and Kaanan slept. Even though it sounded ridiculously outrageous, Flora knew in her bones she was right. She would never forget a beautiful forest. They were all different and unique. Flora chewed on her lip as her gaze locked on the trees. She toyed with the idea that it might truly be the same copse, before telling herself she was being crazy. There was no proof...but her gut squirmed in that telltale sign when she looked at it. With another breath of hesitation, she cemented in her notion.

They were going in the wrong direction. There was no doubt in Flora's mind when she scanned her surroundings again, this time with different eyes, and found everything looking too familiar. Maybe she was wrong, but she was amping herself up too much to let it go. However, she had to drop it for the time being, until she and Anise were alone, and the couple was fast asleep.

It took longer than Flora would have liked, as she smiled falsely and nodded along to the incessant chatter. Eventually, when the moon was high and the fire embers were dying, the couple crawled into their tent, and, Flora hoped, fell asleep.

"Anise," Flora hissed under her breath as her friend lay down in the dirt.

"What?" Anise asked, voice *not* quiet like Flora. She pressed her hands over Anise's mouth with a frantic gaze at the tent only to find it still and silent. Anise scoffed, pushing Flora away and shot her an annoyed yet questioning glance.

"Sshh," Flora said, and Anise rolled her eyes while

sighing.

"What?" Anise whispered this time, raising her eyebrows.

"I think we're going the wrong way. Doesn't this all look to familiar to you?"

"It all looks the same, Flora. That's Woodvale under a curse," Anise said slowly like she was talking to a child. Flora shot her a withering glare.

"Seriously, this place looks exactly like the route Kaanan and I took to the Svart Sea. I don't think we're going to Myrkurden."

"Don't be ridiculous—it all looks the same because it always does. It's all dirt and dead land."

"Anise, please, trust me on this. I'm right. I know I am."

Anise sighed, frowning at Flora, but relented. "I trust you. I do. So how about this: let's just look through their stuff and see if they're telling the truth about who they are. If they have what they said they have, we stay, if they don't, we leave—we flee into the night like proper heroes."

Flora's chest warmed, the cracks in her trust for Anise knitting together as she smiled at her friend. Flora nodded and the two crept toward the cart, barely making a sound, and trying not to accidentally kick a loose rock.

They climbed up into the buggy and rifled through the open crates and found goods to be sold, nothing out of the ordinary. It wasn't until Flora dug deep into a crate of cloth that her fingers snagged on paper. She hastily tugged it free, almost falling from her balancing act, and held the crisp sheet of paper up to her face to read the dark lettering in the moonlight.

Her heart dropped out of her chest and smashed into the wood of the cart as she read the words. King Desmond had issued a hunt for her—he *knew*. Oh Gods, she could barely breathe, her lungs clenched, and her throat locked up tight.

"Flora?" Anise cried and read the paper too. Anise's eyes bugged and she gasped loudly in the silence.

"Well, this is a shame," a gruff voice said from behind them as they both gasped and nearly fell in surprise to the ground below.

The man and woman were standing at the foot of the buggy and before Flora could do something, fight back, call up plant to help her, *anything*—he was on them. A wood plank whistled through the air as it connected with her head. She dropped instantly, limbs crunching and bending awkwardly as a sea of black claimed her for the second time that day.

Chapter Eighteen

Myrkurden is a beautiful place, with thick, luscious pine trees creating an aroma that carries on the breeze. It is lovely, but there are two warnings one must be aware of before visiting.

The first is that it borders the Pitch Woods and many people and animals have gone missing under mysterious circumstances. There are also sightings of beasts and monsters that lurk on the border. So, if you're planning to see the Pitch Woods in person, best stay far away from the tree line—or better yet, skip it.

Secondly, presumably due to the unfavorable living circumstances, Myrkurden is rife with thieves and criminals. Keep your coins close, try to look and act confident or tough, and lastly, do not, under any circumstances, travel at night.

-An Adventurer's Guide to Woodvale: Myrkurden by Gísli

Flora woke slowly, her head aching and throbbing fiercely, screaming at her for her careless actions. The world was still washed in darkness, the tent erect with bodies pushing against the fabric. Flora deduced they were all where they were before.

This is good, Flora reasoned. She took a deep breath, pushing away the niggling worm of anxiety threatening to cause her panic to spill over.

She tugged on her hands, tied in front of her

securely to the wheel of the buggy. She desperately wanted to grab the rucksack *just* out of reach, that held all the things she could use to escape. Flora cursed under her breath and craned her neck to find Anise beside her in the same predicament.

"Are you okay?" Flora asked, noting the swollen dark purple bruise marring her forehead.

"*No.* What the Hell is going on? The King is after us now?" Anise grumbled, casting a murderous glare on the tent where their captors slept.

"We have to get out of here," Flora said, her heart pounding in her ears.

She watched the quiet night, shadows chasing away her hope as she tugged on her hands that were bound tight. She gnawed on her lip, trying to *think*. She could get out of this—she had to. She had to trust herself. She was capable.

"We're adventurers," Anise said, voice sure. "Of course we can get out of here. Try using your magic. Call up a vine with thorns."

Flora swallowed thickly, thinking of the right plant—she would need something sharp and jagged enough to cut through the ropes. Flora perked when the name came to her: the *Euphorbia milii*—the Crown of Thorns.

She took a deep breath in through her nose and released it through her lips, body softening as she focused, tried to conjure an image while pushing herself to the magic running through her veins. She could feel it, a shimmering green that lay dormant unless purposely, or accidentally, accessed by her. She called upon it then, and it came fast with a head rush, casting her vision in a sea of green before softening into the stark and dead world she knew.

"Please, help me," she begged the shards, clutching them in her hands awkwardly as her wrists burned from the rope digging into her skin. In response, they burned a flame into her palm.

Ask and you shall receive. And to Flora's shock, it wasn't the sultry feminine voice, but the deep blue one. The one that felt like sinking through the ocean to the bottom of the deep depths, the one that could make anyone fall into that voice—reminiscent of Kaanan's.

"Really?"

You did enough to fix your mistakes doubled with your attempt under the sea. You trusted yourself and your friend. Now, we have work to do.

A thorn pierced Flora's skin, a bead of blood dripping and rolling down her arm. She strained her hands closer to the thorns and winced as they scratched her wrists, blood welling. She ignored the sting and let the plants do their work. In no time, the rope snapped, and her wrists were free.

Flora wasted no time and lunged to Anise, tugging and tearing at the rope, desperately trying to get her friend free when a noise broke through the night air. Flora whipped around, pebbles skittering. She glanced up into the dark night. What looked like a shadowy wall came rushing down the path, before it washed away in a blink and he appeared like an avenging angel.

"Kaanan!" she cried softly, her eyes widening and a grin blooming. "You're here."

"I am, but apparently you beat me to the rescue," he said, the smirk with the charming dimple flourishing.

"Um, hello?" Anise said, and Flora gasped, flying to help her friend.

Kaanan came up behind her and extended a leather knife handle, holding the wicked sharp blade in his fingertips. "Thank you," Flora said, and sliced the rope in two as the knife cut through it like butter.

"Anytime," Kaanan murmured, and Flora shot him a small smile.

"We should get going," Flora said, hands on hips as she smiled at her two friends.

"I don't think so," the kidnapper's gruff voice rang out. He held a short sword, blade rusting, but nevertheless, deadly sharp.

Kaanan took a swift step so his body shielded Flora, while Anise was left unprotected. She had no shame in hiding behind Kaanan and his big cloak. Besides, he was the only one of them that had envying control over his magic. So, Flora hid and thought about her options. She lifted her arm slightly, about to grab Anise's arm and tug her to safety, when her gaze snagged on her rucksack just behind Anise's feet.

"Good evening, sir. These two ladies will be coming with me now," Kaanan said, silky and smooth and charismatic to a fault.

"I don't think so. You aren't taking them anywhere," the man growled. "These two are for the King."

"The pamphlet said a man was traveling with her," the woman said, clutching her partner's sleeve as her eyes widened, an insatiable, greedy hunger burning. "We can ask for a triple ransom now."

"Now, let's all calm down," Kaanan said, raising his palms forward which created a lovely large shield for Flora.

She took her chance and dropped to her knees

silently and stretched her arm to deftly lift and yank the bag to her. She paused, waiting for a cry of alarm, but none came. Flora immediately honed in on the vials of crushed larkspur, their potent poison begging to be released into the wild. She reached inside, fingers closing on the cool glass before pulling it into the night, letting them bask in the glory of the dark.

The only thing stopping Flora's larkspur from being free in the wind, free to intoxicate someone, to cling to their body and lungs, creating a symphony of pain and paralysis before a cold death, was a simple stopper.

Should she use it? What kind of person would that make her? Flora wasn't sure—part of her desperately wanted to toss it in their faces and run, flee into the night so none of them could be injured or delayed in their journey. But the other part of Flora hesitated—she could do serious damage to these people if she used her larkspur, could potentially kill them, and she didn't know much about them other than that they wanted to sell her, and would hurt them to get what they wanted.

She supposed she could give it to Kaanan and let him decide, but passing the blame wouldn't change the fact that it was ultimately her idea, her larkspur, her responsibility. If she used it, the only person to blame would be herself. But were you a bad person if you hurt someone who wanted to hurt you, who was probably equally as bad?

What kind of person did she want to be? What could she live with?

Flora considered herself a *good* person. She helped her mother whenever she could. She helped the villagers whenever someone needed an extra hand or pair of eyes. More than anything, Flora *wanted* to be good. But she wanted to because she *had* to. It was always the expectation of her, to be good, so her magic wouldn't curse her like it did Anneliese. But no one truly knew what cast her mother's magic away. And really, good and bad were just another shade of gray—there was no black and white. Good people, people who played it safe and followed every single rule, never got as far in life as the people who took shortcuts, who made decisions that could be deemed questionable. Flora didn't want to fall behind, to not get the most out of life by being categorically *good*. No one was perfect, so what was the harm in being gray, in being selfish or cruel when necessary?

Flora reached into her rucksack and retrieved another vial. This one, she kept curled into her palm, and the other, she pressed into Kaanan's hand out of view. His fingers closed around the cool glass, and before he accepted it, he squeezed her fingers gently, causing a flurry of movement in her stomach, and then the moment was gone and he had a vial, and she had a vial. Both were capable of changing the situation, of being dastardly in the face of threat, of protecting those important to them.

"You have one chance to leave here, forget you saw us, and go on with your lives. Fail to do so, and the consequences will be on you," Kaanan said, voice deeply smooth and confident, sending rippling shivers up Flora's spine.

The man scoffed and growled, "Boy, you don't scare me—some wealthy lord with a little knife? Try me."

"Excellent choice, truly," Kaanan said, and Flora

could hear the smile in his voice. "Don't run crying or screaming, please. It's so exhaustingly boring when they run."

The man sputtered at Kaanan's words before shoving them off with a snarl and jabbed his sword in their direction. Kaanan slightly turned back to look at Flora, giving her a quick nod, before he lifted the vial into the air. Flora took a deep breath and stepped up beside Kaanan, the man releasing a cruel laugh.

"Last chance," Flora said, voice sounding weak even to her ears, but she was trying. She spoke to them, giving them warning, and she was proud of herself for that.

"Those should be my words, girlie," he said, snarling with stained teeth. "Give up now, and we'll be gentle to you and your friends."

Annoyance flared to life in Flora's veins, a steady warm buzz racing through her body. With one hand holding the vial, she clutched the shards in her other hand. She pictured a simple larkspur, like the ones that grew on her ankle, and willed it to grow out of the hard ground beneath his feet.

Flora's brow dotted with sweat as her veins turned a shimmering green, and then, a smile bloomed on her face as a pink and blue larkspur shot out of the ground. The man and woman startled, before looking to her, their eyes wide with wonder and haunted with horror, the magic both charming and terrifying them.

"Are you sure you don't want to run?" she asked, a smirk dotting her lips.

The man snarled and lunged for her, sword swinging and glinting in the moonlight. Flora's finger immediately found the stopper and flicked it off, and without a single ounce of hesitation, she thrust the dust into his face.

The man gasped, a silent cry forming on his lips as he dropped the sword with a thud. His hands clawed his face as his skin turned red, the larkspur dust having hit his open eyes, mouth, and nostrils. Flora felt a twinge of guilt as he dropped to the ground, limbs spasming before falling still, the paralysis taking over from the potency. The woman screamed in fury and grabbed the sword, but before she could even swing, Kaanan calmly blew the dust into her face. In the blink of an eye, she was on the ground beside her partner, both still as death, but hearts still beating slowly before eventually they, too, fell still.

"What was that?" Anise asked, eyes wide.

"Larkspur dust," she replied calmly, pushing aside the guilt and focusing on the matter at hand—they were safe and uncaptured. That was what was important.

"Why didn't I get some? That would have been useful for me, too!" Anise said, and Flora blinked at her. She numbly grabbed another vial from her bag and pressed it into Anise's waiting hands.

A smile grew on Anise's face, and Flora said, "Don't unstopper it unless you're using it. It's dangerous, poisonous, and could kill you in potent doses like this. It's not a toy, understand?"

"I'm not a child, but yes, I understand."

"Thank you," Kaanan said, touching Flora's arm lightly.

"No problem," Flora said. She had wanted to ask why he hadn't used his shadow magic, but looking at Anise, she knew why. Anise didn't know yet and she would more than likely react poorly to the knowledge.

"Are you okay?" Kaanan asked, his eyes boring into hers, like he could read what she was feeling.

"I'm fine. Are you?" He nodded.

"Okay, so, while I guess I have to thank you for the help, I will not apologize for ditching you," Anise said, shoulders drawn back as she stared at Kaanan, daring him to pester her. "Also, you sounded like a psychopath back there."

"I wouldn't dream of it," he said, a smirk resting on his full lips. "But I must insist I continue on with you. I have knowledge of Myrkurden, magic, and the Pitch Woods—like it or not, you need me. Psychopath or not."

Anise pursed her lips, a sharp sigh releasing from her nostrils as she clenched her jaw at him before she relented. "Fine."

"Great!" Flora said, clapping her hands together as she too ignored the two lifeless bodies littering the ground at their feet. "Let's get going. I don't want to linger here."

"We should take their wagon and tent while we're at it," Anise said, and went over to start packing their things.

"Did you bring the horse?" Flora asked Kaanan.

"Yes, she's waiting by the trees. I'll retrieve her and meet you back here—don't let her leave. I will catch up easily enough," he teased, a glimmer in his eyes causing Flora to smile.

"I promise."

Kaanan disappeared into the night while Flora helped Anise pack. In no time, the three were reunited, carefully avoiding the two bodies, and hooked their horse to the cart beside the other one. They ventured into the night, the air cold, but not bleak like Flora had expected. She felt good about tonight, as darkly questionable and awful sounding as that was. She was proud of herself for standing up for her and her friends, for pushing away her anxieties and the pressure to do the "right thing" and instead do what she wanted, what she felt she needed to do.

The guilt lingered beneath the surface, lying in wait, but she ignored it, stuffing it deep down and turning a blind eye. She was freer than she had been in years, and with the breeze twirling her hair, she hunkered down in the buggy, letting the rocking sensation and starry night whisk her off to peaceful sleep.

Chapter Nineteen

Long ago, two women began an era of prosperity and wealth. One was a Witch, and one was a good woman.

Two women with diametrically opposed value systems worked together to bring prosperity and happiness to the country. The values were passed down generation by generation in the woman's bloodline and the Witch lived on steadfastly. Their world was green and full of beauty. But goodness could only last so long, and if our folklore is any indication, no one in life is ever truly innocent.

-*The Age of Larkspur* by Cassius Muscari, IV

A lilting caw of crows and morning dew woke Flora the next morning. If she kept her eyes closed, she could imagine the world as green and full of life as it was in her dreams. Plants would dance in the breeze and the world would be spotted with bold and soft colors, smelling fresh and wild and full of pine as those were the native trees to Myrkurden. But the second she opened her eyes, the illusion fell away.

The birds were there, circling the pale sky, a murder of crows stalking their journey. The sun was cresting over the horizon, but there were no plants, no flowers, no pine trees with their luscious scent. The sun was warm against her skin, and that was what mattered in the moment—warmth in the light of all the darkness.

Soon, if all went well, she could make her dreams a reality for everyone. That thought filled her with happiness and hope, and propelled her forward, sitting up and finding Kaanan still guiding the horses on the dirt path while Anise slept soundly.

Flora crawled to the front of the buggy. "Good morning," Flora said, her forearms digging into the wooden railing.

"Flora!" he said, turning slightly as surprise colored his voice. "Good morning. How was your sleep?"

"Good. Are you okay? I could steer for a bit if you want some rest," she said, but he shook his head.

"I'm fine. I'm not tired, and this isn't the place for you to watch over." Flora bristled.

"What does that mean?"

"Haven't you read the guidebook about Woodvale? I saw it in your bag."

"Well, yes, but not recently, I've mostly been going off of memory and adrenaline," she admitted sheepishly, and he smirked at her, the dimple catching in the light.

"Okay, a crash course in Myrkurden. Rule number one: don't trust anyone," he said, shooting her a dark grin. "Myrkurden is full of thieves, con-artists, and criminals—keep your guard up at all times. Rule number two: if someone asks for help, they are more than likely lying—do not help them. Rule number three: street peddlers will try to put jewelry on you and force you to buy it—don't let them. Rule number four: don't trust guards or law enforcement."

"Is there anyone trustworthy in Myrkurden?"

"Me," he said with a maniacal grin and Flora

laughed softly.

"Okay, so trust you, and then what?"

"Just that—trust me. I will get you through this safely, and I will get you through the Pitch Woods safely. We're going to take a shortcut, a straight shot to the Woods, so we shouldn't have to deal with any residents, but it's still good information to have." Flora nodded. "Do you trust me?"

"Yes," Flora said without hesitation. The second the word hit the air, she wished she could take it back, so she could at least attempt to hesitate, to show him she wasn't so gullible and trusting when he wasn't the type of person she should trust easily. But with the grin that lit up Kaanan's face, she couldn't dwell in her regret for long, and forgot what she was worrying about as she stared at him.

"Good. Just so you know, I trust you too." A crimson blush spread across her cheekbones, and she ducked her head as he watched her intently.

Their conversation lulled, minor questions and answers of likes and dislikes passed back and forth. Flora watched the landscape pass them by. It was less hilly than Whaelmere. Instead of a dry desert-like climate, it was rocky, kind of like Sanarbre, and Flora could picture the vast pine forests that once were. It was more enjoyable to watch the land pass by with her imagination, and her shards warmed against her chest at the imagery.

One day, the land will look like that again, the deep voice of the blue shard whispered in her mind. She could hear the longing in its voice, perfectly mirroring Flora's thoughts as she gazed at the barren land.

"One day," Flora promised the shard under her

breath, clutching it tightly in her hand.

Kaanan glanced at her, at her fervent prayer for the land to return to its natural, bountiful state. He nodded at her, like he approved, like he too, wished he could live in a world of green. Kaanan extended his hand to her, palm up, while he clutched the reins tightly in his other. Flora hesitated for a second, glancing from his hand to his face, to his warm and kind eyes, and with a deep breath, she placed her hand in his. Warmth erupted where their skin connected, and he threaded their fingers together. An army of butterflies burst to life in Flora's stomach as her cheeks deepened in color again. But she didn't pull away, and she wasn't drowning from awkwardness. She felt good, and happy, and she never wanted to let go of his hand now that she had it.

****

Two days passed in a blur of barren land and villages on the horizon. It was incredibly similar to Whaelmere and Sanarbre, except for the stone walls. Along the roads were crumbling stone fences that boxed in the path and provided excellent coverage for hiding highway-robbers and criminals, despite their state of dilapidation. The three had good luck so far and had not encountered any vagabonds along their travels, owing in part to their caution. They didn't travel at night—instead, they settled in to sleep with one person keeping watch every couple of hours.

Their eyes were circled with bruises, no one looking worse than Flora as the dark purple and blue stains highlighted how pale she was becoming. Nevertheless, their travels were going well, save exhaustion, but Flora still worried as they traversed the enclosed path. The buggy was doing poorly on the roads as stones from the walls had crumbled into the path, making the ride bumpy.

She was constantly scanning the horizon and the walls, waiting for some sinister person looking to make some money to pop up and take her away from her friends, whisking her away to King Desmond, where all her plans would crumble like ash. She was on edge, waiting with bated breath and tense muscles, but no one ever appeared, and she was beginning to wonder if the guidebooks were wrong, if they were just stereotypes pitting the provinces against one another.

Flora was wrong.

It was on their third day traveling through Myrkurden that their luck ran out and when the first signs of trouble appeared, Flora almost collapsed in relief. She *knew* their luck couldn't be that good, couldn't protect them from the warnings.

It began with a false owl's hoot. Flora's ears perked at the noise, as it sounded slightly off-kilter, and it was the wrong time of day for owls. The sun burned beating rays down on their skin, the time when owls were asleep in their hidey-holes. They had owls in Sanarbre, and Anise and Flora had spent a few evenings listening to their hoots and calls, making up stories about what they were doing or talking about.

"I don't think we're alone," Flora muttered out of the side of her mouth, desperately trying to ensure whoever was out there didn't catch on that she knew.

Anise and Kaanan both tensed and nodded. Kaanan's grip on the reins tightened to a white-knuckle grip and Anise pursed her lips as she gazed at the road surrounding them. Flora rummaged in her bag for a vial of purple, poisonous powder.

Their sword and knives lay against one of the crates directly behind Kaanan, and Flora positioned herself there, limbs tense and heart pounding as she waited for them to make their move. Several minutes down the road from them stood a large boulder. The two horses reared at the sight as Kaanan stood in his seat, trying to find a way around it.

"Shit," he breathed and dropped the reins, tying them to the undercarriage of the bench and clasping his hands together as his eyes fluttered closed. Flora watched with rapt anticipation, but before Kaanan could use his magic to do something to the boulder—Flora hoped he could use his shadows to move or disintegrate it—chaos exploded.

One second, the land was bare, not a soul in sight save for them and the horses. The next, a flurry of bodies wrapped in filthy clothes scattered around the road, hopping over the fence and surrounding them. Flora couldn't make out how many there were as they danced around the buggy, shouting guttural words she couldn't decipher and jabbing the air with glinting and rusting blades.

Flora's lungs seized as her heartbeat roared a crescendo of noise in her ears, blotting out the screams of the robbers and Kaanan's barked words. Her vision blurred as panic gripped her heart, but she needed to focus, needed to help—she could help. The thought calmed her, and she worked as fast as she could to push the terror and anxiety down to a manageable level. A couple figures attempted to mount the buggy, but Anise stopped them, whipping the vial of larkspur powder across their faces, the breeze helping it hit their targets.

They dropped like flies, weapons scattering to the ground, and they twitched and seized before falling still.

"Do you have more?" Anise shouted and Flora, nodded, kicking the bag to her.

Flora turned and threw her vial of larkspur on the people on her side of the buggy as Anise used a couple more vials on her side. Flora watched as Kaanan artfully slashed and stabbed with his sword at each figure that approached him. She could barely tear her eyes away as each deft, masterful slash hit its intended target. He didn't even need his magic—something Flora was jealous of. She vowed she would take proper lessons eventually and become stronger in all aspects of her life.

"Flora!" Anise cried, and Flora turned, her heart plummeting to the ground. A filthy, balding man held Anise against his chest, rusty knife pressed to the soft skin of her neck.

"Give us your gold, and your friend can live," he said, voice guttural.

Flora hesitated, desperately wanting to give in, let him take what he wanted. But Flora wasn't helpless. While she wasn't as skilled at fighting as Anise, her friend being a natural during their stick swordplay back home doubled with a few lessons from flirting with a guard. Or Kaanan with his magical and fierce physical prowess. She wasn't weak and she could defend herself and her friends. Their whole trip so far had proven that to her. She didn't need to cower in the face of death; she needed to fight back just as hard.

Her hand found her shards and she stared at the man with burning eyes, a hatred of a hundred suns. He would not hurt Anise—she would not allow that.

She called upon her magic, feeling the green rise and flow through her veins as a flash of summers with Anise filled her mind, playing in the river and in the copse where blackberries would grow. Her mind latched onto the blackberries, and as the shard warmed in her hand and her body felt like it glittered in green, Flora coaxed a beautiful stem of thorny blackberry to snake through the wooden railing. It curled around the man's leg lightly as he watched her, waiting for a response, and before he could notice, it wrapped around his whole leg. With a whispered command in her mind, the thorny branch snapped tight, sharp, thick thorns stabbing deeply into the man's leg in one swift movement.

He released a cry of anguish, the knife falling from Anise's neck, and she took her chance. Anise elbowed the man in the face and darted away from him, retreating to the other end of the buggy. Flora stared at the man, blood gushing from his leg as she tightened the pressure of the thorns.

"What are you?" the man hissed, eyes shooting blazing daggers at her.

"She is your only hope," Kaanan said, dropping into the buggy, his sword dripping scarlet drops of viscous blood onto the wooden planks. He nodded at the man. "What's it going to be, Flora?"

"We should let him live—he can warn any others not to mess with us," Anise said, but Flora shook her head.

"We don't need him to warn others—the more people who know about me, about what happened here, will only be worse for me." Kaanan's lips turned up, casting her an impressed look as Anise nodded dully.

Flora didn't *want* to kill him, but she couldn't let him walk out of here. He would blather to anyone who would listen about the crazed lost Larkspur Lady, or about the psycho witch traversing the province. Either one would not bode well for her—she needed anonymity, and a chance to prove herself without the prejudice of her mother hanging over her head. If people knew she had killed, had used her magic to hurt others, they would lock her up faster than she could blink. And he wasn't innocent—that much was obvious. She was making excuses, defending her oncoming actions to herself, but deep down, she knew she was crossing a line she may not be able to find again. And yet, she would break through her line, the edge teetering between good and bad. She may regret her decision, would drown deeper in the guilt she already felt, but she also believed there was no other choice, just like with the couple that kidnapped them.

"Do it," Flora said to Kaanan, and he nodded, before running the sword clean through the protesting man's chest. Blood bloomed in a scarlet rose across his sternum, spilling onto the buggy, and Flora watched with lifeless eyes as it seeped into the wood, making a pretty stain that would never come out.

She let out a breath, allowing herself one moment of guilt, one plea of forgiveness to the Gods, and pulled the shutters down over her heart. They had work to do.

Chapter Twenty

Beware the Pitch Woods, for those who enter never return.

Fear the Pitch King, for he will cause you endless pain and suffering.

Avoid the monsters and beasts, for they will tear you limb from limb.

Run from the ghosts, who haunt the living for the misfortunes of their past.

The Pitch Woods are for those who wish for a painful death, so, if you find yourself on the border between light and dark, be sure, and choose wisely as your life will be on the line.

-A sign in the square of the town outside the Pitch Woods.

The sun rose and fell twice more before they reached the last town before the Pitch Woods. Much to her surprise and relief, they encountered no other problems. There were no more criminals or highway robbers to mercilessly kill. There were also no kidnappers or residents who recognized her and decided to take matters into their own hands and attempt to give her to the King. They had a peaceful journey Flora cherished as the Pitch Woods' shadowy darkness rose in the distance.

She could almost feel the spectral tendrils against her skin, the blotted-out sun and cool air. She could almost *smell* the dark, the heavy and thick cloying scent that only dissipated when light burned it away. She didn't mind the smell usually—she enjoyed it in the comfort of her bedroom—but the thought of smelling it and feeling the darkness press against her skin in the Pitch Woods caused her heart to sputter.

Besides the dark, it was the first truly magical place she would enter. The Pitch Woods and the Sage Woods, home to a sorcerer with beasts, and a witch with creatures. Both places so uncharted, and so concentrated with magic she was a contrasting bundle of excited and scared. Her heart tugged back and forth, beating out of her chest with fear one second, and dancing with excitement the next.

The horse slowed as they entered the town. Flora stared wide-eyed at the shacks made out of buckling wood and crumbling stone. They were few and far between, and only appeared to have a couple of shops. It looked vastly underpopulated—she couldn't imagine who would want to live so close to the living darkness, to the fear and threat of being consumed by something more monstrous than your imagination could conjure.

The streets were barren, but faint lights glowed inside buildings in the dim lighting. The sun had risen a couple of hours ago, but dark clouds shoved the sun into a cave. Flora hoped it would be released before they entered the Pitch Woods so she could bask in the bright light and warmth one last time before journeying into the darkness beyond.

"Here we are, the Last Town," Kaanan said, throwing his arm wide.

"What's it called?" Anise asked, peering out of the buggy.

"The Last Town—it's very uninspired, but it's accurate. It's the last town before darkness, before finding the beasts and monsters that go bump in the night," Kaanan said, his voice dropping an octave at the end as he teased the two nervous girls.

"Ha ha," Anise said with a roll of her eyes.

"We just need a couple of things, and then we can be on our way," Kaanan said, steering the horses to the stables.

The three ventured into the town, Anise and Flora trailing behind Kaanan as he moved through the streets with long strides and a confident aura. He led them through the complicated twists and turns, like it was built to confuse any beasts that may venture too close. Kaanan stopped outside a small, rundown building with a thick padlock holding the door securely closed. Flora was about to ask what this place was when Kaanan leaned closer to the door, shielding it from view with his cloak.

Flora frowned, and then directed Anise's attention to a building behind them while she stood on her tiptoes and watched over Kaanan's shoulder as he conjured a shadow key and inserted it into the lock. It fell open with an audible click and then the smoke vanished into thin air just as Anise turned back.

"Stay here," he said, and then slipped inside before they could argue.

"What do you think is in there?" Flora asked, staring at the warped wood of the door.

"Who knows—hopefully nothing to trick us with," Anise muttered, arms crossed over her chest as Flora frowned at her.

"He's not a bad guy. He helped us. We could have

died with those robbers."

Anise sighed. "I know. I just don't trust him. He gives me a weird vibe and I don't like how he separates us."

"Anise," Flora said, her chest tight as she toyed with her next words. She didn't want to hurt Anise's feelings, but Flora felt the need to make something clear with her. So much had changed and the two hadn't been able to discuss something that had been weighing on Flora, and for once, her tongue felt loose, and her anxiety wasn't holding her back. "I can be your best friend and be his friend too. Just like you can have other friends besides me."

"I know, but is it so bad that I don't want you to?" Anise's shoulders caved in as Flora dropped her gaze.

"We have to grow up eventually and growing up means expanding. I love you, and I always want you by my side, but...I don't think it's so awful if we include others, too." Flora hugged her arms to her body, eyes watching the ground as she couldn't quite meet Anise's eyes.

"Hey," Anise said, tugging one of Flora's arms loose. "I'll work on it. I don't want to lose you either and as much as I don't approve—I see how you look at him."

Flora blushed, burning scarlet encasing her cheeks. "I...I don't know what you're talking about."

"*Flora*, if you can't tell me, who can you tell?"

"We're...just friends—he's out of my league anyways."

Anise sent her a knowing smirk. "I don't think so, but we can discuss it later, when there's no chance of him overhearing," she said, jerking her head toward the door. Flora nodded, and Anise smiled before wrapping Flora in a tight hug.

That was how Kaanan found them moments later, arms squeezing each other as their chins rested on each other's shoulders. Flora jerked them apart as he locked the door before shooting them a dark smirk.

"Ready to see where nightmares are made?"

****

The Pitch Woods loomed before Flora, the shadowy tendrils wafting in the breeze, crawling along the ground, reaching for untainted land, waiting for something to get close enough to snatch. It was an ink stain on Woodvale, perfectly dark and frightful. But even with the pitch reaching for her, she could see faint glowing lights inside, catching her eye and drawing her forward.

Her ankle was a low warmth, telling her there was a shard in the woods. According to legends, the Pitch Woods went on for eternity, which meant it was a daunting task ahead of her. Flora was an uncomfortably masochistic mix of fevered exhilaration and terror. She was just so *curious* about what was inside those pitch-black trees. Was it monsters like everyone said? Was it new plants, ones she had never dared dream of? Was there magic so potent you could taste it?

She was desperate to step a foot inside and see for herself, but her feet were glued to the solid, normal ground of Myrkurden. No magic, just deadened, dry dirt—relatively safe in the embrace of her dying land.

A low cry echoed from the trees, causing Flora and Anise to flinch. A growl resounded and a scream of agony flitted through the woods as a murder of crows weaved in and out of the tree line. Flora and Anise's eyes locked, both wide and with clenched jaws as fear blanketed their hearts. Flora glanced over at Kaanan and found him staring at the Pitch Woods with a rapt and longing gaze.

"Should we...should we go in?" Flora asked, voice wavering and throat tightening around the words.

"Yes," he rasped, like he was a dehydrated man and the darkened forest was the only water in sight. He coughed, breaking him out of his reverie, and turned to the girls. "Stick close to me, and whatever you do, whatever you see, do not stray from my side."

Flora nodded and turned to Anise, her face ashen and taut—Flora had never seen her look so scared. Flora reached for Anise's hand and held it tight in hers as the two girls followed Kaanan and his billowing cloak closer toward the tree line. Flora and Anise paused before their toes could step into the shadowy black while Kaanan immediately glided inside. His entire body grew lighter, shoulders softening, like staying in the sun was a struggle and he was finally home, where he belonged—in the shadows and eternal night.

"Together?" Anise asked, voice steady but weak.

"Together."

And with that, Flora and Anise stepped past the border, into the black of the Pitch Woods. The air was thicker inside the Woods, a weight pressing down on Flora's body and lungs as she struggled to adapt to the change. Her eyes were spotting, not quite yet able to make shapes out in the dark. But as she scanned her surroundings, she could make out faint colors and glows from afar, and her legs almost propelled her forward to discover what it was before her brain caught up and locked her legs to where she stood—she had to stay close to Kaanan.

Notes of wet, damp earth and floral tones drifted into her senses, and she breathed in deep before sighing in happiness. While Flora was scared witless of monsters or beasts that may be lurking, her heart beating erratically, the Pitch Woods at least *smelled* good. There were plants and flowers to explore—a thought that sent music humming to Flora's ears.

She turned to look at Woodvale one last time, but it was covered in a sheet of shadow. The second her body had stepped over the border, a wall of twilight blotted out most of Myrkurden. She could faintly make out dried earth, but not very well. She understood how so many had gotten lost in the woods—it practically swallowed them whole. The thought sent a shiver racing down Flora's spine.

But she trusted Kaanan as much as she could after knowing him for a short period of time. She believed he would escort them safely through the Pitch Woods and back out because ultimately, she was only useful if she got back *all* the shards. Regardless of the kind smiles and soft touches, of the glances that spoke hints of a promise of *more*, Flora doubted as much as she hoped for. She was still a pawn, one he had vowed to keep safe until she fulfilled her destiny.

Her eyes adjusted to the dark enough that she could make out more shapes in detail, and Flora scanned for Kaanan. She found him pressing his bare palm to a tree and caressing the rough bark and whispering something under his breath.

"What now?" Anise said, her voice too loud in the silence, like she broke a spell of peace with her words.

Kaanan's head whipped toward her, and he thrust one finger up to his lips as she reared back. Flora wrapped her arm around Anise's as he tilted his head and scanned the dense forest around them.

"Be silent, and limit your speaking—you'll attract unwanted company," he said under his breath and Flora frowned.

"Can't you…you know." She flicked her eyes toward Anise and tried to will him to understand. A small smirk played on his lips and his eyes glimmered with barely concealed amusement.

"Yes and no. I'm not perfect, and if we attract too many threats, I may not be fast enough to save you. Understand?" They both nodded with faintly quivering bodies.

While Anise surveyed their surroundings, body tense at each rustle of underbrush, Flora watched Kaanan. He closed his eyes briefly, his fingers steepling before they fell apart and his eyes snapped open. Flora almost jumped back at the sight—his eyes were more shadowed than usual, like they were swarming with twilight.

Flora and Anise jumped at a crow cawing overheard, and Kaanan finally nodded to them after a pregnant pause. Flora watched him as he walked a pace in front of them. He kept one hand at his side, slightly extended from his body, and was constantly twirling his wrist and fingers like he was controlling something. Flora assumed he was manipulating the shadows and forest with his magic, helping them along.

In addition to watching Kaanan, Flora watched the land with rapt fascination. The Pitch Woods were dense with towering and thick trees, shrubs and roots littering the surrounding ground. They had to be careful where they stepped, a struggle in the dark, but Flora moved instinctively. She had spent so much time in the trees she could speak their language of growth.

Flora's eyes found the glow from earlier and she almost fell from the amazement coursing through her limbs at the sight. Beautiful, blooming flowers grew near the path Kaanan was leading them down. A faint smell of lemon hit Flora's nose and her mouth watered as her eyes drank in the flower. It was a moonflower, boldly white and healthy, and Flora didn't know if she had ever seen such a beautiful sight. Right in front of her, healthy flowers grew in the eternal night of the Pitch Woods when in her world, it was a continuous barren wasteland. It was incredible and *magical*.

"Flora," Anise hissed, tugging on her arm. Flora had stopped moving, and she jerked to attention and followed Anise, glancing back at the flowers a couple times before they faded from view.

Kaanan had stopped too and was gazing at the brush in rapt attention. Flora sidled up next to him. "Is everything okay?" she asked softly.

"No. Be alert. Something is coming," he said, his eyes boring into hers. She could make out a ferocious heat in his eyes she hadn't seen before, his jaw locked tight.

"Okay," Flora whispered, and Anise hooked their arms together again.

Before they could move, branches and roots snapping echoed like cracking thunder through the trees, and Flora's heart dropped as her lungs froze. The ground rumbled beneath her feet, and the trees to the left swung and shook from the force of *something* coming their way. Flora's heart stalled and with an inhuman cry racing through the trees, she almost dropped to the ground from sheer terror at the sight storming into view.

Chapter Twenty-One

One of the many things to fear in the Pitch Woods is a creature so large and powerful, mere mortals have almost no hope if they encounter it. It will burn you to a crisp before devouring your body in one swift chomp.

Magic is one way to defeat it, but if you're reading this book, you don't have it.

So, if you wish to have any hope of defeating it, travel in a group you have good synergy with, keep a close watch on the situation, and be strong enough to impart damage.

What is it, you ask? It is a surprise for those who travel unprepared, but if you prepare, if you know your lore, you already know the answer—so be brave and be strong, or you will most certainly die a quick, but painful death.

-From the one guidebook on the Pitch Woods in all of Woodvale (one of the least circulated books in Vale Centre's Library)

The crashing, cracking, and vibrating continued in time with Flora's heart roaring in her ears. Flora's hand found Kaanan's and he gave it a quick squeeze before unsheathing the sword from his back and stepping forward, planting himself between the oncoming storm and her. Flora's protests died in her throat when *it* came into view again. But it couldn't be—it wasn't possible.

The creatures had died centuries ago and were now

only stories or warnings about acts of character. No one had caught sight of one in at least one hundred years—they had gone extinct along with all the other mythical creatures. But the Sormurinn were still alive, and if the seaworms could still be alive, then maybe in the depths of other places normally left undisturbed could also house creatures everyone thought were extinct.

Flora knew the Pitch Woods housed monsters, but she always assumed they were the garden-variety monsters you find under your bed or lurking around a corner—shadowy with sharp teeth and a thirst for blood and human flesh. But there, thundering through the trees, the trunks bending unnaturally, was a beast Flora assumed she would only experience in folktales.

A dragon.

"I...I thought dragons were extinct?" Flora asked shakily.

"Not in the Pitch Woods—this breed is native here, among a host of other creatures."

The dragon was closer now, and Flora could make out smoke clouds blowing from the flaring nostrils and inky black scales shining in the dark. Flora desperately tried to recollect any stories about dragons, so she could help defeat the one about to eat or burn them, but all she could remember was that they breathed fire and had almost indestructible scales.

"A dragon! How is it here?" Anise cried, gripping Flora's arm tight.

"Dragons are a common feature in the Pitch Woods. They're intelligent creatures that love to test a traveler's strengths and capabilities," Kaanan replied, eyes not moving from the dragon lumbering toward them.

"So, it won't eat us?" Anise asked, her voice wavering.

"No—they will eat you and burn you alive—they just like to play with their food first," he said with a dark tone. "Just follow my lead."

"What are its strengths and weaknesses?" Flora asked, clutching her shards as she tried to think of a plan.

"It can breathe fire and…we call it Nite. If it's not breathing fire then it's breathing this noxious gas that's pitch black and will cover you in absolute darkness, making you horribly tired so their prey is weak."

"How the Hell do we fight it then?" Anise cried, her body taut as the dragon got closer, trying to tug Flora farther behind Kaanan.

"I told you—follow my lead and don't do anything stupid," he said to her, tone so harsh, Flora flinched. "Stay out of the way." Her movement caught his attention, and when their eyes connected, he softened and said, "I'll keep you safe. Trust me and let me handle it."

"Okay," Flora said and watched him as he stepped closer to the dragon.

"How are you supposed to fight off a dragon? You're one person!" Anise cried, but Kaanan ignored her.

Flora watched as he straightened his spine, black cloak falling into a cave around his body as the dragon reached them. It was so much bigger up close, and Flora's heart stopped beating at the sight, like her stark terror had just murdered her in cold blood. But then it beat again in her ears, rapidly fast and loud, drowning out the crashing trees.

Kaanan held his hands together before he extended his arms to the side, elbows jutting up as the shadows crawled toward him. Anise gasped beside her, and as she suspected Anise might do something foolish, her hand snapped out and caught Anise by the wrist, keeping her in place. As the shadows crawled and creeped toward Kaanan, forming a cylinder of darkness around him, Flora came up with her own plan, a way to ensure Kaanan would be okay after going toe to toe with a ginormous murderous beast.

But she was too late.

The dragon released a ferocious roar, smoke billowing from its flared nostrils, sending Flora's heart tumbling down to her toes. Kaanan held strong, feet planted firmly into the ground as his body tensed, lips moving rapidly and shadows creeping faster toward him.

The dragon reared on its hindlegs, making Flora's stomach drop and cry out, "Kaanan!"

Her voice made him instantly turn to her, their eyes locking—Flora's wide and wild with fear and his calm and dark like the sea after a storm. In one moment, she felt like everything would work out, that Kaanan had the situation under control and he would be fine. Except, she made a foolish decision without thinking, one that distracted him too greatly. In a blink, the tables turned and Flora felt an invisible knife pierce her middle as she witnessed what came next. In the second he turned, the dragon had all the advantage it needed because Flora had *stupidly* distracted him.

Kaanan released a bloodcurdling cry as the dragon slashed him with wicked-sharp claws. It connected with his arm, rocketing him off his feet as he grabbed at the wound, a dark substance already oozing and dripping onto the forest floor. His face changed, melding from calm to fury incarnate. He rose, whirling on the dragon and resuming his vigil.

Flora started to move forward of her own accord before Anise grabbed her, dragging her back out of harm's way. Flora shook her off roughly before straightening her shoulders—she would help Kaanan. She couldn't stand by and do nothing. She had power. All she had to do was use it, call upon it and ask for help to save the boy she liked from death. Flora clutched her two shards and extracted them from the confines of her shirt. As they glinted in the almost non-existent light, she focused her attention on the roots and ground near the dragon's feet that exploded with sharp, jagged claws.

As the shadows accumulated around Kaanan, Flora imagined ivy shooting out of the dark ground and winding around the dragon's ankles and legs. Her entire body thrummed in green again, her magic coursing steadily through her veins as pops of dark emerald sprouted from the forest floor. Flora was expecting them to be black, like the trees and the other plants besides the flowers, but they were green.

The ivy wound around one of the dragon's ankles as Kaanan stepped closer, shadows hovering in the space around him as he snapped his fingers at the dragon. The beast immediately cast its fiery gaze on Kaanan, but it didn't hold it. The dragon's eyes jerked around, looking for something, and Flora flinched when its gaze landed on her. Its eyes narrowed, and smoke huffed from its snout as Flora rapidly tried to get her magic to work faster. Another bout of ivy burst from the packed earth and adhered to the dragon's other leg.

A strong gust of wind whipped Flora's hair around her face and rippled Kaanan's cloak roughly as the dragon roared in anger. But, to Flora's surprise, it didn't start spewing fire or Nite. A thin strip of shadow wound itself around the dragon's snout, effectively muzzling the beast.

Flora caught wind of whispered words in an unfamiliar language from a more guttural version of Kaanan's voice. She stepped forward, Anise glued to her arm again, and watched as the summoned shadows convulsed on the dragon in a ferocious force. Darkness wrapped around the dragon's entire body, creating a column of pitch black shooting high into the sky as a sickly-sweet floral note filled the air, with a slight rotten undertone.

One second, the patch of darkened forest they occupied was full of fright and a monstrously large dragon. In the next, shadows encased everything in a blanket of dark before rushing together in a swirling column and dissipating with a soundless blast.

The forest before them was empty save for bent trees, crushed brush, and trampled flowers and roots. The dragon was gone at first glance, but upon closer inspection, Flora noticed a flapping of scaly, leathery wings. A now bird-sized dragon flapped its wings in the air, shooting the three a dark, malicious glare with the promise for revenge before flying away into the thick brush.

The ivy that restrained the dragon slithered to one of the bent trees, before it climbed up the thick limb and righted it. She dropped her shards as they burned her skin—she hadn't realized her magic was still actively following her desires. She wanted to return the forest to its rightful, unbroken state before the dragon appeared, but she hadn't realized she could use her magic to do it without much effort. Although, she could feel her magic slipping away before she could do more, receding back to its dormant state as the threat and sheer panic left Flora in a ragged exhale of breath.

"What the Hell was that?" Anise shrieked, pulling herself roughly from Flora's grasp. She backed away from Kaanan, and Flora could imagine how fast her heart was racing, how desperate it was to escape its boned cage. She had never seen Anise so terrified before.

"It's okay," Flora said, keeping her voice calm and low, but it didn't work. Anise's agitation grew as she thrust her hands into her hair and gripped her skull. Flora turned to her other counterpart with softened eyes. "Are you okay, Kaanan?" Her voice wobbled on the last bit, and he nodded shakily at her, hand pressing against the wound leaking blood down his body.

"It is not okay! Did you not *see* that!" Anise shouted, eyes bugging from their sockets as she struggled to take a deep breath before she rounded on Kaanan. "What *are* you? Who are you?"

"You know exactly who and what I am, Anise. Honestly, I haven't done a high-effort job of pretending otherwise. You're not stupid, and I know you already know—so let's not play any games, all right?" Kaanan said, cool and collected as he kept pressure on his arm and leaned against one of the unbroken trees behind him.

Anise stared at him, her eyes wide as she released a ragged breath. The words were so quiet coming off her tongue, Flora barely caught them, but catch them she did, and it changed *everything*.

"You're the Pitch King."

Flora jerked upright at the words, her eyes flying to Kaanan accusatorily. His eyes weren't on Anise like she expected—they were already waiting for her reaction, for her questioning gaze to come darting over to him. Her concern for his arm disintegrated at the words.

"Well?" Anise snapped, arms crossing over her chest. "Are you the Pitch King or aren't you?"

But Kaanan didn't answer and his eyes didn't so much as flicker a millimeter away from Flora. She stared at him, a pit in her stomach and heart deathly still. It couldn't be true. He was just the Pitch King's apprentice—not the Pitch King himself. Flora couldn't believe it. If it were true, it would change the entirety of their relationship, the bones of the friendship they were building. It would *destroy* her. If he was the Pitch King, that meant he lied to her for weeks, stringing her along like a fool and pretending to be a sweet, caring man when he was a monster in disguise, vile rot writhing underneath his saccharine coating.

"Kaanan?" Flora whispered, her voice weak as it held a thousand questions she couldn't dare her lips to form. His gaze flared, an undecipherable emotion passing across the dark orbs before disappearing into the shadows.

His lips parted as he released a shaky sigh before he ran a hand through his luscious strands, pushing away from the tree and coming closer to the two girls.

"Stop right there!" Anise cried, flinging one arm out toward Kaanan and the other across Flora's chest, guiding her backward.

"Flora," he said, voice like silk, and while his next words sounded genuine, she wasn't sure she believed him. "I'm so sorry."

"It's true?" she asked, lip wobbling as tears stung her eyes. She couldn't reconcile such a seemingly sweet person with the horrors she had heard, and she couldn't bear her trust shattering so thoroughly.

"I never wanted to lie to you. It was never my intention, but I knew you wouldn't understand, wouldn't believe me unless I proved it."

"What are you talking about?" Anise interjected.

"I am very sorry for the lie, but I felt it necessary, and if you could let me explain fully, then we can move past it. I know we can," he said, his desperate tone pleading. "Just let me explain."

"Oh my Gods, just answer the question! Are. You. The. Pitch. King?" Anise said, holding Flora tight to her.

He hesitated, his eyes never leaving her, before a single word escaped his lips that devastated Flora's world, stopped her heart, and crushed her soul, a moment she would relive over and over as she struggled to move past it, struggled to forgive the lie that changed every single idea and feeling she had about him.

"Yes," Kaanan said, his chin dipping lower, voice dripping with something akin to what sounded like shame. "I am the Pitch King."

Chapter Twenty-Two

Similar to Vale Centre, Pitch City is built in circular strokes with a palace lording over the streets below, an apex of power. However, unlike Vale Centre, Pitch City has no interest in maze-like streets. Only one city is a labyrinth meant to trap and the other is full of unexpected happiness.

-An Adventurer's Guide to Woodvale: The Pitch Woods by Gísli (Gísli's last manuscript, unpublished and hidden in Pitch City with the author)

He had lied to her. She couldn't believe it, couldn't reconcile the information in her head. How could he have lied to her?

Kaanan was really the Pitch King, which meant he was a monster, a cruel, ruthless man capable of atrocities Flora could barely even dream of. He killed without thought, siccing his beasts on innocent people who dared walk too close to his Woods. He was the stuff nightmares were made of, a cautionary tale for all those who started to stray into darkness. He was a powerful sorcerer capable of acts no one knew.

Except, none of that sounded right. She knew all the warning tales of the Pitch King, knew you should run if you ever encountered him, but this was *Kaanan*. Kaanan wasn't cruel or ruthless, at least not without cause. He was a powerful sorcerer consisting mostly of shadow magic, but he turned his beast of a dragon into a miniscule version to save her. He was kind, and thoughtful, and prioritized Flora's safety and happiness multiple times without being asked, and she didn't think it was just because he wanted her magic. Flora knew she had little chance with him, and she wouldn't trust that he liked her the way she liked him even if he told her. But she also wasn't completely blind—the way he looked at her, the way he treated her were not the actions of a man whose sole purpose was to use her for his own personal gain.

Her brain was a mess of mixed emotions, a jumble of conflicting thoughts that raced around her mind so fast it was dizzying. Her heart felt like it had been punched, now full of bruises and broken blood vessels seeping into the rest of her body. Her limbs were weak and sore, and her head ached fiercely. Her eyes had been watering constantly, but she refused to let the tears track down her cheeks, to let him know just how deep his betrayal cut her.

Part of her wanted to never speak to him again, to forget he existed and move on. He had his chance at trust, and he broke it. She could write him off. She didn't like to give people second chances for them to shatter the heart they bruised or broke. But Flora knew she wouldn't cut him off this time. She already knew the second after he confirmed his betrayal. Because when she heard those words, she was already making excuses, forgiving the slight and trying to understand why he lied. She needed to talk with him for her to actually move past it and forgive him, let him fully explain his side of things. Flora knew in her cracked heart she had fallen too deep to drag herself back out without a better reason. And really, she *wanted* to know his side of things because she was starting to wholeheartedly believe there was far more to this than what met the eye.

It scared her, that she liked him so much, that she *wanted* to trust him, wanted to forgive him because she liked the way he treated her. She liked that they could talk without her feeling like she would throw up or her tongue had shriveled up and died. She loved that she didn't spiral or overthink as much in his presence. He emitted a calm sweetness she wanted to coat herself in.

But she couldn't forgive him too easily; she knew that. They had to discuss things like adults and decide how to move past it together. More than that, she needed to hear his side, to hear his plans and desires, to know that they lined up with her hopes and assumptions.

Oh Gods.

A river of worry and fear tore through her veins. What if he wasn't the Kaanan she knew at all? She assumed he was still *her* Kaanan in the sense of personality because she couldn't imagine he could lie and deceive so well for that long. She gnawed at her lip, glancing at his broad back, and felt her stomach sink, because she was no longer sure. She may be wrong about her assumptions, and that would absolutely shatter her already bruised and certainly splintered heart. She prayed he was her Kaanan at heart, at his core, and in his soul. She could reconcile him being Kaanan *and* the Pitch King—probably—but she couldn't bear it if the Kaanan she knew was a lie and he was *only* the Pitch King, ruthless monster.

A loud crack of a twig snapping shoved Flora out of her reeling mind and back into the real world. Crows cawed and branches rustled as the twig broke the entire forest out of its stupor.

She tried to breathe evenly—everything was a mess. But she could handle it, and it would all work out eventually. She just had to keep her head on straight and try not to dwell in the negativity.

Flora struggled to register her surroundings on their trek through the rest of the woods. But with a push at all of her problems, she found she could focus enough so she wouldn't be walking blind. Kaanan had briefly said he was taking them somewhere they could rest before setting out to find the shard. She sighed heavily as the birthmark on her ankle remained in a lukewarm vise around her limb. They were at least in the right part of the Pitch Woods, but according to her ankle, she was still a ways away. It was growing slightly warmer, so she held out hope they would find it sooner rather than later as the darkness of the woods was beginning to reflect poorly on Flora's constitution. It felt like the eternal black was pressing down on her, stifling any brightness and happiness as she wallowed in self-pity.

Kaanan kept one hand extended away from him, twirling his fingers in the breeze as shadows surrounded them in a low fence. The shadows were alive with the will from their master, moving at his beck and call. They formed a dense barrier around them, protecting them from the dangers the Pitch Woods harbored. He kept his wounded arm locked tight against his body, hidden beneath his cloak, but with the way his face tensed with a wrong movement, he hurt more than he let on.

He had more power than he had previously divulged—it was practically thrumming from him in black waves of undiluted magic. Flora could taste the floral, sweet, and rotten undertones. While his magic was a mix of honeyed and putrid, Flora always felt her magic to be fresh, floral, and earthy. She longed to talk with him about it, ask him a million questions and get informative answers back. But first, they had to reach a safe location, and she needed to be alone with him. If they talked in front of Anise, they would get nowhere. Anise would only be happy with Kaanan's head on a spike and crows pecking out his eyes.

"Are you okay?" Anise whispered.

"I don't know," Flora said, shaking her head as they followed Kaanan blindly, dodging jutting roots and uneven earth that attempted to trip them.

They walked in silence for a few more minutes before Anise almost fell flat on her face on a particularly nefarious root. She righted herself before she huffed, hands flying to her hips as she glared daggers at Kaanan's still moving form. "Are we almost there?" she asked, full volume. He whipped around, eyes dark and face drawn taut, no hint of the smirk in sight, making Flora pout unconsciously.

"What did I say about speaking," he said, eyebrows raising as he bared his teeth at Anise.

"We've been walking for *hours*. When are we going to get to wherever you're taking us, *Your Highness*," Anise hissed, a ferocious snarl blooming on her lips. Flora leaned against the tree behind her, watching the scene unfold as she inhaled the earthy notes. The trunk was covered in a soft, dark moss that she ran her hands over in a rhythmically soothing motion.

"Your Highness? Really?" he said, scoffing.

"You're not my subject."

"Aw, but I thought your type were all the same—everyone has to call you by your title."

"Call me what you want—just do it quietly," he said, teeth gritted as the shadows pulsed around them. Anise pouted, displeased he wouldn't dignify her with a battle of snarls and jeers.

"How much longer?" Flora asked softly. Kaanan's gaze slid to hers, his eyes softening. Flora's cheeks warmed and she desperately willed the blood to go away.

"Not much longer, I promise—it's just another hour at most," he said, voice soft and gentle when he spoke to her, such a stark difference to his harsh and snapping tone at Anise.

Flora nodded and pushed off the tree. She linked her arm with Anise's and the three set off again. She just needed to get through their walk, and then she could talk with Kaanan, try to make sense of the situation, try to understand how *he* was the Pitch King.

****

The outside of Pitch City took Flora's breath away, stealing it away into the dark of eternal night and shadow, never to be seen again.

One second, the trees were thick and dense, not letting any ounce of Pitch City be seen as the trees blanketed the forest in a wall of shadow. But then, a faint glow in the distance appeared, tricking Flora into thinking it was another flower. As they got closer, she saw it was coming from a lantern. Gilded metal shone against the flickering flame and Flora's ankle sparked to life. She sighed in relief that her ankle was still working, confirming they were still going in the right direction.

The three passed the lantern and walked into another world. One step, they were in thick trees, and the next they were in a clearing that sloped before stopping at a broad cobblestone wall painted black. Trees circled the obsidian stones, encasing the city, making it nearly impossible to find against the midnight dark.

Flora cast her gaze up, eyes trailing over each nook and dent of cobblestone before cresting the top where she could discern a faint glow over the towering wall. She couldn't make out any of the city beyond, but excitement hummed through her veins.

"This way," Kaanan said softly, touching her elbow with the faintest pressure to direct her attention to the right. She wished he had grabbed her, given her an excuse for them to walk arm-in-arm again, but he respected the gaping distance between them, a chasm ever-so-vast.

They walked against the wall, and Flora trailed her fingers over the smooth stones before the wall changed abruptly, giving way to an ornately carved obsidian door. It was one of the most beautifully crafted objects Flora had ever seen. The intricate detail was enrapturing, full of swirling designs of shadows, plants, flowers, beasts, and people.

"Wow," Flora breathed, eyes scanning over every inch of the towering door.

"It's the tale of Pitch City," Kaanan said, voice rumbling down her spine with how close he stood.

"Really?"

"Yes. My ancestor had it commissioned a few years after the city was created, after people started to thrive here instead of just surviving."

Flora swallowed thickly, a thousand questions rising to the tip of her tongue, but it was so hard to choose just one. She opened her mouth to say something when Kaanan held up his hand, stopping her in her tracks.

"I will answer any questions you have, but first, we need to get into the city—to a secure location, all right?" he asked gently, and Flora nodded.

Kaanan cupped his hands to his mouth and made a series of bird calls directed up to the watchtower. Flora and Anise raised their eyebrows at one another and waited as movement reverberated above them. A call sounded back, and Kaanan chirped once more before a creaking groan filled the air. The heavy ornate door began to open slowly. Once it was ajar a few inches and big enough for bodies to slip through, the creaking stopped, and Kaanan turned to them.

"Come on," he said, gesturing them forward and the three slipped through the dark crack and into a place few people had ever dared to venture.

A cobblestone street welcomed them, and a long corridor of buildings with half-lit lanterns. So far, it looked like a normal city entrance to Flora, not that she had ventured into many cities. The buildings were made out of wood, clay, or stone, all painted in shades of black or dark gray, each one in perfect condition.

"Why are they all so dark?" Flora asked, her fingers trailing on the smooth stone as her ears pricked when she heard the faint lilts of music.

"So we don't attract any unwanted visitors."

"But why?" Flora's brow furrowed.

"Because if outsiders think this is a city, a place

they may find refuge, the secret will be out. The Woods are dangerous and the people who live here are private. None of us want more citizens unless they're born and raised. Outsiders only bring trouble, and if they're from Woodvale, they'll destroy this safe haven with their bottomless greed." Kaanan's jaw snapped shut and Flora nodded. It made sense to her—if the city was alive in bright and bold colors, it would definitely attract more attention. Although, her curiosity was still piqued, still primed and wondering as they wandered.

"This way."

Kaanan led them down the road, not a soul in sight, until the lane of buildings ended and opened into a large square full of people dressed in all colors, though most wore something dark. Music threaded through the square from a band playing as vendors sold goods and mouthwatering food from stalls. Flora inhaled deeply at the notes of fried dough and spices, her mouth salivating as she stared with parted lips and wide eyes at the market.

"Welcome to Pitch City," Kaanan said, throwing an arm wide as he watched Flora and her reaction.

"It's beautiful," she breathed, eyes roaming over each and every person and crevice.

She couldn't believe the smiles on people's faces and the laughter floating high in the air. She assumed the home of the Pitch King would have to be dark and dreary, full of bleak faces and terror. But she found none of that—instead, the pure opposite. Her eyes glistened and a small smile formed on her lips as she finally rested her gaze on Kaanan. He was watching her raptly, eyes not moving an inch from her face.

"Do you really think so?" he asked, and Flora

nearly melted. He asked it with such a vulnerable tone and expression, and she couldn't bear it. Was he lying to her? Faking being nice and sweet? The ambiguity was driving her mad—she couldn't go on like this much longer. Her veins were buzzing with impatient and frenzied energy underneath her skin.

"Yes," she said. "But we do need to talk."

"I know," he said. "We'll stay at my home and rest for the night. Then we can figure out next moves tomorrow." And then softly, just to her as he moved closer, "We can talk once we get settled tonight, if you want—if it's all right with you."

Flora nodded, and as Anise hooked their arms together, they followed Kaanan around the square, people stopping and greeting him with broad, bright smiles. He greeted each person by name and asked after their welfare. And Flora felt eternally confused—how could such a seemingly *kind* person have such a monstrous reputation? She knew there were many instances where tarnished reputations were falsified, when there was so much more to a person—or plant, in Flora's expertise—than what was presented on the surface. But something about the Kaanan she knew, and the Pitch King she had heard countless stories about, was a broken bridge she couldn't connect.

Kaanan bought them the spiced fried dough Flora smelled, along with juicy meat that melted in her mouth before they departed, her stomach full and tongue tingling with the lingering delicious flavors. They traveled for several more minutes through less lively cobblestone streets before reaching a wrought-iron gate protecting a tall obsidian castle. It was smaller than King Desmond's palace, but it was without a doubt a palace. There were turrets and midnight ivy crawled up the ebony blocks, snaking around dark stained-glass windows. Beside the castle, attached with twisted limbs of dark metal, was a dome of foggy glass. Flora's eyes danced over the building, making out several birds swooping inside the aviary. She saw crows and ravens, their inky feathers stark against the glass, the majestic birds that seemed to follow Kaanan wherever he went.

Kaanan led them inside the gate, through a courtyard with a variety of flowers Flora longed to inspect. Alas, he ushered them onward through another ornately carved door into his home. Flora's mouth was agape as he led them through halls filled with plush carpet in deep scarlet tones and shelves that held various relics and books. Near the door was an adorned archway leading to a room cavernous and dark, swathed in shadows and luxury, a large throne at the far end of the room that gleamed white from the hall's light. They passed by a dusty dining room and gilded study before he led them up a flight of stairs covered in velvet carpet. The entire castle was decorated in deep red and black, with the occasional silver or gold piece. It was beautiful, but there was a lifeless, unlived-in undertone to every room.

He deposited Anise in front of an embellished wooden door. She hesitated in the doorway, caught between her distrust of Kaanan and longing for the soft bed she had fantasized to Flora about as they ate. Flora gave Anise a reassuring smile, urging her inside before following Kaanan down the hall. He stopped at the very end where a towering set of elaborate ebony doors lay, before veering to another carved wooden door just a foot before. He held the door open for Flora and she walked into an explosion of life.

Chapter Twenty-Three

A long time ago, before any of us were born, this forest, our dear Pitch Woods, was a place of dark life, of plants and monsters, and the death of humans. It was a place you never went, unless you were interested in dying a painful death, or wanted to become a hero.

Our beloved King's ancestor was the latter—he wanted to be a hero, a conqueror of the Pitch Woods. And while he did just that, he also became a pioneer and savior of the Pitch Woods.

Adrien was a young man with big dreams, and a lion heart. He strode into the Woods with a sword on his back, and vanquished beast after beast before he found other people hiding in the woods, having gotten lost and somehow lucky enough to still be alive.

He took them with him, and they stumbled upon a valley with an obsidian jewel, black as night. When he touched the jewel, it imbued him with magic with which he could control shadows and perform miraculous feats. He looked at the valley, and the people whose lives were in his hands, and with the magical jewel that almost melded into his skin in the center of his chest, he created Pitch City.

It was not the city it is now. It was small, but it was safe and protected.

And so, we owe our lives to the Pitch Family, to our benevolent Kings who always put us first, to respect our wishes of secrecy and make Pitch City the perfect place to live.

-Written account of Pitch City's origin

Kaanan slipped past her and turned on several lanterns to illuminate the compact space as Flora cautiously walked into the room.

The room was much smaller than she had anticipated—he was the King after all—but it was cozy and full of life. Books and plants covered every surface of deep mahogany furniture. Paintings and maps hung on the walls and a small stained-glass window let in the faintest light from the revelry in the City below. It was perfectly representative of Kaanan.

"Please, sit wherever you like," he said, and Flora noted her options: a single, small, neatly made cot, or a worn chair in front of a desk piled high with books and trinkets. Both choices felt personal, but the desk held so much that it exuded *him*. She daintily sat on the edge of his bed, which was closer to her anyways.

"So…" Flora said, a thousand questions dangling from the tip of her tongue in the extended silence. He just watched her, sitting in his desk chair so it faced her, elbows on his kneecaps, face resting in his hands.

" 'So,' indeed," he mused, glancing up to face her, a faint smirk growing before it was extinguished. "I first want to start by apologizing. What I did was unforgiveable, and I know you may not forgive me. I just want you to know I wouldn't blame you—I don't want you to feel guilty about this. I'm so, so sorry for lying to you."

His face was perfectly sincere, and Flora fought against forgiving him immediately because she needed more information. Even though her lovesick, twisted heart wanted to give in right then and there.

"Thank you," Flora said, nodding for him to go on.

"All right, well, what do you want to know?" he asked, holding his hand against his injured arm, which Flora had forgotten in the shock.

"Are you okay?" she asked tentatively, and his eyebrows rose.

"I'm fine. Ask any question you want. Don't be concerned over my arm."

Flora sighed and rose, extending her hand to him. "You're hurt, Kaanan. And Pitch King or not, I feel a sense of obligation as...*friends* to make sure you're all right. So lift the sleeve and let me see."

Kaanan stared at her blankly for a second before he complied, removing his damaged cloak and unbuttoning his shirt. She could see the dark patch on his arm where the blood had seeped. It was adhered to his skin and she winced, knowing how painful it would be to remove the cloth. Flora looked around his room, spotting a small ensuite. She found a cloth near the sink, and a length of gauze and a small flask in the cabinet below, before returning to sit beside Kaanan.

Flora gulped. He had half removed his shirt, exposing a long line of brown, toned skin that had her biting her lip, cheeks flushing, and gaze darting to anywhere but him. She cleared her throat and mentally prepared herself for the challenge of playing nurse.

The wound on his arm was deep and bloody, the claw that connected with him sharp and viciously thick. Flora squeezed the sopping cloth onto the wound, letting the blood wash down his arm before gently patting it. She took the flask and after a quick apology, she poured the pungent alcohol on the wound, causing him to tense and groan under his breath. Flora called upon her magic, summoning a sprig of *Calendula*, mashing it between her palms and spreading it against the wound.

She wrapped the wound with the gauze and secured it with a pin. All the while, a pair of eyes burned a hole into her skull. When she was done, she finally glanced up, their eyes locking. "What?"

He shook his head and said, "Nothing. Just—thank you."

"Anytime," she said with a shrug. "But please try not to get hurt again—I'm not that good of a nurse."

"I think you're a perfect nurse," he said, and she smiled. "But please, I'm sure you have lots of questions and are tired. So, ask away."

Flora took a deep breath and leaned back so their faces weren't almost nose to nose. She bit her lip, racking her brain before settling on something obvious, but something she needed confirmed. "So...you're the Pitch King?"

He sighed with his whole body before saying, "Yes. I am the Pitch King, and please believe me when I say this: I am not the man people think I am."

"You're not a murderous, malicious monster?" Flora asked breathily and he smiled lightly.

"No. I am not. I'm Kaanan and I was more myself the past couple weeks with you than I've been in a while."

"What do you mean?"

"I'm the King. I have responsibilities and things I can't do because I have to stay here and protect my people—it's my duty. But with you," he said, ducking his head so he gazed at her through his thick eyelashes,

"I could be myself; I could forget my responsibilities."

"Okay."

"My ancestors weren't monsters either—well, some were, but not for many years. We're not perfect, and we've all killed before in the name of protecting our City and ourselves, but we're not stone-hearted psychopaths. The rumors and stories about me and my family are lies. When my ancestor first created Pitch City, he made it a safe haven for the people who were trapped here. He ensured the Pitch Woods and City would be protected by creating rumors and scary stories. It worked, and people have mostly left us alone. We can live here and not have to deal with politics or frightening magical feuds. My magic is passed down through our bloodline, like yours, and we're able to control the shadows, and with effort, control the creatures a bit. We have it all under control here, and the people are content. The last thing I want is King Desmond to come in and raze the place."

"That's fair," Flora said. "It sounds like a noble cause, and I think it's smart you lied about yourself and the City. It's dreadful out there, especially King Desmond."

"Thank you. That means a lot to hear, Flora. But I am not that noble." Kaanan smiled softly, before his eyes flashed and the curve of his lips dropped dramatically as a darkly hesitant look settled on his face like a carefully constructed mask. "I will be honest here, Flora. I have killed people and kidnapped them and tricked them, even some that may not have deserved it. I try to do my best, but sometimes my best has to be cruel to get the outcome I want or to protect the people I care about. Please, do not heroize me. I would rather be the villain in the story than bind myself to the rules of the so called 'good.' "

Flora nodded, chewing on her lip. She found his statement didn't bother her as much as it would have before. This trip had exposed her to different things outside and inside herself, and she was able to realize just how gray the world was, and that to survive, things couldn't be black and white. Things had to be gray, or chaos would destroy everyone and everything.

"Please say something?" he said, gazing at her with such a vulnerable expression, Flora melted internally.

"I…don't know what to say. I don't think less of you, Kaanan, I understand why you might feel the need to do that. It doesn't change the way I feel about you," she said, trying to articulate her words as she felt them. "I guess, what I'm trying to say is, I hate that you lied to me, I hate the way you made me feel. But I…like you, and I've enjoyed spending time with you. So, I tentatively forgive you—though you'll have to work to rebuild my trust, if that's something you want to do."

"Really?" he asked, face bright and hopeful.

"Yes." Flora really did mostly forgive him because she believed him. His words sounded sincere, even though they went against a lifetime of being told otherwise. Even though she was well aware if Rosie could see her now, she would be having an aneurysm over Flora's decision to trust Kaanan again. But Flora felt like she knew Kaanan in the ways that mattered most, and it made sense to her why he would lie to everyone. Fear was both a powerful weapon and guard—it was more effective than asking nicely. And she wasn't so crazy as to ignore and blanket everything he had done, the trust he had broken. Kaanan would have to rebuild her trust—she wasn't going to roll over for him. She would see how he behaved in the coming days, see if he was trustworthy and stopped lying to her.

Kaanan gaped at her for a minute before his face cracked into a blinding smile. "Thank you. That means so much more to me than you'll ever know."

Flora flushed, cheeks igniting scarlet as she shyly smiled back.

"So, why did you help me?" Flora asked, the question falling from her lips, unbidden without her express thought. "You…you said the Pitch King wanted my magic."

"He does—I do. Flora, as much as I may detest Woodvale, and the abhorrent greed Desmond has, I want you to fix it. Your magic is valuable, and I want you to fix Woodvale, because…the cursed death is starting to affect my land."

"*What*?"

"I noticed it several weeks ago now, near the border. It was just a small patch, nothing major really, but a leaf on one of the trees had gone brittle and disintegrated in my fingers. I thought it was a one-off, but I found another a couple of weeks ago. So, I went searching for the lost Larkspur Lady, hoping she was still alive," he explained. "I found out who you were, from—actually, I don't think I ever got his name, but he lived in Sanarbre and knew about you somehow. Anyways, I went to your village and found the place ransacked. Then I went to the *Króna* and with some persuasion—mostly after I begged and reminded her of a favor my father did for her—she informed me of your quest. Since Vale Centre was your first stop, I headed there to wait for you."

"But how did you know where we would stay?"

"I didn't—my magic guided me there. It's hard to explain, but as I said, magic is sentient, and a tad omniscient. It led me to you."

"So what now? You're not going to *use* me, are you?" Flora asked, biting her lip and wringing her hands.

"No," he said, voice stern. "I would never dream of using you, Flora. All I want is for you to come into your magic and save Woodvale, as I hope that will save the Pitch Woods. When I went looking for you, I never imagined I'd find I someone whose company I enjoy as much as I do, that we'd share commonalities. You're kind and brave and vivacious in a way I didn't expect. You're beautiful and smart and I hope I haven't ruined everything. You can do what you please, of course. But, I hope we can stay…friends, or whatever this is, but I won't hold you to anything."

"Thank you," Flora breathed, body sinking into the firm mattress as a weight lifted off her shoulders.

Beautiful.

Flora nearly fainted at the word. A heady warmth spread through her belly, tangling through her limbs as a crimson flush splashed across her cheeks. Flora wanted to bask in the compliments, melt into the ground at his feet. But a voice in her head held her back, reminded her that she couldn't let her heart get ahead of itself. Friends called each other beautiful too.

Ice chased away the scarlet flush and Flora twisted her mind back to where it belonged. She could wonder and worry for an eternity whether or not Kaanan liked her as a friend or as something more. But in that moment, Flora had bigger battles to worry about, pressing issues and an hourglass that was rapidly losing sand. Her priority had to be her magic, her mom, and the road ahead. Her future, her feelings and his, could be broached when she wasn't actively dying. If she ever found the courage at all. Time would be the judge on that anxiety-inducing conversation, on the heart she would have to bear on her sleeve to do so.

"You don't have to thank me for that," he said with a smirk and quirked eyebrow.

Flora swallowed thickly and quickly changed the subject as she tried to keep the crimson off her cheeks. "You said magic is sentient—does it ever...talk to you?"

"Yes, it does. It whispers in my mind sometimes, usually when I'm actively using my magic, but sometimes it appears when I'm struggling with something. Magic is a part of you. It's like the blood running through your veins—it's always there, watching, helping—so, it talks to me. Nothing much or anything serious, but I've heard its voice in my mind countless times."

"Good." Flora breathed a sigh of relief. She had hoped that was the case, but there was always the possibility she was going crazy. "It talks to me too—my shards."

"That's good—at least, from my understanding of magic—it means it likes you, is okay with being used and housed by you. It will stick by you unless you do something drastic of course." Flora nodded—it was how it felt in her mind and body, that the magic that had eluded her was clear and strong enough to latch onto her, and apparently didn't hate her the way it must have hated her mother after whatever it was that she did. "Do you have any other questions?"

And Flora did. She asked Kaanan countless questions about him, Pitch City, the Pitch Woods, magic, and everything under the sun she could think of. He told her about his dad and the burden of ruling on his own for four years, trying to do the best for his people. The two spent hours talking, until their eyes were blurry, and yawns filled the space instead of words.

Flora didn't want to say goodnight, didn't want to go to sleep and break the crystalline bubble they had constructed. She felt like she knew Kaanan so well after talking, almost as well as she knew Anise. He was special to her in the way most people weren't. He liked her for who she was, and she could see and believe that now. No matter what happened during the rest of her journey, she didn't want to lose him.

****

A searing pain from her ankle woke Flora the next morning, or what she assumed was morning as the dark sky through her window looked the same as when she went to bed. Her hands clutched her ankle, the pain receding. She frowned; the pain didn't feel like it did when she was near a shard—this was something else. Concern bloomed in the pit already lodged in her stomach.

She crawled out of the plush bed and when her feet hit the floor, she swayed. Flora clutched the edge of the bed, willing her body to fix itself. Her limbs and muscles ached, brittle as a dry twig. Her stomach twisted into knots at the sensation.

Flora couldn't make sense of why her body felt so weak. She knew her ankle was slowly sucking the life out of her, but mentally she was more alive than she ever was. She supposed it could be that her curse was only drawing physical strength and nutrients, leaving her mind active and alive. Flora's face scrunched—that sounded infinitely worse to her, having her mind fully present while her body withered to dust and her heart slowly stopped beating.

Gods, I need to get a grip, she thought firmly to herself, mentally scolding the dark thoughts threatening to flatten her.

There was no use dwelling in the what-ifs—she needed to use her time wisely and focus on retrieving the shards. Flora breathed out deeply, letting every drop of air out of her lungs, before lingering in the emptiness as she tried to put her mind at ease by focusing on something else.

Her room was pretty, with swatches of gold and pale pink on top of blacks and grays. It was bigger than Kaanan's, with a larger bed and untouched furniture, lacking any personality and homey comfort. It was objectively nice, but Flora was used to cozy and lived-in spaces, which was why she liked Kaanan's room so much. When she asked why his room was so small, he had told her he didn't need much, and was more comfortable in a smaller room—something Flora found relatable.

Her stomach heaved, sending Flora stumbling to her feet, and as her tongue contracted, she flew to the ensuite, just making it to the porcelain bowl in time for bile to surge out of her. She heaved and vomited until it felt like her insides were no longer there, her forehead was sweaty, and her limbs were even weaker. She swallowed thickly as she lay down on the cool tiles, trying to find strength. But it was hard, and she was so tired.

In the end, she allowed herself ten minutes of wallowing on the cool bathroom floor before she carefully righted herself and got ready for the day. Flora exited her room, ignoring the lingering, faint tremors attacking her body, with her rucksack safely tucked against her back and jolted when a raised fist met her eyes.

"Good morning," Kaanan murmured, lowering the fist he was about to use to knock on her door.

"Good morning," she replied with a smile. He was dressed in his usual head-to-toe black but instead of road-worn, the cuts were crisp and clean. "How is your arm?"

"Much better, many thanks to you," Kaanan said with a bright smile that sent Flora's heart fluttering in its cage of bones.

Kaanan lifted a book in his other hand and pressed it into Flora's waiting fingers. "This is for you. It's the book of folktales I was telling you about."

"Thank you," Flora breathed, running her hands over the smooth leather cover. "I'll read it as fast as I can and get it back to you."

"It's okay. This is for you to keep—I have two copies."

Flora thanked him again profusely, her heart warm as she hugged the book to her chest, a rosy warmth spreading across her cheeks. Kaanan led them down the hall to Anise's room before the three went downstairs and into the kitchen for a quick breakfast.

Anise was quiet that morning, and from a glance, Flora could tell her friend was leery of Kaanan. She watched him constantly with a narrowed gaze, shooting her questioning eyes to Flora. Each time, Flora nodded reassuringly—trying to tell her it was all okay. Flora understood Anise's hesitation, but Kaanan had helped them countless times and Flora decided to put her faith in his truth.

"Can you give us a minute?" Flora asked Kaanan softly and he exited the room with a silent nod. She waited a minute before turning her attention to Anise. "Are you doing okay?"

"You forgive him, then?" she asked, her nostrils flaring lightly. "He lied to you and he's the Pitch King. How can you trust him?"

"He and I talked a lot last night, Anise, and while he did lie, he's not as bad as the stories make him out to be. And on the subject of trust and forgiveness, he's not the only one who hurt me this trip." Flora swallowed thickly, angry tears stinging her eyes as a faint flush bloomed on Anise's cheeks.

"Flora," she said softly, her lips twisted in guilt. "I'm sorry."

"I know," she said, blinking back the tears and shoving away her emotions. "I don't want to get into this now. We have things to do today, but I need you to trust me on this and therefore, I need you to trust him, just a little bit. Stop doubting him and making things difficult at every given turn. If we are going to get through this, we need to be a solid team. No backstabbing and petty comments. You don't have to like him, but I need you to at least pretend to be civil. Maybe he'll surprise you and you two can be friends once he proves even more that we can trust him."

Anise pursed her lips, doubt clouding her eyes, and

Flora thought she would fight her on the subject, her hatred and distrust of Kaanan running deep in her bones, but apparently her guilt and value of Flora's friendship was stronger. Anise softened and nodded haltingly. "All right, but if he lies or betrays us one more time, he is out. Promise me."

"I promise," she said and hoped in her very bones the words were not a lie, for her own sake as much as her friendship with Anise.

"So, into the Woods then?" Anise asked brightly, changing the subject swiftly. "Or do you think the shard is in the City?"

Kaanan poked his head back into the room. Flora narrowed her eyes, wondering if he had been listening in or was just uncanny in his timing.

"I think it's outside. My ankle felt hotter outside the City. But it is close," Flora said, rubbing her warm ankle as a stem began a slow crawl out of her bone. Her body felt better now that she had moved around, but she could feel a tremor rising in her ankle. Flora tried her best to clamp down on any weakness lest Kaanan and Anise react poorly and force her to take a break. Her body was quite literally telling her she was running out of time—she needed to hurry. Her mom, her country, and her health depended on it. There was no time for rest anymore.

"Are you okay to come with us?" Flora asked Kaanan.

"I wouldn't miss it," he said with a smile.

"But don't you have King things to do?"

"Not right now. My people are fine as they are for the time being. Besides, this is more important." Butterflies burst to life at his words.

"Are there any folktales that take place close to the city?" Flora asked as she remembered the Sormurinn. It was as good a starting place as any.

Kaanan pursed his lips, steepling his fingers as he pondered. "There are a few. You could try Myrka's Ghost or the Dreki—they're near the beginning of the book."

Flora flipped to the pages, the story of the Dreki coming up first. She read with bated breath as the story told of a different kind of dragon—a protector. The Dreki protected Pitch City centuries ago when a particularly rebellious and violent group of young dragons rose and wished to attack the city. The Dreki called on the other Pitch Woods creatures—serpents, toads, and insects that could spew poison. There was a battle, and ultimately the Dreki and his friends won, and Pitch City remained unharmed. The rebelling dragons' attacks lessened over the years as the story of the battle was told to each generation as a warning.

Besides the battle taking place near Pitch City, there were no distinguishing landmarks, so Flora assumed they would need to walk around the perimeter should the shard be linked to the Dreki.

Then, she flipped to Myrka's Ghost:

A long time ago, many decades before Pitch City was created, a man named Myrka ventured into the Pitch Woods. Myrka had a girlfriend, Guðrún, whose parents did not approve of him. They thought him impotent and deficient. But Myrka loved Guðrún—she was his first love—and wanted to marry her. He had the perfect proposal set up—all he needed was a blessing as Guðrún would not relinquish her family.

So, Myrka devised a plan. There was a legend that

there was a valuable gemstone deep in the Pitch Woods, only worthy for those with brave hearts and souls. Myrka thought it was the perfect way to prove to Guðrún's parents he was worthy of their daughter.

But a terrible accident befell Myrka on his journey to achieve great heroics. He was overconfident, cocky, and did not realize just how dangerous the Pitch Woods were. He encountered ferocious beasts and monsters, and in fear, he ran. But in his haste, he lost his footing and tumbled down a steep ravine into a raging river below. The furious water claimed Myrka, drowning him, cold and alone.

Guðrún had no idea her love had drowned and died. The ethereal night of their date held a breath of promise. To Guðrún, it whispered sweet nothings of her love's courage. To Myrka, it hissed a vow of eternal love. When he appeared at her doorstep, she felt no alarm at the sight or his silence as her giddiness for her pending proposal overshadowed the warning signs. When Myrka drowned, and his ghost rose, the Pitch Woods cursed his arrogance. His possessive nature he had in life amplified in his death. Myrka's love for Guðrún was magnified into a vicious, haunting obsession. His cursed, vengeful spirit set on claiming his beloved at last.

The full moon was hidden behind a cluster of clouds, so Guðrún was unaware of how fast she should have run from Myrka. For as they continued on their journey, Myrka led her into the Pitch Woods and even then, Guðrún was too swept up in her romantic fantasies to let any alarm puncture the cloud she floated on. The trees thinned to reveal a small field when the clouds parted, letting the full moon penetrate the thick, dense black and shine brightly down on the couple. It was the Pitch Woods' callous warning to the innocent girl and a way to ensure she was properly petrified. Guðrún glanced at her beloved, and terror struck her core.

Myrka's face was gone and in its place was a translucent, bone-white skull gleaming in the moonlight. Guðrún screamed, shattering the illusion of a peaceful night, and Myrka tried to calm her. But he could not say her name, as Guð was the old word for God, and Myrka was now a ghostly demon—a monster incarnate, forbidden to speak holy words or ever know peace in death.

Guðrún ran, but in the wrong direction. She fled toward the field Myrka's ghost was leading her to—a graveyard. She stumbled into an open grave Myrka had dug and he smiled maliciously down on her as she screamed into the dead night air. Dirt walls rose around Guðrún, boxing her inside a coffin of horror. Plots of earth surrounded the couple, full of bones and death, and Guðrún looked at the illuminated moon once more before her body began shutting down in stark terror.

"Please," she begged her beloved, sure some part of him was still there. But Guðrún was foolishly mistaken.

"You will be mine for eternity, my love," Myrka said, voice rough as stone.

There are some that tell the tale that Guðrún's parents found her in time, saved her from death at the hands of her beloved. But this is not a fairy tale.

Myrka buried Guðrún alive, listening to her pleas, screams, and then soft whimpers as dirt filled her lungs and cut off her oxygen. When her cries could no longer be heard, Myrka's ghost pushed a stone on top of her grave, trapping Guðrún and her soul for eternity. Then, Myrka lay on top of the stone, and sank into the deep earth where Guðrún was waiting for him, and the two stayed connected forevermore.

Chapter Twenty-Four

Purple shard properties: first love, royalty, beauty, and uniqueness.

(An easy shard to wield if you have been blessed with the experience of first love—innocent, pure, and sweet. Focus on the things you love, yourself included, and the shard will be putty in your grasp. [Even easier if you are of royal blood.])

"Wow," Flora whispered, breath caught in her tight throat as she finished reading the story.

It was so darkly poetic, with love and passion, but possessiveness and cruelty. It reminded Flora of the Pitch Woods and Kaanan, of reputation and perception versus reality and truth. Flora felt dreadful for Guðrún, for the woman whose life was cut so short over something she had no control over. Guðrún was the victim in the story, prey to a man who loved her so much he had killed her so they could spend the afterlife together. It was despicable.

Although, as awful as it was what Myrka had done, Flora sympathized with the man. He acted that way because of his death, because he had been cursed to turn into a shadowed version of himself—a demon in disguise. All Myrka wanted was to spend his life with Guðrún. She couldn't quite decide if his actions were forgivable or not. She was leaning toward not, as the idea of being in Guðrún's shoes sounded terrifying, someone loving you so much they would murder you in cold blood so you wouldn't live apart. Regardless, Flora loved the story, and was so overwhelmed with bubbling joy in her chest at reading something *new*, something based on truth and passed down to generations. She loved the book already, and a smile lit up her face as gratitude for Kaanan rose like a larkspur blooming.

"It's an interesting read, yes?" Kaanan asked, leaning back in his chair.

"Very," Flora murmured. "Do you know where the graveyard is?"

"It's just outside the city," Kaanan said with a dark grin full of gleaming teeth. "No one goes there—we have a different graveyard where we bury our dead. Everyone is too scared of Myrka's graveyard. There have been some…unsavory stories passed around from far too loose lips."

"What kind of stories?" Anise asked, leaning forward in her chair.

"Where to start," he said, eyes cast to the vaulted ceiling decorated in swathes of gilded gold designs. "There are rumors and stories of people hearing or seeing things when they visit the graveyard—a man made of bone, a woman screaming, chilled air—pretty much anything you can think of connected to the tale."

"And?" Flora asked. Kaanan had a look in his eye, a hesitation in his words, and she wanted to know exactly what they were getting into.

"I would like to preface this by saying I find it highly unlikely this story is fact. I'm certain it is fiction—there's no real proof."

"Just say it," Anise said through gritted teeth.

"A few years ago, someone died in the graveyard,"

Kaanan said, eyes darting between the two girls, hesitation written clear as day on his face. "There was one witness, so there's no real way to verify the story. But the witness claimed she saw the ghost of Myrka, and while she was scared, he didn't approach her. But then her boyfriend got closer, and apparently, the ghost of Guðrún rose and killed him."

"*What*?" Flora asked as Anise's mouth dropped open and face blanched.

"It is very, *very*, unlikely any of that is true."

"Then how did he die? Do you think the girlfriend killed him? Were they fighting? Were they happy?" Anise asked.

"Everyone said they were happy," Kaanan said with a grimace and Flora's stomach dropped. "But who can really say the nature of another's relationship behind closed doors, in private moments privy to no one else?"

"Say it's true, the ghost—Guðrún—killed her boyfriend. Why?" Flora asked.

"Exactly—why? What more do you know?" Anise asked.

"Not much, truly. All I know are theories. When the death happened, my advisors and I tried to determine the truth so it wouldn't happen again. The girl was too distraught to have killed him, so she's free but under surveillance. If she didn't do it, and she didn't see another living being, all we could think of was that, if the story is true, Guðrún's ghost may be angry enough to kill men or people who come close enough to her."

"That makes sense—she was murdered," Flora said softly.

"She has every right to be angry, even kill," Anise said.

"I know. I agree," Kaanan said. "We'll be prepared—I have weapons and some guards can come with us."

"Okay," Anise said with a determined nod, then glanced at Flora. "Hopefully the shard will be easy to get this time. I'll keep my distance."

Flora nodded, squeezing Anise's hand in thanks, an overwhelming surge of gratitude that Anise was playing by the new rules. It would make her life so much easier, and whether it was the reprimand or Anise just turning a corner, Flora didn't care so long as the three of them could work together. Once the three got up from the table, Kaanan disappeared as the girls finished getting ready. He went in search of his guards and supplies and would meet them outside. Flora's stomach tossed and turned, the bundle of nerves refusing to sit still. Her chest was tight as they walked into the dark courtyard. She wished there were lighting changes in the Pitch Woods—going to a graveyard in the dark sounded dangerous, like an omen that death was near.

****

The forest loomed before Flora, towering pitch trees shooting to the dark sky. Her stomach heaved as they stepped out of the creaking gilded door and into the woods beyond. Kaanan walked beside her, and Anise beside one of Kaanan's guards. She was clinging to the man's armor and attempting to hide in thin air beside the thick man in black-coated silver. A unit of guards Kaanan trusted led them into the woods. Three in front, two beside, and five trailing behind them. Flora felt safe, but she didn't think it had anything to do with the guards. Flora gazed at Kaanan out of the corner of her eye, and she knew at the sight of him that he was the reason she felt safe in the merciless woods.

Myrka's graveyard was close to Pitch City, located in a small field to the left of the City walls. Flora's chest was tight with excitement and fear as her ankle warmed, a scorching ache as heat radiated off it. She noted a flower blooming on the edge of the trees: evening primrose, burning yellow petals with orange seeds, a beautiful sight and floral scent amongst the midnight.

It calmed her, the sight of the flower, the sight of life growing in the dark. It made Flora understand Kaanan more, how he was sweet for someone who was raised in the dark by a line of men dealing in black and shadows and danger around every corner.

To Flora, Kaanan was a bright, bursting flower blooming in the pitch black.

A small smile rested on her lips as his head turned to her. Their eyes connected and a grin blossomed on Kaanan's face as Flora blushed pink once again.

"Are you feeling okay? Ready to face a potential ghost?" he asked, lips quirking as his dimple deepened.

"I think so. After seeing a dragon and the Sormurinn, I don't think a ghost sounds all that bad," she said with a sigh.

"That's fair. It also opens more possibilities."

"Of stories being real?"

"Exactly," he said, his eyes almost glowing in the dark with wonder. "You wouldn't believe some of the tales they tell, the worlds they speak of in such detail that I can't help but believe they're real."

"So, if you're King, without an heir I assume,

well…I hope. You don't have any kids do you? Oh Gods, please tell me you don't! You're so young and I li—" Flora bit down on her tongue so hard blood burst and splattered against the back of her throat. She swallowed the warm, tangy liquid as Kaanan's lips quirked in undisguised amusement.

"No, Flora," he said, his tone gentle and warm. "I don't have any kids. I hope you don't as well?"

Flora shook her head profusely. "Gods, no. I don't even know if I *want* kids."

His eyes sparked to life at her words, and he nodded like he was realizing they may be kindred spirits. She shyly smiled back, tucking her hair behind her ears and clearing her throat. She was being ridiculous. And even worse, she almost told him she *liked* him. Last night she only admitted to liking him as a friend, not romantically. She was only just coming to terms with that herself—let alone comfortable telling other people. And she knew there was no way he genuinely liked her back in that way. She wasn't pretty enough, or smart enough, or enticingly dark enough. Her throat closed tightly as she spiraled down further, her stomach and heart sinking.

"Flora? Are you okay?" His melodic voice pulled her back to their conversation, dragging her body out of her tunnel of agonizing thoughts kicking and screaming as her anxious mind wouldn't let go that easily. But she made it out alive and managed to have enough sense to remember what she hadn't finished asking him.

"I'm fine. As I was saying, will you chase the stories?" she asked, holding her elbows as the light dimmed from his eyes.

"I honestly don't know. It's my duty to protect and

serve Pitch City, be the best King my people can dream of..."

"But?"

He sighed. "But I want more. I want freedom and adventure and new worlds with new people. I want to live a life of my choosing, and then come back and rule my people when I feel like I'm worthy. When I can offer them more than what I can at nineteen. I mean, I'm still just a kid myself."

"Well, you could do just that—explore and then come home when you're ready, or never if that's also what you want," Flora said. "You deserve to pick your future, Kaanan, to follow your dreams."

"Thank you, Flora," he said with a small smile. "But what about you?"

"Me?"

"Yes, what do you really want? Do you have your answer for me yet?"

"I don't know."

"I think it's a good dream to save Woodvale, fulfill your destiny—I get all that, I really do—but after that? I hope you do the same thing you told me, Flora, and follow your own dreams and desires—not follow what people expect or want from you." He smiled gently at her, nudging her lightly with his shoulder. "And if you need a place to hide out, my city and I are always waiting for you."

Flora nodded, her chest tight with so many emotions—happiness that he cared for her and her future, pressure of the life she was given, anxiety that constantly followed her for a plethora of reasons, and fear of...everything. Fear of making a mistake, saying the wrong thing, messing everything up, and letting people down. She wished she could snap her fingers and have all her problems solved.

But that was impossible, and as they neared the graveyard, the field of matted, dry dirt and headstones poking up, the stem of larkspur twined up her ankle and calf, effectively distracting her. Flora sighed as the larkspur crawled up her leg, tickling her thigh beneath her flowy pants. The world spun around Flora as the larkspur continued to grow. Bile climbed her throat as her vision blurred and she shook. She breathed deeply through her nose, trying not to alert anyone to her weak state, and stayed in line with Kaanan.

She could feel his gaze burning a hole into her cheek, but she refused to turn his way, mostly because if she did, she was sure she would vomit her breakfast on his leather boots. Flora's hand snaked to her shirt and clung to the two shards beneath, steadying her as she begged and willed the larkspur to stop in its tracks. She had never tried to will her larkspur to stop growing before. Usually she just plucked it and felt nothing, but now, she felt like she was seconds from passing out—like all her nutrients were being sapped out of her with the growing larkspur.

An elbow brushed against Flora's limp arm, and she glanced at Kaanan out of the corner of her eye and found him looking forward at the approaching graveyard. Before she could stop herself, she slipped her fingers through the crook of his elbow and let him guide her through the remainder of the forest with its snaking and jutting roots.

The night was dark, the only light coming from the lanterns the guards held. Flora's nose wrinkled as a musty smell rose when they entered the ungated graveyard. Headstones and plots scattered the small field. Flora's hand brushed against the first one, trying to read the name in the dark as her ankle burned an inferno into her bones.

Flora gasped as she saw what her fingers had landed on—a larkspur was carved into the headstone. The name was too chipped for her to read, but the larkspur was there, clear as day. She sighed, relief flooding her that they were in the right place.

"What's wrong?" Kaanan asked, jerking to a stop at her gasp.

"It's a larkspur," she murmured, eyes still caught on the flower engraved thereon. When she looked up, she saw Kaanan's face darken, eyes hard and cold. "What?"

"I just don't understand how it's here," he said, shaking his head. "I know everything that happens in these woods. Who put it here? How? There are magical protections everywhere close to Pitch City—it makes no sense."

"Maybe you're just not as good as you think you are, Your Highness," Anise said with a sneering smile. He cast a dark glare at her while Flora turned away from the exchange and back to the larkspur. She touched it once more for luck, praying to the Gods she could get this shard easily.

"Where is Guðrún's grave?" she asked, eyes searching the field as clinking steel filled the air when the guards shuffled.

Kaanan led Flora over to a few plots shrouded in shadows and darkness. A chill raced down Flora's spine as her breath became visible in the air. The pit in her stomach dropped as the air shifted and converged upon the area around the grave.

A shadowy figure rose out of the ground, hair trailing in the oncoming breeze as Flora's heart stopped. *Oh please, oh please*, Flora chanted in her mind, begging any Gods to be merciful with her. Another shadowed figure climbed out of the ground a pace behind what Flora assumed, and hoped, was Guðrún.

Flora squeaked as Guðrún stepped closer, stumbling backward into Kaanan. His arms closed around her, encasing her in his firm body and flowing cloak. A quick glance at their surroundings revealed Anise and the guards were gone. In their place was a wall of shadows that looked alive as pieces of sharp thorns snaked in a rhythmic pattern.

It looked vastly different to Kaanan's, yet also similar. Where Kaanan's magic was moving shadow, pure black and smoky in substance, like a sinister fog rolling in, these shadows were tinged with dark crimson and shapes forming in the writhing dark.

"What do we do?" Flora gasped, her lungs clenching and squeezing.

"Your magic—call upon it," he instructed, hands soothingly running along her biceps as she quivered.

"What about you?" she hissed, hands flying to her shards as Guðrún moved closer, an arm outstretched before she stopped in her tracks, frozen in time.

"I'm trying," he said through gritted teeth. "My magic isn't reacting well to whatever this is. Just breathe, Flora. You can do this."

Guðrún's ghost cocked her head to the side, shadows in place of hair. Flora stared at her, chest aching with sympathy and terror. She clutched her shards until they bit painfully into her skin. Flora let out a deep breath and called upon her magic, sparkling green coating her veins as she imagined stalks of ivy bursting out of the ground. Ivy exploded from the earth packed with bones and bodies in front of her and Kaanan, creating a short wall between them.

An echoing laugh escaped one of the ghosts, sending an icy finger down Flora's spine. In seconds, the shadows surrounding them tore into the ivy, pulverizing the green until the space between them was empty once more.

Flora swallowed thickly as Guðrún moved closer. "Please, we want to help you," Flora whispered, throat too tight for her voice to raise an octave.

Guðrún's head craned to the side, looking right past Flora to Kaanan. He noticed the same thing Flora had and immediately used his arm to push her behind him.

"Stop," she hissed peeking over his shoulder as Guðrún moved close enough to touch.

"Flora," he said, turning his head to face her, "if anything happens to me—run."

"What?"

"Run. Forget about me and run as fast as you can. My guards will protect you with or without me."

"Kaanan," she whimpered, her throat tight with rising emotion.

"*You protect her?*" the air around Guðrún whispered. Flora blinked, her mouth dropping open as the ghost moved another millimeter closer. "*Even in the face of death, you protect her?*"

Flora's hand clenched Kaanan's shoulder she was using as leverage. She swallowed thickly as Kaanan said, "Yes, I do."

"*Good,*" she whispered, intently staring at the two while Myrka loomed in the backdrop. "*You're not a coward. I respect that.*"

"Why does that matter? What do you want, Guðrún? Death? Do you want to be a murderer of my people?"

"Kaanan," Flora hissed in warning.

"*What do you speak of? The boy? He deserved it.*"

"What gives you the right to decide that?" Kaanan growled through gritted teeth.

"*My murder does.*"

"What do you want, Guðrún?" Flora asked.

"*I want to be removed from* him." Flora's eyes flicked to the ever-looming presence of Myrka's ghost, a shudder racing down her spine at the menacing figure.

"How can we do that?"

"*Remove me from my prison, and I will give you what you desire.*"

"It sounds too easy," she whispered in Kaanan's ear.

"I know," he muttered.

"*No strings, no tricks—I want to spend my afterlife unshackled from my killer. Is that so much to ask?*"

"We'll do it," Flora said, moving past Kaanan as he lightly grabbed her arm.

"Flora."

"We have no other choice, trust me," she whispered, locking eyes with him. She watched him scan her face, noting her even paler skin and eyes. His eyes darkened—in what, Flora wasn't sure—but he nodded reluctantly.

"*Move me across the field, where the flowers are—*

far away from him."

"We will."

Kaanan clasped Flora's hand in his and they walked past Guðrún to her grave. Myrka rose taller as the two approached, but Flora was already expecting a struggle. She called upon her magic and sent thorny vines to snake around the ghost as Kaanan got some control of his magic, trapping the ghost in his shadows. He fought her fiercely, and her vines buckled and broke. But for each that crumbled, she called upon another until he was subdued. Her magic felt stronger and in that moment, she didn't care if she tapped herself dry—so long as they got out of the mess alive and saved Guðrún from an eternity shackled to her murderer.

Flora called upon roots and gentle moss and slowly brought Guðrún's bones to the surface. With Kaanan's hand clasped in hers, and Myrka indisposed, Kaanan used his shadows to lift the bones, and they walked through the wall of living dark into the Pitch Woods beyond.

Chapter Twenty-Five

An interesting thing to note is of all the records known of the Larkspur Ladies, from Alouette to Anneliese Larkspur, their ruin was ultimately brought by love. While each situation varied, like Anneliese's love being shadowed by greed and her legacy being ruined by the cataclysm she caused, or Willow's love being too passionate, or Peony's father's wrath, their destruction all came by the hands of a loved one.

-The Age of Larkspur by Cassius Muscari, IV

As soon as they stepped past the barrier, it came down around them, exposing them to the guards and Anise, who shrieked the second she saw Flora. A flurry of frantic limbs hit Flora, jolting her away from Kaanan as Anise clung to her.

"Are you okay?" Anise asked with shaking breath.

"I'm fine. We just have to finish this," she replied, extracting herself from her friend's arms. Anise glanced down at the bones in the space between Flora and Kaanan and reared back. She nodded shakily, and Flora turned to Kaanan.

The two walked across the graveyard, trying to avoid stepping on any plots, before they deposited the bones on the ground at the opposite end, far away from Myrka. Flora breathed deeply and envisioned the ground before them tearing up with roots so a hole would be left in its place. Flora watched as it did just that but with a mix of Kaanan's shadows. A deep hole lay before them, and they gently lowered Guðrún's bones into her new grave.

When they finished pushing the dirt into the grave, Flora noted the moonflowers just at the tree line and used her blooming magic to grow gleaming moonflowers around the edge of Guðrún's grave in a glowing halo of protection. From the black night air, the ghost of Guðrún appeared. Her wispy arm extended, palm up, and in the twinkling waning moon, a purple shard appeared.

"*Thank you,*" she said with a wispy voice.

"Thank you," Flora said softly. "I hope you rest in peace now."

Guðrún dropped the shard into Flora's waiting palm, and then disappeared with the breeze. Flora closed her fist around the shard, tucking it against her chest as her shoulders sagged. "We did it," she said, turning to Kaanan who was waiting with a soft smile on his face.

"*You* did it. You were amazing."

Flora stared at Kaanan a moment before she threw her arms around him, hugging him tight. He stiffened for a second before he softened and closed his arms around her waist. Flora pulled away just as quickly as she had hugged him and smiled up at him in the dark before she heard Anise come bounding over to them.

"Did you get it?" Anise called and Flora held up the shard triumphantly before tying it to the other two shards.

Now her chest held a collection of pink, blue, and purple. She wondered what the last color would be— what it would mean and how it would help her.

Already, Flora felt stronger in her magic with the purple shard humming through her veins at the contact. Her body was weak, but her mind, spirit, and magic were alive.

She couldn't get over how much magic she was gaining. With each new shard, the magic that lay dormant exploded in bursts of passion and energy. It was starting to be as natural as breathing. She couldn't imagine a world without it, but she also felt as though there was an end to it. Her magic wasn't bottomless or eternal—not yet at least.

Flora cut her connection to her magic, letting it sink beneath her surface, out of reach until she needed it again. But the second she did, a wave of dizziness knocked her down. She stumbled and Kaanan's arm shot out to steady her, firm hand holding her back against his chest.

"Are you okay?" he asked, voice low and concerned.

"Fine," she said, voice strained, "just tripped over the ground."

He turned her so she faced him, eyes narrowed as he scanned her, but Flora shrugged him off and collided with Anise. "Flora, are you okay?"

"Great!"

"Okay, well we should get going, right? We have to go to the Sage Woods and the new moon is coming sooner rather than later," Anise reminded.

"You can resupply at my home before departing," Kaanan said, and Flora couldn't help but flinch at his choice of "you" instead of "we."

****

The second they got back to Kaanan's castle, Anise

bolted to her room to pack quickly so they could be out of there before night fell in Woodvale. It was hard to tell time without the sun, but Kaanan kept track and Flora's internal clock told her it was daytime.

Flora had already packed, having kept all her personal belongings in her rucksack glued to her side. The only thing she had done was excuse herself to the bathroom to hastily rip off the larkspur twined around her leg and mash it into a chunky paste in some of the empty vials. It wasn't as easy to use as dried larkspur dust, but she felt better having the insurance.

When she left the bathroom, she navigated back to the entry hall. Kaanan was right where she left him, but he had evidently left for a period of time. In the entrance hall on a once empty table were two bags stuffed to the brim with supplies.

A flutter erupted in her chest, warmth spreading across collarbone and ribcage, her heart rattling in its bony prison. Flora swallowed thickly as a burning sensation hit her skin where her shards lay. She glanced down and saw the purple one glowing lightly, but it made no sound in her mind, so she pushed past it and focused on Kaanan.

"Is that for us?" she asked, pointing at the bags as she toed the edge of the rug.

"Yes. I packed it with food, a medical kit, and some sleeping bags," he said, leaning with his arms crossed against the wall beside the bags. A large, immaculate painting of someone who looked faintly like Kaanan hung on the wall behind his head. "I also arranged for two horses you may use for your journey. I would recommend keeping close to the Pitch Woods tree line to avoid anyone seeing you—people tend to give the Woods a wide berth."

"So…" Flora mumbled, tongue leaden as she dared herself to say the next words, but it didn't work.

"So?" he asked, quirking an eyebrow as he kicked off the wall so they could speak without a distance between them.

"I…"

"You?" he teased, grin forming and dimple appearing.

"You're not coming with us?" she said, spitting the words in haste, eyes burning a hole in the carpet as she refused to look at him. She could feel her cheeks burning and convinced herself she looked like a tomato.

"Do you want me to?" he asked, voice deep as the ocean with twinkling eyes.

"I…I." She paused, tongue thick around the word, "Yes."

A grin sparked and burned on his face as he said, "Then I'll come." Flora nodded and swallowed thickly as he leaned forward, tucking a loose strand of hair behind her ear and whispering in her ear, "I'll follow you for as long as you want me to."

Just as quickly as he approached her, he stepped back and went into another room for a second before returning with another pack and two sheathed swords he strapped in a menacing X across his back. His grin was feral as he strode to Flora with a bag extended in his hand. Their fingers brushed as she took the bag from him, goosebumps erupting on her exposed arms and a warm shiver trailing down her spine. He didn't let go of the bag, just let their fingers rest against one another as they both stared at the other, her blinding pale to his stormy dark.

They sprang apart as Anise thumped down the stairs, and Flora fiddled with her bag. A lump resided in her throat, and she was second-guessing each action she had taken. Did she look awkward? Do something weird? Did Kaanan really look at her the way she looked at him or was it just wishful thinking? She couldn't stop the questions from racing around her mind as a furrow arched across her eyebrows.

"Ready to go?" Anise said, snapping Flora out of her sinkhole.

"Yeah, let's head out."

Just beyond Kaanan's courtyard, three horses waited for them. Flora shot an accusatory look at Kaanan, and he chuckled softly. "Sometimes you have to ask, Flora—I can't read your mind."

Flora scoffed. "You could have asked too."

"Very true, but I wanted a genuine, unbiased answer."

Flora nodded, breaking eye contact with him as she patted her tawny mare. "Her name is Honey," Kaanan said, the name causing a bittersweet pang of longing for her mother to ring through her bones, the reminder of honeybuns too much to bear. "Anise, yours is Chestnut."

"And yours?" Flora asked, noting the largest and pure-black horse with shadows dancing around his hooves.

"Jet."

Kaanan boosted Flora into her saddle and the three set off into the Pitch Woods. Flora soaked in every sight of Pitch City before they departed, wanting to commit it all to memory in case she never returned. As they breached the tree line, Flora glanced back at the walls, and was surprised to find she actually *wanted* to come back one day.

****

Nothing bothered them in the Pitch Woods, not even when all light was snuffed out and pure darkness reigned. Nothing jumped out or attacked them—the only thing keeping them company were the dark shadows Kaanan toyed with at their feet.

They made excellent time and found themselves at the edge of the precipice in a matter of hours. Flora could faintly make out gleaming light from beyond the almost impenetrable wall of shadows and trees. Her fingers trailed the trunks and tall ferns as Honey took her out of the Woods and back into the burning sunlight.

Flora breathed deeply and closed her eyes as her face warmed and eyes burned from the contrast. She had missed the sun. As much as she had gotten used to the Pitch Woods in the short time they were there and enjoyed the change of scenery, she truly loved feeling the sun on her face and light dangling from her fingertips.

She basked in the dying sunlight as they increased their pace, trying in earnest to get as far as they could out of Myrkurden and into Skógur. Kaanan said there was a town two days ride where they would stock up on supplies if necessary, but their main goal for the remainder of the day was getting out of Myrkurden.

It was difficult, and the horses were exhausted along with their panting riders, but the three made it just across the border into Skógur as the sun dipped behind the mountains, casting the world in shadow and cool air of the night. They stopped in a gully, erecting their large tent provided by Kaanan, and immediately crawled inside, not bothering with a fire. Flora was between Kaanan and Anise, blanketed by shadow and dawn, protecting her from any potential intrusions or threats. She was warm and cozy, heart full, when she drifted off to a sleep full of dreams.

****

Flora was on a pane of glass, firm beneath her bare feet as she looked around. Her eyes met clouds and blue sky, so close she could almost touch them. Her stomach dropped when she realized she was above the clouds, in the sky on a measly piece of glass holding her weight. Before she could succumb to the panic clawing at her throat, three silhouettes appeared before her.

Three women swathed in pink, blue, and purple hues rose before Flora, floating in the clouds. She couldn't make out their faces, just their silhouetted bodies of pastel colors. Flora's body hummed with magic, gleaming through her veins and lightening her body in the sun on the blurry horizon.

"What is this?" Flora asked, wrapping her arms around her waist as she shifted away from the glowing figures. Her ankle ached as her eyes darted between each of the women.

"*Hello, Flora,*" the purple one said.

"…hi?"

"*You have much work to do, Flora, and not much more time to do it. That curse is sucking the life out of you faster and faster,*" Blue warned, sending Flora's heart racing.

"I'm trying."

"*Try harder! And prepare yourself, for your tryst with the Sage Witch will be more difficult than you can imagine."*

"How do you know that? What does that mean?"

"If you manage to succeed, your life will change. There are things you don't know, but you need to."

"Then tell me." The harsh demand fell from her lips before she could soften the tone—but she didn't care. They were being too cagey and vague. She wanted real, specific answers.

"It's not our place to say. Magic is complicated, and our lips are bound with the secrets we carry."

"Just give me a hint, then! What area of my life is at risk here?"

"Every area is at risk, Flora, always. But I am speaking of your family, your mother and father, and your ancestors. Your mother ruined herself by breaking the rules, by tempting fate and falling for greed instead of generosity. And your father, well, he was no better than your mother," Blue warned.

Flora's mouth dropped open. Rosie had never shared much information on her father, but she spoke of two men in her mother's life—a priest and the King. Rosie only spoke neutrally or faintly bitterly about King Desmond but was always warmer toward the priest. Flora had no idea which man was her father, if it was either at all. There were too many holes in her mother's story that had yet to be filled—no one truly knew what happened in her mother's life. It was mostly speculation and assumption. Nevertheless, Flora longed for the truth, so she could understand her history and her mother.

"But—"

"Follow your heart, and you will be safe. Generations of women held the boon before your

mother, and they were fine. They followed the ebbs and flows of magic and kept true to the original purpose of the boon," Purple interjected. *"Just follow your heart and surround yourself with love."*

Flora blinked, sputtering as she said, "That's so vague! Can't you tell me more? Who is my father? Tell me more about the boon and the curse—will getting my magic back in full stop my…disintegration?"

"Yes. You can save yourself by regaining the shards, and you will be fine so long as you don't follow your mother's footsteps," Blue said.

"We'll help where we can. The magic is already yours—it likes you; we like you. So, it will listen to your desires and wishes. Just be careful," Purple said, as Pink fluttered in the background.

"I—" Flora couldn't finish her sentence. Instead she slipped as the glass cracked and then shattered beneath her feet. Flora fell for what felt like hours, stomach and heart flying out of her body and fear squeezed her tight.

Just before she hit the ground, Flora woke with a soul-wrenching gasp.

Chapter Twenty-Six

The question on everyone's lips in the castle is this:
who is the Larkspur babe's father?

Gossip riddled the halls, insidious stalks of poison
cutting through truth.

Was it the priest forever caught in the tangles of a
fated woman?

Or

Was it the King destined for greatness and power?

-Gossip pamphlet circulated after Anneliese's
pregnancy was announced.

Flora's sputtering gasp woke Kaanan. He was on
her immediately, hands touching her shoulders and
cheeks to get her to focus on him. She tried nodding her
head to tell him she was okay, but her head felt like it
was detached from her body. She attempted to utter the
words, but in the end, all she could manage was ragged
breathing and miniscule nods while he watched her
with concerned eyes.

"I'm okay," she wheezed, as his hands tightened on
her shoulders.

"What happened?" he whispered in the dark. Anise
was still soundly sleeping beside her—Flora knew from
experience Anise could sleep through anything,
probably even an earthquake.

"Just a bad dream," she said, her breathing righting
itself.

"Come here," he said, and pulled her against his chest. Warmth flooded Flora at the sensation, and she melted in his arms as he wrapped her tight, flushing out the feeling of falling and replacing it with stability and heat.

"Thank you," Flora murmured, closing her eyes as she pressed her cheek against his chest. The firm muscle grounded her, and she slipped back to sleep, except this time it was dreamless and deep.

****

Flora had ample time to process her magical manifestation on their ride through Skógur the next morning. Her sleep had been restful and deep, and when she woke, Kaanan was outside the tent cooking breakfast. She almost thought she imagined their encounter last night, but it was too vivid and the feeling of him against her burned deeply into her mind until she had no doubt it was real.

Flora was concerned about the dream. The shards were too vague and threatening. She already knew she had limited time and everything was at stake—she really didn't need the reminder. Regardless of the pressure it mounted on her, she was pleased to glean some information. Like how her magic was cooperating with her, something she already partially knew from use, but it was a nice confirmation. It was such a powerful feeling, using her magic—it was like a limb that had been lost was returning to her and she was constantly jittering in anticipation to get the fourth and final one so she could be complete.

Her only real concern was running out of time and confronting the Sage Witch. She may have originally granted her family the boon, but she was also the one who embedded a curse into the boon directly affecting Flora. The Sage Witch had eons of experience on her, and Flora wasn't sure exactly what would become of their meeting. Would they fight? Duel? Or would it be a simple exchange? She had no idea what to expect. Her shards were no help on that front, and her stomach was roiling as a result.

They were making good time, however, something Kaanan was evidently pleased about with the small smiles he threw Flora. But their progress was stopped in its tracks when Anise's horse tired too much for it to continue. They were just outside of a town a ways into Skógur when it happened. Anise hopped on behind Flora, and they towed her horse into town where Kaanan would attempt to exchange it for a new one.

The town was similar to the ones Flora had already seen in Woodvale. The starkest difference was that the buildings were made primarily out of wood, and there was barely a chiseled stone in sight.

The stablemaster exchanged their horses without a hitch, and because they were there, they decided to stock up on supplies. Flora followed Kaanan as he led them through the town streets to the open square market full of life. She gawked at the people, the peddlers, and the life vibrating from the square.

Everything was going fine, she was flying under the radar, and had completely forgotten she was a wanted woman. Being in the Pitch Woods afforded her a safety that made her forget the reality of being the most sought-after person in Woodvale.

It all changed in the blink of an eye, in a split second, and it wasn't even her at fault. Flora was quiet and drew no attention to herself, but the square held someone with a different past and agenda, and looser lips than her.

"Anneliese?" The name sent a shockwave through the crowd, and you could have heard a pin drop in the silence that followed. Her name echoed in the square, a ringing in Flora's ears as she stared at the man before her with wavy brown hair cropped close to his skull, blue eyes boring into her so intently, with such barely restrained emotion she could feel the pressure of it as it shot tingles up her spine. Flora stared back, with a furrowed brow and frown cresting her lips at the man who was evidently a priest. He wore navy robes and white collar, a gold cross hanging around his neck like a noose. No flicker of familiarity rang through Flora, but that didn't surprise her with the name he used.

Flora knew she looked like her mother. Rosie had always struggled to find ways to disguise her, but Flora also knew Anneliese was vastly more beautiful, more elegant. According to Rosie, the Larkspur line looked very similar—at least the women did—but Flora had never been recognized before, and was always described as plain, so she had assumed the genes were lost on her.

Flora swallowed thickly as the crowd moved as one, looking at her, scrutinizing her, and then, fearing her. She could feel the terror and hatred rising in the people surrounding her, it was so potent and pungent. Kaanan and Anise closed around her, trying in earnest to block her from view.

But the damage was already done. Someone had finally recognized her, someone who knew her mother, and while she should be shaking from terror, all she felt was burning curiosity. She wanted to talk to the man who exposed her, find out how he knew her mother and anything else he may have known.

The priest was shaking his head at her, eyes wide as he whispered the name once more, like a prayer, "Anneliese."

Flora shook her head and took a step forward but was blocked by Kaanan. He was standing tall and erect in front of her, holding her close as the crowd started to close in on them.

"Flora," he murmured out of the corner of his mouth, eyes never leaving the growing mob. "On my signal, duck and let me get you out of here."

"Okay," she said, clasping his waiting hand in hers and then grabbing Anise's so they wouldn't get separated.

Kaanan's hand rose from his cloak, and Flora could feel the magical energy radiating off him and zapping into her. She wondered if her magic could help him at all. She bit her lip and willed some of her magic to flow through her hand and into his, aiding him in his attempt at their escape. Flora wasn't sure if her assistance did anything at all, but it made her feel better to try to help.

Shadows rose and in one fell swoop took out the entire mob. The three were encased in a bubble of shadowy protection as the rest of the crowd fell away to the black abyss. Kaanan's hand clenched around hers, and he shoved them through the shadowy substance scattered in the air where people stood moments ago. Flora stumbled on uneven ground, but they cleared the square quickly with ease. She turned around once they were back in the sun and found bodies littering the square. She gaped and then whirled on Kaanan, shrieking, "What did you do?"

"It's fine—it was just Nite. The dragons have their uses." He winked with a devilish grin. "They're asleep now, but they'll be fine in an hour or so. We need to go," he said, tugging her along as she glanced back at the bodies. She could just make out chests rising and falling.

To her surprise, she barely felt any guilt at the field of bodies they left in their wake. Sometimes necessary evils had to be committed—people had to be hurt for the greater good. She was fine with Kaanan's actions after the initial shock, and with each passing day in his company, and away from the pressure Rosie had placed on her to be good and pure. Flora was enjoying her moral freedoms. She didn't have to follow Rosie's rules to be *good*, she just had to draw her own lines and be okay with the consequences that followed from her actions.

It wasn't like Flora wanted to go on a murder spree, but she didn't necessarily want purity either. She wanted a balance, where she didn't have to be eaten up with guilt if she did something bad and allow herself to make hard choices some may disagree with. She wanted to be selfish for the first time in her life, wanted to find out for herself what right and wrong were. Bad people got away with dreadful things all the time whereas good people were constantly being stepped on. Flora was tired of being stepped on—she didn't want to be feared, but she didn't want to be taken advantage of either. Flora wanted her mind to allow her to be less anxious, less inherently good at the cost of her sanity, and focus on what *she* wanted.

They had just rounded the corner leading them to the stables when they crashed into brass and silver.

Flora's heart started rapidly pounding when she saw the emblems on the men's silver-plated chests—the King's Guard.

"Grab her!" the one in front barked and Flora stumbled backward, tripping over Anise as Kaanan desperately tried to snatch her.

His fingers just missed her falling body, fabric slipping through his hands as Flora fell away from him onto the dirt. Flora shrieked as rough hands closed around her biceps, hauling her forcefully up as she heard shouts of her name. She turned and found her friends in the same predicament. The guards holding her tightened their grip and she whimpered from the pain.

"Be gentle!" a stern, deep voice shouted. "That is my *daughter* you are holding—your Princess."

Flora's head whipped to the voice, mouth agape and eyes as wide as the sockets in her skull as she stared at the presence before her. A tall, stocky man with straight brown hair and blue eyes stood with a twisted gold crown of jewels resting on his head. He smiled brightly at her, eyes gleaming as she shied into the guards, swallowing thickly as her throat closed.

Her tongue was caught in a cage of thorns, and she was helpless as King Desmond came closer, inspecting her as he caught her chin in his firm grip. He moved her head side to side, an unreadable expression on his tan face. With a quiet, emotionless voice, he said, "You look just like your mother."

"Ready the carriage and find Jeremiah. We have a lot of ground to cover and little time to do so," he said to his guards, before focusing on her once more.

Their eyes met, his sinking ocean to her pale dew.

Flora longed to speak, to overcome the hands holding her throat and talk to this enigma of a man. A man who claimed to be her father. But if that were true, it would mean she was a *princess*, in line for a throne. The possibility had crossed her mind once or twice, but after Rosie's reluctance to speak of her father, Flora had washed her hands of the matter, leaving it in the past because the potential for this man to be her father was too much for her to bear. She didn't want to be a princess, the heir. She stopped breathing at the thought.

Flora's face reddened as her breath was cut off completely. She couldn't be a princess, couldn't be a queen. She wasn't prepared, wasn't smart enough, wasn't able to rule a whole country. She couldn't even go on a quest by herself without needing help from Kaanan and Anise. And she couldn't be caught in a gilded cage, in all the expectations the monarchy forced upon royals, wings clipped. She needed freedom and wind beneath her spread wings as she explored and *lived*.

Agony erupted in her burning lungs as she doubled over, black spots clouding her vision. "Flora!" Kaanan yelled, voice concerned, but with a hint of promise of destruction at the hands that put her in this current state.

Her father's face loomed closer, lips moving rapidly, but Flora's hearing closed off as her vision swam in a pool of black. The last thing she felt was hands slipping from her biceps, allowing her to kiss the dirt before she was swept away with the current.

Chapter Twenty-Seven

I HATE HIM. I HATE HIM. I HATE HIM. I HATE HIM. I HATE HIM. I HATE HIM.

I HATE HIM.

I chose the wrong man.

Rage is consuming me and I can't keep it in any longer. I will destroy him, and everything he has worked me so hard to build if it is the last thing I do.

His legacy will be ruined at my *hands.*

-Diary entry by Anneliese Larkspur.

Flora woke slowly, eyelids fluttering as she regained consciousness. She had to swim through thick, inky tar to return to the land of the living. Her breathing had regulated itself, her lungs having opened once she blacked out as her mind could no longer play tricks on her body.

"Flora?" She heard Kaanan's strained voice ask. Her eyebrows furrowed as she struggled to blink open her dry eyes.

"Flora, wake up," Anise hissed, helping draw Flora further from the claws of sleep gripping her. With a violent mental shove, she breathed in deeply, opening her eyes.

Her eyes were met with wood paneling painted black, light hitting the corner of her eye from a pane of fogged glass. A rocking sensation hit Flora, her empty stomach quivering in disagreement.

They were in a carriage, plushness and luxury cradling her exhausted body. Her head was on a warm muscle, and legs elevated on something soft. Flora swallowed thickly as she glanced down, finding a worried Anise holding her legs. Her cheeks flushed as she realized what her head was resting on. Flora daintily looked up to find a burning gaze. Kaanan's jaw was taut, but his eyes were softly smoldering as he caught her gaze.

"Are you okay?" he asked, voice honey and velvet. Anise squeezed her un-birthmarked ankle, voicelessly asking the same sentiment in the quiet.

"Fine," she said, voice croaky from disuse and assault from her own body. Fainting was never something she could ever truly get used to. It was the oddest sensation, like your body was no longer your own, control slipping through your fingers like sand.

"You gave us all quite a scare," a voice across the aisle from her said. Flora's eyes darted over, catching expensive-looking silk pants that hung on a man Flora had hoped to never meet in person.

King Desmond sat across from the trio, fingers steepled in his lap as he watched each of them, eyes narrowed and all-seeing. Flora jolted when she caught sight of who sat on either side of him. A guard—which didn't surprise her and she was sure she would find more outside the moving carriage. What surprised her was the priest from the market sitting beside King Desmond. He was sound asleep, head leaning against the side of the carriage. Even in sleep, he looked uncomfortable and out of place in the luxury, and Flora was sure she mirrored him.

"Where are you taking us?" Flora asked, her

tongue having loosened from her blackout. Apparently her body had given up on trying to punish her. But she still felt weak, weaker than she should have. Her ankle itched and she resisted the urge to scratch it.

The reminder of the ticking time bomb living on her ankle drew her to another solution for the potential hellscape she entered unwillingly. Because on her ankle was a rapidly growing larkspur. A beautiful, deadly purple flower. A larkspur that could incapacitate someone with ease. She wondered if her mother had ever used her larkspur like this, or if she even grew a larkspur from her ankle. Flora wasn't sure if it was part of the boon or the curse.

"I'm taking you home," King Desmond said with a smile. "Flora, is it?"

"Yes," she said, hesitantly. His mouth tightened at her confirmation, a sour expression racing fleetingly across his face.

"I would have chosen something...more in line with your status, not something with such a reminder of what you possess."

"So? You weren't there and her mom did her best, better even. Flora doesn't need you—if you're even her father," Anise said, tone snarky and biting as she glared at her King.

"Anise," Flora scolded under her breath, "he's the *King*." Anise rolled her eyes, crossing her arms over her chest and leaning back in her seat, continuing her distasteful stare at the King.

"These are who you surround yourself with, Flora? A brooding boy and biting girl? I would have thought you had better taste, considering where you come from," he said, lip curled.

Anise opened her mouth, and Flora pinched her friend out of sight, knowing exactly what she was about to blab. Anise was going to brag about Kaanan being a King of the Pitch Woods—but if King Desmond didn't know yet, Flora had no desire to reveal their cards so early. Kaanan rested his hand on her bicep, giving her an approving squeeze. She almost smiled, but she kept her face flat, trying not to let any pertinent information out. They had to be a cold, united front—the only way to deal with greedy royals who had more power than they should.

"Yes, they are," Flora said, sitting upright so she could sit and face the man who claimed he was her father. She couldn't tell if it was true or not. Flora's features were so washed out and her mother's so vague to her, she had no idea if she resembled the man before her. "I don't want to go wherever you think home is— let us go."

"No," he said with a bored tone, quirking an eyebrow. Flora's jaw clenched and her nostrils flared as she let out a sharp breath.

"Let us go, before you regret not listening to me." Flora wasn't sure where the words came from, somewhere deep inside her where she didn't care about hierarchy or saying the wrong thing, where she only cared about getting herself, and her friends, to safety.

King Desmond raised a thick eyebrow, a scoff escaping his throat. "Really, Flora? Threats? To your own father?"

"You're not my father."

"Why do you say that?"

"You didn't raise me. I don't care if we share blood. I know all the things wrong in my life are

308

because of Anneliese and *you*."

"What have people told you?"

"Enough. I've heard rumors my entire life, and I don't care what's true and what isn't. I have things to do that don't involve going to your home or spending time with you," she said, eyes burning.

"You're right. The things wrong in your life, and mine, are because of your mother and my actions. We made mistakes in our youth I would like to fix. But I need you to do that."

"Why me? My magic?"

"Yes, I need your magic," he said, leaning forward.

"To do what?" she prompted, eyes scanning his face. There were so many rumors floating around about Anneliese and Desmond. Even more so that she had heard from other villagers still cursing the two, keeping them all in the past as stories were retold with fervent lips. The stories all told the same things—destruction brought on by greed. But no one could agree on who was at fault.

"To save Woodvale, of course," he said with a smile. It rang false to Flora. She wasn't sure if it was just her reading into it, or if it was true. Either way, Flora didn't trust King Desmond.

"I have something to finish first," she said as King Desmond's eyes hardened.

"Yes, I suppose you do—rumour has it your 'mother' was taken?" Flora's face dropped, along with her heart and stomach, all tumbling to the floor of the rocking carriage. Anise gripped her wrist as Flora's eyes narrowed on the King.

"How do you know that?"

"I make it a habit to know what is going on in my

kingdom."

"And yet you couldn't find me for almost two decades," she sneered with bared teeth.

"An oversight on my part—I didn't realize *magic* extended past your mother and two sorcerers who haven't left their respective Woods in hundreds of years," he said with a snarl. "Regardless, the chambermaid is gone. The question is, my darling daughter, do you really think you can defeat one of them to get her back? I know the woman who took you. She would have made you hide your magic, forget it existed—so be smart, Flora. Come with me, help me save Woodvale."

"Rosie is my mother. I won't leave her to the wolves."

"She is your caretaker—not your mother, not your blood. She is one person and there are hundreds of thousands in Woodvale with an hourglass of sand about to run out—save them. I know you want to," he said, eyes watering with emotion as he begged her. But Flora felt nothing, not at his face, or his words. She wanted to save her mother, wanted to finish things *her* way. She didn't want to be used, and following King Desmond would begin a precedent she wanted no part of.

"You're right," she said, the lie slithering easily from her lips as her chest warmed. Her ankle tickled up her calf, the larkspur growing in earnest. She didn't want to kill him, just incapacitate him—he was the King after all.

"*Flora*," Anise hissed as Flora pinched Kaanan's wrist where it rested beside her thigh. It was the only warning she could give him, and she prayed he understood.

"Excellent. I knew you would be smart about this—you are my daughter," he said with a grin.

"You're right, I am smart," she said with a saccharine smile and in one movement she tore the larkspur from underneath her skirt and lunged across the carriage, ramming it into King Desmond's waiting face. "But I'm my own person—not yours."

King Desmond collapsed backward into the carriage wall, face reddening and slackening, a trickle of drool escaping his mouth as Flora hit him dead on his nose, eyes, and mouth. The paralysis came on fast from the orifices Flora contaminated with a potent dose of her poisonous curse, and he was down for the count instantly, a looming threat vanquished in the blink of an eye.

Meanwhile, Kaanan had thrown himself at the guard in the carriage, slamming his head into the wood repeatedly before the guard collapsed too. Anise had shrieked and pushed herself out of harm's way as Flora half-stood over the man claiming to be her father. From the ruckus, the carriage slowed, and Kaanan nodded at Flora as he drew the shadows around him and threw himself outside to deal with the rest of the guards.

Flora breathed heavily as she stared at King Desmond's weakened state. The priest in the corner was still fast asleep from Kaanan's Nite dosing, so Anise and Flora grabbed their things and followed Kaanan out. She looked back once more at the incapacitated King, trying to find some semblance of guilt, but she came up empty. To her mind, he deserved it—even without the full story, she had heard enough, and she didn't want to be a pawn in his grasping game of chess.

There would be consequences to her violent actions in the carriage, but she hoped they wouldn't find her for weeks, maybe even years if she was lucky. Whether King Desmond would live or die was undetermined—it would depend on if anyone was left to save him once they ran. Flora wanted to feel guilt over the thought, but the King was also to blame for the way her world was. She would leave the carriage with one thought to comfort her: an eye for an eye. Every action she had taken was deserved—he finally got what was coming to him for his despicable greed.

Several guards were bleeding or passed out on the dirt road, Kaanan wiping a stolen sword clean with a fallen guard's cloak. He glanced at them as they approached him and said, "You two okay?"

"We're good," Anise said, nudging one of the guards with her shoe.

"Thank you," Flora said, gesturing to the littered bodies. Those ones she did feel bad about, but she didn't care to dwell on their actions. Instead, she gestured to the horses. "Can we take these ones to the Sage Woods?"

They looked healthy enough with luscious, thick coats and strong muscles gleaming in the afternoon sun. Kaanan looked at them, assessing, a smile toying on his lips and said, "Finder's keepers. Let's go."

"Wait!" a man's croaking voice yelled. A hand clasped the doorframe of the carriage with a white-knuckled grip. The priest's head appeared seconds later, eyes unfocused and evidently struggling to remain upright.

The whistle of a blade being drawn through the air hit Flora's ears as Kaanan directed the angled, deadly point toward the priest. She stood behind him and grabbed his free hand.

"Stay back or die—I have no issue killing a holy man, especially one with ties to Desmond Vale," Kaanan said, voice cold even as Flora squeezed his hand.

"Please...just wait," he said, releasing his grip and stumbling from the carriage. Kaanan tensed and Flora took a deep breath, readying herself.

"Stop right there." Kaanan's voice was cold as a blizzard.

"What do you want?" Flora interjected as Anise huffed behind her.

"Can't we just go?" Anise groaned as she stomped her foot.

The priest stopped where he stood, swaying in the wind as his hand clutched his heart over his shirt. "Anneliese."

"I am not Anneliese—I'm Flora," she huffed, her free hand balling into a fist at her side.

"I know," he muttered, eyes drifting to the ground, face crestfallen.

"Who are you? How did you know her?"

The priest hesitated, deep lines befalling his face before saying, "I loved her."

Flora sucked in a breath as the pieces fell into place. The man in front of her was the other man vying for her mother's attention and love who Rosie had spoken about.

"I just...wanted to tell you how sorry I am for my part," he said, voice cracking as he finally let his eyes meet Flora's. "I was a coward, and things would have been different if I spoke up."

"What do you mean?"

"I loved your mother, but my priesthood came between us. I should have chosen before she did, before she gave herself to Desmond."

"Are you my father?" Flora asked, eyebrows drawn together as she tried to decipher exactly what he was saying.

"I don't know," he said, shaking his head. "I would have loved to be—but your mother was unfaithful to Desmond and me."

"Oh," she said, mouth tightening as disappointment pressed on her chest.

"I just wanted you to know how sorry I am, and please know I will provide any assistance you may need now or in the future."

Flora nodded, unsure about how she felt. She mostly just wanted to escape from the conversation and conflicting emotions threatening to crush her. Even if he was her father, she felt very little for the man standing before her. Flora held each potential candidate in distaste. They were both strangers with different and ulterior motives she had no interest in uncovering. Her mother's past love life was hers alone—Flora wanted no part of that area of her life.

"We'll be going now," Kaanan rumbled, eyes watching Flora throughout the entire conversation. He saw she was ready to go before she knew it herself.

"I wish you all the best," the priest said. "If you ever need to find me, I will be in my church in Vale Centre. If you ask around for Jeremiah the Priest, someone will direct you to me. Or, just look for the church covered in larkspurs."

"Thank you," she said, and offered him a small

smile before turning away. Her chest was tight and her eyes were watering, but when Kaanan gave her a smile and squeezed her hand, her turmoil started melting away. Her eyes were wide at the implication they had been in his church, that one of her shards had been protected there for the last eighteen years. She didn't know what it meant—if it was a clue to her parentage, but that was a theory to solve another day.

Anise hooked her arm through Flora's and led her to the side while Kaanan went to retrieve the horses. They all mounted the borrowed beasts, power and strength thrumming through the creatures' muscled bodies. Flora waited for Kaanan to depart first before she followed him off the path, into the flat, hard earth toward the Sage Woods.

They were too far away to know, but a tugging in her navel told her they were going the right way, that soon enough she would see the inside of another forbidden place. Mountains rose in the distance to the left of them—the Línu Mountain Pass that kept the Pitch Woods and Sage Woods separate. They always looked like a beacon to Flora in paintings and in the distant view from her village. While the Norn Mountains looked unpassable to her, the Línu Mountains looked like an exit hall. She was wrong though—many people had tried leaving that way and were unsuccessful. After speaking with Kaanan and flicking through his folktale book, she wondered if more was out there. Flora felt it would be too lonely of an existence if she didn't hope and believe there were other cities and people beyond their insurmountable landscape. And if there wasn't, well, there was a burning thread of desire growing to find out those answers for herself instead of just reading about them in books.

Chapter Twenty-Eight

*The Sage Woods are beautiful and light,
prosperous and good—the pure opposite of the Pitch
Woods.*

*Where the Pitch Woods are dark, with an evil
sorcerer, the Sage Woods are bright, with a witch who
has been known to grant boons.*

*But neither is very different from the other and
misunderstanding their similarities and differences will
be the downfall of everyone.*

*What people fail to realize, is that monsters and
beasts hungry for flesh and foolish humans don't only
live in the dark—they live in the light too.*

-Proverb

Flora ached all over and each second on the horse
sent waves of pain and discomfort coursing through her
tired and weak body. It was their second day traveling
since Flora had disarmed, and potentially irrecoverably
hurt, King Desmond. Maybe even killed him and she
wasn't wallowing in guilt yet. It would come
eventually, but right now she had shoved so much down
she knew when everything was said and done, she
would be a shattered vase to be glued back together.

They had traveled as far as they could the previous
day before stopping for the night. It was tense until
Flora tripped trying to sit down at the smoldering fire,
and then laughter erupted in the silence of the night.

After, they were all calmer and smiles and laughs flowed freely.

Flora's stomach was in a constant state of motion, her nerves sending waves through her belly almost making her heave from anxiety. The closer they got to the Sage Woods, the more unease gnawed at Flora. She wasn't worried about getting the last shard—she was worried she wouldn't make it in time.

She woke in the space between midnight and dawn, and when she went to relieve herself a gully over, a coughing fit overcame her. When she moved her hand from her mouth, scarlet specks littered her palm. Her stomach dropped, bottoming out as she swallowed a mass in her throat. The crimson decorating her palm had her heart stuttering and stopping as she imagined what could be happening inside of her body. Maybe her intestines cracked, or her heart valves or tubes splintered. Anything could be shutting down, petering to a halting stop that would end her life sooner rather than later.

Oh Gods, Flora thought, her breath coming out in a wheezy gasp she desperately tried to keep quiet. She just needed to get through the next couple of days. It was no time really, but it felt like an eternity when she had no idea if the next dizzy wave would be the one where she would keel over and never wake up. All she needed to do was keep it together until she could save her mother, something that sounded so simple, yet so difficult.

But they were close to the Sage Woods. The sun had almost finished burning beneath the horizon when they decided to stop for the day. Kaanan said they were only about a two-hour ride from the tree line. The information sent a ripple of anxiety through Flora's navel as her ankle tingled with fire. She tried to calm herself, but her pulse pounded in her ears as she lay back down to sleep between Kaanan and Anise, trying to drown herself in their support.

****

Flora was a jumble of nerves and worries when she woke again. The sun had yet to rise, the sky a washed-out dark blue with just enough light she could make out the words in Kaanan's folktale book as the other two slept. The folktales were fascinating. Flora devoured them, flipping parchment rapidly, narrowly avoiding papercuts as she drank the words in. Each story held a message, and each was more beautiful than the last. They spoke of new places, new people, new creatures with different histories and Flora longed for them to be real, to experience them for herself.

A bird's caw broke her out of her reverie, and she glanced up at the ignited sky, expecting to see a crow or raven, and instead found a vulture circling overhead. The distraction made her recenter, and she forced herself to slow down as the stories began to speak of the Sage Woods. She wanted to glean any information she could before they entered, but most of the information was about magical plants and elves called Huldufólk who lived in rocks all around the Woods. The tale said those who dally with the Huldufólk should be careful to never speak to the elves or accept their gifts as they would steal your mind before tearing your body to shreds.

Flora believed the warning, choosing to assume the words were true. When Kaanan and Anise finally woke, once the sky had finished smoldering, she relayed the information before they went on their way.

The Sage Woods came upon them quickly. Luscious, towering greenery filled Flora's eyes as far as she could see. It was beautiful and intimidating, inviting and unwelcoming all at once. Flora couldn't decide between wanting to go into the deep green trees and feel the plants against her bare skin, or if she wanted to run as fast as her legs could carry her, screaming her head off all the way. It was simultaneously a contrasting forest of magic and trickery, of fascination and perversion. Scanning the treeline brought up the differing feelings so formidably it was hard to put her foot forward. She had to dare herself.

Flora was the first to break the little line they formed, all watching the trees dancing in the faint breeze, and once her feet moved closer, Kaanan and Anise followed close behind. Cool confidence radiated off Kaanan, while Anise exuded a contradicting air of fear and cockiness. Flora paused, her lips quirking as laughter bubbled up. Her shoulders shook as she stopped walking, trying to contain her hysteria, but failed miserably.

"What's so funny?" Anise said, giving her shoulder a light shove as Flora turned to face both Anise and Kaanan, finding a smile on her and a smirk on him.

"Nothing. It's just I'm more frightened of going into the Sage Woods than I was the Pitch Woods, and only one is known for monsters and death," Flora said, her voice light and giggly even as anxiety thrummed through her. She was going crazy with the constant fear assaulting her the past few weeks—she had reached her breaking point.

Anise's face cracked in two, light washing away

her fear as she burst out laughing along with Flora. Kaanan watched the two, eyes warm and amused, the smile growing on his face until his dimples appeared in full force. The three drank in the happy moment, basking in it as they procrastinated going past the tree line.

Another vulture cawing overheard shoved them from the moment, the laughter dying in their throats while their smiles dimmed. And with that, they strode forward into the trees, Flora leading with Kaanan keeping close behind her. Flora's ankle warmed the second she stepped past the border, her shards pulsing lightly against her chest as she drank in her surroundings like a person dying of thirst in the desert without a mirage in sight.

The Sage Woods were gorgeous and full of life, so potent and vivacious Flora's eyes shined and a smile blossomed on her lips. Awestruck, she trailed her fingers along the nearest tree trunk and bush of red-tart colored berries, a focal point of bursting color in the sea of green. Flora breathed deep, inhaling the earthy tones, finding a home in her lungs as her mind settled from the comforting smells.

"Be careful of the rocks," Flora reminded, her gaze clocking the stone a pace away sitting in a small clearing, sunlight streaming directly on it. If the folktales were true, it looked to Flora like a good spot to make a home, with direct sunlight and a clear patch of grass in an otherwise densely packed forest.

Kaanan unsheathed a knife at his belt, whipping it into the air so fast it whined as he nodded to Flora to lead them on with her rapidly warming ankle. Flora stepped carefully through the thick underbrush, absentmindedly brushing aside leaves to uncover beautiful gems underneath. She found several species of flora, each more stunning than the last. She wanted to burn the visuals of the Sage Woods into her head so she could go anywhere, travel past Woodvale for the hope that more existed in the world, and still transport herself back to the healthy, bright life inhabiting there.

Flora's heart was in a steady state of unease, a strong pulse beneath her breastbone that distracted her from the calm energy of the forest attempting to flood her system. Bushes rustled and branches cracked, their snaps and shuffling echoing into her ears as fear flooded her middle, but nothing appeared. From the looks of things, they were alone.

Nevertheless, Flora could feel the pulse from the Sage Woods, a livelihood hiding in plain sight, or beneath the surface—she could *feel* it. Something lived in the Sage Woods, magic and more, and Flora wanted to know exactly what. Her ankle burned fiercely, but there were no larkspurs or shards in sight. She wanted to ask someone where they were supposed to be going because her legs were getting sore, and the sun had passed over them without notice. It would be dusk soon, and Flora assumed that unlike the Pitch Woods, light was in flux, not a constant—but only time would tell. Flora didn't want to be in an unknown, magical wood at night when so much was at stake.

"Anything, Flora?" Anise asked with a deep sigh. She had been trailing behind farther and farther the past hour, growing tired and bored, but still keeping up with Flora—it was their quest after all, and even the boring spells were an experience she and Flora had only ever dreamed about.

Flora stopped in her tracks and turned, shaking her head at Anise. Sweat dotted her brow, accompanied by rosy cheeks and tired eyes. It was warm in the Sage Woods, and with the thick vegetation, they were constantly overexerting themselves by slashing or shoving plants out of the way.

Flora's eyes flicked over to Kaanan, who was still wearing his all-black ensemble complete with his thick wool cloak Flora had no idea how he was still wearing. She and Anise were wearing short sleeves and they were sweltering. Except, the dark was a cold place, and a halo of shadows surrounded his body—his magic was keeping him enviously cool.

She had no idea how King Desmond didn't see it, the sheer power and regality Kaanan held, the shadowy magic he exuded without even trying. His entire ensemble screamed "Pitch King," and yet, no one called him out on it. Even she had missed it when they first met. But people saw what they wanted to see, and no one wanted to see the Pitch King in the flesh.

"I don't know what to do," Flora said, hands falling to her sides limply. She was at a loss—everything in the Sage Woods looked the same. "Maybe we should look for the Sage Witch."

"No," Kaanan said immediately, straightening at Flora's suggestion. "If we go after her now, we're on her turf—her home. She has all the advantages. And you don't have your full magic back, Flora. We have to find the shard, play by her rules. She's not an inherently bad witch; she has some sympathy. She's as fickle as magic, but she can be fair. If you follow her instructions, she will do as she promised."

"Are you sure, though? Have you met her?" Anise

asked, arms crossing over her chest.

"I...not personally, no, but my father met her," he said. "Look, the only thing I know is seeking her out now will be next to impossible—we don't know where to look—and she will be furious and have the advantages."

Flora nodded meekly, her body sagging with another punch of exhaustion. She didn't want to look in a mirror—she was scared to see her reflection. But neither Anise nor Kaanan had said anything other than a few concerned glances so she hoped she didn't look too close to death's door. She was almost there, but the end kept slipping from her shaky grasp.

A rustle in the branches nearby halted their conversation. Six narrowed eyes fell on the shaking brush, and Flora stilled in her spot. Kaanan glided in front of her, shielding her with his cloak as Anise sidled up next to her. The two exchanged a glance, both mirroring frightened expressions as the girls clasped hands.

They waited with bated breath, three hearts pounding in ears, but nothing appeared. Kaanan glanced back at them before he strode forward, inspecting the area. He called, "There's a rock, but nothing else."

Flora nodded shakily, the encounter reminding her of the dragon in the Pitch Woods. Maybe they had just missed one of the Huldufólk returning home, or it was the wind or another creature. Regardless, Flora was glad nothing chose to bother them as she wasn't sure her weakening heart could handle another terrifying scare.

"What if you tried using your magic to find the last

shard? Like calls to like sort of thing?" Kaanan suggested, looking appraisingly at Flora. "Maybe growing a larkspur could help."

Flora nodded, the idea sounding feasible to her—all the other shards had a trail of larkspur leading to them and at this point, they were out of ideas and options. Based off their surroundings, her magic appeared to be their only hope of finding the last shard.

Flora closed her eyes, tucking her hair behind her ears as she breathed out deeply, centering herself in the trees. She nodded to herself and snaked her fingers up to her shards, bringing them out into the light and holding on so they bit into her palm. Flora focused on her shards, her magic running through her veins, and on the last shard somewhere nearby waiting for her to claim as her own. Lastly, she thought of larkspur, the burning sensation on her ankle, and the gorgeous bulbs her eyes could find anywhere.

Her chest and palm warmed as her mind exploded with images of larkspur while her senses flared alive. Her eyes fluttered open, and she gasped, her spare hand flying to her lips as she blinked rapidly, trying to ensure what she saw was real and not a figment of her imagination. Flora's brows creased as she leaned forward, raising her hand to touch what lay in front of her eyes.

A path of brilliant purple larkspurs had popped up, extending and weaving through the trees in front of Flora. Her fingers brushed the petal, and she inhaled sharply at the confirmation of reality. She had made a trail of larkspur with her magic, and hopefully, it led to the last shard. She swallowed thickly as her vision dimmed and fought against the birthmark trying to wash her away.

"You see this too, right?" Flora asked, keeping her voice steady amidst the rolling nausea and quivering limbs.

"Yes," Anise breathed, eyes wide as she stared at Flora.

"That was excellent," Kaanan said with a blinding smile. "I could feel the magical energy—you had admirable control."

"Let's follow it," Flora said, eyes unwavering from the larkspur. She swallowed thickly, knowing if she moved too fast she would surely fall. Her heart ached in her chest as she struggled to find the strength to move forward. She issued one warning to her friends before they could move closer to the larkspur. "Be careful not to touch it."

Flora stepped forward onto the magical path, Kaanan and Anise following beside her, both taking care to not even accidentally touch the poisonous plant. They walked deeper into the Sage Woods, green the only thing they could see, save for a few pops of purple. Flora was almost in a trance the way she moved, sure-footed in the unknown location, and barely pausing to catch her breath as her body begged her to keep going, to find the end of the path where the shard had to be.

Flora felt like they had walked for kilometers as her legs burned and shook with each step. The sun had fallen from the sky without her knowing, the sky dark with specks of white, but the forest was still bright as though the sun reigned supreme in the sky. It was a very disorienting view. Just as Flora's ankle felt like it was being dipped in acid, they finally arrived at the final larkspur, bigger than the last and instead of deep purple, it was a pure, stark white.

"Wow," Flora breathed, fingers moving of their own accord to touch the petals. They were warm to the touch from the mysterious sunlight, and softer than the petals that grew from her ankle. "What now?" she whispered to the air of the forest.

A crashing, rumbling sounded from all around Flora, and she flinched, hands flying over her head as the ground beneath her feet shook violently. One second she was standing a pace away from Kaanan and Anise, and the next, she was falling down a rocky ravine that opened from thin air.

Chapter Twenty-Nine

White shard properties: Innocence, purity, and joy
(This shard is easiest to control if you stay true to yourself and be a good person, at least a little bit. There's no such thing as innocence or purity, but there is such a thing as being evil. Be kind and true, and care for others. Try to be happy and the shard will reward you for it. Just follow the rules.)

A scream pierced the air and it took Flora a second to realize it was coming from her. Her lips clamped shut and she heard a faint echo of her name from Kaanan and Anise. Her stomach swooped as her eyes closed, as she prepared herself for impact, for death. But nothing came.

Flora opened her eyes to find she was at the bottom of a ravine. Rock walls rose on either side of her, and she could just make out trees and arms waving at her from above and a vulture circling overhead. Flora sat up, tenderly touching her back and skull, expecting to find blood even though she felt no impact, but she was fine. She twirled around, eyes scanning the rest of the ravine only to find it was average save for the white larkspur behind her.

It grew from the rocks unnaturally bold, healthy, and large. It beckoned Flora closer, her feet moving to it on their own accord. And then she was there, eye level with the blooming petals, brushing the soft velvet with her fingers as she admired its beauty.

A noise sounded from behind her, rocks sputtering against one another as a miniature figure climbed out from behind a loose rock. Flora's mouth dropped open, her stomach roiling as she stared at the creature emerging—a Huldufólk, looking just like it had in the illustrations. They had distinct humanoid features, just immensely smaller with viciously sharp teeth. If you ever saw a Huldufólk's teeth, you were apparently as good as dead for you would have done something to offend the tiny people.

Flora swallowed thickly as it looked her way, and immediately dropped her eyes, begging and pleading to every God she knew to please, *please* let it ignore her. She squeezed her eyes shut tight, face scrunching. Rocks continued to sputter, clanging noises echoing in the cavernous ravine. All the while Flora's heart raced and stomach contracted. If the folktale were true, all she had to do was not talk to it and she would be fine. It didn't say anything about eye contact, but Flora was far too frightened about angering the Huldufólk and potentially ruining her chance of getting the last shard to open them.

It was only when the rocks stopped moving that she cracked an eyelid open. Her eyes widened immediately at the sight, as round as saucers as she gasped. Flora only just held herself back from lunging forward and snatching it up. Because sitting in front of her on the ground was the last shard, gleaming white in the sunlight, calling her name so the other shards could finally reconnect.

But she couldn't.

Right?

No. Flora couldn't—it went against the rules, it went against the little information she knew about the Huldufólk.

But it was the last shard, just sitting there, waiting to be claimed by Flora. It was the answer to all her problems, the only way she could live past eighteen. Her limbs shook as she held herself back, clenching her fists until her nails made crescent moons of pooled blood in her palms. She let out a gasping breath as the pain helped her stay away. But hurting herself could only do so much because she had stepped forward. Now the shard was that much closer, that much shinier and her stomach dipped as the overwhelming pressure of desire crushed her.

"Pick me up, Flora, we can go save your mother," a silky voice said as it slithered into her mind. Flora stepped closer, shuffling her feet against the rock as her eyes locked on the shard.

"Don't listen to her Flora—this is a test," a different voice hissed in her head—Blue.

Flora caught her bottom lip with her teeth, biting down until sharp, tangy blood matted her tongue. She didn't know what to do, didn't know what the right choice was. She needed that shard, but the rules said she couldn't take it—so what was she to do?

An anchor hooked into her navel, tugging her forward, closer to the shard. Flora reared back, desperately digging her heels in as the forceful presence dragged her closer.

"Stop resisting. You know you want it," the voice whispered seductively. And oh, did Flora want it.

Her magic rose. The world was bathed in a hue of green, magic simmering in her veins as the headiest desire to reach out and pluck the stone struck her like a sledgehammer. She wanted nothing more than to be selfish, to be greedy, to forget about rules and do what was right for her, damn the consequences.

But as appealing as that sounded, she couldn't close the gap between her and the twinkling, shimmering, crystalline white shard.

Stones sputtered behind the shard and Flora flinched as the Huldufólk came into view. It stared at her with dark eyes, black pits absorbing most of its skull as it watched her, waiting for her to move. It was taunting her, mocking her inability to just *make a decision* and hope it was right, hope it was something she could live with.

"What are you, Flora? What do you stand for?" Blue asked, nudging her mentally.

Flora let out a sharp breath, her eyebrows furrowing into a deep crease across her forehead.

What was Flora? What did she stand for? It changed and shifted like water running, so how was she supposed to know? Was she only a rule follower? Or did she also act impulsively, ignore warnings, and do what would further herself? She was only eighteen and constantly growing and changing—so how was she to know?

Flora breathed in deeply, filling her lungs until they felt like they would burst, and then let it out along with her worries. Flora knew herself; the quest had proven a lot for her, had shown her aspects of herself Flora had reconciled with.

Flora was sometimes selfish, sometimes greedy, but she liked helping others, especially those close to her. She liked helping herself too, but not without looking at the consequences. Because at the heart of it all, Flora was a rule follower—she respected rules and liked them. Society couldn't function without rules and people following them. And Flora respected the stories too much to ignore their warnings. They were there for a reason—you just had to listen to them.

So, with a heavy heart, Flora stepped backward, rocks crumbling around her noisily until her back brushed against the white larkspur. Her legs gave out from under her without warning, and she collided with the solid ground, groaning as pain ricocheted up her spine.

A vision appeared before her eyes, a blinding white silhouette in the shape of a woman. The light bathing Flora was warm and she softened as she basked in it. Twinkling charms flittered into her ears, her body relaxing at the sound as the white surrounded her completely.

"Well done, child. Your task is complete, and you have been found worthy. Do well, respect the magic, and all will be fine," the white shard whispered lovingly into her mind and Flora's lips curled in a hesitant smile.

"Thank you," she whispered, her palm warming as the white shard appeared in it. It was beautiful, just like the others, and Flora could feel the magic pulsing from it into her.

Flora tugged the rope holding the other three shards together over her head and laid them out on her lap. She placed each shard next to each other, and cupped her hands around them, furrowing her eyebrows as she called upon her magic. The Sage Witch had written of an amulet, and Flora hoped she would be able to create that.

Magic flooded her veins, an intoxicating feeling as her body and hands warmed around the shards. A bright kaleidoscope of light erupted from the shards, causing Flora to gasp and faint cries of her name to carry on the wind.

The light faded as quickly as it appeared and in its place was an amulet composed of the shards, an exquisite mosaic of pink, blue, purple, and white in the shape of a larkspur petal. It was beautiful, and alighted Flora's world in vibrant, magnificent color as she slipped the amulet over her neck, letting it rest on her breastbone.

She gasped as her body tingled all over, nerves buzzing to life as her skin electrified. The sensation was too great, and she collapsed to the ground, the dark sky raining down on her as she twitched and groaned. Her body felt fuller, her mind complete, and as the sensations faded away as fast as they came on, she stood, her vision neither blurring nor discoloring.

She felt better than she had in years—her lungs breathed deeper, her legs powerful, and her heart felt stronger as she reveled in the sunlight streaming down on her. She heard cries of her name again and glanced at her friends rapidly waving at her. She had forgotten how far down she was, with no rope or pulley to help her back up. But she had something stronger now.

Her magic was like breathing. Instinctive and pure.

It was like a switch had been flipped inside of her. Like her very soul and livelihood had been completed, fixed in an instant. Like she had been drowning and struggling to tread water for years, like all the puzzle pieces fell into place to create a shimmering, colorful mosaic that was wholeheartedly Flora.

A grin sparked to life as she realized she knew exactly what to do. One hand slipped to the amulet from habit, and the other she cast straight out, palm facing the ground as she called upon her magic—her plants. She closed her eyes as she imagined what she wanted: a lift to the top.

A thick stalk shot from the ground, a stronger than normal leaf sprouting up, cupping her bottom as it continued its journey to the sky. Flora held onto the stem tightly, her heart hammering as the rocky ravine faded from view. She swallowed thickly, very aware of her own mortality and that if she fell, she would surely die.

But she didn't fall, and the stalk didn't falter—her magic was sure and strong and would never let such tragedy befall her right after she proved herself.

Kaanan and Anise came into view, both staring at her with wide and worried eyes, mouths open as she smiled at them, hopping off the stalk and patting it gently, releasing it back into the wilds as her magic simmered in her veins. Flora's feet touched grassy earth and she ran for her friends, throwing her arms around their shoulders as she hugged them tight. Gone was the dizziness and weak limbs—she felt good and strong and healthy. There could still be risks. She didn't know everything about the curse, and magic was so fickle, but in that moment, she felt alive and well, and so happy her friends were okay and waiting for her.

"Are you okay?" Anise asked, pulling back from the hug and inspecting her friend.

"I'm great," Flora said, beaming in the sunlight.

"You did amazingly," Kaanan said, his eyes warm and bright as he looked at her.

"Thank you," she said, and pulled the amulet from underneath her clothes into the light. "I got the last shard, and I completed the amulet."

"And you feel good? Your magic is strong?"

"Yes, I feel better than I have in a long time." Flora beamed at her friends, heart full as she ignored her worries and anxieties and focused on the joy. "I know we need to get to the well, but we have a day's buffer—we should just…relax for a few hours."

"As long as it's out of these woods," Anise said, shuddering.

"Deal."

And so the three departed the woods, Flora leading them as she asked the flora and fauna which way to go and in no time they were back outside in the warm glow of dawn, sun low in the horizon, gleaming onto their faces.

They spent the day frolicking around the area, recuperating their bodies and souls before they would face what was to come. Flora finished the day with the cracks in her heart patched up and almost mended, her limp bones strong, like nothing could break them again. She practiced her magic, calling upon plant after plant, and when they found an abandoned, dead crop field, she filled it full of ripe, plump strawberries and they feasted on the lusciously sweet fruit.

And then, in and amongst the joy and celebration and avoidance of thoughts of the challenging battle ahead, Anise softly, gently pulled Flora away from Kaanan so the two could have a brief reprieve alone. They waded into the wildflowers and fruits and vegetable garden Flora had created. She smiled at her friend tightly, already sensing what was to come. Flora wanted nothing more than to avoid talking about the emotional turmoil, and the petrifying possibility things might not work out how she wanted. And that wasn't even taking into account the traumatic encounters she had already faced and only somewhat processed.

There were so many parts of Flora that felt like they were being held together by a thread, by glue that was peeling. She was a mix-matched amalgamation of broken pieces that would come undone with a light gust of wind. But in the next breath, she knew she had grown so much, had become stronger in spite of and because of her hardships. And she knew in her heart of hearts she would not be broken, that she may have shattered in some regard, but she was more powerful because of it. She was broken and bloody and bruised, but she was whole and complete and fierce. She was an enigma like everyone else and she was proud for it— she could face what was to come and when the dust settled, she could genuinely and completely process and work through her trauma. It would take time, but she also knew, had grown to realize, she was worth the investment of her time. She was worthy and valuable, and she would spend the rest of her days trying to learn to truly love herself instead of tearing herself down at any given opportunity. It would never be an easy journey, but she was tired of constantly belittling herself and letting her frightened thoughts win.

"Flora," Anise said, voice soft and probing, "are you okay? Truly? Sorry, that's a dumb question. I just wanted to make sure you know I'm here for you— *always*." Anise paused, her lips pursing as she chose her next words. "I know it couldn't have been easy with King Desmond..." She trailed off, face pinching in a wince that spoke volumes. "He deserved it. You know that, right? I know you, and I don't want you to feel bad or guilty. He was an awful man and he got what was coming to him. You did the right thing."

"I know," Flora said, voice soft and hesitant. "I *know* that in my mind, but I still feel so bad. I *killed* him, Anise. There is no way he survived, and while part of me is okay with that, part of me feels disgusted. It's just so hard to cement myself in some of my actions, to accept what I've done."

"I will always support your decisions. As long as you keep your mind and heart intact, I think you'll always make the right choices. And if you don't, then I'll be here to help patch you up and make sure you can move forward."

"Thank you," Flora whispered, her heart lifting. It would take more than one conversation to move past her deeds, to truly come to terms with her actions, but it was comforting to hear Anise's support. Flora was in knots about King Desmond, but she also stood by her actions—he was a bad man, one who helped drive Woodvale to ruin and destruction. His suffering was long overdue. Flora believed what truly held her back from moving on was the loss of a father. While she had never had one and had accepted that fact, being presented with the figure and then violently ripping it away from herself was a blow she would need time to recover from.

Anise clasped Flora's hand as her voice took on an awed, urgent, and fervent tone. "I'm really proud of you, not that it really matters what I think. But I hope you know that." Anise's eyes watered, a well of tears forming but not yet falling. "I also wanted to make sure *we* were okay. I know I've not always been a good friend—I see that now. I'm selfish and self-absorbed and to be honest, I liked that you were shy and anxious and always needed me. I liked being wanted and needed and I know I haven't let you grow because of that. I never wanted you to be strong, and I know that's awful, especially seeing how much you've grown and matured, and now I can't believe how much I was holding you back."

"No, Anise," Flora breathed, tightening her grip on her friend's hand as her face fell. "You don't have to apologize—it's not like I didn't let you. And besides, look where we are now. I will always be grateful for our time together, and our friendship. Yes, we've had some…difficulties"—Flora quirked her eyebrows and Anise barked a soft laugh—"but I wouldn't want anyone else by my side. We're different people now, but I hope we can still stay together, *grow* together."

"I'd like that," she whispered. "How did you get to be so mature?" Anise asked with a watery smile, tears slipping down her cheeks she hastily wiped away. Flora smiled softly at her friend, a rush of lavender rising to her senses, calming her light panic at the heart-to-heart and the exposure she let herself succumb to. She tucked her heart on her sleeve for Anise.

"I think I finally let myself." Flora shrugged, searching her mind for the right words. "I spent so long closing myself off, shutting myself down and giving in to my anxieties that I never really grew. Exposing myself to new things and the world just…allowed me to breathe, allowed me to find myself in a new way and let me break down my fences and expose myself to a never-ending open field of new possibilities. I want to constantly grow and change and be *me* and the only way to do that is to keep moving forward and not let myself get in my way."

Anise smiled at Flora widely, their connected eyes saying a thousand unspoken words and feelings before Anise and Flora crushed their bodies together in a tight hug, spending longer than they ever had just holding each other and offering support after a tumultuous journey not quite over.

"You're going to be fine. I just want you to know I believe in you, and you are more than capable of getting your mom back and making sure the Sage Witch doesn't screw you over. You're going to be amazing. And if you stumble, I'll always be your safety net—just like I know you're mine." Anise pulled away, her eyebrows twisted in worry while her lips curved up.

"Thank you." Flora caught the other girl's gaze. "But, I'll be fine. Don't worry."

"I know. Just make sure of it, okay? I need you too, Flora. I want us to grow old together and still be best friends when we're gray and wrinkled and cursing the little kids who think they know so much when they don't. I want to stay by your side, so I need you to make it through this."

"I will. I promise." Flora's vow cut through the space between them like a knife, slicing a line of scarlet in each of their hearts, connected and sworn for life.

The two stayed together for a little while longer, Flora's head resting on Anise's shoulder, and Anise's head on hers. They watched the breeze tickle and twirl through the grass grown from Flora's magic and filled each other up in their endless well of love and support for one another. They had grown and changed a lot throughout the course of their adventure, and while their friendship was not what it used to be, Flora preferred the new one that emerged. Their relationship was stronger and healthier, and Flora would cherish it forever.

Before they fully crossed out of the wildflowers caressing their ankles, Anise bit her lip and narrowed her eyes at Flora. "You know, I can't believe you forgave him so fast." She sighed, rolling her eyes and smirking at Flora. "I mean, I get why—he is gorgeous, and he doesn't seem to be like the stories. I honestly think he's even *good* for you, but still."

"I know—me too, but I realized closing myself off is just as bad as never trusting anyone or never letting people change or earn forgiveness. People aren't perfect and when you find kindred souls, like you or Kanaan, you have to hold onto them as tight as you can. They're scarce. That kind of connection is rare and special, and I won't let either of you go without a fight. You're stuck with me." Flora watched as Anise's eyes sparked to life and the two hugged swiftly again. Flora's arms were like stone around her friend, and she wished she didn't have to leave the comforting, safe embrace of Anise. Her heart raced and thundered at the thought of confronting the Sage Witch, and at the burgeoning truth that would utterly complicate the matter.

"I love you." The words were whispered from Flora's quivering lips, the confessed truth earnest and sweet like flowers surrounding them.

"I love you too."

It was a day Flora would never forget and would cherish in her heart always. It was a day that cemented her feelings, that she loved Anise, no matter their difficulties and struggles, and Flora wouldn't let anything come between them even as they grew and changed with the wind.

And as for Kaanan, well, Flora fully accepted she liked him as more than a friend, and she decided she wanted to do something about it. Once she saved her mother, she would tell him, and if she were lucky, maybe he would say the same back. Because he looked at her with such intensity and warmth, Flora was begging to question her doubt, and trust what her eyes and heart were telling her. Whether it was familial, platonic, or romantic love, she would strive to hold onto him no matter what came next. But she hoped, dreamed, he felt the same brush of golden, rosy light when he looked at her, just as she did when she looked at him.

Chapter Thirty

If it is a Witch they want, then it is a Witch I shall be.

-Unknown.

The moon climbed into the sky, resting on a bed of clouds before it drained away behind the horizon, winking goodbye as Flora stirred awake. She stretched deeply as she sat up in the tent, joints creaking and popping. She crawled outside to find the sun starting to bloom behind the trees in the distance.

After their day of fun and relaxing, they had spent yesterday traveling to the well at the base of the Línu Mountain Pass. They had barely stopped to rest, and all three plus their horses had slept deeply last night, sleep claiming them as soon as they lay down.

Now, today was the day. The day Flora had been dreading and anticipating, fearing and hoping. Today was the day Flora would save her mother. After that, she didn't know. All she knew was that the Sage Witch wanted to exchange her family's amulet for her mother.

But Flora was having second thoughts.

After experiencing and using the completed amulet, after it restored her cursed-away magic, Flora never wanted to let it go. It was powerful and satisfying. It made her feel *good*, and she couldn't imagine letting it go. Even so, she loved Rosie and couldn't let anything happen to her or her friends.

Except, she wanted to keep the amulet, wanted to hang onto her full magic, restore Woodvale to its formal glory and then...and then she wanted to go away, find new adventures and work on her anxiety to a point where it didn't need to be "manageable" and could just be a minor blip in her existence that sometimes appeared but that she could largely ignore or work past.

Flora sighed, crunching into an apple she picked yesterday from the newly grown tree she made beside their campsite. Sticky sweet juice dribbled down her chin as her shoulders relaxed, the burst of flavor on her tongue enough to calm her momentarily. She would figure it out, and until she saw the Witch and her mother, there was no point in planning ahead—she was on uncommon ground and there was the possibility of the Witch letting her keep the amulet.

"Or you could just take it," Pink said in her mind causing Flora to jump.

"Take it?" Flora whispered to the air, a frown forming on her rosy lips.

Taking the amulet would not be easy. She had no idea what exactly the Sage Witch wanted with it, and she knew if she could be cursed once—as a baby no less—the Witch must not be outrageously kind. Flora's mind cast to her victims, the people she had used her larkspur on, the people Kaanan had killed for her. Strong-willed people could rarely be cowed unless drastic action was taken.

If she wanted her mother *and* the shards, Flora would have to kill the Sage Witch and take it for herself.

Flora startled at the thought, her eyes widening as

her mind raced. She hated to admit it, but the idea was intoxicating. If the Witch was indisposed, Flora could have everything she wanted. She could have her mother and her full magic. But killing another person over it? Flora hesitated—that wasn't something she thought she could do.

The Witch had been alive for centuries if the stories were to be believed, so she would have lived a long and probably good life. Flora was young with a birthmark that could kill her excruciatingly slowly and painfully. Because even with her magic restored, and body healthy, the birthmark was still on her ankle like a stain on her existence. It looked malicious to her—like one wrong move and she would return to her weakened and husk-like state.

But Flora wasn't a killer, not unless there was just cause, like those who were after her. But what was the difference, really? It was still a life snuffed out like a candle's flame. Flora didn't know what to do. Her magic had a point—she could have everything she wanted if she looked past morals and goodness. She just didn't know if she could, or what would become of her if she did.

"Good morning," Kaanan said softly, his voice deep and silky from sleep, startling Flora out of her mind, allowing her to push aside her dark thoughts and pretend they didn't exist for the time being.

"Good morning," Flora said with a smile. "How did you sleep?"

"Good, you?" And at Flora's nod he continued. "Are you ready for today?"

"…yes…no—I don't know," Flora said with a nervous giggle. "Part of me is ready. I feel good and I don't want anything to happen to my mom. I need to see her, make sure the Sage Witch didn't hurt her—I've been avoiding thinking about that."

"But?"

"But…what if I'm not ready?"

"Ready for what? The Sage Witch didn't threaten you, right? Just an exchange?"

"Yes, but I don't want to give her my amulet. I don't want her to take away my magic—I want to use it, to keep it," Flora said, biting her lip and not meeting his burning gaze.

"Flora—that's not a bad thing," he said, lifting her chin with his finger so their eyes connected, now a bright green to his dark, almost black brown. "But you don't know if taking away the amulet will take away your powers. It may be fine."

"My birthmark was killing me, Kaanan, literally sucking the life from me. I almost died the other day—I could feel myself shutting down and I coughed up blood," she said, voice rising an octave. His eyes widened comically in horror, but she ignored it and continued on. "I don't think I can have both—magic without the amulet. The boon's true power clearly comes from the amulet like the *Króna* said. I don't just have access to magic without it! That's why I spent years living without even feeling it. But after touching that first shard, *everything* changed. I finally felt my true potential."

"But this was a test, and the magic found you worthy. The Sage Witch will probably allow you to keep the amulet and the same magic your ancestors had so long as you follow the rules," he assured with a smile.

"What if she doesn't?"

"Then we make her, and if that doesn't work, we kill her—end the reign of the everlasting Sage Witch," he said with a shrug and Flora blinked.

"Really?" she asked, eyes boring into his.

"Yes, really. Sometimes the end justifies the means," he said. "Plus, having no competition for who has the best forest would be nice." He cracked a blinding smile and Flora laughed briefly before she sobered. "However, I would like you to tell me if you're ever hurt again—I'm here to help."

"Okay," she whispered, and watched as a dimple appeared in his cheek as his eyes darkened.

"Excellent," he murmured. "You don't have anything to worry about, though. I'll be right behind you. I just hope you know that you are worth so much more than your magic. You're incredible and powerful without it." Kaanan tentatively reached out to cup her cheek with his sultry hand, nearly causing Flora's knees to buckle. "But really, you don't need me there—you can do it Flora. You're strong with or without your magic, and I know you will get what you want."

"I will." She nodded. She would take what she wanted, or she would die trying. It was all too important for Flora to roll over—she was tired of how her behavior was dictated in the past. Now was the time for New Flora to take the reins of her life.

****

Flora was going to throw up, or faint—she wasn't quite sure, only that it would be one of the two. So much for New Flora. The old her was still alive and kicking. It would take so much more than a simple string of words and a thought for her to truly change—

she needed action. Nevertheless, her stomach was far too unstable, and her vision and hearing were going in and out of focus. Something was coming. It was inevitable—like the sun rising or her anxiety making mundane situations difficult for her.

The sun was about to slip below the horizon, the sky smoldering as it burned away the pale blue. There were maybe ten minutes until sundown, and Flora couldn't take the waiting. She glared at the sun, willing it to go down faster so she could get this all over with, so she could move on with her life. The past few weeks were filled with anxiety and excitement, and while Flora enjoyed herself at some parts, she was tired and wanted a break from the fast-paced, high-stress life.

She was leaning against the ancient well that had no water in it—Flora had checked; her stones had come back pinging instead of splashing. Kaanan and Anise were waiting a stone-throw away at an abandoned farmhouse. It was the only place that provided shelter for them to watch at a distance so she wouldn't be completely alone.

Flora sighed through her nose sharply, her hand pressing against her stomach as it tossed and turned. It felt like it was being eaten by tiny little insects, crawling around and munching until it was all she could focus on.

The only plus side was the view. The sun falling behind the Línu Mountain Pass was gorgeous. It cast shadows and light glinting off the rocky peaks and kept her cool in the warm, almost suffocating air of Skógur.

The smell was different here too, mustier yet earthier than the other provinces. Flora couldn't decide if she liked it. It reminded her too much of the dead earth under her feet and what should have been. What she could fix if she could keep the amulet, if her power were strong enough. Making fruit and vegetable plants for their meals was taxing enough as Flora assumed it had to do with her inexperience. Her ancestors before her were raised to take care of the land, while Flora was raised to hide. She needed time, the only thing she currently didn't have.

Flora looked over to the dilapidated farmhouse, trying to make out Kaanan and Anise. They couldn't come any closer or make themselves known as the Sage Witch had said in her letter to "bring no one or their life is forfeit."

So, she was alone, but she didn't feel alone. She caught sight of a hand waving before it disappeared into the shadows. A small smile tugged at the corner of her lips as her stomach settled a bit. Her friends were a shout away. She wasn't alone—she could do this. She could find her voice, her confidence in front of an all-powerful stranger. She would try at least.

As the last of the light burned away, navy and shadow rolling in, Flora felt a disturbance in the air. She shivered as a cold finger trailed down her spine, and her eyes darted around the area.

From what appeared to be out of thin air, Rosie materialized bound and gagged on the ground in front of her. Her eyes widened frantically when she caught sight of Flora and she rapidly shook her head, muffled noises escaping the cloth shoved between her lips.

"Mom!" Flora exclaimed, dashing over to her mother and dropping to her knees painfully. She ran her hands over her mother, checking for injuries and went to grab the gag from her mouth when a silky voice called out.

"Hello, Flora."

Flora's hands stilled on her mother, casting a quivering glance over her shoulder. Her blood ran cold, turning to ice, freezing her all over as she stared at the woman before her. Flora's eyes widened as her hands fell from Rosie, her mouth opening and closing. Her brain stalled and her tongue was in a cage of frozen glass.

"Do close your mouth, dear. You look unbecoming," the Sage Witch said, voice commanding and regal.

Flora stared hard, her eyes straining to make out features in the darkening night. All she could see was that the Sage Witch was tall, dressed in an elegant, flowing gown made of a deep green velvet that brushed against the dirt. Her thick hair fell in loose curls down her shoulders, the bright blonde illuminated in the growing moon's glow.

Flora frowned, her stomach uneasy as she looked at the Sage Witch, eyes squinting as familiarity sparked. Goosebumps pebbled along her arms as her heartbeat increased. Something was wrong. She could feel it— there was something she was missing.

"Well? Are you going to greet me or are you incapable of speaking?" she asked, baring her teeth that gleamed as moonlight hit them. Flora could see her canines were sharp even from the distance between them.

Flora unglued her tongue from the roof of her mouth, swallowing thickly as she tried to speak, but the words tangled in her throat, and she just slumped to the ground. Her eyes burned with frustrated tears at the terror gripping her heart, but a blessing rose for Flora.

A warm hand mixed with rough rope squeezed Flora's hand. Her mother had strained her tight bonds to grab her daughter, to offer her support in her weakness. And it helped more than Rosie would ever understand. Sometimes all she needed was a nudge, nothing major, just a small touch that reminded her she could do it, to bring her out of her anxiety and just *speak*.

"Hello," Flora said, voice cracking, "Sage Witch." Rosie gripped her hand tighter, a whimper escaping the cloth, and Flora's stomach dropped as she envisioned what must have taken place the past few weeks for her mother to react like that.

"Do you have what I want? Or did you fail?" she asked, voice teasingly biting as she waltzed closer.

"I have the amulet," Flora said, rising to her knees, and she shoved and kicked and stomped her anxiety down, down, down until it was nothing but an ember instead of a forest fire. "But I wanted to talk to you about that."

"Oh? Do tell."

"You gave the amulet and magic to my family for a reason, and while my mother may have broken that—I proved myself. The magic accepted me and I...I think I should keep it. It's rightfully mine and as far as I know, the boon didn't have an expiry date, just apparently a curse attached to it should anyone screw up," Flora said, words spilling and piling over one another, but they were clear enough to understand, and she was proud of herself for persevering by voicing her wishes and beliefs.

The Sage Witch stared at her with dead eyes and a blank face save for a lightly clenched jaw—like she was restraining herself. "What do you know of your mother?" she said, lips curling, and then she shook it off, switching topics. "You honestly think you're worthy of the boon? That the amulet is *yours*?"

"Well…isn't it?"

"Gods," she cursed, eyes casting to the sky as she ground her teeth. "You know *nothing*, Flora."

"Then explain it to me!"

"Explain it to you?" she scoffed. "I owe you nothing—you owe me *everything*. Give me the amulet or I will kill Rosie right now. I hear larkspur is a lovely way to die."

Flora blanched, hands scrambling behind her to touch her mother. "You stay away from her—she has nothing to do with this!"

"Oh, she has *everything* to do with this," she hissed, stepping closer, and the moonlight fully hit her face, casting her features in light. Flora reared back, sucking in a sharp breath as she inspected her. "Do you see it now, dear? Or are you as stupid as you look?"

Flora's eyes hardened, her skin turning to stone as icy water crashed over her head. She swallowed thickly as her brain worked overtime.

The Sage Witch rolled her eyes and sighed sharply, snapping her fingers together, and magic erupted in the air. It hit her like a tidal wave and all hope of beating her faded away—the Sage Witch was too strong. Rosie yanked her hands free, the Sage Witch having sparked a thorny stem to life, slicing her captive's bonds, and tore the gag out of her mouth.

"That is not the Sage Witch, Flora," Rosie said, wrenching her daughter close. "Just let her go. She doesn't deserve this, Anneliese."

"Anneliese?" a breathy, wheezy gasp fell from Flora's lips as she rounded on Rosie, mouth dropped open. "*Larkspur?*"

Flora gaped at her *mother* standing before her, the woman she was told was dead, the woman who destroyed Woodvale and cursed Flora for her own carelessness and greed.

"Thank you for that, Rosie. It seems you raised an unobservant and dense young woman. I really don't think that was what I asked of you," Anneliese said, cocking her head as she snarled at Rosie.

"Go to Hell, Anneliese, and stay there," Rosie hissed, hugging Flora to her chest as she batted her away.

"Go away, *both* of you!" Flora screeched, scrambling away from the two women who were both her mother in equal right. "What is going on? Someone, explain right now."

"Would you like to do the honors, Rosie?"

"Anneliese," she growled through gritted teeth, "stop insinuating I had anything to do with this. This is *your* mess, *your* problem—explain it yourself."

"Fine," Anneliese said with a shrug. "I'll explain it, dear, simple, Flora. But first, we should start at the beginning—there is something you should know. Rosie"—she cut a glance to the woman in question— "has been lying to you. Rosie here knew exactly who the Sage Witch was, has even been in contact with me, and that you were slowly dying without lifting a finger to help for all your little life."

"*Anneliese!*"

"Is that true?" Flora whispered, heart cracking her chest.

"Flora," Rosie said, eyes watering and voice shaky. "I wanted to tell you when you were ready, when you were old enough, but...each year passed and you were okay. Your coloring was pale, but other than that, you seemed fine. I thought she was lying—exaggerating! I thought you would be fine."

"But you were talking to her? You knew she was alive? Does the Sage Witch even exist?"

"Anneliese and I have only spoken a handful of times over the years—but only briefly, only enough for her to berate me and pester me with questions about you," Rosie said, her voice cracking. "I'm so sorry for not telling you, Flora. I was just trying to protect you."

Flora nodded stiffly, tongue caught in a cage of thorns again. Her heart was in a tug-of-war of wanting to tell her mother to stay away from her, get out of her life. But she also wanted to run into her arms and forgive Rosie, to try and remove the image of her crying and her heart breaking at the thought of Flora abandoning her.

"How are you the Sage Witch?" Flora cried, rounding on her biological mother.

"Blah blah blah." Anneliese rolled her eyes. "You're not asking the right questions. You should be asking me *why*."

"Fine. Why?"

"Because Flora dear, I was ruined by your father and left to rot in an eternity of villainy all because I was *born*."

Chapter Thirty-One

Magic can be passed from person to person, but it rarely goes well. If the receiver is lucky enough to be able to cast magic, it comes with a steep price.

-A Guide to Magic, by Anonymous

"What are you talking about?" Flora cried, hands clenching in furious fists at her sides.

"You are so unbelievably lucky, Flora. You don't even realize how much. You were *spared* from the courtiers and pressure of disgustingly greedy men who never leave well enough alone! My entire life was laid out for me without my choice—I never truly loved your father, but I was forced to bear *his* child so he could have a legacy of power! I was forced to do his bidding whenever and wherever *he* wanted. I let the man I loved slip through my fingers, and he would have treated me with *respect*."

"Sure, but he couldn't offer you power, right?" Flora sneered as Anneliese shot her a withering glare. "So what? You're bitter? That's why you cursed me and sent me on a quest for something you could have just done yourself? Why you kidnapped my mom?" Flora shrieked, her voice rising higher and higher as her vision clouded red instead of her usual green. "It's not like my life was perfect either! Everyone has issues!"

"Oh, Flora. I know you. I watched you grow up—I watched you need a hand to hold constantly. I knew you would never go after the shards unless you had a good reason, and unfortunately, your life isn't one of them," the Sage Witch said, no longer looking like Anneliese to Flora. To her, Anneliese was dead, and always would be. The person before her was a selfish, power-hungry witch driven mad by a burning vendetta.

"But *why*? Wasn't turning the amulet to shards a punishment? Wasn't locking my magic up one too? I don't understand how you're the Sage Witch!"

"Gods, you're thick. I am not the Sage Witch!" she shouted, spittle flying from her mouth as she glared daggers at Flora. "At least, not how anyone knows her to be. I killed that miserable old hag and stole her magic, her title, all because your father drove me to it! But it backfired on me tenfold."

"*What*?"

"The quest was a punishment from her—one you were supposed to know about sooner so you could prove your worth of the boon. I've been watching and waiting but that damn locket ensured I couldn't touch you. But once I saw you heading toward the Norn Mountains, I knew Rosie or any magic wouldn't be able to block me anymore. The *Króna* would repay her debt and so long as I used your precious Rosie for leverage, you wouldn't be able to be weak anymore. I've waited for you to grow up, but you still want to hide behind your mother's skirt."

"I don't understand. You're doing this out of some kind of kindness for me?"

She pursed her crimson lips. "Oh my Gods, you stupid child. *No*, I am doing this for *me*!" Flora's cheeks flushed scarlet, shame pressing down on her, but she couldn't help her brain being slow—too much information was being told to her and in her panicked state she couldn't process things quickly.

"So...you want the amulet...for yourself?" Flora said under her breath, the pieces finally clicking together—if the real Sage Witch were still alive, Flora would have probably been able to keep the amulet. But because Anneliese had murdered her, Flora was stuck with an impossible choice—lose her magic or...lose Anneliese.

"*Yes*," Anneliese hissed, baring her teeth.

"So you killed the Sage Witch, stole her magic, and what? It didn't work like you wanted?"

"Yes, Flora. She wanted more, but the magic didn't appreciate Anneliese's greed or her ravenous need for revenge. Anneliese wanted enough magic to decimate the King and take Woodvale for herself—but it didn't like her enough. It rebounded the original boon, making Woodvale and you suffer until it dies, unless someone worthy came along," Rosie said, clasping Flora's hand. "The shards wouldn't allow her to claim them since she was the one who cursed them apart. She broke their trust—that was why she needed you to find and fix them. She only has access to a fraction of the Sage Witch's magic but it's not enough for her diabolical plans. The restored amulet is her last hope—if it even lets her wield it again."

"I am worthy of that magic—I was vilified! The monster here is the man sitting on that throne!" Anneliese spat. "I deserve the amulet—it is rightfully mine. I will protect Woodvale. No monstrous man will ever sit on the throne again."

"King Desmond is likely dead," Flora said, swallowing the lump of guilt in her throat.

"What?" Anneliese said, her voice a whisper as her body went unnaturally still.

"He…he attacked me, tried to kidnap me, and I used my larkspur to escape. He got a full stalk of larkspur rammed into his face. He is likely dead, or at the very least, comatose and paralyzed."

Anneliese sighed, her head tilting up as a blinding smile overtook her face, ecstasy radiating off her and a maniacal cackle escaping her lips. "That is the best news I have heard in many years," she said, then her smile dropped and she glared down at Flora. "Now, give me the amulet—I have nothing else in my way. You can even be my heir, darling, with some teaching."

Flora swallowed thickly, the amulet biting into the palm of her clenched fist. Her heartbeat pounded a furious song in her ears, and she struggled to stay calm and think things through.

"*Kill her*," Purple whispered in her ear. "*She deserves to die. It is her fault the world is broken—just end it.*"

A deep darkness was awakening in her. Her light was being shadowed, and she *liked* it. Because really, where was the fun in being good? In being looked over and abused because the selfish people always seemed to win—never the good people. Flora wanted to be good when she was younger, because she was told good always conquered evil—and who wouldn't want to be a winner? But she was kidding herself. While she tried to be good, deep down inside, her core was leeched of light, sucked away by her birthmark and she didn't know how to get it back. Maybe it hadn't always been that way, but what did it matter? The light was snuffed out now, and the insidious thoughts were planted.

"You and Kaanan can rule, can make things better, the way they should be—the way it was before your mother and father ruined everything by letting greed and corruption rule them," Purple continued, guiding Flora's thoughts with her words, sending her an image of her and Kaanan standing together holding hands as a crowd of people cheered for them, and then a kiss shared between the two.

Her cheeks warmed at the image. Just because shadow snuffed out light didn't mean it was bad. Under Kaanan's and Flora's rule, things could improve. The hateful witches would be gone for good, no more curses cast as boons in disguise or power-hungry, vengeful villains. Kaanan could be cruel, but he was fair. And there was something so intoxicatingly delicious about the idea of having to answer to no one but herself. Besides, she cared about the citizens of Woodvale and could provide them with bounds of happiness and prosperity.

Even so, something inside stopped her from jumping on the possibility. Her heart may have tugged in two directions, but Flora could tell the way it leaned. At the core of it all, Flora didn't want to rule. She didn't want that kind of attention on her, or responsibility. And she knew Kaanan didn't either unless it was for Pitch City. They both wanted to travel and explore new worlds, find out what else was out there beyond their miserable existence. They wanted to find new stories and hear new words, see new things. Not rule a country that would always fear them.

Kaanan showed her how good it was to be what the world perceived as bad, and let her release her selfish side. No longer would she let herself be tossed around.

Because what was the fun in being good if you were continuously used and stepped on?

Except she had to be careful. She had lines drawn in the sand she could not cross. She would not hurt or kill for the fun or ease of it. She didn't want to maim people who did not deserve it. However, she would not balk at defending herself and her loved ones brutally and viciously. She wanted to be kind and forgiving, but she would not allow herself to be stepped on and walked over because she was nice. Death and murder had a purpose and so long as she believed in her reasonings, and they were truly valid, Flora would not hesitate as she once would have. She had her beliefs, and she would defend them. While Anneliese may have given birth to her, she was dead to Flora. Anneliese the Sage Witch was not worthy of power or title in Flora's eyes.

"It's mine—I earned it. It's rightfully mine," Flora said, sticking her chin up, trying to pretend she felt as confident as she sounded, but even that was a struggle as Anneliese let out a cruelly sharp laugh.

"Please," she scoffed, jaw tight as she bore down on her daughter. "Flora, you forget I know you and, darling, your friends aren't here to help you. You're alone, weak, and helpless. Now do as I say."

She threw her hands together and out, the ground instantly rumbling beneath Flora's feet, causing her to crash painfully to the dirt. Thick, unbreakable stalks of ivy burst from the ground sending dust flying at Flora. The ivy shot high into the sky, linked tightly together, blocking out the outside world. Flora glanced around, heart beating erratically in her chest as they closed into a circle around Flora and Anneliese.

"Flora!" Rosie screamed, a mother's desperation and love so heavy in her voice Flora wanted to cry. She heard scraping and fists pounding against plants as Rosie desperately tried to break through Anneliese's ivy. "*Flora!*" Another cry sounded and Flora's eyes burned fiercely.

"I'm okay," she called to her mother, fingers delicately touching the ivy. "I'll beat her, Mom, I promise." And with that, an unbreakable vow ripped through Flora. She would beat Anneliese, the fraud Sage Witch—she had to.

A thorny stem flew from the ground, wrapping its stingingly painful prongs around Flora's ankle, causing her to cry out as she turned to face Anneliese. She could feel the crimson blood bursting and dripping down her ankle, feeding into the earth as Flora grasped her amulet and called upon her magic.

Rage and fury lit like a match in Flora as magic flooded her veins, the restored amulet working together to imbue her with more magic than she had ever felt. Her vision turned a hue of green as she imagined a stem of *Atropa belladonna* wrapping itself around Anneliese a pace away. She watched it fly from the ground as the thorns dug into her ankle until it touched bone.

Flora let out a bloodcurdling scream as the thorns dug deeper and deeper. Her vision spotted, and she almost tipped over, but she flung her hand out, coaxing and guiding the belladonna higher and higher until it was level with Anneliese's head behind her. Dull green leaves with deep-black berries danced in the wind, waiting for Flora's next command.

It confused Flora as to why Anneliese wasn't using poisonous plants, only thorns. But, she supposed in her haze of pain, Anneliese could be using poison. Flora was just in too much agony to know for sure. Or maybe, underneath it all, Anneliese didn't want to kill her daughter, her only flesh and blood, the little girl she carried inside of her. The thought made Flora pause, but she shook it off—it didn't matter if Anneliese was only maiming and not killing. Flora knew both couldn't live. She could feel the furious revenge radiating off Anneliese and Flora knew that Anneliese would never rest until she got what she wanted. And Flora wasn't giving up the amulet. There was one answer, one already blooming with petals of guilt, but she was backed into a corner with a beast bearing down on her. This was the only way forward.

Flora longed to delve into her biological mother's psyche, if only to alleviate some of the incoming guilt and despair—but there wasn't time, and Flora felt Anneliese was too far gone after eighteen years of stoking her ravenous revenge.

Flora wasn't sure what Anneliese was thinking, where her emotions truly lay as Flora tried to take stock of her strength, trying to reserve it for a final gust of power to end it all, if she could be so lucky to win against a woman who had honed her craft for her entire life compared to a measly week or so for Flora. But her power was true, and Anneliese's was stolen and revolting against her for the theft.

Flora's heart rate was rapidly dwindling, shadows blotting out her sight as the pain reached a crashing crescendo when Anneliese crafted a new thorny vine that cinched around Flora's middle, digging jagged points into her torso.

A bloodcurdling scream tore from Flora's lips, a

gush of blood and moisture wetting her stomach and hips as her knees crashed to the ground. And then, out of nowhere, like an avenging angel, a familiar shape tore through the magical barrier, face contorted in unadulterated rage, so pure and potent it could level a city just by the sight. Flora's heart dropped in her chest as Rosie, somehow miraculously, ran toward Anneliese, her face twisted in hatred. She collided with Anneliese, the distraction effective as the thorns digging into Flora retreated, giving her a brief reprieve.

Flora took a deep breath, filling her lungs as she tried to ignore the absolute agonizing pain plaguing her insides. She watched in horror, desperately trying to get a new grip on her magic, as Rosie attacked Anneliese with her bare hands, deploying some blows before Anneliese snarled and shoved her to the ground. She towered over Rosie, muttering something and arching her hands to the sky beside her head, a devilish grin growing on her twisted face as Flora grasped her magic and attempted to surge something, anything to protect her mother. But it was no use, Flora had been too distracted, in too much pain, and was not quick enough.

Anneliese cast stalks of larkspur from the ground, pure pink as it arched through Rosie's back and exploded from her chest cavity, blood and tissue and muscles gushing and spewing a scarlet river all around the two of them, a horrific sight to witness. Flora's breath snagged on her heart and stopped altogether as she shook her head, unable to accept what she saw. It could not be true. Her mother could not be dead, bloody and heartless, when Anneliese stood healthy and whole over her, grinning like a mad woman.

And just like that, in one miniscule moment,

Flora's heart and soul were pulverized, shattered into a million pieces, broken irrevocably.

Flora's rage grew swiftly, sparked to life by the sight she would never unsee, never move past. A part of her would always remain in that moment, with her mother forever. She grabbed hold of her magic with a firm grip, her body humming with a white-hot heat as her vision tinted green and renewed stalks of belladonna burst to life around Anneliese's feet, careful not to touch Rosie.

Anneliese slowly returned her attention to Flora, her chest heaving like her act of sheer power took a lot out of her. But the thorny vines snaked back around Flora, finding the same holes and blackening out her vision once again. Anneliese's face was contorted with effort, sweat dotting her brow as she kept pumping her magic at Flora, another thorny stem meeting the other and wrapping around Flora's free ankle. A scream bubbled and boiled in Flora's throat as blood gushed down her ankles and stomach, pooling stickily in her boots as she directed two more tall stems to grow beside the first.

Flora would never go down without a fight. Not anymore, and certainly not after the unforgiveable crime committed. Whatever guilt or sympathy she felt for Anneliese was snuffed out like a flame, gone forever because there was nothing she could do or say to stop Flora. She was ready, rejuvenated with the all-consuming desire for retribution.

The sharp thorn hit her bones harder in both ankles, her teeth chattering in the backbreaking effort to stay awake, stay focused, and keep her magic on task. The thorn scraped against muscle, sinew, and bone, the sensation feeling so *wrong* and excruciating she wanted to give up, toss the amulet at Anneliese and sob into the ground, let the rising pain and sorrow for Rosie overtake her need for vengeance.

But she would do none of those things.

"I'm sorry," she whispered to the wind, to what was once Annalise and to her true mother, Rosie. With her eyes burning, she directed the *Atropa belladonna* to wrap itself around Anneliese's neck, head, and face.

The effect was instantaneous. Red, angry welts bloomed where the belladonna rubbed and burst against Anneliese, and Flora bottled up her feelings into an unbreakable glass jar as she directed one stalk to squeeze her throat, Anneliese's mouth dropping open as she clawed at the poisonous plant beginning its journey into her system.

Flora made another stem slip in her mouth, guiding the berries to burst against her teeth, and then she drove the stem down her throat. Muffled gags and cries hit Flora's ears and she flinched as she walked closer, her ankles in such ferocious agony she could only manage a stiff shuffle. While the shards' voices were quiet in her mind, she could feel their pleasure at Flora's actions and choices.

Atropa belladonna was one of the deadlier plants Flora knew of. It contained atropine and scopolamine and captured and claimed hearts by paralysis with the ingestion of the enticing midnight orbed berries housing death.

Anneliese's face turned purple in the night's dark light, and Flora waited as she pulsed her magic harder against her biological mother. She collapsed to the ground, the ivy falling slowly to the ground with her.

Flora knelt beside Anneliese, and being careful not to brush against the belladonna, she pressed her hand to her knee, their eyes colliding. Flora found a lot more than she would have thought lurking behind her eyes, and she couldn't help but wonder if what drove Anneliese to such horrific lengths was really the effect of magic and a man that poisoned instead of helped. Regret and guilt writhed in her eyes, a silent apology when there was nothing she could truly do to right the wrongs she had committed.

While Flora believed Anneliese was not solely to blame for the atrocities plaguing their land and Flora herself, she also believed Anneliese's actions could not be excused as it was she who wielded her own hand. It saddened Flora that both her parents succumbed to greed and power, and she vowed on her biological mother's last breath she would not follow down the same path.

Anneliese was a sickly shade of purple, and with the belladonna covering her neck and face, she looked like a cut down goddess, one Flora would find in a folklore book. Flora watched the life leave Anneliese's eyes, and then dropped her head, offering a quick prayer for her mother before she rose. She wished she could ask Anneliese a million questions, secrets and intimate, intricate details of her life and plans involving Flora she hadn't gotten a chance to ask. But some secrets were bound to stay hidden, left to be forgotten in the past and hopefully to never be repeated. Flora dropped her hand to her side limply, letting the belladonna sink back into the earth as a wave of magic crashed into her, threading itself through her veins and muscles, claiming Flora for its own.

Flora gasped, the feeling of so much potent magic ecstasy in her veins. She wanted to slump to the ground and ride out the wave as her body healed itself, the damage the thorns had done stitching themselves back up. Flora crawled through the blood and sinew toward her mother, tears steadily streaming down her face as she collapsed on Rosie's body.

So much magic filled her veins that Flora assumed part of it was the Sage Witch's with the sheer, raw power it radiated—a terrifying thought as she wasn't sure of the effects it may have on her. The stolen magic caressed her own, a boon and a murder righted at last. All Flora could focus on was the power coursing through her veins, bubbling and boiling and ready to burst out of her when a hazy gold string hooked around her pinky finger.

Flora followed the magical string to where it was tied to Rosie and she gasped as the gold blossomed to life, even more magic filling her veins. Flora couldn't believe how alive she felt when moments before she felt as though she could die in between her two mothers with how much pain she was in and how much power and energy sapped out of her.

Flora bolstered herself up into a sitting position beside Rosie and dug her fingers into the ground, life pulsing beneath the surface, waiting to be called on, to be nourished back to health with magic. She pictured the paintings she had seen of Woodvale before her mother destroyed it, before she caused the boon to rebound and curse her daughter and the land she was sworn to protect.

Flora closed her eyes and imagined green grass fields, massive crop fields with plump and healthy plants to feed the hungry nation. She pictured rolling hills covered in a rainbow of colorful flowers and massive forests of tall, healthy trees covering every province. The dust and death washed all away, leaving Woodvale strong and green once more.

Flora could feel her magic, the Sage Witch's magic, and the warm feeling of Rosie's pure love burgeoning in her veins and flowing steadily into the earth, her rage and sorrow spurring her magic onward, but her body was tiring as she pushed all of herself into the task at hand. Her eyebrows were furrowed into a firm line across her forehead, and her heartbeat was erratically fast and then perilously slow, but still, she persisted.

It felt like hours had passed when her magic finally slowed to a trickle, the earth plump and damp between her fingers. A ragged sigh escaped Flora's lips as her magic helped Woodvale grow into a picturesque country again. Her eyes fluttered open to find exactly what she had pictured, exactly what she had seen in all the paintings. Her heart felt like it would burst from joy, and she breathed in deeply, inhaling the fresh and floral smells intoxicating her nostrils.

She had done it, saved Woodvale and brought it the glory it should have always had. Tears burned in her eyes as her lip wobbled. She hadn't thought she could really accomplish such a feat, but she had. The larkspur magic running through her veins had shown true, and she had completed her destiny, her birthright. She had righted the wrongs of her forebearers and done exactly as the original Sage Witch wanted.

She didn't know what would come next. Her body was tired, and her magic was dampened, like a wet blanket had smothered her flame. But she was alive, albeit exhausted. She would bound through the fields filled with flowers and taste ripe fruit and spend her hours with Anise and Kaanan—her wild and dark forest of light and support.

Flora had saved Woodvale and herself in the process. She had found herself in the journey and while she had lost more than she would have ever bargained for—her innocence, her mother, and so much more—she was alive and breathing at the end of it, and that was what mattered to her in that moment. With another ragged sigh, the last of her energy leaking out of her, her vision slanted and colors distorted as her eyes rolled into the back of her head as she succumbed to the abyss of sleep.

Chapter Thirty-Two

I fear that when the Lost Larkspur is truly found, her life will be one of strife. She will be pulled in multiple directions, watched constantly, and pressured to the point of breaking. While I, of course, want Woodvale to be healthy again, I can't help but have a small part of me wish she is never found. As someone with daughters, I cannot imagine letting one of my own walk into this particular wolf's den because I honestly am not sure she would survive.

-*The Age of Larkspur* by Cassius Muscari, IV

"Flora, my darling, it's time to wake up now."

Flora groaned and shook her head, snuggling deeper into the warm and soft surface she lay on, ignoring the call of a familiar voice, soft and sweet and full of love. Rosie never let her sleep in as much as Flora longed for, and her bed was just too comfy to get out of.

"No," she whimpered, eyes squeezed tightly as her brain woke up and reminded her of the one thing she could never truly forget. "Please, no."

The previous day's events came back to Flora slowly but surely, and she pressed her hands into her eyes, the sting of pain grounding her as she swallowed thickly, the sight of her mother's destroyed and mutilated body burning her mind like acid.

"Flora! You're okay!" she heard Anise cry and

burrowed deeper into her mind, trying to erase the sight of her mother.

She wanted to wallow in the space between, in her mind that plagued her with horrific sights because that was what she deserved. She had been too weak, too slow, to save her mother and Rosie had *died*. Flora didn't know how she could come back from that. She was broken and bruised, her heart cut into tiny little pieces that scattered with the wind.

"Hey," Anise said softly, warm hands closing around Flora's wrists. "Stop hurting yourself and look at me."

Flora let Anise tug her hands away and she glared up at her friend. Anise just gently smiled and pulled her into a seated position. Flora gasped and her mouth dropped open as she gazed around her in pure astonishment. Rosie's murder had taken precedent in her slow-to-wake mind and somehow she had forgotten the one highlight to her actions yesterday.

The world around her was an explosion of color— mostly green, but vibrant and dynamic. No longer was her world dull and dry and dead or dying. It was alive and healthy, thriving as grass danced in the breeze and thick trunks of leafy trees exploded from the ground. Rolling hills covered in plants and flowers rose around her, the intoxicating smell of grass and nature heavy on the wind.

It was beautiful, more than she could ever have imagined.

But for Flora, there was a shadow lurking around the edges, a painful reminder that Rosie would never see the world whole ever again. The thought sent Flora into a fit of tears, streaming down her face and fogging her eyes as Anise sputtered and hugged Flora tight.

"She's dead," Flora blubbered.

"Who?"

"My mom," Flora said with a hitching sob into Anise's shoulder. "Anneliese murdered her and then I killed Anneliese. She was the Sage Witch all along."

Anise tightened her arms around Flora, the pain hitting her too before she said darkly, "But you killed her so it's all right—it will all be all right."

Flora nodded into her friend's shoulder, appreciating the sentiment, but knowing in her heart full well that the healing process of this particularly open and gushing, bloody wound would take a long time to even scab over, let alone heal. Flora pulled away from her friend and looked around her for the other familiar face she was hoping to see. It appeared they were in the same valley as before, the stone of the well covered in ivy now, and the wall of magic dispersed completely. She twisted around and her breath hitched when she saw what was behind her.

A beautiful, bountiful bush of roses.

"Rosie," she whispered, her finger brushing the velvety petal, and while she would not truly be okay for quite some time, seeing that her magic had created a monument to her mother was enough to give her the strength to stand.

Anise clasped Flora's hand in hers, shooting her a watery smile Flora returned, the two bowing their heads before Rosie's rose bush and sending their love and thanks to a woman who deserved the world. Flora didn't care about the betrayal, that Rosie knew Anneliese had been alive and had spoken with her. Rosie was only ever trying to protect Flora, and she would be forever grateful to her mother for providing her a childhood free from Anneliese and dangers. Flora only held love in her heart for Rosie and everlasting grief.

Several moments passed before Flora explained more of what had happened, what she witnessed, and what she had done. Anise was an attentive listener to her tale, her hand rubbing soothing circles into Flora's back.

When she was done, Flora dared to ask, "Where's Kaanan?"

Anise shot her a wry grin. "He's trying to keep the masses away from you."

"What?" Flora's eyebrows were furrowed as she tried to make sense of what Anise was talking about.

"Flora, it's been three days since you fixed Woodvale." Flora gasped and Anise kept explaining. "We were going to move you, but when we tried these roots came out of the ground and wrapped around you, so we decided to wait and hope you would wake up. Kaanan figured it might be a bit since you used a massive amount of magic to heal Woodvale and yourself. I'm honestly surprised it only took you three days."

Flora's eyes were wide as she nodded along and blinked rapidly at the lost time, but her body felt so much stronger than it had in years that she was grateful for the time to heal. With a pit in her stomach, she dipped into the reserve of magic coiling inside of her, her breath held before whooshing out of her when she felt it there, full of unimaginable life and waiting for her next desired command. Flora wasn't sure what happened to the Sage Witch's and Rosie's magic, if it fully dispersed into the earth through her body as a conduit or if it still lingered in her veins, buried deep. It was something she would figure out another day. She was just overjoyed that her own magic replenished and lay waiting in her veins. She couldn't quite believe how it had all turned out—she got to keep her magic and she would not be plagued by the cursed pair that was Anneliese Larkspur and Desmond Vale ever again. While she lost the most important person to her, she tried to count her blessings that both Anise and Kaanan had made it out unscathed. She at least had two other loved ones to draw on.

"And Kaanan?" she prompted again, Anise grinning.

"Well, that battle with Anneliese—absolutely wild, by the way—was not inconspicuous. Apparently, you could see that magic wall for kilometers. Once it came down, the world magically fixed itself and all life was restored in what was an instant for us. Everyone who saw the barrier came running. They all want to see and meet our savior."

"And Kaanan is keeping them at bay," Flora finished, and Anise confirmed with a nod.

"You would not believe how many people are there and how fast word has spread. Kaanan said there were multiple guards and people from the castle looking for you." Anise paused, a hesitant line between her eyebrows. "Everyone is calling you Queen Flora."

"*What?*"

"Apparently Desmond is on his deathbed and since everyone only knows about one person who could save Woodvale, everyone is looking to you now. I don't know how exactly, but someone figured out your name, and someone in the palace is claiming your birthright to be true."

"I don't want to be Queen," Flora said, her voice hollow in horror, but the words were true.

"I know," Anise reassured. "That's just what everyone is saying. But we'll find a way out of it."

"What do we do now?"

"What do you want to do?" Anise asked, and Flora's heart warmed.

"I want to get Kaanan and I want to get out of here. I want to be somewhere less open, somewhere safe where they can't find us."

Anise nodded swiftly and hooked their arms together. "Then that's what we'll do."

****

Flora and Anise reunited with Kaanan by tossing pinecones at him until he turned around, a wall of shadow protecting them from the shapes of hundreds of people on the other side. Their reunion was cut short as Anise hissed at him to hurry. They fled back through the woods, Kaanan gazing at her wide-eyed, thousands of unspoken words and questions lingering behind his eyes just waiting to be spoken. He released his hold on the shadows when they were several paces away to where they had let the horses graze. When they were mounted on the magnificent creatures, he led them back the way they had arrived days ago, back toward the Sage Woods. It was the only place Flora could think of that was close enough where they shouldn't be followed.

Walking into the Sage Woods tree line was a completely different experience. The Woods welcomed her home like she was its new daughter, warming her and blanketing her in sunlight and floral aromas. She found an alcove, collapsed onto a log, and retold her tale to Kaanan, delving into more details as she held both of their attentions in full. Flora was comforted once again by both her friends, and she let herself mourn and wallow in her grief with their companionship.

Flora wiped her cheeks dry and asked Kaanan a question that had been plaguing her for hours. "Do you think my mother somehow gave me a form of magic? I swear I felt something different from my magic and the Sage Witch's magic."

"I haven't heard of such magic, but it wouldn't surprise me," Kaanan admitted. "A mother's love and a selfless act are very powerful."

Flora nodded softly, the conversation lulling as Anise dozed off, and Flora racked her brain on what she wanted to do. A noose was closing around her neck and she didn't know how to stop it.

"Flora," Kaanan said, drawing her out of her thoughts. His gaze burned into her as he gestured for them to move to another clearing, letting Anise rest. Flora trailed her fingers along the ferns, sniffing the roses blooming around her as Kaanan leaned against a tree, the moss shying away from him.

"Are you okay?" she asked him, spinning on her heel to face him fully.

"That should be my question. How do you feel?" he asked.

"I feel much better. Honestly, I feel brand new. My magic is still mine and my body feels stronger than it has in years." She beamed at him, her breath hitching as a magnificent grin broke out across his face.

"I'm so glad," he said, "and I must say, you've done an incredible job fixing Woodvale. It's wonderful."

"Thank you," she said shyly, toeing the roots around her feet as her teeth plunged into her lip. "Kaanan, I want you to know how important you are to me. I know we've only known each other a few weeks, but I truly enjoy your company and if you're okay with it, I would be so grateful if you would want to continue to spend time with me."

Flora's cheeks burned a scarlet hue as she kept her eyes locked on the ground. Boots crunched twigs and leaves before black leather shoes come into her line of vision. A warm finger brushed her chin, gently guiding it up so their gazes met.

"I would be honored, Flora," Kaanan said softly. She swallowed thickly, her heart hammering in anticipation as he brushed his finger up her jaw, his hand lightly cupping her cheek. "I am so happy you survived, *Kærasta.*"

"What?" Flora asked with a blink, her mind snagging on the foreign word, but he only smiled, a wry and amused twist of his lips, as a twinkle sparkled in his eyes with the promise of an explanation she would have to work for.

"Flora, you know I feel it too, this connection. To me, you're a kindred spirit, a gorgeous lifeline I never expected to find. But now that I have," he said, drawing her attention back to him as he brushed over explaining the word and asked her a question she could barely let herself hope was real. "May I kiss you?"

Flora's heart stopped, her breath halting in her lungs as she nodded once before finding her voice and whispering, "Yes."

That was all the encouragement Kaanan needed and he dove forward, swooping his mouth onto hers, their lips slotting into place. His hands slipped to her hips, tugging her against him as she slung her arms around his shoulders, gasping against his mouth as he deepened the kiss.

Flora was in a haze of pink, her heart beating steadily in her chest as all her wishes came true, her hopes confirmed, that Kaanan liked her the same way she liked him.

He pulled away, his eyes blown wide as she looked to his swollen lips, biting her own as she longed to press hers against him again. And she did just that. He laughed against her mouth before the birds' tweeting drowned out the lovely noise and Flora sank into the moment, a dream come true.

It was hours later, after Anise had woken and Flora and Kaanan had returned with rosy cheeks and swollen lips, rumpled clothes that had Anise rolling her eyes, that the three of them hammered down on their plan.

Flora wanted to run. She didn't want to be Queen and she didn't want to be around a mass of people who would only see her as such. She wanted to flee, explore new places, and then she would come back and deal with the consequences. Just because she was of Larkspur and apparently Vale blood, did not mean she needed to rule, and she hoped her absence would confirm that in the people's minds.

With a deep breath and a boldness she didn't know she had in her, she asked Kaanan to join her. He responded enthusiastically, the two of them in agreeance in terms of their lacking desires to rule. They would deal with their respective thrones and reigns another time—they believed more was out there, and they both wanted to explore that for themselves first and foremost.

While Flora extended the invitation to Anise, her friend declined to Flora's surprise. "But why? Not to pressure you or anything, but I thought you would want to come."

"It sounds fun," Anise assured her, "but honestly, Flora, I'm exhausted. I had a good time, don't get me wrong, but I need a break and you need someone to make sure things don't go too south around here. I can try to get people to change their minds, to elect a new ruler, and when you're done exploring new places with your new boyfriend," she teased as Flora flushed crimson, "we can build that life we always dreamed of, with both of our desires met."

Flora didn't want to leave her friend, abandon her in Woodvale with people who would seek her out just for being friends with Flora, but she had also grown enough to know when to choose herself, and Flora wanted to explore new lands, take the risk and run, even if it meant leaving her best friend behind.

It was a few days later the three parted ways in the cover of night, their paths diverging greatly, but their beginning was forever connected to one another and one day, Flora knew in her heart they would find each other again. After a great deal of new experiences and adventures of course.

Epilogue

It is today we celebrate our Lady Flora Larkspur, our Princess and heir to the throne of Woodvale. She has risen like the flower she is and saved us all with her magic.

Magic is nothing to fear with Princess Flora at the helm. Our sources say she has defeated the Sage Witch and struck a deal with the Pitch King.

People of Woodvale, we are safe, but still have a task at hand:

Our mighty King Desmond is dying and actively unfit to rule, and we need our Princess to come home to Vale Centre. It is every citizen's utmost duty to find her and urge her home so we may continue into the next prosperous era of Woodvale.

Long Live Queen Flora

-Notice distributed to every town in Woodvale

When Woodvale was saved, mass gatherings were held to celebrate and thank their savior—a woman most of the kingdom had only seen in passing without realizing it was her. After the dust had settled, and the King's advisors had informed the people about their dear King, they knew there was a new task at hand: bringing the Princess home and ensuring she fell in line. The King's Governors and advisors had big plans with the confirmation that magic was back on their side.

But the woman they hunted had other plans and

379

while they may have wanted her to do their bidding, they had to find her first.

A flyer was distributed to every city and village of Woodvale the day after Flora saved the land. But she paid no mind to the written words for she had other plans that did not involve becoming a Princess, a Queen, of replacing her biological mother and father and ruling over a population.

She knew she was being hunted, and would have to move quickly, because there was one person she wanted to take a chance on and one dream she wanted to fight for.

It was hours after the letter was distributed that a young woman with flowing birch hair and a healthy glow to her skin was found at the border of the Pitch Woods, a rucksack on her shoulder and a blooming, excited grin dancing on her lips. A young man dressed in all black, with a velvet black cloak to boot, appeared at the tree line, cheeks on both parties flushed bright pink. Each held matching grins of pure joy and excitement as anticipation hung thick and heavy in the air and tentative names of endearment from a lost language were tried on like new clothes that fit perfectly.

But the pleasure didn't last long as shouts echoed in Myrkurden behind them. While the instant threat wasn't what they planned, they knew they had all the time in the world to chase their dreams, and many avenues to explore so they could discover something new.

The young woman and man looked at one another and clasped their hands tightly together before they flew through the trees, daring the hunters to chase them into the eternal, malicious pitch-black Woods and beyond.

A word about the author…

Aleighsha Parke is an avid reader who first fell in love with storytelling as a young child. Young Adult Fantasy and Sci-Fi are her first loves and the two genres she enjoys reading and writing in the most, however, she is interested in dabbling in other genres. When she's not writing, reading, or crocheting/knitting, she is working in a library, so she's always surrounded by books. She lives in British Columbia with her adorable cat and family.

You can find her on Instagram or
Twitter or
TikTok @aleighshaparke
https://aleighshaparke.com/